The Writers of Minnesota 1996

CrowbarPress
P.O. Box 8815
Madison, WI 53708

Collection Copyright © 1995
Crowbar Press
P.O. Box 8815
Madison, WI 53708

All Rights Reserved

Water	© 1994	Bill Meissner
The Five Window Grail	© 1995	John Early
Me and Ronnie	© 1995	Jim Redmond
Brave Punishments	© 1995	Christine Mack Gordon
Paychecks and Other Handouts	© 1995	Chaunce Stanton
Lady-Slipper	© 1995	Joyce Basore Wilson
That Particular Summer	© 1995	Jeffrey Wilkes
Backfire	© 1995	William Reichard
Golden Girl	© 1995	Jane Cowgill
Covering Home	© 1987	Joseph Miaolo
Stupid Animals	© 1995	Brian Batt
They Gathered at the River	© 1995	Lawrence Owen
Van Meter	© 1995	Kent Cowgill
Night Fishing	© 1995	Patrick Martin
A Hint of Things to Come	© 1995	Matt Kruger
Into the Eyes of Sorrow	© 1995	Ethan A. Wells
Designated Drivers	© 1995	Melanie Mallon
The Guest Conductor	© 1995	Roger Sheffer
Clair	© 1995	Julia Klatt Singer
Road	© 1995	Diane Glancy
Bitter Wine	© 1995	Carol Mohrbacher
Eventual Revenge	© 1995	Peter Gilbertson
Party of One	© 1995	Jess Lang
Skeeto Bites	© 1995	Jim Palmer
We Oughta Write a Book	© 1995	Grace Sandness

All Stories Used By Permission

"Water" Courtesy of Random House, from *Hitting into the Wind*, © 1994 by William J. Meissner.

All Rights Reserved. No part of this publication may be reproduced, stored in a retrieval system, or transmitted in any form or by any means, electronic, mechanical, photocopying, recording, or otherwise, without the prior permission of the publisher.

For Reprint Rights Contact Publisher

ISBN 0-9647347-1-0

Printed in the United States of America

Contents

Water--Bill Meissner	1
The Five Window Grail--John Early	6
Me and Ronnie--Jim Redmond	19
Brave Punishments--Christine Mack Gordon	27
Paychecks and Other Handouts--Chaunce Stanton	63
Lady-Slipper--Joyce Basore Wilson	74
That Particular Summer--Jeffrey Wilkes	88
Backfire--William Reichard	96
Golden Girl--Jane Cowgill	106
Covering Home--Joseph Maiolo	119
Stupid Animals--Brian Batt	129
They Gathered at the River--Lawrence Owen	137
Van Meter--Kent Cowgill	141
Night Fishing--Patrick Martin	155
A Hint of Things to Come--Matt Kruger	164
Into the Eyes of Sorrow--Ethan Wells	188
Designated Drivers--Melanie Mallon	199
The Guest Conductor--Roger Sheffer	220
Clair--Julia Klatt Singer	227
Road--Diane Glancy	251
Bitter Wine--Carol Mohrbacher	258
Eventual Revenge--Peter Gilbertson	264
Party of One--Jess Lang	274
Skeeto Bites--Jim Palmer	280
We Oughta Write a Book--Grace Sandness	286

Water

Bill Meissner

If you've ever ridden on a team bus for nine hours toward Medicine Hat or Great Falls, as I have, you'd know what I mean. If you've ever followed that dry, straight road to a sun-bleached Wichita ball field and back, you'd understand. You'd understand what distance is, and what it means to be a minor leaguer. You'd understand what the drive's like--beneath the floorboards, it's that steady droning sound, and ahead, through the bus's dust-caked windshield, all you can see is an endless mirage of shallow water that keeps pulling farther and farther away. No matter how many miles you drive, you never seem to catch up with it.

If you understand this, you'd understand a minor leaguer's yearning for water. You drive through lakeless states, drive in a tin bus that heats up like an oven across the parched fields of the Dakotas where there's not even a scrub brush for shade. You keep seeing, outside the oval side windows, the empty bowls of dried watering holes like blind eye sockets in the land. You're always by yourself on the bus, even if a buddy is sitting in the seat next to you. Even if he mutters to you now and then, or even if you play a hand of cards, you're always alone.

If you knew all this, and more, you'd understand why each night, after a ball game on some crippled field where the outfield grass is piled with gopher mounds, after a game where my socks are decorated with burrs that needle my ankles, after a game where my sweaty jersey clings to my skin like it'll never let go, after a game like that, I dream of water.

I dream of my small home town back in Wisconsin, dream of riding in a sleek aqua Fairlane convertible with my girlfriend Melissa through the downtown, past the theater where we used to neck in high school, to the lake a mile outside town. The lake water is deep, everyone says; it's the deepest lake in the state. There are even Indian legends about the dark green dropoffs along the lake bottom. I dream of stepping my bare feet slowly into that water off the steep rocky shoreline, dream of that cool water rising as I lower myself onto a submerged rock slab, slippery with algae. I dream of Melissa, facing me, wearing that bright blue two-piece, lowering herself into the water, too, as she stares straight into my eyes. The spring-fed lake water's not too cold. It's never too cold. She lowers herself and the water rises to her waist, to her smooth breasts, to her slim, long neck. I watch the woman I love sliding into the liquid and I always think: *Water that touches her everyplace touches me everyplace.* This thought keeps flowing over and over in my mind as her blonde hair swirls on the surface of the water around her bare shoulders. I submerge myself to my chin and feel the ripples from the water lapping at my face. She leans toward me and I lean toward her, and we're about to kiss, a deep, long, moist kiss, the kind of kiss that could last for years. Then I wake up. I always wake up at that moment, just before our lips touch.

I wake up on a dry white sheet in some motel room on the road and it all comes back to me: I'm on the minor league circuit, six hundred miles from home. No way I can touch her lips.

Tonight I have the dream, and I wake up, and then something strange happens. I sit up and try to picture Melissa's face, her lips, but I can't. Like that water mirage on the highway, the harder I try to reach it, the further away her face seems to be.

I stumble to the small desk lamp, click the light on, and pick up the phone. It bugs my roommate and I see him glare from his pillow, his face pinched like a fist, then grunt and roll over.

I dial her number. In the split second after I finish dialing, there's a hiss in the receiver before the connection, and I picture the electricity flowing through the thin black wires across the darkness of these arid flatlands, flowing from telephone pole to cracked telephone pole, to Wisconsin, where streams rush through back yards, where the lawns are green. The phone rings once, twice, three times. When she answers, her words are groggy, sleep still coating her voice.

"Closer," I hear myself saying. "I want you closer."

"Denny?" she says. "What's wrong? Is anything wrong?"

"Yeah," I say. "We're wrong. You're at home and I'm here in some crummy motel in Kansas."

"Do you know it's three-fifteen in the morning?"

"I don't care what time it is," I say. "Jesus, Melissa, I miss you. I want you out here."

"You know I can't," she explains softly. "You know I can't leave my job."

I suddenly feel foolish for calling. I know she'd never come out here, and it's impossible for me to go back there. So what's the point of waking her up?

"The end of the season's not far off," she says, her voice trying to soothe me like liniment. "We can make it until then, can't we?"

"Not far off?" I say. September's almost two months away."

"It's not forever," she says.

"It's a million years to me." I feel like there's sand in my throat when I say the words.

"I know. I know." Melissa says, her voice trailing off a little. "This isn't exactly easy for *me*, either."

The way she says this bothers me, and I pause for a few seconds, thoughts rushing through my head. I have a feeling things are going to be rocky when I get back. Before I met her, she had other boyfriends in town, and I know with me gone they wouldn't mind asking her out. I wish I could feel more sure about her. It's been so long since I've seen her, we'll hardly know what to say, how to look into each other's eyes. I picture her with a nervous half-smile, leaning on a wooden pillar on her front porch, twirling a small lock of her blond hair by the side of her face. I picture myself, my hands uncertain what to do, so they hide in my jeans pockets.

I finally break the pause. "Been to the lake lately?" I know it's a dumb thing to ask, but it's the only thing that comes into my mind at the moment.

"Lake?" Her puzzled voice tone rises.

"Yeah. You know, swimming."

"Well, a few weeks ago. But not lately."

"Don't go. Not until I get home, I mean. That's the first place I want to take you."

"Well...okay. If that's what you want." She laughs lightly, and when she laughs, it makes me think of ripples on the surface of water. I want to swim in those ripples.

I think about saying goodbye and hanging up the phone and I miss her already. That's the strange thing about being in the minors. You get a chance at something you love, but in order to get it you always have to give up something else. There's a balancing in this life, a strange balancing, and sometimes it gets to a point where you just have to chose, because things don't stay balanced for long. It occurs to me that maybe I'm just thinking too much; sometimes the guys laugh at me and poke me with an elbow and say I'm thinking too much. Melissa and I talk a few more minutes, and before I hang up, I balance the black receiver in my hand.

   The next day the team's on the road for hours after a game, and it's getting close to evening. One thing you learn in the minors is patience. Patience. You learn not to think more than a day ahead, or it will practically kill you. I've met guys like that in Class A ball. They always talked about getting to the big leagues, *The Show*, they call it, as if they were going to appear on Johnny Carson or something. As if their whole life was spent hiding behind a thick curtain, being nobody, and then they'd get to The Show where, all of a sudden, they were *somebody* in the spotlight. I wanted to tell them, *Hey, you* are *somebody. You're somebody now. Just be yourself. Just appreciate it.* But guys like that would have just scoffed and spat out their tobacco and turned their back to me. But the truth is, guys like that didn't last long. Guys like that thought too far ahead, as if their minds jumped years ahead of their bodies, which were still sitting on the slashed beige vinyl seat of a team bus, feeling each jolting pothole in a county highway. Guys like that went slowly crazy, saw their averages dwindle to nothing, swatting at batted balls with their gloves and came up empty. Guys like that threw their arms out on plays at the plate and you saw them after the game, pacing near the end of the bench, a bag of ice on their shoulders, swearing to themselves. *God damn arm,* they might be saying. *How the hell am I gonna make it to The Show now?*

   We won't reach our next stop for hours. Some of the guys on the bus are snapping cards on the slippery arm rests. Some are talking and chuckling softly. Some sigh and write letters home.
   But me, I'm just fingering the frayed hole in my jersey as I stare out the window through the reflection of my own face in the glass. I'm staring at the junk cars parked on the front lawns and the kids running free along the sidewalks. There's a small, scrubby baseball field with the silhouettes of the outfield floodlights on wooden posts, like crosses on the dusky horizon. Ahead of the bus, the sun sets and the road quickly darkens. I imagine, somewhere on the other side of the world, the sun rising, the water mirages just beginning on the roads, those mirages always just out of

reach.

    I'm thinking about things most ballplayers don't think about, I know, but I think about them anyway. I'm thinking about my girlfriend and me, and how time is passing each day, like something being pulled out from under us, and we don't even know it. We'll just look up one day and we'll be older, our hair splashed with gray, and we'll think back on these days. *Remember when you used to travel with that team?* she might say. And I might reply, *A million years ago. A million years.*

    But maybe I'm thinking too far ahead. So I pull my thoughts back a bit closer to now.

    I'm staring out the window and thinking about my first day back from the minors, about how I'll jump into the battered Fairlane convertible with the woman I love and cruise through the downtown, past the theater with the darkened marquee bulbs and toward the deep-water lake. Two months is not too far to think ahead. Two months is just right. When we get to the lake, I'll grab Melissa's hand, pull her out of the passenger's side, and without even closing the door we'll run toward all that cool liquid that's been waiting for us.

    It's night now, and we pass another small town; in one house, through a big picture window, I get a glimpse of the husband and wife, facing each other across the dinner table. As the window clicks past, they sit unmoving, frozen in the blue glow from the television set. There could be a ball game on. Or maybe it's a Johnny Carson special. Or maybe they don't even care what show's on, and all they're thinking about is looking deep into each other's eyes.

    I hear the last few murmurs of low conversation as the guys on the bus gradually run out of talk, and though it's way too early, I think about sleep. I think about dreaming. About things ballplayers never think about. A million years go by. I stare through my reflection, then slowly tilt my head to the glass that's clear and smooth as the surface of water.

"Water" appears courtesy of Random House, from Bill Meissner's collection ***Hitting Into the Wind*** ©1994

The Five-Window Grail

John Early

Walt phoned just as I started in on supper, a mild urgency in his voice. He required assistance unloading something, he said, though I had never known Walt to need anybody's help before. So I ate and then drove the two miles to his place just as night began to thicken. Roy and Jim were already there in the garage. Walt must have called them, too. I nodded, and Roy told me Walt was still in the house. The three of us waited in the big, bright garage--two-and-a-half stalls wide and two deep, with banks of fluorescent lights everywhere--and stared at the canvas-tarped car that needed rolling off his rusty trailer. We knew better than to lift the tarp and ruin his secret.

Walt and Sue had a small house on 10th Ave., and the first thing Walt did after they bought it was knock down the old and leaning single-stall and hammer up this garage with more floor-space than the house. He needed room for his cars, his welders and floor jacks and compressors and engine stands. Walt was a hot-rodder. They call those painted, plated and pleated cars street rods now, but, though Walt had owned a lot of old Fords and Plymouths, he'd never owned one like that. No, for about forty-one of his forty-three years, ever since he'd learned to make exhaust sounds with his lips, Walt had been a hot-rodder. He wore wrinkled work pants and a shirt with his name embroidered on the pocket, never cleaned the eternal grease under his nails; a tall, thin ratchet of a man, born too late, perhaps.

The garage emptied onto a gravel alley, but the stones had been worked into it so long that it was mostly dirt now, potholed and muddy from the rains we'd had. Across from the garage lay an old market some enterprising realtor had converted into an apartment. You could drive down this alley anytime Walt wasn't at work and find him in the garage. The overhead doors would be up in warm weather, and the smell of gas or oil or paint or sanding dust would float on the moist air above the potholes filled with gas and oil-streaked water. On cold nights, when the mud lay frozen, his garage lights were always on, and all you had to do was knock and go in. There were usually three or four of us standing around talking to Walt or watching him work, listening to him preach about some right or wrong way to do a job. He was an awfully good mechanic; things came out right when he fixed them.

I'd never seen him so proud of a car; he came out of the house after a few minutes and sat on one of the trailer's fenders, keeping us in suspense. We'd attended this evening service often enough that we knew what he wanted: for us to form a congregation as he leaned against the canvas pulpit and delivered the sermon regarding just how he came to possess what lay shrouded on the trailer. Walt always needed an audience; he'd asked us to help, though he could have done the job himself. Said the cooler was full, so we came.

"Heard about this son-of-a-bitch a little more than a year ago," he began. "TJ told me about it first." TJ was another guy we'd go over and talk to once in a while, though not nearly as often as we would to Walt's. TJ was a car guy, too, but his love was mid-sixties musclecars-- Barracudas, Road Runners, Chevelles, Mustangs. They both worked at the local Ford dealership. That night TJ wasn't in the garage with us.

"I remember when I first got serious to look for it," Walt went on. "For an hour I was sitting at a round table in somebody's kitchen I didn't even know, and probably ain't never gonna see again, when I decide I've had about thirty minutes too much of this graduation shit. This was a year ago May. Bad cake, lousy coffee, and these dick-heads all talking about certificates of deposit or doing some sandbox thing for the Jaycees." He led us in a laugh.

"Sue tells me the day before," he continued, "that we're going to her friend's daughter's graduation, and for some reason I agree. A couple hours, I figure, we're gone, but I know sitting there I'll never make it that long. I look at Sue in the living room and she looks pretty much settled in for the duration. Well, I figure, she can stay, but I'm leaving. I got a wild hair that I'd go start looking for that fucking deuce five-window." Walt took a sip from the beer sitting on the workbench, then set it back exactly on the circle of water it had sweated. Beer cans were like parts of his tool collection. We were all holding one, sipping as we might of wine at communion.

"I'm sitting there smiling at these jerk-offs but I was hearing TJ's voice over the winter keep telling me about this '32 five-window that was about the cherriest original hot rod ever built in North Dakota, late fifties/early sixties, all steel, channeled, flathead with Strombergs, all the neat old stuff.

A *hot* rod, not some show car. He said he'd heard about it from somebody who knew where it was, but he sure as hell wasn't telling me where. I watched him strut around this garage like a big cock"--he paused--"pheasant, listened to him gloat about how he knew where the car was and I couldn't find it.

"So I come right out and tell him, 'Bet I could find the fucker,' I say.

"He says, 'Even if you could--which you no-way can't --wouldn't matter.' Then he just shuts up like he's in on this big secret. I'm thinking, *fuck you.*

"I ask him why that was that it wouldn't matter.

"'The guy won't sell it, is why', he says. 'He lives out in California now. Keeps it at his brother's place, where they grew up. Hasn't driven it in years. Gonna trailer it out someday and restore it.'

"I say to him, 'Bet I could find that sonofabitch.' All the time I'm thinking, Jesus, an all-steel deuce five-window. You don't exactly fall over them every day. Put it back like it was late fifties, that thing would be worth some serious coin." We all knew that Walt'd had a five-window maybe ten years before, but he'd had to sell it. And that he viewed Henry Ford's design and construction of the 1932 Ford as Moses might have viewed the parting of the waters.

"And TJ said--you know he can't keep his mouth shut-- 'I'll give you one hint: it ain't past the river.'

"I'd heard rumors about some old deuce. Hell, you hear 'em all the time about all sort a cars, but they're mostly bullshit. Nobody knew if the car was for real, let alone where it was. So I'm thinking it'd be pretty neat to get that fucker. TJ'd got me pissed off so that I really wanted to find it.

"I tell Sue I'm breaking out of the prison. I can walk the mile home here and get the truck. She smiles in front of her friends and tells me that's fine, like I need her permission, but I know her voice well enough after being sandblasted by it for sixteen years and I know she doesn't like it. *Tough shit,* I think. I had better things to do on a Sunday afternoon when it wasn't hunting season."

A couple of us found some stools, and I got a box to sit on. It looked like we might be a while. That was all right; Walt could tell a good story, beer-induced or not, maybe because he never failed to believe every word he uttered.

"But walking back here I started thinking about how

big half of North Dakota is. Knowing the deuce wasn't past the river wasn't knowing too goddamn much. Then I start considering TJ--where would he have heard that bit about the deuce? Who would have told him?" Walt cocked his head like a dog, listening. "I couldn't think of him being out that way recently. He never hunts but with us. But then I remember him talking about some relatives somewhere in some little town.

"When I get home I go into the garage and grab a map I keep with all the hunting spots I use." Walt turned and picked up a wrinkled and torn map folded into a plastic holder. The map wasn't greasy but the holder was. "This one right here," he said. "Names, phone numbers, routes. I start looking at all the little towns within maybe fifty miles of the river, hoping a name will register. And I'll be damned if that don't work. I spy this wide spot in the road, Wishek, and I remember TJ's brother-in-law or some other fucker lives there. Not quite half-way between Jim-town and Bismarck, maybe an hour south of the Interstate. Maybe just shy of three hours from here.

"Well, it comes to me that I just can't drive out to Wishek and start looking around. Sure as hell not go knocking on doors. And sure as hell not that day. Been five o'clock by the time I got there, dark around eight-thirty. I could go the next weekend, but I don't want to wait that long to get something more concrete.

"So I spot this *Deals on Wheels* magazine I got laying around for a couple weeks and I figure maybe I can find some guy advertising an old car who lives somewhere by Wishek. A long-shot, but what the hell. Call him up, ask about the deuce. If he was a good car man, maybe he'd know.

"I sit for over half an hour on the stool right here by the workbench. Shit, I haven't read that long since high school. But I find this guy, Clarence Wagner, advertising what he calls a "cherry" '46 tudor out of Napoleon. I check the map. North of Wishek, maybe thirty minutes. Old Clarence even has a picture with his ad, and from what I can tell, the '46 does look pretty decent. For a sedan.

"So I get him on the phone. 'Clarence,' I say to him, 'you still got that '46?'

"He wasn't much of a salesman. 'Yup,' was all he says.

"How nice is it?' I ask him.

He says, 'It's all there, and there ain't no rust. Not on

the rockers, not on the floor, nowhere. Been took care of.'

"I say, 'The hell.'

"He says, 'That's right. This car's about as nice as you can get.'

"I say, 'How much?'

"He says, 'Takin' offers.'

"'How many so far?'

"'Ain't sayin'.'

"I say, 'Give you a hundred.' Then I start laughing to let him know I'm joking.

"But he didn't laugh. Just says, very calm, 'It'll take more than that.'

"I say, 'I know it will, Clarence. I know. Maybe I better come out and look. You home next Saturday?' I felt like I shouldn't just blurt out something about some hot rod deuce. And I wouldn't mind getting out in the country.'

"'I get off at noon.'

"I'll be there twelve-thirty.'

"Then he give me directions and I mark my map. I'm thinking maybe I'll get lucky. Course, that's what I thought about Sue, too, and look how that turned out." He bent over like he was sick to his stomach. We laughed some more and visited the cooler.

When we'd reassembled in our make-shift pews, he continued: "The next Saturday I take off exactly at 9:30 and go down 29 to 46, which goes directly west. Hadn't been down that way in a while. Usually hunt up by New Rockford, you guys know. But 46 isn't a bad road and I hammered that old Chevy pickup down past Kindred and Enderlin and Litchville, a straight shot all the way to Gackle, then south on 20 to 34, then over to Napoleon." Walt always seemed to know how to get places. "I'm listening to the radio and all I hear about every five minutes is a news update on this guy escaped from some deputy between Bismarck and Dickinson. I mean that's all they talked about."

One of us said, "They caught that guy pretty quick, didn't they?"

"Couple days," Walt said. "But anyway, I pull into town around noon, hang around at the little podunk cafe and eat lunch. I follow Clarence's directions and find his place a mile south on 3 and a mile east. He apparently farms plus works in town at the elevator. Just after 12:30 I pull into the long gravel drive leading up to his place, and when I park in front of the house I don't see the '46 anywhere. But there were a lot of buildings around. Nice place.

"Clarence, he come down the steps and we shake hands and he takes me to a big new metal building to the north. Inside is his combine and tractor and a big grain truck, and way in back the '46. Christ, looks small compared to the John Deere.

"Clarence doesn't say anything, just lets me look it over. I pretend I'm pretty interested in it, and actually I am, because he was right, that fucker was cherry. About as nice a '46 as I seen. Odometer read 47,633, and the interior cloth good yet. A few dings, but the chrome isn't pitted. Buff the black paint, it'd be good as new. A guy'd hate to rod something like that.

"I ask him, 'Does it run?'

He just grunts and pops the hood. Then he gets in-- the door swings open without a sound--and turns it over. Flathead starts right up and idles smooth as a teenager's ass. But what the hell good's a car you can't stuff a big Chevy in and tear some folks some new ones? I look it over real careful for about fifteen minutes, just to make the right impression. Then I figure I've played it long enough, and I say to Clarence, 'You know, driving over here, I'm thinking I want something older than a '46. This one here's nice, but...' I shake my head. I added on, 'I got a '48 back home, not near as clean, but I didn't give much for it.'

"He says to me, 'This is a awfully good-looking car.'

"I say, 'I know it is, Clarence. I know it.'

"We stand silent for awhile.

"I say, 'Well, I guess it's got to be something older. Thanks for your time.'

"He just grunts at me.

"We walk out of the metal building and back toward my truck. 'Say,' I say to him, 'anybody else around here got anything for sale? Long as I'm out here?' I don't say anything about a deuce.

"He rubs his chin and I can tell he's thinking why the hell should he tell me where someone else's car is when I ain't going to buy his. Up to then he hadn't appeared overly friendly.

"But finally he says, 'Guy I know of, lives on Green Lake, he's got a '39 for sale. Pretty rough, though. At least that's what he says.'

"'How rough?' I ask him.

"'I ain't seen it, but he said there wasn't much straight on it. Rockers and floor rusted. Shot up good with a rifle.

Sitting outside a long time.'
 "'Coupe?'
 "'Yup.'
 "'Where's Green Lake?'
 "'Down past Wishek,' he says. And I'm thinking, *getting warmer.* Clarence gives me directions and I take off.

"Guy's name is Ray Larsen according to Clarence. Lives with his wife on an old farmstead right on the lake, but works around the area as a carpenter and doesn't farm. Owns a couple hundred acres but rents them out. Clarence talked to him a couple times in the cafe in Wishek and they'd got to talking cars once, and that's how Clarence, who's never been to Ray's place, knew about the '39.

"It's a pretty goddamned hot day by the time I get over to Larsen's. Still and quiet, humid. As I pull in the driveway, another long piece of gravel, I see someone in the front window of the house. It's a big white two-story, old farmhouse with these gables all over hell. I see the curtains in the big front window go closed.

"The '39's sitting under some big old trees between the house and the barn. Only car there as far as I can see. I don't want to act too interested so I go to the house first rather than the car. I knock on the old storm door and it makes a god-awful racket, but nobody comes. Bang some more, but still nobody. Go around back. I knew I'd seen someone. There isn't a doorbell, so I figure fuck it, whoever seen me just ain't too friendly, or sick or something. So I walk over to the trees and through this tall grass to the '39. It's a pretty neat old rig, chopped and lowered. I raised the hood first thing and it make a terrible squawk, and I figure that might roust someone from the house. Big flathead with three two's. And from the levers inside looks like maybe a Columbia two-speed differential. Some pretty choice parts, maybe, worth some good cash. Whoever'd built it was sure as hell a hot-rodder, but I don't know if Larsen knows what he has.

"I hang around some more, checking the car, waiting. The trunk lid's all shot through about ten times. I can't really see the floor, but it's got to be rusted as hell, sitting down as it is near the ground. But I figure I could fix that.

"I go back to the house again and knock, look in the windows. It doesn't feel right to go in. But I hadn't come all that way for nothing. Jesus it was quiet out there, eerie. Shit, I don't know.

"Well, I say to myself 'fuck it' and head back to the highway. I go into Wishek and sit at the cafe and have some more coffee, thinking. That '39 was good for parts, and maybe the body can be salvaged. I see this old black phone hanging on the wall and look up Larsen's number, just on the chance someone might be around or willing to talk by then.

"A man answers, and I ask him if he's Ray Larsen.

"'You're talking to him,' the man says.

"I explain who I am and what I want. Make sure he knows that Clarence had pointed me in his direction.

"He says to me, 'You out here about an hour ago?'

"I says, 'Yeah.'

"He says, 'When I come home my wife says someone been around knocking and hollering, looking at the Ford.'

"I don't want to piss him off, so I say, 'Sorry I scared her.'

"He gets apologetic, says, 'Oh, not your fault. She thought you were that guy, that convict got loose last night up by Medina. We heard he might come this way. She wasn't about to let anyone in the house. She went upstairs and sat in the chair holding the gun.' Jesus, I think, I'm glad I didn't walk in the house and get plugged.

"Ray,' I says to him, 'I am truly sorry about that. I shouldn't have called. I thought I saw someone when I pulled up, but I couldn't raise nobody. I've been called worse than a criminal, but I ain't one. Sorry I scared her.'

"'She's a woman, jumps to conclusions all the time. I think I just about got the '39 sold, but you could come back out if you want.'

"I sure as hell was going to. Since I'd seen the car, I didn't like the idea of anybody else getting it. Shit. I like that kind of challenge.

"So I drive out there and we shake hands like we're old buddies or something and the very first thing he says to me is, 'My brother and me, we used to roll this coupe from here to Jamestown or Bismarck, and nobody could catch us.' I'm thinking, *his brother?*, because TJ had said this guy who owned the deuce lived in California and kept the car at his brother's place. I let Ray talk. His wife brings us out some lemonade, but she doesn't say anything at first. We lean back against the '39. Finally she apologizes for not answering the door. Turns out they were really good folks.

"He tells me all about how some friend of theirs got drunk one Saturday afternoon, some ass who didn't know cars, and shot the holes in the trunk for target practice. They threw him off the property and he's never come back.

"Finally I say to Ray, 'Tell me how much you've got to have for the car.'

"Well,' he says, 'I know I can get a thousand for it.'

"I want to ask him how the fuck he knows that, but I don't.

"I just say to him, 'A thousand, huh?'

"He says to me, 'There some good old stuff on this car.' He lists off the motor, differential, shifter, steering wheel.

"I want to ask him why the hell he didn't take better care of it then, cover it or put it inside. But it was plain Ray knew what he owned.

"Then he drops the big one on me: 'The other one me and Bill used to rod with, now *that* one I keep inside.'

"'Bill's your brother?' I say.

"'Yup.'

"What other one do you mean, Ray?' I play real innocent.

"'Oh, it ain't for sale,' he says. 'It's Bill's, and he said he'd never sell that car.'

"Where *is* Bill, Ray?'

"'California. Comes back here every couple of years. First thing he does is head for the machine shed over there, goes in and sits down in it.'

"*Bingo.*

"I say, 'Well geez, Ray, I don't mean to be pushy, but sits down in *what*?'

"Come up and see it,' he says.

"We walk maybe 150 feet to an old style wooden quonset, built back in the forties or fifties, maybe, but the shingles are new and it's straight. Ray unlocks the walk-in door and steps inside and turns on the lights. I follow him. Inside there's a collection of antique furniture strewn around, dressers and chairs and shit like that. But right by the door there's a car under a tarp.

"Ray steps over to it and pulls back the dusty canvas and there that son-of-a-bitch is.

"'This car hasn't run in twenty-five years,' he says. 'Bill, he left for California and parked it right here, said he'd be back for it. But he never come to take it.'

"'You mean it's sat right here all that time?'

"'That's what I mean. Not one inch it's moved.'

"It was a deuce all right. And it was a hot rod. I

pictured the two of them thrashing around the gravel roads back when they were young bucks out for a good time, chasing tail. Hardly anything was even painted on the car. Well, hell, it's right here, see for yourself." Walt turned to the car and began to undo the ropes holding the tarp on.

He described the car as he worked. "Body's straight. You can see it's just the body--no fenders, running boards, no hood. Body and grille, that's it. Channeled a couple inches over the rails. Body's just like the frame there, that rust-color primer. Bench seat but no headliner and no door panels or mats. Look here," he said as he finished pulling the tarp off and swinging open the driver's door, which groaned as he did so. "Original gauges, '40 banjo wheel. Big Sun tach."

The car had wire wheels with big old bias-ply tires in back, smaller ones in front. It had a dropped axle but still didn't sit that low in front. Pitted chrome Ford hubcaps on the wheels. It exhaled a musty breath when Walt opened the door.

But it was the engine that fascinated Walt. A big flathead with a blower on it, carbs on top of that. He just stood looking at it, a kind of awe on his face. "Jesus," he said, "I bet this fucker used to fly. Ray told me some stories about how they used to drive. By rights they should have been dead a couple times over. He looked like a man who'd done some goddamned things when he was young, but maybe even nothing like Bill, and couldn't believe he'd lived to tell.

"I stood there picturing what I'd do to this baby. Gave me a hard-on practically. Wouldn't change a thing except do the brakes and tear down the mechanicals and get them working and leave the rest alone. There was just something about imagining how it was when it was brand new, original, innocent.

"So I come right out and say it: 'Ray, I want this car.'

"He says, 'Get in line. But Bill, he won't sell.'

"'I respect that,' I say, 'but I still want the car. Give me his number and I'll call him.'

"'He don't talk to nobody about this car. Quit that ten years ago.'

"'What's he do out there?'

"'Computers, got his own company. Worth a goddamn fortune. Drives a Mercedes. Told me once that he sold every kind of thing there was to sell when he moved out there, but there were two he'd never sell--the farm and this car.' I swear there were tears in Ray's eyes. "Something about this Ford Bill loves more than anything.'

"I did everything but get angry to get Ray to give me his brother's number, but he wouldn't. Wouldn't even say where he lived, what town. So I left him my number, explained very carefully what I'd do with the deuce if she were mine. Then I stood for maybe thirty more minutes just looking at her, and then I took off. My only consolation was that I could tell that asshole TJ I'd found his precious deuce, found the goddamned thing he told me I never would.

"For a month or so I couldn't stop thinking about that car, but then I just sort of gave up on it. I was pissed that TJ had been right about the one thing, that I'd never be able to buy it. Nights out here I'd think that sweet thing wouldn't ever sit in *this* garage. But I was wrong." Roy and Jim and I looked at each other; I doubt any of us could remember Walt owning up to being wrong.

"I was wrong because Bill Larsen, he was real sick. Told me that on the phone a month and a half ago. He'd been home for a visit a couple months after I'd been there and Ray had told him about me and gave him my name and number. Ray must have done alright by me, because Bill told me I was the only one he thought of calling because I wouldn't tear "her"--he never called it a Ford or deuce or five-window, just "her"--apart and chrome every goddamned thing in sight, put electric windows in and upholster the interior or some shit like that.

"We'd been talking a while and he says to me, 'Walt, I'm not going to live long enough to see her run again. Maybe I don't even want that. Looking at her, remembering, that's about enough.' He talked slow, like Ray, low and gravelly.

"I didn't say anything. I was on the phone right here, sitting on a stool right here by the bench.

"'When Ray and I were young,' Bill says, 'when we built her, everything was exactly the way it should be, but we didn't know anything then. Seemed like everything was new and the whole world had been made just for us. I've done well, but things just aren't ever as good as they were when they were new.' He spoke like someone who'd lost the only thing worth keeping, though I don't know what that was for Bill Larsen.

"'I hear you, Bill,' I say. Shit, there were tears in *my*

eyes.
"'I've got money coming out my ears, Walt, but I got no time now. Couple of months, maybe.'
"I told him, 'I don't know what to say, Bill. I don't want to take your car off you. I see how much it means to you.' That wasn't exactly true. I still wanted that fucker bad.
"'I can tell you do. But I might as well let it go. That's why I called.' Then his voice got firm and steady and he says, 'It'll take eight thousand to trailer her out of there, Walt.'
"'How about the '39?' I ask. 'I'd take 'em both.'
"'Another grand,' he says. I bet he made real good money selling because he had the kind of voice you knew was straight. Quick, straight and firm, like my dick, which you can count on every time.'" Almost all of us laughed.
"'Done,' I said. I wasn't going to argue with him.
"'I'll be back home the end of September,' he says. 'Let me check the date. 30th. You be there, and you can take her and the other.'
"I say, 'I'll treat 'em right.'
"'One thing, Walt,' he says. 'You have to promise me you'll keep her just like she is. Get her running, but no major changes. No lacquer, no chrome or aluminum, no fancy interior. I've got a '37 Cabriolet with billet aluminum sticking out its exhaust pipes. Not that deuce. It stays a hot rod.'
"The last thing I say to him is 'Count on it.' And I aim to keep that promise."
Walt paused a moment. Then, "I never met Bill Larsen. He died about a month after we talked. They buried him in the family cemetery on the farm. I knew he was a good man because he knew cars and he was straight. And he was there at the beginning, when gas was cheap and there were fucking hot rods, not these pussymobiles...." He gestured with his hands, almost spilling his beer.
"I didn't know Bill was dead when I hauled the trailer out there. Ray met me, explained it. He says, "Bill told me you'd be coming. He said you'd agreed on nine thousand.'
"'That alright with you, Ray?'
"'That's alright with me. Bill was the one who knew cars. I just rode along. I got no good use for them.'
"I wrote him out the check. I'd had to do a little haggling with the bank--bankers don't know shit when it

comes to *real* cars--but any payments I'm making are damn well worth it. Ray even had the original title. Bill'd bought the car in '52 from a farmer over by Kulm. I said, 'I'll take the deuce now, come back for the '39.'

"'That's fine,' he said.

"I get out the air tank and fill the front tires and by God them bastards hold and we winch it onto the trailer. And here it is boys.'" We stood in a circle around Walt's miraculous deuce. He looked heavenward. "Eat shit, TJ," he grinned.

I suppose we all knew what it was Walt really loved. He looked at us as a man might before he asked disciples to cover the world and tell as many others as they could. And, of course, that's all any of us was good for. We couldn't ever be like Walt, and that's why we kept coming back to his garage, why we'll always talk about him. He'd resurrected old bodies and performed miracles on bent frames, done things beyond what our clumsy hands were capable of. He knew that, and knew how well we could sing his praises. He hoped those that we told would spread the story, and eventually maybe everyone would know Walt had something ancient and holy. Something there was only one of. Only one. And his.

Me and Ronnie

Jim Redmond

    Me and Ronnie went fishing last Sunday. We did a little drinking, too. Some people think that's bad, though, 'cause Ronnie's a retard. But they don't know him like I do. They didn't grow up with him.
    I woke up early that morning because of a hangover. I still had some beer in the fridge, and thought about pounding a few and going back to sleep. But I really wasn't tired. So I sat there, at the kitchen table, thinking about how shitty life is. You know, about fair shakes and all that crap. So it was no surprise that my thoughts turned to Ronnie. I felt a little guilty about not doing anything with him lately, so I thought I'd take him fishing. He loves to fish. Can't get enough. Earlier in the season I used to take him out all the time. At least two, three times a week. But then summer came. The water gets warm, the fish don't bite. It's a law of nature. Try telling that to Ronnie, though. And lately I've been pretty busy at work. I drive forklift for Swift-Ekrich on the graveyard shift. It isn't too bad, but it takes up a lot of time. I have to do inventory and stuff at the end of the nights, really it's morning by then, so when I get home, I sleep. When I get up it's time for work. So that's why we hadn't been out for so long.
    I drank three beers, then put a six pack in the trunk of my car. I drive a '71 Chevelle. The motor purrs, but it needs a little body work, so I don't mind taking it out fishing. Maybe one of these days I'll have Ronnie help me sand off some of the surface rust. Anyhow, after loading up the beer, I picked up some bait, and went over to Ma's house. Ronnie's a few years older than me, must be 25 at least, but he still has to live with Ma. He's not one of those real bad retards that have their heads twisted and carry their arms like a broke chicken wing and have spit running down their face. Sure, he drools now and then, and does those goddamn yelps, but he understands a lot of stuff that goes on. Don't let him fool you.
    When I got to Ma's the sun wasn't even up yet. I went around to the back door, the one she always leaves unlocked. I went upstairs to Ronnie's room and woke him. He saw it was me, jumped out of bed and hugged me.
    "Tom, Tom," he said. "Where you been?"
    I backed away from him. His breath stunk. "Get dressed," I said. "Let's go fishing."

"What about Mom?"

"I'll take care of Mom," I said. "You just get dressed."

You know how some people have pictures of naked women in their rooms? Well Ronnie has fish. He has pictures of fish all over the damn place. And he knows what kind they are. That's what I mean when I say he's smart. You take an average Joe off the street and he won't know the difference between a walleye and a sauger. Ronnie does.

Downstairs Ma was still sleeping. I opened her door a little. "Ma," I said.

She made a startled sound. Like an "ah" or an "oh" or something.

"It's me. Tommy."

"What is it?" she said. "Is something wrong?"

"Nah," I said. "I just came to take Ronnie fishing." I heard movement from in there. "Ma, stay in bed. We're just going fishing."

"But he's sleeping. Why don't you come back later, after he wakes up?"

"Ma, he's already up. Just go back to bed."

"He's awake?" she said. "Then just wait. I'll get him ready."

I squeezed the door knob until the muscles in my forearm hurt. I hated it when she pulled this shit. Don't get me wrong. Ma's a good woman, and she tries hard, but sometimes she just pisses me off. I mean, Ronnie is a grown man, he don't need her to dress him. She treats him like such a fucking baby sometimes.

"Ma, he's getting dressed now." I spoke through the crack in the door. "Stay in bed. We're leaving in two minutes. If you get up now you'll never get back to sleep. Then you'll be bitchy all day."

"Will you help him get ready?"

"Yeah," I said. Jesus.

I met Ronnie halfway up the stairs. His clothes looked like they were on right to me. He didn't have his T-shirt tucked in or nothing, but had his pole and tackle box, and his Minnesota Twins hat on--the old kind, the kind with the TC for a logo. He asked me if it was okay to go and I told him damn straight it was. He got all excited. He ran down the stairs and then ran in place, his stupid feet slapping up and down, waiting for me to catch up. The goofy fucker.

There wasn't any wind, so we went to Duck Lake. We would probably have had better luck down at the river, but then we would have to use jigs, and it's easier for Ronnie to just cast out and leave the fucking bait sit. He can cast and jig a chub across the bottom of the river pretty good, don't get me wrong. But sometimes reels backlash and the line gets like a rat's nest. If we can't get it fixed, he cries. So I figured we'd just slap on a chub and a bobber and kick back and see if anything hit.

When it comes to fishing, Ronnie can do about anything a normal guy can. He sets up his own tackle, baits his own hook, and he can even run the net pretty good. And he can take the hooks out of fish, though I usually do it. Once he got bit by a northern. He didn't even notice it. He kept trying to pull the fish's stupid mouth open so he could get the fucking hook out. His finger looked pretty bad for a while after that. So I usually do it now.

Really, Ronnie's quite handy at things. He used to work for the retard center. They'd send all these goons out to electrical places where they'd sort bolts and shit like that. They only got paid like a buck seven an hour. But the supervisor, he kept sending notes home to Ma saying that Ronnie was one of their best workers.

So anyhow I got this bright fucking idea that if Ronnie was such a good worker, I should try to get him on out at the plant, let him make some real money. Not that five-fifty is a ton, or anything, but it sure beats the shit out of a buck something.

My boss wasn't too keen on the idea, but I told him Ronnie could be a de-icer. All they did was unpack plastic bags of turkey meat from combos of ice, then cut open the bags into a vat so the meat could be dumped into a mixer. My boss didn't think it wise to have Ronnie fucking with knives. De-icing is a two man job. One guy holds the bag and the other guy cuts it. I told my boss this. Ronnie could hold the bag over the vat while somebody else cut. I even told him they could pay him three-fifty instead of five-fifty. He said if Ronnie worked there, they had to pay him scale. He also said they'd give Ronnie a shot.

It took Ronnie a few days to get into it. He was pretty fucking slow at first. I thought they were going to fire him. But he caught on. He really liked it when I had time to go back into the freezers and talk to him.

Well, about a week later I had to drive my forklift back there to get some old re-work that had to be dumped. Ronnie was working with this kid, eighteen or nineteen years old. They must have been waiting for a new combo or something, 'cause I saw Ronnie walking to get a drink. Ronnie's a retard, so he walks kind of funny. You know, sort of bowlegged and his feet stick out at weird angles. This kid was walking behind Ronnie imitating him. I got real pissed, jumped off my forklift and grabbed this kid by the throat. I backed him up against the wall. I kept asking if he thought he was funny. He grabbed at my arms as his face turned red. When he started turning blue he clutched at my face like an old woman. He didn't have a chance. I would have killed the fucker, but Ronnie was behind me, saying the kid didn't mean it, to let him alone. When Ronnie pulled on my neck and started whimpering, I let the little bastard go. Word got back to my boss, and he said Ronnie couldn't stay.

The fish weren't biting. Ronnie had one strike, but he lost it. He let the fish run long enough, and set the hook good, but somehow it got loose. Those things happen. Ronnie knows that. I mean, something bad can happen and Ronnie don't give a fuck, he's on to the next thing.

Myself, I was getting bored, and the beers had worn off, so I pulled my sixer out of the trunk. It was mid-morning by now so it was no big deal. After I had a couple I asked Ronnie if he wanted one.

"Sure Tom," he said.

This kind of surprised me. I didn't think he'd ever drank beer before. But I thought it his right to have one.

Ronnie tasted the beer, then held it and watched his bobber. From the side he looked like any man. His dark hair and sideburns sticking out of his hat. His profile. Hell, even his posture looked relaxed, normal. From that angle you couldn't see his big forehead and goofy eyes. He looked like anybody.

When I ran out of beer I left Ronnie by the lake and went to get another twelve pack. The liquor store wasn't that far, about five or six miles, so it wouldn't take me long. Ronnie couldn't get into much trouble while I was gone.

As I walked back down to the lake with the beer he said, "Tom! Tom! Look!" Then he let out that high pitched yelp of his. It sort of starts out like it's going to be a laugh, but it just rises in pitch until it's this sharp piercing noise. He only does that when he gets real excited.

At first I thought the beer had really done something

to him. Or he'd really fucked something up. Dropped a bunch of shit in the water or something. "What, Ronnie?" I said.

He grabbed my arm and showed me the pail. There were two sunnies in there. Nice ones, too. The smart fucker'd switched his tackle, cut the leader off and put on a smaller hook and a waxworm and a small bobber and caught a few fish while I was gone.

"Hey, that's great," I said.

He yelped.

I set the beer down and patted him on the back. "You're a good guy Ronnie. You know that?"

"Yep," he said.

"Do you?"

"I know, Tom," he said.

I squeezed his neck lightly and shook him. "Are we buddies, Ronnie?"

"Yeah, Tom. We're buddies."

I gave him a light tap on the shoulder. Ronnie's a good guy, and I'm glad I got him for a brother, but for a second there I felt pretty bad. I got to thinking about fair shakes and hard knocks again. So I quick ripped open that twelver and dived right in for the both of us.

We sat around the whole afternoon fishing and drinking beer. We didn't hammer them or anything, the fish or the beer, but we had fun. At one point when we were watching our poles, and not talking much, I got to thinking. I remembered when we were young and had gone fishing out to this other kid's place. He lived on a farm, and a river ran through the back of it. This kid was in my grade, and he was pretty cool. I was pissed when Ma said I had to take Ronnie with. Back then I didn't really like him. When people found out Ronnie was my brother, I was afraid they would think something was wrong with me, too.

The fish weren't biting and we just fucked around. Me and this kid started walking around and throwing sticks at each other. Ronnie, he just watched his pole. We ended up going quite a ways down stream. When we came back Ronnie was wacking off. I was only about ten or eleven years old at the time. Ronnie had a big prick, I knew that from seeing him around the house, but I didn't really know what in the fuck he was doing with it. I mean, I sort of knew, but not really. I knew it was bad from the way this other kid acted. He started laughing and making jokes. Fucking Ronnie kept right at it, as if we weren't even there. Finally I told him to stop or I was leaving and not coming back to get him. He quit. The other kid was making jokes and saying how he couldn't wait to tell everybody. I tackled him and got on him. I started pounding my knuckle into his chest as hard as I could. I didn't stop until he started crying. I told him if he ever told, I'd give him a hundred more. Then I gave him one really good shot before I got off him. The funny thing is Ronnie could have kicked both our asses together, but he either didn't know or didn't give a shit about what was going on.

That was probably the first time I stuck up for Ronnie. A few years later, when I started wacking off heavy duty myself, I realized some things about Ronnie. The first was that he was a person, not just some fucked up piece of shit. I mean, I already realized that he was my brother and all, but I guess I had always thought of him as something other than a human being. Almost like a pet. You know what I mean? The second thing I realized was that Ronnie, for whatever reason, would probably never get a chance to live like a real person. He probably would always have to wack off. What woman would want him. Nobody even wanted to be his friend, except for other retards. So somewhere around this time I decided that Ronnie needed me, and since I was his brother, I wouldn't let him down.

We probably had an hour or two of daylight left when we quit fishing. But we were out of beer. I was half fucked up, but Ronnie seemed the same as always, which I guess is a little more than half fucked up. I was just going to drop him off at home and let Ma bitch at me for feeding him beer. But when I saw the Grain Belt sign swaying from Boots', I pulled in.

"How about a drink, buddy?" I said.

"Okay, Tom," Ronnie said.

We went in and I led him back to the pool tables. There were only three, and these four hotshots were playing on two of them. They all had their own sticks and were doing pass shots and calling fouls. None of them even had a beer, or a smoke. But I thought we'd sit there anyway, knock back some drinks and shoot a few games of stick. Just call your pocket and hit the fucking ball--the way the game was meant to be played. I put the money on the table, and told Ronnie to rack the balls. I went to get me a Jack Coke and Ronnie a beer.

When I came back with Ronnie's beer he had the balls racked. Not right, but racked. I broke. I showed Ronnie how to make a bridge, and how to stroke the ball. I told him that if he fucked up and tore the felt on the table I'd take his fishing posters. He concentrated real hard every time he shot. He didn't make too many. He didn't shoot hard enough. Half the time he just tapped the cue ball and didn't even hit another ball. He didn't give a shit. He sure got excited when I made a ball though.

His excitement is what got us into trouble. The more we played the more he started getting into it. He started doing those goddamn yelps. Pretty soon the hotshots left. I noticed this right away. It was nothing new. When we were kids, and playing outside, people would come up and talk to me, ask how Ma and my dad were doing, but they'd never say anything to Ronnie. It was like the fucker wasn't even there. This one old bag that lived down the street would walk way around us when she came down the sidewalk. The bitch would step out into the street so she wouldn't have to walk near Ronnie.

In the bar it didn't bother me. I thought, fuck 'em. Me and Ronnie were playing pool, tipping a few, and having fun like people do there every fucking night. So if those hotshots were afraid of a retard, fuck 'em.

After that it wasn't too long before the waitress wouldn't bring us any more drinks. We weren't even drunk. I'd probably had six or seven whiskeys, and Ronnie probably had two beers.

I went up to the bar to find out what the problem was. I looked for the four guys, but they were gone. I talked to the bartender. He told me the bar couldn't be liable for serving liquor to a mentally handicapped person. I told him we weren't hurting nobody, and were just having fun. He said, "Sorry."

I said, "How about a double shot of Turkey for the road."

"Can't do it," he said.

"Just for me. Not Ronnie."

He served it up, and I knocked it down.

We got in my Chevelle, and I started it. By this time my vision was pretty cloudy. But I was still in plenty good shape to drive. I wasn't seeing double or anything. And even if I was I'd have just covered one eye and driven home like that. I know all the back streets, so cops are never a problem. So I thought, since it's never a problem, why not let Ronnie drive?

"Ronnie. You know how to drive?" I said.

"Tom, I can drive a little," he said.

We got out and switched seats. I asked him if he knew which pedal was the gas, and which was the brake.

Ronnie revved the car. My tac was buried. "This is the gas, Tom."

"Stop it," I yelled. All I needed was for him to blow my motor.

Ronnie let up on the gas. He didn't say anything.

"You can't press on the gas so hard, buddy." I gently squeezed his neck. "Just take it a little easy."

"I'm sorry, Tom."

"I'm sorry I yelled at you," I said. I let go of his neck and pulled his hat down over his eyes. "How about we get rolling?"

At first he drove rather jerky. It was like being on a ride at Valley Fair or something. It was a good thing I was so drunk, or I'd have been scared. I pointed out which streets to take, so we could stay off the main drags. By the time we got to our neighborhood he was doing OK. He drove a little slow, like seven or eight miles per hour, but at least we weren't jerking all over the goddamn place. I had him stop, right in the middle of the street. There was no way he could park. We switched seats. I pulled the car up and onto the curb. I left it like that.

When Ma saw what kind of shape we were in she was pissed. She started fussing over Ronnie like he was a goddamn baby. She grabbed him by the shoulders and said, "Ronnie, oh, Ronnie." He just looked at her without saying anything. She petted his hair, then led him to the stairs. Before they went up she gave me this look. Her mouth opened, then closed. Tears were in her eyes. Then she said, "Tommy, how could you?"

Ma took Ronnie upstairs. I looked around the kitchen for a couple seconds. I could hear them, Ma getting him undressed, muttering to herself. All I wanted out of Ronnie was a brother. I'd never hurt him. Never. But I knew Ma wouldn't listen to this. She'd say I'd gone too far, that one of these times he *would* get hurt, and it'd be my fault. So I just went back out to the car, climbed in, locked all the doors and slept. The next morning I left before the sun came up without going inside. I thought I'd try the back door, but figured it'd be locked. Even now, she's probably still pissed. Maybe she has a right to be. Maybe all I've ever done is let him down. Made him do things he can't. Who knows? All I know for sure is that I haven't gone over there since, and she hasn't called me. At least not when I've been home.

Brave Punishments

Christine Mack Gordon

For KCR and the Garden

"Think not on him till tomorrow. I'll devise thee brave punishments for him."
Much Ado About Nothing, V. iv. 126-7

He wondered if, after all, this was where he was meant to be. In the dark, alone, abandoned. The darkness was somehow comforting as always; in it he became no one, nothing--the way in which the world perceived him, its pretty words to the contrary. The manacles on his wrists and the stale straw in the cell were not especially conducive to meditation and yet he could not sleep. The world beyond would enact its revenge on the morrow and his death was not unlikely. Then it would be as if he had never been born, which should please all the righteous among them. John the bastard, John the blackguard, John the ingrate. And what would be lost in his dying?

"No one can hate me as I hate myself," he muttered into the silence. "You have all taught me to hate so well." He leaned onto the chill wall, his memory reaching back to a time before hatred became the energy on which he fed.

* * *

Twenty years earlier, as a boy who lived from day to day in the wild countryside, working with his hands in the garden, learning the crafts of the everyday--those that kept the small household he shared with his mother in good working order. Occasionally they would ask assistance from neighbors or from those in the nearby village, and so he learned a bit of many trades: blacksmithing and carpentry, weaving and pottery making, leather mending and basketry. People commented on his quickness and his skill, and he found pleasure in all the work of his hands.

Yet he was not like the neighbors and the villagers; undefined yet clear was a line between them he could not comprehend. When he spoke with his mother about becoming an apprentice, she reacted almost in fear. "No, Johnny, no. Another life awaits you." But when he pressed her with questions, she refused to speak further. She taught him to read and to write, skills beyond nearly all the others he knew save perhaps the village priest. For a woman to have such skills was extraordinary; though he knew little of the larger world, that much he recognized. If his mother could read and write, she was not like other women, nor many men.

After a reading lesson one early summer evening, John looked over at his mother's shadowed face, her eyes closed in thought, and asked, "Where is the rest of our family, Mother? Where is my father?" Her brown eyes blinked open, startled. "That is not something I can speak with you about, John--not now."

"But why not, Mother?"

"I cannot--you must accept that."

He reached out to touch her cheek, burnished by the summer's sun. "Is that why I cannot be an apprentice? Is that why you teach me to read and write? What am I to be then, Mother? And when shall I know?" He looked up into her wide brown eyes, which seemed to him torn between knowledge and anxiety.

"I cannot talk with you about this now, Johnny. Someday, when you're older, I'll try to explain."

But I am eight now, Mother. How much longer?"

"I do not know, Johnny, I do not know." She pulled him to her and embraced him, stroking the straight black hair, caressing the sun-warmed arms. Then she pushed him an arm's length away and looked at him intently. "I love you more than anything in this world, Johnny, and I hope to do what is best for you. Can you be patient?"

He focused on her with a fierce intensity that reverberated through his young body. "I shall try, Mother, I truly shall."

She embraced him again and he surrendered to the warmth of her body.

* * *

He started out of his reverie as something crawled across his hand. Small, most likely a bug of some sort. A time before hate then, so long ago.

* * *

A few months later, as the autumn days grew shorter, the nights cooler, his mother became ill. Anna, the local purveyor of herbal cures, shook her head in dismay and sent John for the priest. He performed the last rites shortly after his arrival, and took John aside to convey the inevitable.

"No! She cannot die, she must not..."

"John, hush, hush...you must be a man now. Go to your mother. She will not be with us much longer; it is time for her to return to God..."

"Why must she return to God? God does not need her. I need her. Mother!" He ran toward the bed in which she lay. "Mother?"

"Johnny...?" she reached out her arm toward him and he took her hand and sat on the edge of her pallet.

"I'm here, Mama. Can I get you something? Would you like some water? Or something to eat?"

"No, John, not now. Just sit beside me." Her voice was barely a whisper. "John, I want to tell you about our family."

"Later, Mama, when you are better. You need to rest now, so you can get better."

"John, my love, I must tell you now; I have waited too long already and dare not wait longer." She paused briefly as if to catch her breath, a breath so shallow that he could barely see her breast rise and fall. "My father is a wealthy landowner in the next province. I have asked Father Herrera to take you to him when I...to take you to him. I pray that he will care for you until you are ready to enter priesthood-- that is what I wish for you, my son, to give your life to God, to making this world a more sacred place, a better place for all those who live here. You are a good and intelligent boy, and I know you will grow to be a strong and good man."

"But, Mama?"

"Yes, John."

"Must I be a priest? I would rather stay here and work on our land and..."

"John, you come from a noble family. It is your responsibility to take on a more difficult task than that of a farmer or craftsman. You will find all the skills you have learned useful in the life of a priest, especially a village priest, like the good Father. I hope that this would be a good life for you, John. And you can pray for me..." her voice drifted into silence.

"Mama, you will get better! We can live here for a long time yet. When I get older, then we can talk about this again...Mama?" He leaned closer to her face, and felt the breath move slowly in and out. "Mama?" he whispered. She did not respond.

Father Herrera walked over to the pallet. "She is asleep for the moment, John. Let her rest. She may wake again soon."

John remained at his mother's side, holding her hand,

occasionally wiping the sweat from her brow with a damp cloth. The late afternoon waned, the sunset quietly brilliant in the western sky. Still she slept. Father Herrera offered John some food, but he could not eat. As night drew on he climbed onto the pallet beside his mother. The priest started to object, but could find no words to challenge this last gift. He sat quietly in a chair on the other side of the room.

Midway through the night, she cried out, "Johnny! Johnny!"

He was awake at the instant, "Mama, I'm here."

"They will not take you from me, Johnny, they will not. I do not care what happens. I do not care what they want. Johnny!" But she had gone back to sleep, or had lost consciousness. Her breathing was labored and intermittent. John turned his eyes to the priest, asking a question the man could not answer. Her breathing suddenly stopped.

"Mama? Mama?" He fell upon her body, hugging her fiercely to him as if to pour his own youth into her. "Do now leave me, Mama. I do not want to be alone. Mama!"

The priest came up beside him, drew him away from the body, and clasped him in his own arms. "John, your mother is gone now. She has gone. We must pray for her soul."

"No--" he sprang from the priest's arms and raced out of the cottage.

He remembered running for what must have been many miles that night, far into the countryside around the only home he had known, until he threw himself exhausted onto a silent hillside and gazed obliviously at the night sky.

* * *

"The end of innocence," he thought as he pressed his hands against the wall and brought himself to his feet. He walked across the cell and back, no more than four strides each way, and wondered how many hours yet till the morn. At least they had not shackled his feet; the freedom to move even so small a distance was precious.

* * *

The moment of his mother's death was in some ways not only the end of innocence, but the end of freedom as well. She was buried in the village churchyard, and the next day Father Herrera had ridden with him to his mother's family. Whether the simple priest had anticipated the welcome that awaited them was something John never knew.

The household of the Las Robles family was a large one; the family estate embraced a huge tract of land that included several villages larger than the one near John's home. The family home seemed a palace to the young boy who approached the doors hesitantly, suddenly embarrassed by his simple clothing and work-roughened hands. Surely this was a place where princes lived--how could it be his home? A servant had carried Father Herrera's message from the anteroom where they waited to some inner depths of the house. He returned and glanced with a peculiar intensity at John before motioning them both to follow him. John could barely disguise his curiosity about the grand rooms through which he passed, but the servant walked briskly and he had little time to admire the lavish furnishings and the elegant tapestries that adorned them. Suddenly the servant halted and said to the priest, "The boy is to wait here," and pointed to a bench outside the room where he had paused. John took a seat and Father Herrera was shown into the room.

The servant came out, looked once again at John, and returned the way he had come. John could hear the murmur of voices in the room, but could not hear the conversation clearly. He contented himself with gazing at a series of paintings hung across the corridor, wondering if these were members of his family. He tried to detect a resemblance to his mother and thought that in one or two the wide eyes and full lips hinted at a relationship. But if this were his home, why had his mother left it? Why had no one from their family come to seek them?

"I am glad the slut is dead. Would that she had died ten years ago, before she disgraced our name!" The voice from the other room was fierce, imbued with a harshness that held no measure of sympathy. John heard the murmur of Father Herrera's reply.

"No, I will not have the bastard here. He is no part of this family."

The quiet voice responded again.

"You do not know what my father would have wanted. He never forgave her for what she did. He would act as I am acting."

John edged closer to the door to try to hear the priest's reply.

"I do not care what you do with him. Drown him. Sell him to brigands. We will have none of him here."

"But will you not at least see him...think of your sister, her sorrow, her hope that you would..."

"No! Now get out of here! Here is something for your pains."

John heard the coins as they fell upon the floor and moved quickly back to the bench. The priest's voice, quietly persistent, made one final attempt to speak.

"Now, Father, or I will personally throw you out." The voice was quieter, but no less harsh.

The priest soon appeared in the doorway and motioned to John to join him. They walked slowly back to the courtyard where they had entered.

"Father?"

"Not now, John. Get on your horse."

John obeyed silently and followed the priest as they rode out into the fields that surrounded the estate. The sun was halfway to the horizon and he wondered where they would go. The ride back to the village would take a full day. The priest rode on in silence, not the way they had come, but continuing east. Shortly before sunset they came to a small farm where the priest begged hospitality for the night. They ate in near silence with the farm family, then went to the outbuilding where they would sleep.

John had been in turmoil since the afternoon. What had happened? Why did his family not want him? What had the man meant about his mother? About him? He feared to ask the priest and yet desperately needed to know.

"Father?"

"Yes, John?"

"Where are we going now?"

I'm not sure, John. I have to think about this carefully. I do not know if..."

"Father, was that my mother's family?"

"Yes, John, it was your uncle--your mother's brother--with whom I spoke."

"But what about my mother's father? She said he..."

"He is dead, John. Your uncle is his heir."

"Those things he said, Father, I did not understand...why does he not...what did it mean..."

"It is late, John. Try to sleep. I will try to explain tomorrow." The answer was a final one, and John was silent.

"Goodnight, John. Say your prayers."

"Good night, Father." He did not tell the priest how hard it had been to pray since his mother's death. He knew he must, that only God could hear him now, yet he could not forgive God for taking his mother. He could not believe in God's goodness. And now the fierce man who was his uncle wished him dead, would not see him, said that his mother was...but he would not think of that. He struggled toward sleep, fearing what his dreams might bring.

When they rode on in a drizzling rain the following morning, they followed an eastward path, continuing away from their village. John refrained from questioning the priest for half the morning's ride, but when they stopped to water their horses, he could contain himself no longer. "Father, where are we going?"

"I am taking you to your father, John."

"My father? Who is he? Where does he live?"

The priest maintained his silence for a moment the boy found endless. Finally, after he mumbled what seemed to be a silent prayer to himself, he placed his hand on the boy's shoulder and said, "John, this is a difficult story for me to tell you, and it will be a difficult story for you to hear. But I can think of no other way. You do not belong to us in the village. Your mother wanted you to be with her family, but clearly that is not possible. Your uncle refuses to accept you. Your mother told me her story when she first came to our village and swore me to silence. But it is your story, too, and you must know it if we are to continue on this journey."

John sensed the fear in the man's voice, and sought in his youthful way to reassure him. "Please, Father, I need to know. I am sure my mother would want you to tell me. I do not understand why my uncle hates me so, when he has not even met me--or why he hated my mother..." his voice cracked.

"Your uncle is a stubborn man, John, and unforgiving. Let us ride on and I will tell you the story."

They remounted and continued across the nearly empty countryside. "Your mother was the daughter, the young daughter, of a noble house. One of the visitors who came frequently to the family estate was a noble lord of our country. He was very attracted to your mother and paid her a great deal of attention. She very naturally responded to him--he was handsome, wealthy, and a significant figure in the land. He seduced her, and not long afterward she found herself with child. What she hadn't known was that he was also married. When she revealed her situation to her father he was outraged, but there was little he could do since his own estate owned allegiance to this lord. The best he could do was to hide her shame, and the way in which he did it was to send her to our village, and to tell the rest of the world that she had chosen to enter a nunnery. He sent monies to her to assist her in her new life, but she refused to accept any help shortly after you were born. She learned to live the life of a peasant woman, and struggled to make your world as loving as she could. She hoped that eventually she would be able to return with you to her father, that he would see you as a gift to his old age, but that is not to be."

"But my father, what of him? Did he never return to see her? Does he know of me?"

"Your mother wrote to him--first, when she became aware of her condition, once more after your birth. She said that he never replied."

"What is a bastard, Father? That is what my uncle called me, is it not?'

"Yes, John. But it is an ugly word. It means that you were born outside the marriage contract, that your parents were not wed."

"Is that a terrible thing, Father?"

"In our world, John, it can be. It means you cannot inherit from either of your parents' families, at least not according to the law. You are looked upon by some as a child of sin and therefore an outcast in society."

"It was wrong, then, what my mother did."

"She was weak, John, but we are all weak in different ways. She was young and trusting and she made a dangerous mistake, a mistake most fatal for women, since we prize them above all when they maintain their purity despite all assaults against it."

"She was a slut."

The priest, startled, turned and raised his hand as if to slap the boy and only at the last minute pulled back. "Never, *never* let me hear you use that word again, John, not about any woman, but above all not about your mother. Your mother gave all her being to give you a good life, to teach you what was important and right. Do not think you have the right to judge her because she sinned. She spent her last eight years in exile from her family, living a life that was totally alien to her, because she made a mistake. And yet she lived those years in humility and goodness, and brought joy to our village. And she raised a son of whom she had every right to be proud. Or so I thought until now."

The boy, astonished by the vehemence in the priest's voice, did not reply.

"John, John, do not heed the rules of the world. Heed the rules of God, and grow to be a good man. That is what your mother wished for you."

"But what if my father feels the same as my uncle? If he would not even reply to my mother's letters, why should he see me now?"

"I do not know, John. But this seems the right way to me. We will go to him and see. If he refuses to acknowledge you, we will find some other course."

"Please, Father, let us go back to our village now. I do not wish to go on, I do not want to see him..."

"John, despite what I have told you about these events, perhaps we have not heard the full story. I believe we should give your father a chance."

John rode on silently. He thought back to one of his earliest memories, of walking through a blossoming field at his mother's side, chasing butterflies and picking up unusual stones. He remembered his mother's warm hand encompassing his own, and found himself suddenly wiping the tears that streamed down his face. He hoped the rain would hide them from the priest's ever watchful eyes.

* * *

"Damn memory!" The night seemed deeper than ever, and the memories more vivid. He tried to vanquish the long dead face of his mother, the one face whose love he had known, whose care had been without cease, without limit. She haunted him now as he remembered his crimes, and the woman he had wronged, who looked perhaps too much like the mother he remembered. No punishment could be enough. It did not matter about the others, the men whom he had betrayed. But she had been innocent, and he had abused her. For that he could not be forgiven.

* * *

His father, he soon learned from Father Herrera, was Don Alejandro, Prince of Aragon and one of the most powerful lords in the land. The terror he had felt as he approached the home of his mother's family was a mere shadow of what encompassed him as they approached Don Alejandro's palace. For a palace it certainly was, fortified against assault, surrounded by a grand village through which they rode as the late afternoon warmth dissipated into cool evening breezes. A guard at the castle gate demanded their business, and the priest politely requested to see Don Alejandro.

"Don Alejandro is not seeing petitioners today, Father.

Come back in three days; that is when he considers requests from his countrymen."

"I believe the Prince would be willing to see us today."

"Father, I know him well, and he is most unwilling to change his habits."

"My son, I beg you this favor. Carry a message to the Prince for me. We will await his reply."

"I still do not believe he will see you, Father, but I will carry this message."

Father Herrera, who astonished John by being prepared with scrip, ink, and a quill in his saddlebag, quickly prepared the brief note and handed it to the guard.

"I thank you, sir, for doing us this service. What is your name?"

"Pablo de Abuelos, Father."

"God will bless you for this, Pablo de Abuelos." The guard walked through the gate, and John and the priest dismounted from their horses and walked them to a small patch of grass nearby where they might graze.

"What sort of man is Don Alejandro, Father?" John could no longer bring himself to say "my father." The idea that he was the son of a prince of the land was still beyond his comprehension, as was his peculiar status in relation to this man.

"I do not know much about him, John. My sense is that he is a good ruler, that he cares well for his land and people. But I know little about him as a person. I have had no reason to travel outside our village these many years, and the Prince has never traveled there. What I know I have heard from others. But we may soon see for ourselves."

"Father?"

"Yes, John?"

"Father, I'm afraid. I do not know how to act here. I will disgrace myself and you. I..."

"John, stop. You need only be yourself. If your father will see us, we will go in together. Watch what I do and do the same. You are a good, intelligent lad, and you need not be ashamed of who you are. Always remember that. You are a child of God, whatever men may say."

John remained doubtful, but disguised his concern from the priest. He watched the village around him as it slipped into dusk and thought how much he would like to be back in his own cottage, his own village. He feared he would never see them again. A few villagers passing by the gate glanced with some curiosity at the damp and dusty travelers. The guard returned, and with a grimace of astonishment informed the priest that he was to escort them into the palace. He led them through a maze of corridors and into a room where a servant awaited.

"Bernardo will help you bathe, and will find fresh clothes for you. Don Alejandro has requested that you join him at supper." Pablo de Abuelos saluted and turned to depart.

"I thank you again, my son," the priest called after him.

John stood silently in the middle of the room, astonished by the richness of his surroundings. The priest urged him forward and helped him strip off the dusty clothes of their journey. A large tub in an adjacent closet was filled with heated water, a sight John had never seen, a pleasure he had never experienced. At home he had bathed in the stream, or washed with water they carried from it to the cottage. As he slipped into the tub, he wondered anew at the world in which he suddenly found himself. He might have stayed in the bath forever, but Bernardo was very efficiently rubbing his youthful body with a soft rag and something that smelled faintly of roses. Then he found himself wrapped in a huge length of cloth and led back into the other room where the quietly persistent man helped him into clean clothes so soft that his skin felt as if it were being gently embraced. The priest bathed after him, but refused the clothes that had been provided, agreeing only to a careful brushing of his stained traveling clothes. Then the still silent Bernardo left the room, and another man appeared.

"This way, please, gentlemen."

They moved through several corridors and passed many darkened rooms; night had fallen and torchlight illuminated only those rooms that were occupied. They could hear raucous laughter as they approached a well-lit room and soon found themselves in the dining hall of the palace. The man who escorted them led them to the head of the table, bowed, and departed. Father Herrera bowed as well, "My lord, I bid you good evening."

John hesitated a fraction of a second, then did a precise imitation of the priest. As he stood upright again, he glanced at the man seated before him. He appeared to be about five and thirty, dark-haired and blue-eyed, his face aging at the corners of his eyes and mouth, but still remarkably youthful. He wore a splendid tunic of red silk, embroidered with small pearls, and a jeweled medallion hung from a chain about his throat. Several other men sat at the table with him but John was scarcely aware of their presence.

"So, this is the young pup, eh?" A laugh rose from deep in his throat. "Come here, boy."

John approached the large chair in which Don Alejandro lolled. He bowed again. The man's large hand reached out and rested on his shoulder. "So, boy, what brings you here?"

Father Herrera took a step forward. "My lord..."

"Not you, Father, I want to hear what the boy has to say."

John's lower lip quivered as he began to speak. "My mother is dead, sir. We buried her but a few days ago in the village where we lived. She had asked Father Herrera to take me to her family. We went there first, but my grandfather was dead and..." he paused and took a carefully controlled breath, "...and my uncle did not wish me to remain there." He glanced quickly at the priest, who nodded. "Then we came here." He did not know what else to say.

"I see. And it is your belief that I am your father?"

"I do not know, my lord, but that is what my mother told Father Herrera."

Don Alejandro's blue eyes peered intently into John's brown ones, then his hand stroked the boy's dark hair, and moved down again onto his shoulder. "All right, boy. Antonio!" The man who had escorted them to the room reappeared. "Take the boy to one of the guest chambers. I am certain he must be tired after such a journey."

John had started to follow Antonio, then suddenly turned to make a final bow, "Thank you, my lord."

"Off you go, boy. We will speak again in the morning."

As John left, he heard another deep voice cross the room, "He is a remarkably attractive lad, Alejandro. Do you really think there is a chance he might be yours?" The question ended with a laugh that was joined by the others at the table, and John's chest suddenly felt as if all the breath had been forced out of it. He nearly stumbled as he walked, but caught himself and followed Antonio into the torchlit hall.

* * *

He remembered the bed in which he slept that first night--the first real bed in which he had ever slept. The straw in this cell was much more like home, save that no cloth protected him from its inevitable prickings. He wandered back in memory to that bed, and to the others which had succeeded it. Now he had come full circle and beyond, to this cell and to this night, perhaps his last. Whatever his fate in the morning, he would make peace with himself tonight. The manacles were chafing against his wrists; he lifted them to his face and licked the skin, tasting drops of blood where it had broken. Would his blood redeem his crimes? Would his death resolve the dilemma which his life posed to the brother he had betrayed? He scraped the sides of his hands against the wall, almost as if to increase the pain.

* * *

When he awoke the next day, the sun was already quite high in a brilliant sky, and Father Herrera was seated at his bedside. "Good morning, John; God be with you."

John rubbed his eyes, and observed for the first time the full dimensions of the room in which he had slept. It was twice the size of his cottage, hung with heavy draperies and filled with two magnificent wooden trunks, several chairs, and the huge bed, which itself seemed the size of a small room. A large window gave entrance to the sunlight which shone across the foot of the bed. "Oh, Father, am I dreaming?"

The priest laughed quietly, "No, John, indeed you are not."

"Am I late, Father, should I have risen earlier?"

"No, my son, Don Alejandro wanted you to sleep as long as you wished. We spoke together last night after you left, and he will see you whenever you arise."

"Is he my father then? What is to happen to me?"

"Yes, John, he has acknowledged that he is your father. He would like you to remain here and to be raised as befits his son."

John suddenly recalled the strange laughter as he had left the dining hall the night before. Something peculiar about it made him tremble. "But, Father, I am not his true son, I am only his..." he could not bring himself to say the word.

"Yes, John, and that will make some difference. Don Alejandro has an older son, a son by marriage. That son is his heir. But he has agreed to take responsibility for your care and to bring you up as a respectable gentleman. While you will not inherit his estates, you will receive an education and learn skills that can provide a good life for you. You might become a soldier, or perhaps help manage your father's lands."

"My mother wanted me to be a priest, Father."

"Well, that would be possible, too, John. If you receive a calling from God, I'm certain that your father would respect that. But for now, you must look to learning the ways of the nobility of our land, for it is among them that you will live."

"Could we see him now, Father?"

"Break your fast, first, my son. Then we will seek him out."

"Father?"

"Yes, John?"

"Will you return to our village now?"

"Soon, John, as soon as I see you settled. The people need me there, too."

"Father? I am not certain I wish to stay here."

"It is all very new to you, John, but this will become your home now. I know this change will be difficult, but I also know you, John. You have great gifts to offer these people, though they may not know it. Bring your knowledge of our lives to them; you have lived among those who have little, and now you will live among those who have much. You have learned from the poor, and now you will learn from the wealthy. You are young and healthy and intelligent; your mother had great hope for you. Remember her, and do good with what you learn, John. Never forget what she sacrificed for you."

The boy saw his mother lying before him in death, and a cry escaped him. "Mama--"

"She will always be with you, John. Remember that. Remember her."

"Father..." the boy flung himself from the bed and into the priest's arms. "Father, I'm still afraid."

"It will all be fine, my son. All will be well." But his voice spoke as if he were petitioning God, rather than reassuring the trembling boy.

The priest had left two days later and John adapted himself as best he could to a life radically different from that he had lived before. His father hired as his tutor the same priest who had tutored his elder son and John spent his mornings in the quiet library learning Latin and Greek, mathematics and bits of history. Religion was omnipresent, yet disregarded. The Church made its presence felt, yet the men who ruled the land were secularists at heart. Their hypocrisy astonished John as he grew older and more aware of its implications. He noted how ruthless his father and his allies were in their treatment of those who worked the land. They exploited their labor, they recruited them for endless petty wars, they took the women to their beds and deserted them the next day.

All this he observed, retreating more and more into himself, while at the same time taking on additional responsibilities for the running of the estate. He had a gift for detail, for the maintenance of records, and he soon found his place in the estate's hierarchy. He learned soldiery, too, as befitted his father's son, and the training served him well. Several times by his sixteenth year, he had ventured forth in his brother's ranks to confront some hostile invader and acquitted himself well.

Yet nowhere was he at peace, nowhere at home. He continued to develop the skills he had learned as a boy and spent time among the estate's laborers, where he earned respect with his ability rather than because of his status. He discovered an affinity for animals and learned to care for them, to heal their diseases. The animals and the peasants knew him as himself, for he felt no need for pretense among them.

In Don Alejandro's palace, he became silent, withdrawn, melancholy. Although his father included him in his council and welcomed his abilities in the running of the estate, he felt more often like a clever clerk than a son of the household. Doubtless his own reticence was in part responsible, but he could not join in their debauchery. The ghost of his mother remained too clearly in his consciousness. They teased him fiercely for his refusal to join their revels, yet though his own desires often tempted to succumb, he would resist and retreat to his account tables or to his room.

He found it hard, as he neared his seventeenth birthday, to imagine how his life would proceed. He thought that his father might marry him to the daughter of some minor nobleman--even his bastardy would not preclude that; his bloodlines were noble if illegitimate. But he did not want a life like his father's or his brother's. Pedro spent most of his days leading his father's military forces in excursions to increase their own land holdings or to prevent any incursions by others into theirs. John found it rather stupid and pointless, though he admired his brother's military prowess and his apparent affection for the soldiers with whom he surrounded himself. But he barely knew Pedro, who was a full ten years older than he. And while he was content doing the work he did around the estate, he felt a restlessness to go beyond its limits, to see a larger world in which he was not defined by his blood or his station. He wondered if he might persuade his father to allow him to venture forth on his own.

A sullen September day brought Don Alejandro's closest ally to the palace. Don Aurelio arrived with a small band of men to discuss a recent military triumph and to ask permission to hunt on Alejandro's lands. John had sat somnolently through the roisterous dinner, trying to ignore the persistent glances Don Aurelio directed at him. He had ever despised this man, who seemed to him the most foul of his father's allies, though clearly he was one of the most powerful. Aurelio drank to excess, took his pleasure with any who came in his path, and despised all who did not join him in his ludicrous pursuits. John had done his best to excuse himself during Aurelio's previous visits, but his father had requested his presence tonight.

"John, come here." It was his father, calling him to the head of the table, where Aurelio sat on his right.

"Yes, my lord, how can I be of service?"

"Don Aurelio would have you accompany him on the morrow's hunt."

"I am honored, my lord, but I have many tasks here to which I must attend." John's voice exuded a graciousness which demanded all his attention.

"The work will wait, John. I expect you to attend his lordship."

"As you wish, my lord." John bowed discreetly and began to withdraw.

"John!" Don Aurelio's voice was slurred, though the evening was still early.

"My lord?" John glanced directly at the man before him. Aurelio was his father's age, but looked older. His auburn hair was streaked with grey, and the colors of his eyes ranged from grey to green to brown, depending on the light and his mood. He was of a fiery temperament, fierce in battle, rowdy in company. When he graced Don Alejandro's household with his company, the halls rang with his laughter and the servants did their best to keep out of his way. His wrath was not pleasant to behold.

"I am pleased that you will accompany us. I hope you

will enjoy the hunt."

"I am certain I shall, my lord," he replied, though he knew the opposite to be true. He did not relish the thought of spending several days in Don Aurelio's company. But he knew better than to defy his father's will.

The next day dawned fair and the hunting party set out before mid-morning. The land was abundant in game and the first day's hunt proved energetic and fruitful. John enjoyed the fierce autumnal air as it broke against his face, and the powerful feeling of his horse's muscles as they crossed the open land. As sunset neared, they took refuge in a lodge at the eastern edge of his father's domains; John and a few of the others prepared a meal that succeeded in satiating everyone's hunger. Several of the men drifted outdoors to sleep, while a few kept Aurelio company. Wine warmed them more than the fire they had built, and seemed likely to put them to sleep as well. John sat silently near the fire and hoped the evening would end soon. He felt obligated by his father's command to remain with Aurelio, but would have preferred to be out of doors, where he might test his knowledge of the stars in the clear night sky.

"John."

"My lord?"

"Come here, John."

He rose and walked to where Aurelio was seated in a rough wooden chair. "Yes, my lord."

"Closer, John, bend down." John bent down toward Aurelio's face until he could smell the wine on his breath. Suddenly a hand pulled his head forward and forced his lips to Aurelio's mouth. He struggled and broke away, turning towards the door.

"Hold him!" The two men beside Aurelio, who John had thought had drifted to sleep, sprang to their feet and attempted to grab his arms. He fought their approach as best he could in the dim light, but a third man came at him from behind and with a swift blow knocked him into the others' arms. They gripped him firmly and turned him to face Aurelio.

"Now, John, do not struggle. It will do no good. And you will forfeit your pleasure as well."

"I see no pleasure for me here, my lord." John's voice rang with anger.

"John, I have desired you for so long. Let us take this opportunity to learn to know one another better."

"I have no desire to know you better, my lord."

"Ah, John, you are such an innocent. I think that is

what makes you so attractive." Aurelio had approached him now and was stroking his cheek. John continued to strain against his captors and kicked fiercely at Aurelio's legs. But the blows struck only the air. Aurelio took his face in his hands and kissed him again. When he drew back, John spit into his face.

"You bastard!" Aurelio screamed and struck him full force, one blow, then another, and another. "All right, then, we will not worry about your pleasure. Turn him, hold him over the table."

The two men pulled him to the table in the room's center, while the third began to pull off his clothes. John fought as well as he could, but the two men clearly knew their task, and his efforts achieved nothing. Suddenly someone's hands were running down his naked back and over his buttocks, "What a fine young body you have, John. It is truly a delight to see it at last." He was suddenly pierced by a lacerating pain as Aurelio plunged into him. He screamed.

Everything after that was terrifying chaos. He knew Aurelio had taken his pleasure and then had turned him over to the others; at some point he began to vomit and they laughed and tried to pour more wine down his throat. When they were finally exhausted they let his body sink from where they had held it against the table to the floor beneath, and had gone off to sleep in the other corners of the room. He lay there for what may have been hours, cold, unmoving. He could feel the dampness on his thighs, where semen and blood anointed him; his face was swollen from Aurelio's blows. Slowly, he began to move on his hands and knees. He sought his clothing and found it in a crumpled pile near the fireplace. Some of it had been torn, but he put it on as best he could. He rose to his feet and made his way to the door. The horses had been hobbled on the other side of the lodge, but he knew that taking one would disturb the rest and awaken the hunting party. It would be best to make his way on foot. He glanced up at the sky to ascertain his direction, then slipped away from the sleeping camp and back toward his father's home.

He walked through the next day and night, stopping only briefly to sleep. They had come a fair distance on the hunt, and some of the terrain was difficult for a man on foot. His body was a pattern of bruises and only his desperate need to get away had allowed him to go the first few miles when even to walk was excruciating. It became easier as the sun rose and the air warmed slightly. He stopped to drink whenever he reached a stream, but several times he vomited water and bile. When night fell, and he tried to sleep, he was tormented by dreams in which the previous night's torture was enacted again and again. Long before dawn, the dreams and a burning fever drove him onward. He moved more slowly, the fever and hunger exacerbating his pain. It must have been nearly noon when he reached the village; he made his way by a less-traveled path that brought him into the stable yard of the palace. He glanced up at the bright windows glittering in the sun, and collapsed.

When he regained consciousness, he was in his own bed. The windows were draped and he could not tell whether it was day or night. A torch burned on one wall, and a candle was alight on the table beside him. As he turned to rise, a groan escaped from his lips and he sank back upon the bed. He was naked beneath the bedclothes, but he was aware of the medicinal smells that indicated someone had seen to his battered body. "Ah, but who will see to my battered soul," he murmured to himself, and drifted to sleep again.

The next time he stirred, he sensed someone in the room. "Who's there?" The terror in his voice startled him.

"My lord, it is I, Bernardo." The servant drew closer to the bed, bringing with him a cup that he offered to John. "Please, my lord, take something to drink. The fever has broken, but your body is famished for water and food."

"I cannot."

"You must, my lord. Please let me help you." Bernardo brought the cup to John's lips and as he felt the liquid pass the cuts on his mouth he grimaced but managed to swallow as well. It was wine, well-watered, the way he used to drink it when he was a boy.

"Thank you."

"My lord, do you wish us to call a physician to you?"

"No! No one, no one must see...must know..."

"But, my lord, the injuries may be..."

"No. I will be..." he didn't know what to say. Would he ever be well? He would never again be the young man he had been only days ago. "How did I come here, Bernardo? I remember only entering the stable yard."

"Amelia found you my lord, and she carried you into the kitchen, and came to fetch me. We brought you up here and bathed you and did what little we could to soothe your pain and fever. She has a true gift with herbs."

"I know. We have worked together with the animals

many times. Did anyone else...? Does anyone know...?" His agitation had increased with his questions, and he had tried again to rise.

"Do not try to get up, my lord." Bernardo reached out a hand to restrain him.

"Do not touch me!" The words escaped him without thought, to be followed by a howl of pain so shattering that John himself was frightened by it. "I'm sorry, Bernardo, I..."

"My lord, shall I call Amelia? Would it be easier for you if she..."

"No, stay, please. Please. I do not know why...I, please, Bernardo..."

"Oh, my lord, anything I might do for you, I..."

"Could I have some more of that tinted water you're passing off as wine?'

"Yes, my lord. Of course."

John drank several more sips of the wine, then glanced almost shyly up at this man who had know him since the first moment he had entered this world, and reached out to take the hand that lay upon the counterpane. "Thank you, Bernardo," he whispered.

"May I bring you some food, my lord?"

"Only if you know Amelia has some of her wonderful soup over the fire."

"She may well, my lord. It's been a brisk few days recently."

The conversation had become almost normal, ordinary. But John felt the edge of madness very close to his barely regained control, and knew it would be a struggle to contain it. Ordinary words might do it best.

"How long have I been home, Bernardo?"

"Two days now, my lord. It was the day before yesterday, about midday that Amelia found you. And the night is just upon us today."

"Was I unconscious all that time?"

"You were at first, then you seemed to sleep. But the fever ravaged you and you cried out in dreams. It was only late today that the fever ended."

"With much thanks due to the fine remedies of our Amelia, I'm sure."

"Indeed, my lord, without them..."

"I might be dead. But perhaps that would be better." A deep bitterness imbued his voice.

"Do not think so, my lord. Your life means much to us."

"To you, perhaps, though God only knows why. To no one else, I think."

"I am sure that is not true, my lord."

"Has my father asked for me?"

"Yes, my lord. We told him you were ill, and that it would be best if no one see you until we could determine the course of the disease."

"Ah, Bernardo, what wise dissemblers you and Amelia are. What about Don..." he could not speak the name, but it proved unnecessary.

"He returned before we found you, my lord, and told Don Alejandro that you had decided to remain and hunt another day on your own."

John turned away from the compassion in Bernardo's eyes. He did not deserve such care from anyone. He felt himself slipping toward sleep again as Bernardo turned to leave the room.

* * *

He was weeping. Weeping for himself, for the boy he had been, for those who had loved him, and whose love he had never truly acknowledged. He remembered Bernardo's gentleness and concern, the quiet conversations they had shared in his rooms on the many evenings he had escaped the entertainment in his father's halls. When he was a boy, they had played games both foolish and challenging, and Bernardo had encouraged all his exploits. And Amelia had been as close as he had come to a second mother. He had wandered into her kitchen from the yard shortly after his arrival, drawn by the scent of some astonishing delicacy that turned out to be a delicious soup that easily took the chill off his young bones. She had welcomed him with a casual acceptance that was the antithesis of his father's court, who didn't know quite what to make of him. After he had his fill of soup, she took him to a corner of the kitchen where she was nursing a young puppy. When she noticed his delight at the sight of the fuzzy black ball, she had him sit on the floor and placed the pup in his lap. "You help take care of him, lad, and he'll be a good friend to you always." And so he had. And she. And Bernardo.

* * *

The murmur of voices nearby stirred him to

consciousness, but he lay quietly and listened.

"What have you said to Don Alejandro, Bernardo?" Amelia's husky whisper carried well.

"What could I say? I told him he was ill, that he had been hurt..." Bernardo hesitated. "I did not know how much I should say. Don Alejandro knows well enough what sort of man Aurelio is."

"Pah. He is the devil. I would I had the strength to murder him myself for what he has done. And Don Alejandro, for..."

"We do not know that Don Alejandro..."

"He is not a stupid man, Bernardo, he must have suspected Aurelio's intentions."

"But surely he did not think it would be like this..."

"What did he think? Knowing Aurelio as he does? This is his son, his own son. How could he..."

"He is not always as strong as he should be, and Aurelio's support..."

"This is his son, Bernardo! I have done what I can to heal his body, but who will heal his spirit? He has been such a blessing to us because he is not like the rest. He has helped us in so many small ways, all the ways he could given his position. And he has done so much for his father as well--and this is how he is rewarded: perhaps Don Alejandro thinks this will make him into a brute like them."

Amelia moved to the bed and placed her hand on John's forehead. "The fever has not returned. Did he sleep well?"

"Much better than last night. He dreamt little, if at all."

"His body must be exhausted, between the fever and... We should encourage him to get up today, he needs to regain his strength. Find him some clothes, Bernardo. He may wake soon." Her voice drifted away from the bedside.

"Amelia?" John called.

"You are awake, my lord!"

"Just waking, sweet maid..."

"Ah, la, you are such a tease. I have brought these for you."

He noticed her small stockpile of herbs for external application and internal consumption.

"Here, have some of this," she said, holding a cup to his lips.

"Phew! It tastes awful."

"Just drink it down, my lord. It will aid the healing."

"Or take me to my grave."

"My lord!" Amelia's attempt to sound outraged barely concealed the relief she felt in response to John's mild levity.

"Amelia, will you tell me what happened when you found me?"

"Yes, of course, my lord. The morning had been quiet as most everyone was aiding in the harvest or had gone to the market in the village center. I heard the horses first, and glanced out but saw nothing. But something had disturbed them, and then Trago began barking. When I came out into the yard he was standing over you, and would put his paw on your back as if trying to gain your attention. I tried to rouse you, but could not, so I lifted you and carried you into the kitchen, then sent for Bernardo."

"Was there anyone else about? Did anyone..."

"No one but Bernardo and I saw you, my lord. We brought you here and I did what I could to treat your injuries. I feared the fever--truly your whole body burned-- and thought it best that we call the physician, but finally we did not. I hope we were not wrong."

"You were not wrong, Amelia. See what wonders your herbs have wrought!" He cracked a dry smile, but it failed to reach his eyes.

"I wanted to find them and kill them, my lord, for what they did."

He had never heard this gentle woman sound so fierce. She must be fifty years old, robust and healthy, but always maternal, always nurturing. Suddenly she appeared as an amazon before him and he found himself able to laugh.

"Amelia, my love, I thank you for that. But," and his voice suddenly changed, "I shall have to take on that task myself."

"My lord," she drew closer to the bed and reached out to stroke his hair. He drew back and she pulled away in turn, her eyes cast down. When she raised them again, she saw the tears in his. "Oh, my lord." And suddenly he was in her arms, and she was clasping him to her breast. "Oh, Juanito..." It was the name she had called him when he had first come to the palace and found her a friend he could trust with his secrets. My dear lord."

"No, Amelia," his voice escaped between sobs, "Not a lord, not ever a lord. Just a bastard. Just a..."

Her hand covered his mouth. "Hush, John, hush. I'll not hear you talk so. You are a better man than any who grace themselves with titles. They will find their punishment in time. Shhh, rest now, and heal."

"Will you ask Bernardo to come in?"
"If you will promise to rest."
"I will try."
"All right, then. Drink some more of that potion."
"Must I?"
"Yes." She smiled slyly, "It will do you good."

When Bernardo came in, John asked him to ascertain Don Alejandro's whereabouts. "I must speak with him." He spent the day in his room, eating sporadically, rising and walking about to help restore some measure of strength to his limbs. He had dressed himself, and washed his face, trying to ascertain by feel the extent of the bruises. Much of the flesh was still tender, and he imagined he would not present a very attractive picture to anyone he confronted. Bernardo returned with the news that his father had ridden to a nearby village that morning but was expected back later in the day.

"Where are the clothes, Bernardo?"
"Which clothes, my lord?"
"The ones you found me in."
"My lord..."
"I want them."
"Yes, my lord." Bernardo went into the adjacent room and brought back the remnants, torn, dirty, bloodied.
"Will you let me know when Don Alejandro returns?"
"I will, my lord."

All afternoon John moved restlessly between his bed, the desk, and the window. He longed to be outside, to wander in the fields beyond the village, to be away from this reputed outpost of civility and law. Yet he also feared to leave his room, uncertain how he might respond to those he would meet. He felt safe here, safe with Bernardo and Amelia. Beyond this room, the others waited, those whom he had trusted, those whose concern he had assumed, his father primary among them. But had his father ever cared? Certainly he had accepted his responsibility for John's birth, and had provided this home, an education. But love? A rough affection when he was younger that in recent years had disappeared. A grudging respect for his skills in soldiering; a respectful surprise in response to his more bookish talents; a dismay at his lack of interest in the other pursuits of the nobility. He did not know what his father wanted of him. An now he feared what he might learn.

Twilight was fading into full darkness when Bernardo entered with word that Don Alejandro had returned and was in his chambers.

"Has he eaten?" John inquired.

"Yes, my lord."

John picked up the bundle of clothes and left the room. His father's rooms were not far from his own, and the short walk in the near darkness allowed little time to gather his thoughts. He hoped the afternoon had been time enough. As he approached the door, he hesitated. Taking several moments to breathe deeply, he knocked on the door and immediately entered. "I would speak with you, my lord," he said, almost casually dropping the bundle on a chair near the door.

"What? John!" his father's surprise appeared genuine. "Then you are...better?"

"Better, my lord?" John's voice rang sardonically through the chamber.

Don Alejandro rose from his seat and moved toward John, "Bernardo told me that you had been ill."

"Ah. Yes." A long pause. "Then I must be better." His voice was low, deliberately so, that his father might strain to hear it.

"Come and sit down by the fire, my son, and we shall talk."

"I would prefer to stand."

"As you wish. I hope you will not mind if I sit; it has been a bone-wearying day."

John could detect the exhaustion in his voice. His face was difficult to discern in the combination of candle and firelight. As Don Alejandro moved to reclaim his seat, John took a place before the chair. He noticed where his father had left his dagger on the table nearby; he must have removed it from his belt when he sat down to examine the map that was spread across the table.

"Your brother has been busy in the east, making new alliances for us. See here, and here," he pointed to several positions on the map.

"Did you love my mother, my lord?" The question was clearly unexpected and the reply long in coming.

"She was very beautiful," he murmured as if to himself, then glanced up but refused to meet John's eyes. "You favor her."

"Did you care for her at all? I have seen the way you use women, my lord; was she just another conquest, a hunter's quarry? Did you take such pride in your status as lord of the land to think it entitled you to deflower the daughters of those who owed you allegiance?"

"No, it was not like that!" An edge of anger had crept

into his voice, and then it softened. "She was beautiful, and I was entranced."

"She was the daughter of your liegeman and you seduced her. Did she know you were married?"

"No. But I was still young..."

"As was she. Younger. Much younger. A virgin. One who knew nothing of the ways of the world. One who loved you. Did you care about her?"

"I did care. If I had not a wife already..."

"But you had. And you seduced her. And she found herself with child. And you did nothing." The contempt in John's voice was unmistakable. "She wrote to you. Did you ever reply?"

"I thought it best not to."

"She wrote again, after she gave birth."

"By then there was no point to a reply. I had heard that she had entered a holy order, and I assumed the child had been taken in by the family, or..."

"But you never inquired. You never knew what had happened to her."

"No." The voice had become a whisper.

John turned to stare into the fire. He tried desperately to recall his mother's face, but it had faded now, beyond memory. Her voice, too, had vanished from his heart, and her absence was suddenly a searing wound that time could never stanch.

"You were surprised, then, when I appeared?"

Once again, Don Alejandro glanced toward his son, but failed to meet his eyes. "Yes. It came as quite a shock. I was relieved that my wife was dead; at least I was spared the task of explaining your existence to her." The voice was attempting a casual intimacy, almost a lightness.

"You mean you had never lapsed before, my lord? Why is it that I find that so difficult to believe?" John was treading very close to the edge, but the provocation was intentional if wholly intuitive at this point.

"John..."

"So you kindly took me in. Thinking, perhaps, I might ultimately be of some use to you, I suppose. As my mother was of some use to you." John's breath grew shorter and shorter; he found himself nearly gasping, and stopped speaking. His hand moved to his face, as if to caress the bruises that still lingered there.

Don Alejandro's voice was barely audible, "John, please, you are my son and..."

"And I was of some use, was I not, my lord? What

was the price, my lord? My body to maintain your alliance with..." The name refused to come. "My body, my lord? Just a bastard's body. The son of a whore. Here, my lord," he stepped to the chair near the entrance, picked up the bundled clothing, and threw it at his father's feet, "Here's the proof of your contract. My blood, my shame. May you rot in hell." He crossed to the table, picked up the dagger, and stepped quickly behind his father's chair, holding the knife at his throat. "Perhaps I should send you there now."

"John," his father's voice barely escaped his throat. "I did not know, I did not think Aurelio..."

"Do not tell me that you did not know, do not lie to me about this." He flung the dagger to the floor. "For the love my mother bore you, I will spare your pitiful life. But I will have my revenge, my lord, though it take me a lifetime." Once more he stared at his father's face, in which anger and terror struggled. "Look at me!"

Don Alejandro turned deliberately away. He tried to speak, but no word escaped his lips. John turned and left the room.

He never saw his father again.

* * *

John could sense the approach of dawn; the stillness of night had given way to a gentle movement of air that stirred even here. The darkness too had softened, as if in anticipation of the morn. Everything waited, silent, for what another day might bring. He wondered how much longer he would linger in this cell until he was taken before the sexton to hear his doom. It could not be soon enough, he thought. "Let it all end at last." How ironic to face death at his brother's hands when he had spent the last ten years or more so far from his home.

* * *

The morning after he had confronted his father, he had packed the few belongings he considered his own, left a purse of what money he had with Bernardo to share with Amelia, and had ridden away from the palace and the village with no thought to his destination. What he soon discovered was that his skills as a soldier would serve him better than any others he had acquired, and his survival demanded that he sell his services to the highest bidder. So he, who had had such contempt for the petty wars he'd seen being waged by his father and others, found himself amidst them, fighting for tyrants who coveted the land of other tyrants.

He made a name for himself with his skills, and his leadership gained renown throughout the minor kingdoms of the European world. While he felt no true loyalty to those he served, he did his job well and was well compensated for it. The camaraderie among his fellow soldiers was sufficient to meet some basic need, though he never grew close to anyone in all those years. He grew distant from himself as well: violence came to him more easily. Yet he still restrained his men from wanton revenge against the innocent--peasants were spared everything but the requisition of food supplies and anyone who assaulted a farmer or villager was subject to harsh discipline. There were whores enough following the carnage to meet the demands of the soldiers; he would not allow them any other privileges of victory.

Among the men who served under him he elicited a fierce loyalty. Not only were his tactics in battle admirable, but when skirmishes ended, he took as much time as he could to aid those who had been wounded. The farmer's skills he retained from the village and much he had learned in his father's world served in this rougher world in unexpected ways. The lords to whom he had sworn allegiance prized his talents and exploited them until he was no longer of use to them. Thus he had made his way from fiefdom to fiefdom, ten years and more a wanderer.

* * *

He could hear someone stirring outside the cell. Time began to press in on him. "Ah, mother, how far from your dream I have traveled." A soldier, but not of God, he thought. A soldier for the worst sort of men. He had become what he despised though he struggled to hold onto some fragment of belief, if not in God, then in the goodness of others. He had found it sometimes among the lowest ranks of soldiers, the peasants whose villages he invaded, even the women who followed the wars; much more rarely among the others, his fellow officers and the men for whom they fought. These wars, this world, brutalized all who were a part of it. And he had no longer sought any other world.

* * *

His latest commission had been with an Italian force:

one prince struggling against another. And it was on that battlefield that he was knocked off his horse from behind, then beaten into unconsciousness by four soldiers of his brother's army, which had allied itself with his prince's enemy. The exquisite Count Claudio had apparently been the mastermind of the attack, having learned that John was Don Pedro's renegade brother and thinking that his capture would ensure the particular gratitude of Don Pedro. He remembered being dragged, his hands bound before him, to be thrust at his brother's feet in a tent on the edge of the battlefield.

"A special prize for you, my lord," Claudio's voice had dripped with triumph.

"John," his brother's response was a simple moment of recognition.

John looked up from where he knelt, his face still bleeding from the battle, attempted a smile, then winced with the pain. "My lord."

"Leave us," Pedro said. He drew John up and led him into the tent, then cut his bonds and looked at him with a measure of astonishment and dismay. "I did not think to meet again like this, brother."

"I did not think to meet again at all," John replied dryly. "Would that I had known you were embroiled in this war."

"Would you have left your service?"

"Perhaps. I have no quarrel with you, my lord."

"You know that our father is dead."

"I had heard as much."

"He spoke of you before he died. He wondered where you were, how you fared."

John did not respond.

"Why did you leave, brother? What was it came between you?"

"It does not matter, my lord. It is not something of which I need speak to you." John heard the harshness in his voice, and knew his brother heard it as well. But he had not sought this reunion, and he would not ingratiate himself with his brother to save his life. What would happen, would happen. Once more, he had lost the ability to control his own fate.

"Don Pedro," the call came from outside the tent, and Pedro walked to the entrance.

"Count Claudio?"

"We are preparing to execute the other prisoners, my lord, and..."

"We will execute no prisoners today, Count; send a notice of ransom to their prince."

"For all of them, my lord?"

"All but my brother, Count, and his aides; I would have them remain with us."

"Yes, my lord."

John wondered if he imagined the disappointment in Claudio's voice; perhaps his own cynicism now extended to everyone he encountered. Don Pedro turned back into the tent.

"I would have you remain with us, brother."

"As you will, my lord. I do not see that I have much choice."

"John...I would have us renew our friendship. I know you did not choose to fight against me."

"Do you, my lord? Perhaps you are wrong; it has been many years since you saw me last, and I am a different man than I was then. I have learned the ways of princes in this world, and how they kill for sport and profit. I have learned to take what I need from their victories, and have no need of friendship. Not even yours. My execution might serve you better."

"No, John, that I cannot do, however much you might long for it. I would have you live."

"Then so I shall, my lord." John glanced at his brother's eyes, noting with resistance the questions that lingered there. He wondered what his brother knew. He wondered how his father had died. But he would not ask.

That battle had essentially ended the war, with Don Pedro's forces assuring the triumph of his Italian ally. And then they had come here, to Messina, and he had perpetrated his small drama of revenge on Claudio. And had failed. Claudio had his lady, after all, and now John would at last find the death he had unconsciously sought for so long. Yet when he remembered the devastation he had seen in Hero's eyes as Claudio accused her, he hoped that his death might be delayed long enough to beg her forgiveness. In this ugly act, he had betrayed the deepest vow he had ever made, never to hurt those who had done no harm. He had betrayed his mother and Father Herrera, Bernardo and Amelia. He had betrayed himself by wounding her, and only her absolution could comfort his soul.

* * *

As the light brightened in the cell, a guard entered

with water and a pasty gruel. John drank the water gratefully, but could not stomach the food. He tried to remember when he had last eaten; it had been the feast the night before the wedding that had been so dramatically disrupted, two and a half days ago now. He should be more light-headed from such a fast, yet he felt more in control than he had since before his defeat in battle. How much longer would it be before they came for him? He wondered if Claudio would be part of the proceedings, on the morn after his finally achieved wedding night. He wagered the lusty Benedick would stay abed, but knew somehow that Claudio would find this event more to his taste.

    He was astonished once again by the memory of how easily Claudio and his brother had been gulled. And Leonato, too, he had heard. Believing that his own child was the whore John had painted her. Why had any of them believed him? But he knew, only too well. They were all only too eager to believe that all women were whores, and not to be trusted. Their only true loyalty was to one another. He pitied the women who loved them. That they would give their trust to him, a proven traitor, rather than to a lovely, gentle woman whom they knew so much better: what a twisted world this was, in which his maleness had such power. Suddenly it did not matter that he was a bastard son, that he had fled his father's home, fought against his brother; the alliance of men stood him in good stead. Yet such an alliance sickened him. It was what had exiled his mother, and what had violently destroyed his belief in the possibility of love and trust. Now he would pay for all his treacheries. Suddenly he longed to recover the boy he had been before he had known of his history, when the ordinary work of the day had blessed him and he had been loved. He felt a sudden pang for that boy's lost innocence and the too brief joy he had known.

    At mid-morning, the cell door opened again, and two members of Leonato's watch escorted John to a quiet, sun-lit chamber in the villa. The sexton, Leonato, and Don Pedro were seated at a table at the front. Claudio stood to one side, and several other members of Don Pedro's troop were scattered about the room. The guards escorted John to a place before the table, then withdrew. The sexton cleared his throat, glanced at Don Pedro and at Leonato, and began.

    "Prince John of Aragon, you are accused of conspiring with your confederates Borachio and Conrade to slander the Lady Hero, and to deceive the Prince, your brother, and Count Claudio. These acts causing the supposed death of

Lady Hero, after which you fled from this land to avoid capture for these crimes. How do you answer to these charges?"

"The plan was my own, and Borachio and Conrade acted under my orders. Their only error was their loyalty to me, and I would petition their release. The crimes were mine alone."

"No, they are just as guilty as he," Claudio's voice rang out across the room.

"Silence, my son, you are not called as a witness here," Leonato replied.

"You acknowledge, then, this vile and reprehensible deed."

"Yes." He spoke clearly, looking directly into the sexton's eyes.

"And do you wish to say anything more to this body about such a heinous act?"

"No." He wondered if Don Pedro and Claudio had already successfully erased their guilty complicity from their memories. It would be easy enough, he thought, since he provided such a convenient scapegoat. Would it ever gnaw at their consciences, even a little? He thought there was a possibility in his brother's case, almost none in Claudio's.

Leonato and Don Pedro rose from the table and withdrew to a corner of the room. Claudio took the opportunity to cross to where John stood.

"You bastard, I hope you die for this," he muttered, then spit into John's face, and raised his fist to strike.

The blow knocked John off his feet, but before Claudio could continue his attack, two of the soldiers had pinioned his arms and pulled him away. The disruption brought Don Pedro and Leonato back to the table. Don Pedro walked over to Claudio and spoke to him quietly. Claudio shook off the restraining arms of the soldiers, walked to the far wall of the room, and collapsed into a chair.

As the room came back into focus, John slowly rose to his feet. Claudio's spit still dripped down his face, and his mouth tasted of blood. Perhaps they'll let him beat me to death, he thought, it would certainly give him great pleasure. Don Pedro had rejoined Leonato at the table, and it was the old man who began to speak. John remembered the kindness of his greeting when he had arrived at the villa, a welcome that had seemed absolutely genuine. He looked into Leonato's eyes and regretted the pain he had caused him.

"Don Pedro and I have determined your punishment." He hesitated. "You will be flogged in the presence of the company, stripped of your rank and your titles and any privileges that they would accord you, and exiled from your homeland and from any lands in which your brother has developed alliances. This sentence is to be carried out immediately."

Not death, then, not death. The rest scarcely mattered.

"Do you have anything you wish to say?"

"No, my lord."

"Then take him outside."

The two members of the watch who had escorted him from his cell took his arms and marched him into the courtyard. The manacles were removed, his shirt stripped off. Then he was bound again, his wrists tied together then looped through a metal hoop on one of the posts in the yard, his waist bound by another rope around the pole. He vowed not to cry out. The blows came fast and fierce, and his body exploded with pain. His breath grew ragged and tears streamed from his eyes, but he made no sound. He fell into a whirlwind of terror and grief, felt death's approach and moved to welcome it, then struggled back toward life. He would live. Through the incomprehensible agony, he would return to claim his life and make it his own.

It was over. He longed to sink into unconsciousness. He nearly fell as they removed his bonds, but one glimpse of the grim satisfaction on Claudio's face brought him back to himself. Then his brother's voice broke through the silence, "You must leave by dawn tomorrow. A horse and what goods you have brought here will be ready. Return him to the cell." Don Pedro glanced once more at his brother, then he turned and moved back toward the villa.

"My lord," John's voice was scarcely more than a whisper, but it was enough.

"Yes?" Don Pedro turned back.

"I would beg one favor."

"What is it?"

"I would see the lady."

"No!" Claudio placed himself before Don Pedro. "No, my lord, he has done enough harm already. She has no wish to see this vile..."

Pedro glanced at John, then at Claudio. "I will ask her. It must be her decision."

"Thank you, my lord." John looked for the first time into his brother's eyes, and saw a sadness that mirrored his own. He longed to say some word that could erase that sorrow, but found none. Another fierce regret, that he had not known this man better, that the link that should have brought them together had driven them apart. It was too late now.

"Take him back into the chamber for now; put the manacles back on, and keep a guard with him. I will speak with the Lady Hero." Pedro strode off, followed by Claudio, still voicing his protest at this turn of events.

"Let me help you with your shirt, my lord." It was one of the men of the watch. John slipped his arms into the sleeves, winced as the delicate cloth came into contact with the lacerations, felt the blood seeping into the fabric. Then he put his hands out before him for the manacles, and noted with interest the raw state of the skin on his wrists as they were fastened. Both the men walked him back into the chamber where his fate had been sealed; he walked over to the table, sat, stretched his arms out before him, and laid his head down upon them to wait.

He must have slept, if only briefly; the guard's hand on his shoulder awakened him, "Lady Hero is here, my lord." He pushed himself up, a groan escaping his lips as the pain from the flogging burst into his consciousness. Suddenly she was beside him.

"Please, my lord, sit down again." Her voice was low but firm. He glanced up into her face and saw the shock in her eyes. "I pray you, my lord."

What had he done? Once again, he had thought only of himself. What a disgusting portrait he must present her with.

"I am sorry, my lady, I should not have asked you to come. I only hoped..."

"Hush, Simon," she turned to the guard. "I want you to take off his bonds, then go find Marianna. Tell her to come with warm water and soft cloth, and to bring her salves and unguents, and any herbs she has for pain."

"But, my lady, I was ordered to stay in the room with you, and..."

"Simon, there is a guard outside the room, is there not?" Simon nodded. "Good. I will be fine. Now release him please."

"My lady," John spoke again. "Please, do not do this. You should not be here at all; your father...your husband...would not wish..."

"It does not matter. I am here. Please, my lord, let me do what I can."

"But you should not...you have no reason to..." He sank down into the chair once again, as Simon came to him to remove the manacles. When he moved back across the room, Hero called out to him, "Simon! After you fetch Marianna, find some fresh clothes, take some from my father's rooms."

"Yes, my lady."

John stared fixedly at the table before him, willing his pain into submission. "My lady," he whispered. "About Borachio and Conrade...I beg you to intercede for them. They took part in this crime because of their loyalty to me. They did not know how deadly our mischief would prove. Borachio cares for Margaret, I know, and thought this all a carnival game. And Conrade has fought beside me for three years now, and would not betray me even in such an act."

"I will do what I can, my lord. I know how distressed Margaret was when she discovered the nature of your play. She took it all for a wedding frolic." Suddenly, she laughed, and John looked up startled at her radiant face. "She's rather too lusty for her own good at times." Then her glance fell again on his tormented face, and she turned away. "I will do what I can, my lord. I think my father will listen to me."

A stirring at the door announced the entrance of Marianna, arms filled with jars and cloths; Simon trailed behind her with a pitcher and bowl, as well as some clothing flung over his shoulder. Simon had clearly informed Marianna of the task at hand, and she simply set her materials on the table beside John and went to work. She helped him to remove his shirt, poured the water into the basin, and began very gently to wipe the drying blood from his back.

Hero sat down beside John, looked closely into his eyes, and asked, "How else, my lord, might I help you?"

"I have no right to ask you to help me at all."

"Let us not speak of rights. You have suffered--"

"A well-deserved punishment, my lady. Perhaps even this is not enough."

"Do not say that. I do not understand why you did what you did, but there is much of the world I do not understand. I believe, in truth, you are an honorable man--"

"No. What I did had no semblance of honor. What I did was provoked by a rage for revenge that violated any last shred of honor that remained to me. I slandered you, my lady, you who had done nothing to harm me. That I have lost my name and my home is nothing; they were lost to me long before this. But that I could injure one who had only been kind, who embodied the grace and beauty I remembered from..." he stopped.

"My lord..."

"No lord any longer, my lady," his voice had dropped again to a whisper.

Marianna had completed her ministrations, and nodded to Hero as she left the room. Simon, who still hovered about the table, looked to Hero as if for directions. "Simon, would you wait outside, please?"

"But my lady, I..."

"Please, Simon."

"Yes, my lady."

Hero turned again to John. "Will you tell me, my lord, about your life?"

John glanced once more into those patient brown eyes and recognized the compassion from which her question had sprung. He spoke for the first time in many years of a life he had tried to forget, of another woman betrayed who haunted him still. He spoke little of his life in Aragon, for he could not tell her all, but she pursued him gently with questions, and seemed to understand all that remained unsaid. She returned his life to him, transformed. He would take it, this time, away from this world to a place in which he could live differently.

"My lady, my life does not excuse what I have done." He rose to his feet, then dropped to his knees before her. "I beg you to forgive me. If you cannot, I will understand--"

"John," she placed her hand on his head, "If I can take this burden from you, yes...yes, I forgive you." Her other hand reached to take his, and she brought it to her lips. "I pray that you will find some joy in your life..."

"My lady," he kissed her hand in return. "Your blessing is my grace."

"I must go. Farewell, my lord." She rose from her chair, and he rose beside her, then watched as she walked slowly across the room.

"Farewell, dear lady," he whispered.

The guard who entered after Hero's departure escorted him not to the cell, but to the room where he had lodged earlier. He slept the rest of the day and through the night, awaking to find the stars still illuminating the heavens. What little he possessed he carried with him out of the villa and to the stable, where he found a horse saddled and awaiting him. He bid a silent farewell to foe and friend. The stillness around him remained unbroken as he rode, alone, into the dawn.

Paychecks and Other Handouts

Chaunce Stanton

They call it the skids because you got nothing to stop you. No job. No money. And nobody. You just keep on coasting, missing the occasional rent payment and a lunch every now and again. And all those friends you thought you had--well, they aren't missing lunch, and they aren't missing you.

Today I was on the skids. But I sure wasn't going to let that stop me from missing a lunch. I was already decked out in my best clothes and pounding the pavement for a job. That wasn't going too well. Filling out all those applications made me hungry.

Trying to find a job in St. Cloud is like trying to get milk from wringing your hands. They hire all of them college kids for four bucks an hour, part-time. Any leftover jobs you've got to type for, cry for, or lie for, and I can't type.

I got told the same thing at the temp agencies, the kitchen--even the parking ramp: "Not too much hiring this close to Christmas."

Got to love this time of year. Ho ho.

I crossed over the Germain bridge and into the east side. The streets always look like God spit-up fresh on them. Everything happens on this side of town: the bridge people, the AA clubs, the Goodwill, the junk-yard. Even the animal shelter.

All the sirens wind up here at some point every day. The drunk panhandler who won't take less than a dollar for his "coffee." The Little Duke's convenience store gets hit. Again. A squat fire gets out of hand on the river shore.

Occasionally you see a college teacher jogging through the neighborhood. You can spot them a block away. They look like hippies except they have new running shoes and those CD players.

They know this isn't their neck of the woods; I guess that's why they're running. They live mostly on Riverside in yards full of shrubs. They recycle their *New York Times*. I waved to one, once, as I passed him on the bridge.

He handed me a dollar and kept running.

So when you're on the skids, there's nothing stopping you from taking money or a free lunch. About the only reason I ever come over is for the soup line at the Salvation

Army, because free food happens to be my favorite kind.

You got to eat regularly. Otherwise the chill gets you when you're out walking. You get tired easy. And sick. And you feel as slushy as the gutter.

I had my hands in my pockets 'cause I lost my gloves, but my buddy Ken said he had an extra pair for me. Told me to meet him later at the coffee shop.

The cars winged by, their exhaust fouling the already gray breeze. A scummy blue Chrysler let off at the corner of Wilson and then gunned away leaving the wig lady there on the curb adjusting her vinyl skirt.

I think her real name was Roberta. She was Asian-- probably Korean. Forty, maybe older. She got released from the state hospital 'cause they couldn't afford "minimal risk" patients like her, so she took care of herself by instinct.

As far as I know, she is St. Cloud's only regular prostitute. There were some women who were dishing on Saturday, but they always seemed to find religion again on Sunday. Others didn't think anything of taking dinner and drinks but considered it "indecent" to accept cash. Roberta was practical; she took cash, food, and housewares.

It's unnerving, the way she leers at me whenever I pass her. She's capable of bending steel with her face, so I've never figured out how she stays in business.

Maybe she's that good.

Maybe some guys are just that hard-up.

Me, I'd never pay for it; too many free lunches to pay for spoiled apples.

She adjusted her flaming red wig and said hi to me. She got that wig from a quarter bin at the Goodwill.

I said hi and side-stepped her.

"You want a date?"

I raised my palm to her, "Got one, and she don't eat much, either."

Roberta, on the other hand, ate like a horse. Guess she must work up quite an appetite in her line of work. I'd see her sometimes in line at the Salvation Army. Some of the guys would give her their crackers and bread.

Soon enough, I was staring at a semi-rancid bologna sandwich on wonderbread and a glass of "fruit drink." It isn't much, but I've come to appreciate little kindnesses in all forms: charitable tax write-off, free lunches, and the amazing shelf life of wonderbread.

I've started to eat more slowly. I chew every bite twenty-five times. It sure doesn't help the taste, but the pale potato lumps get an extra moment of attention each time. It draws lunch out a good fifteen minutes. That's fifteen more minutes of being out of the cold and fifteen less minutes til next day's lunch.

These soup kitchens work on a shoe-string. Volunteer servers and the day-old bakery breads and borderline sandwich meats from groceries. They would throw the stuff out anyway, so I guess they figure if they donate it people would stop digging in their dumpsters.

But old habits die hard for some, like "Dumpster" Bill Thompkins. Born and bred here in the granite city. The only time I see him he's got his head poked in some apartment dumpster picking out aluminum and whatever else catches his eye.

I've had some intense conversations with him when all I could see was his butt while he was digging in the trash.

The first time I met him I was passing through an alley across from Coborn's. I watched an orange cat crouch in the weeds, ready to pounce on a chattering squirrel. The cat's tail quivered, its belly tensed. Right at the moment of truth, Bill saved that squirrel's life, coming down the alley whistling. The cat's claws came up empty, and the squirrel looked down at the three of us from a telephone pole, chattering angrily.

"Nice cat you got there."

"Thanks," I said. "He ain't mine, but he's a cutie."

"What's his name." Bill unheaved two bags from his shoulders. They hit the gravel, ka-klunk, sending the cat skittering behind my leg.

"I don't know. He ain't mine."

Bill scratched his head. I could tell he wanted to be friends, but he didn't know whether to start with me or the cat.

"Name's Bill," he said, his slimy leather glove encased my hand. Then he bent down to scratch the cat's head, trying to make nice. It purred for him but shied away from the smell. He shrugged his shoulders and looked the alley up and down.

"Must be moving day for the college kids," The alley was lined with stained couches and splintered desks. "Good day for me!" He rocked himself over the edge of the nearest dumpster so that I had a fine view of a wide leather belt and a slab of back-crack.

A holler echoed from the bin, "Whoee!"

"What'd you find?"

He wiggled out of the trash. "Three girlie magazines!" He handed them to me. "These kids are so wasteful! They'd throw away their lungs if they weren't using them now and again smoking pot!"

Little treasures like these magazines, old cassette players and lamp cords are the only incentive a man like Bill needs to keep diving dumpsters.

"What's the best thing you ever found?" He asked me once.

"I don't know. I guess one time I was standing in this empty parking lot, and out of nowhere a twenty dollar bill came blowing right up to my feet."

"Hey, that's pretty good. You know what the best thing I ever found was?" He patted his back pocket.

"You found your pants in the trash?"

"No. This letter here," he pulled out a folded piece of paper. "I found this a couple years ago behind a place over on sixth. See, I'm an orphan, or thought I was. I grew up in that children's home by the river. Then one day I'm going through this barrel and I come across this letter. Had my name in it. Some sort of update from the children's home! So this lady turns out to be my mother!" He put the letter back in his pocket. "I'd figured she'd have left town or something, and then, boom, I find out I've been living in the same town with her all my life!"

"She was still alive?"

"Oh, yeah. Alive and kicking. Got two kids of her own, but her husband died some time back. He wasn't my dad, though."

"So, did you meet her?"

"Yeah, I met her. Went up to her door one day and introduced myself."

"Well, what happened? What'd she say?"

"She said, 'Stay outta my trash.'"

"That's it?"

"Yup." He put a bent-up old fork into one of his bags.

I still see Bill around. Of course, he doesn't stay out of his mom's trash. Sometimes he even leaves especially good finds on her door-step. He comes here to lunch now and again, gives Roberta his crackers sometimes.

If I don't meet the down-and-outers in alleys, I'm sure to meet up with them some day at lunch. I see a lot of the vets 'cause we got a VA hospital in town. Today I sat across from a couple guys from Kentucky. They'd been in Nam and now they collected their checks and drove from casino to casino, staying at VAs and Salvation Armies across the country.

They wondered about the women in town, so I told them about all the college cuties that go downtown to the bars. These guys practically stumbled over one another to get out of their chairs and make for the door.

"But, fellas, they don't go there til night, and, besides, since it's almost Christmas, they might have gone home."

That didn't slow them down. They said they needed to go find a place to shower and get ready. Maybe I should have told them about Roberta--at least with her they wouldn't need to shower.

The food-line filled up around noon. Everyone there is nice to me. A line of old folks dish up the slop every day and ask me how I am, and I do the same. Sometimes this old lady gives me an extra cracker and winks at me. I wink back at her...

It pays to be nice to people.

On the way out, I thank the workers 'cause it is real nice of them to do this for us every day. The winking lady asked me why I was dressed so "spiffy" today, so I told her I was looking for a job.

"Oh, doing what?"

"Anything," I said.

She took my arm and led me to a hallway, telling me how tough it is now-a-days to find good work and how she should know 'cause she used to have a job herself, forty years ago stitching car seats at Fingerhut.

"Would you like to take home a couple loaves of bread?" she asked.

"That'd be great."

Then, pointing to a door at the end of the hall, she told me to help myself to whatever I found and that it all should still be fairly fresh.

"Take as much as you like," she said, winking.

I'm sure she meant a different door, because the one she had pointed at was the lady's room. I tried the room next to it and found some wheat and rye that said SELL BY DECEMBER 22. It was already the twenty-third, but they weren't green or anything.

I met up with Ken at the coffee shop a little later. Coffee shops are weird. They get all kinds of people, like the decaf cappucino-drinking, pinkie-in-the-air yuppies who talk on their cellular phones between bites of biscotti. And then there's Ken, the other extreme. He's big--probably the fattest guy I've ever seen, and he's real conscious of his weight. He even wears a little bell on a necklace to warn people that he's coming.

He's also one of the nicest people I've met. He never judges anybody for their appearance, and he'd give you the shirt off his back, except it would probably be way too big. He has a hard time finding clothes that fit, so he wears a lot of sweat pants and flannel shirts.

    I took him to the gym once, because I wanted to help him lose weight. I know it's hard for him to do on his own. He panted and grunted and was sweating and swearing--all in the locker room when he was changing clothes.

    I heard his bell tinkling before I saw him. He was waiting for me on a sofa in the smoking section. He thought cigarettes might help him lose weight. So now he was fat, and he coughed a lot.

    "Find a job yet?"

    "Nope. And you?"

    "Nope." I knew between the two of us, I was the only one who actually needed to work. He lived with his mother still. She fed him and let him bum cigarettes.

    "Oh," he handed me a pair of gloves. "I found them. They should be okay. There's a little tear in the thumb."

    "No problem. Thanks, buddy."

    We went up to the counter to look at the drink board. The manager was making his deposit from the till into a little gray safe behind the counter.

    "What can I getchya?"

    My lips started to move for "coffee" when I remembered I didn't have any cash.

    "Ken, can you spot me a coffee?"

    "Oh, you don't have any money, either?"

    Marty, the manager, licked and sealed his deposit envelope, sending it into the safe's drawer.

    "So you guys won't be ordering anything, then?"

    "I guess not."

    He rolled his eyes at us. "You're gonna have to leave. No more loitering."

    When you're on the skids, loitering happens to be your primary occupation.

    We had just began buttoning our jackets when a booming voice went off behind us, "Hold up, there, boys. Three coffees, Marty!" An older man shoved his hand at Ken. "Name's Howard. Vietnam combat veteran. Three tours. I killed more people than you ever seen. Like it black?"

    Ken and I knew the routine. These guys were itching to tell stories, so they'd buy us coffee and we'd listen to them talk about missing toes and how their first wives ran off with the kids. Eventually, they'd have to catch a bus out to the VA before lock-down, but for that hour or so, we were an audience. Sometimes they'd leave me a five for a refill, so it pays to be nice to people.

    "You boys look like hippies!"

"Yes, sir."

"When I was your age, I had even less hair than I do now! Kept so short I could feel my brains squirming in the top of my head! Course, when you're in the jungle, it's so goddam hot, you don't want any hair!"

Ken tried to ease into a pleasant prattle, "Thank you for the coffee, Howard."

"Hell, don't mention it! I got money! See, I set myself up. I did my time over there. And whatever the wife didn't take, I sold. I'm serious! You boys need to set yourselves up!"

"Do you play chess, Howard? 'Cause Ken and I were just gonna play a game if you wanna watch. You can play winner."

He leaned back in his chair, "No! I fought a real war. I don't play games." Then he leaned forward and slapped us both on the shoulders, "But my brother. He could whomp both you guys!"

Ken automatically set up the white pieces every time, forcing me to be on the defense, "Is that so?"

"Oh yeah! I'm serious. It's all he used to do when we were kids. Everyone in the neighborhood would be out playing ball or swimming, and Pete'd be practicing in his room all day."

I don't like queen openings, and Ken knew it, "You mean, he'd play by himself?"

"Oh, yeah! He was president of the school chess club!"

"Why don't you give him a call and get him down here for a game, Howard?"

"Aw, he lives in Tulsa. Got a real nice spread. You're pushing your bishop's pawn?"

Ken had opened his king's side a little early, "Yeah. That's my move. Did you want to play?"

"No. No, I'm just saying that's kind of a dumb move."

"Well, it's the move I'm making, so we'll just see how it goes."

It didn't go well at all. Howard offered chess advice between stories about drunken chopper rides and the prozac he was getting for free.

Ken was easily distracted, and I beat him in the twelfth move. He's a little thin-skinned, too. People always offer him unsolicited advice about how to lose weight. I learned pretty quick that this only makes him hungry and depressed.

"You know what you need to do. Marching. Marching is the best exercise." He patted Ken's gut. "It'll get rid of that lickety-split. I'm serious!"

I tried to lift Ken's mood, "You know what we need, Ken? We need a good war! That'd keep our minds off of food. And they give you free guns!"

Howard's cheeks took on a color, and he smiled loosely. Then, slapping a five on the table, he told me to get us refills while he told Ken about the beautiful hookers in Saigon.

"Found some money, huh?" Marty looked up from his newspaper as he rested his elbows on the counter.

"Guess so," I said.

He was typical of all the underpaid slobs in the world. Whatever little power he possessed, he flashed like a ceremonial sword. Even though he was the "manager" he still wore an apron, still poured coffee, and still got paid an hourly wage, but he could feel better than me. He was probably thinking to himself, "At least I ain't bumming coffee money from VA crazies."

"Two bucks is your change."

"These are refills. I want the refill price."

"Today, that is the refill price. There ya go."

Back at the table, Howard lit his cigarette from Ken's lighter. "That medication is strong stuff! But I need it! I'm one nasty SOB. I'm serious. I almost got kicked out of the marine corps for being too wild! Can you beat that?"

"Here's your change, Howard."

"Two bucks? That's it?"

"That's all the dude would give me back."

"Christ! They're already making a ton on this stuff. No need to skim off of good customers!"

That's how it works, though. Marty charges you what he wants, pocketing the difference, and if you don't like it, he kicks you out. And if you don't like that, he calls the cops.

"Ain't no living in a perfect world," Howard growled and glared towards the counter, shaking his head. "You boys gotta set yourselves up. Me, I did my time!" He pointed at Marty, "You gotta set yourselves up so you don't end up like him! What time is it?"

"Quarter til."

"I gotta fly boys! I gotta catch a bus outta here, but maybe I'll see you back down here tomorrow, Huh?"

"Thanks, Howard."

"No problem. And good luck finding a job!" he said to me.

It was luck alright, but I don't know if it was good.

After leaving Ken at the coffee shop, I stopped by one

more temp agency downtown. It turned out that the agency rep was an old girlfriend of mine. I smelled her perfume the minute I walked in.

"Tracy, is that you?"

"Oh, my God! What are you doing here?"

"I'm looking for a job! Boy, do you look good!" She didn't. She had filled out like a tent in the wind, but it pays to be nice to people.

"Oh, that's too bad. Don't you work in the warehouse anymore?"

"No, all that work was getting to me. You got anything else?"

She told me what I had already heard a dozen times today: Not much hiring this close to Christmas.

I pointed to a file on her desk, "What's that there?"

She folded her arms on top of it, "Oh, nothing. Well, I mean, nothing really."

"Oh, c'mon, Tracy. I really need a job."

"This is supposed to go to one of our long-time employees."

"I can do it! I know I can." I gave her the same wink I gave the sandwich lady.

"Well..." she was easily charmed. That was part of the reason why we broke up; I found her in bed with a guy who told her she had nice eyes. "Can you start tonight?"

"I guess. If I have to."

"Well, do you want to work or not?"

"Okay, okay. Tonight's good."

"You have to be there at seven and you work until 3:30 in the morning. Five dollars an hour. Are you interested?"

I wagged my head, "Yeah! What do I do?"

The night was hell. I was "collating" piles of paper during prime time, late night and early morning. I couldn't see straight by ten, and I couldn't walk straight an hour later.

I had to walk up and down this table full of paper piles and take one item from each pile, put them in folders, then put the folders in envelopes. Some other poor sucker had to seal the envelopes.

The ink smell of the press floor was narcotic. The fumes and the hum of the printers set me at a mindless rhythm. Except for the nagging aches in my neck and shoulders, my only contact with reality was the wall-clock and the songs that I was making up in my head.

I started singing. It kept me alert, and no one loves the sound of my voice better than me. Into my third or fourth number, I noticed my supervisor eyeing me suspiciously from across the warehouse.

There was no one near enough to hear me--especially over the racket of all the machines, but suddenly I was staring across the table at this woman with rubber gloves and a matching facial expression. She took out her ear plugs and leaned close to me.

"Whaddya doing? Talking to yourself?"

"No, I'm singing!" We both had to yell to be heard.

"Well, don't sing! You'll get yourself in trouble!"

"Trouble?" I cupped my ear, unsure if I had heard her correctly.

"Yeah! Like fired!"

"For singing?"

"For being distracting to others!"

"But no one can hear me!"

"But they can see you! It's disturbing! No singing, humming, whistling or clapping your hands!"

"Good thing I didn't bring my tambourine! How about snapping my fingers?"

"Fired!" was all she said.

It was already past one in the morning by then. I figured Tracy was in bed with her new boyfriend. Howard was medicated and safely strapped in bed at the VA. And those guys from Kentucky were chasing coeds out of the bars. Me, I was staring at a woman whose face made meatloaf seem sexy by comparison.

"How about Christmas carols?"

She just shook her head. So I flipped her off and wandered out of there. Oh, well. At least I made thirty bucks there tonight. Not that thirty bucks is going to go far, what with back-rent and the coffee money I owed Ken.

Winter nights are always twenty degrees colder when the moon is out and you can see all the stars. It's the clouds that keep things warm, but tonight all the heat had escaped into outer space, and the stars are huge, quietly sizzling in their airless void.

My ears are deadened by the ringing of the press floor, like I just got out of some god-awful heavy metal concert where you can't make out the music through all the noise. Even the sirens from the east side sound muffled.

"Probably a stick-up over at the convenience store again." I was thinking this as I passed the dim window of the coffee shop. The words of my thoughts took on a new voice.

I heard Howard saying, "They're making a ton on this stuff..You boys gotta set yourselves up!"

Click. The door lock snapped just as easy as a guy like Howard could snap. As easy as Tracy. As easy as free lunch.

When you're down, you can only go lower.

The place was only partially lit by a deli case. I found the register keys conveniently located on the counter next to the register. Inside was only a hundred bucks in small bills and change, but that would cover the rest of October's rent. I pocketed the money, wondering what to do about November and December, wondering if Tracy would be able to line up something better for me. Maybe I'd lie to her and tell her I learned how to type.

I hit my knees against the safe on the way out. It isn't more than three feet high--not like those one-ton safes most places have. Marty was a cheapskate manager, didn't want to waste money on a heavy-duty safe or bolts to secure it to the floor.

By this time, drunk with the thrill of breaking in, I felt like I was avenging Ken, and Howard, and me of our over-priced refills. I felt like I was working hard when I rolled the safe upside down, feeling in the money chute to see if the cash came out.

It did. My fingers felt a pile of doughy envelopes, stuffed with about two weeks of the shop's take.

I immediately stuffed my pockets, taking only a moment to peek in one of the envelopes and breath in the currency smell. Only two other things I can think of smell better than money: a good dinner and a good woman. Now I can afford both.

Maybe I can go get groceries so I don't have to keep walking over to the east side for lunch every day. Maybe I can go to the bars and meet a nice girl, play some pool, get a hotel room. Maybe I'll take a trip, buy some clothes.

I guess I have plenty of places for my money--I mean Marty's money. "The great thing about money," my dad used to say, "it gives you options."

I started singing "Silent Night" while I wiped the places where I may have left fingerprints. Then I wrote a little note that I'll leave on the register so Marty can see it bright and early when he starts brewing his first pot of coffee in the morning.

All it says is "Thank you," because it pays to be nice to people.

Lady-Slipper

Joyce Basore Wilson

Delphine glanced out the window above the kitchen sink. Her eyes briefly lingered over her husband. Emmett Clodfelter, oblivious to his uncombed hair and his manure-caked boots, was standing near the cattle pens and was, Delphine knew from experience, swapping bull-breeding jokes with their pasty-faced neighbor.

She thought, *This neighbor, others, folks in nearby Bentonville...what did they know about her husband beyond the externals of his vulgar bluster and sexual guffaw?*

If they actually knew him, as she did, would they congregate in their churches and pray over his immortal soul, ignoring hers, and preach that all should be forgiven in the name of...What? A deity? What deity? A Supreme Being of Understanding?

Unlike Bentonville's citizens, she understood that Emmett was a verbal, physical replica of his crusty, unwashed father, and that he had married, in Delphine, a perfect cringing replica of his mother.

But what did this understanding change?

"Damn stupid dame!" old Mr. Clodfelter would call his wife in front of company, demeaning her cooking, her housekeeping, her child-rearing, her sexuality, and Mrs. Clodfelter would mumble something painful like "yessum," in the manner of an indentured servant. And Emmett took it to heart, during those days when he still had a heart.

Oh, yes, Delphine understood. A gullible seventeen-year-old country girl, she believed it when Emmett told her, "Yessir, baby. Aren't we gonna have a sweet little life up in Becker County?" and when he insisted, "Shure, I love 'ya, gal. Why do you keep askin' me to repeat it, by Christ?"

Understanding. In that only. Forgiveness? How, how, when every second in every day was tied up in her survival?

Yes, Delphine decided, *requiring herself to dwell upon the semblance of his past humanity, and excusing, in the name of holy matrimony, his present griminess and dumb devotion to animal reproduction--was a penitential act for her.*

And, too, his words were always ordering her to recognize his spousal dimensions. For hadn't he, just as he *informed her daily for the past eighteen years so she wouldn't forget it, "given her everything"? Hadn't he paid for every "blessed cotton-pickin', fancy rag that hung in her closet"? Hadn't he paid for every "soft sofa, thick rug, and unnecessary knickknack on his farm"? Wasn't he the one who fathered those two "big, strappin' boys who were bred to lay waste to the entire female population grown past puberty in Becker County"? Didn't he have "the healthiest, horniest sonofabitchin' Brahman studs in the Midwest"?*

Delphine mouthed, "Yes, Emmett, you did, you do, you have."

Cold non-penance performed, she looked away from the window. She flipped a page of the book she had propped up on the windowsill between a jug of Ivory liquid and Bon Ami cleanser, then plunged her hands into hot soapy dishwater, scrubbing greasy plates and silverware by the Braille method as she read *Passion Under the Pines*.

She believed fervently that places and people like these in her poetic novel existed somewhere, beyond dusty roads and miles of limp highline wires abuzz with country gossip, beyond hay bales and beyond dogs barking around mailboxes, beyond the lonely motions of snaking out the plumbing and dragging brooms and mops over a wasteland of floors where no one had ever danced.

Women she read about wore bluebells under their sashes and loosened their clothes gingerly and tentatively, and only after some suitor professed undying ardor and desperate longing for completeness.

Book women were her only friends: Miss Velvet, dark, boisterous, emotional and tearful, repenting nothing erotic; Miss Sophie, white-robed princess, demure, breathy; and Miss Angelique, dazed by vapors, primly sitting on the tuffet of her virginity, ready, ready to rise from her seat for sugar on her lips, to lie down and receive sweet death and give away soft heather.

Such women.

They puckered rosebud lips and pressed them to love letters they saved passionately in cedar hope chests. These women married for love, not to escape a father's lash and a mother's tongue, and they blanketed themselves in this *amour*. Love kept them warm.

Men she read about were lean, rolled their mustaches between slender fingers, then swept a woman into a thicket and whispered comparisons between her and the moon, giving her the greater glory.

She adored them all: Charlie Pendragon, the laughter, the tickler, the joker; Daniel Rake, mouth twisted, eyes narrowed, a sweetheart of a villain with whom any woman would willingly lie on a bed of spikes; Mr. Glass, silent, his feelings hidden behind steamy window panes; and HIM, the most loved, Percy Dreamkeeper, his form still in mist...pulling her further and further away from herself, from reality.

Such men.

These men didn't drag out what hung between their legs and call it the persuader, never jabbed that persuader into unlikely orifices. No. They kissed a woman's earlobes and toes, laughed at her womanly moods, praised, worshipped, kept vigil at the door of her heart until she opened it to them.

Tears stung in Delphine's eyes.

It was just the lingering strength of onions she had fried for last night's liver, she reasoned.

She read aloud.

Lady-slipper. She grows in the shade, hidden.
knowing his gentle hand approaches her.
Plucked from obscurity, she will rest against
him, hard membrane of the earth.
Oh, love boundless that stirs her delicate petals
taking her onto himself, to root...his soil...
her soil...soil souls...mingling.

Too much. Her hands came out of the foamy dishwater. She lightly touched her cheeks, her eyes muted, and she imagined that her fingers were the gallant fingers of Percy Dreamkeeper, stroking.

She visualized her vivid face, a good face, no matter what Emmett said, not a "plain puss that sucked lemon" but a pale oval complimenting her dark pixy eyes and her pouting mouth that awaited kisses to die for instead of kisses that bruise.

Swathed in the aroma of baking bread, she said to herself in Percy Dreamkeeper's stead, "I love you," then stood very still so his presence could ravish her as he lauded her abilities, ending with the ejaculation, "My God, must you do everything so well? You even bake your own bread!"

She mentally strained to see Percy, momentarily caught a glimpse of the back of his head, his curly black hair, and the swell of his shoulders. And from memory, she recited a line from her book.

Open wide, Lady-slipper, for he comes, he comes...
Percy's breath was against her face, and she shivered, every petal of herself unfolding for him. Then, then...

WHAM. A slamming door disturbed her reverie. She guiltily wiped desire and dishwater onto her apron, and turned her attention to the oven.

"Bred!" Emmett announced to the room.

Though she knew better, for a second Delphine forgot that he meant matters of animal husbandry and thought he was being appreciative of her baked goods.

Fool. Emmett Clodfelter had no place in dreams with her. He was like the name he gave her, a ruddy, stocky, smelly, weathered animal, a clod. The thought of aromatic bull dung writing with the scent of pastries, the knowledge that Emmett's shout had pushed Percy Dreamkeeper's sensuality back into her imagination, was unbearable.

She turned out the bread onto a cutting board. Steam rose from the load as she sliced it.

Emmett had seated himself at the kitchen table. He slapped his hand against the yellow oilcloth, his way of ordering her to serve lunch.

Delphine ladled beef soup, thick with fat homemade noodles, into a green ceramic bowl in front of him. He silently ate, broth dripping from his spoon and the soup-sopped bread he brought to his lolling mouth. He paused just long enough to wipe his runny nose on the edge of his hand.

Her inner scream, during the moments Emmett and she were in body-to-body proximity, quivered behind her lips and threatened to escape.

He didn't deserve baked bread.
He didn't deserve service.
He didn't deserve her! she thought.

Finished with his meal, Emmett sucked his teeth and said, "Bred old man Graham's cow this morning," as if he had stood in for the bull. "You should do as much," he insinuated, "for a thousand bucks."

Delphine hurried the dirty dishes off the table and into the sink, into re-warmed and re-soaped water. When Emmett talked about money and breeding in the same sentence it usually meant a quick trip to the bedroom, and to have him touch spots on her body that she reserved for her dream people, appalled her.

"She sure got her money's worth out of old Vic," he was explaining behind her back. He cackled, throat glutted with enjoyment of his favorite topic. "Five minutes, tops. That's the best most bulls can manage. But old Vic, now, he stayed at her for nine minutes, and--"

"Oh," she interjected, desperate to interrupt. She questioned, "Emmett?"

He talked on unimpeded. "Damn but I get a kick out of that beady-eyed look Vic gets when he mounts some bawling heifer and--"

"Emmett, please. Do you think I could--?"

"Old Vic likes tail almost as much as I--"

A near scream came out of her mouth. "Emmett!"

"What!" he bellowed, irritated by her interruption of his prelude.

Her voice faltered, was pleading. "Could I get some seeds for the flowerbox? It looks so empty without something growing in it."

His chair scraped against the wood floor as he pushed away from the table. "How bad do you want 'em?"

"Maybe some pansies," she said, turning around gaily, vibrant with possible joy. "They're bright and cheery, and they don't cost too much. My flowerbox will be filled with flowery people in no time."

He showed a mouthful of bridgework in dire need of toothpicks. "Just what I had in mind," he said, "filling your flowerbox with seed."

Delphine pretended to not understand. It was a coercion she was subjected to about three times a week. She mentally tallied busy work to put between herself and belittlement.

She would carry out the trash. She would boil pasta, perhaps those interesting curlicues, for a cool salad. She would iron all the bedsheets. She would squeeze lemons for lemonade, then save a little juice to press behind her ears and on the pulse point of her wrists so she could imagine herself to be refreshing and drinkable all day. Then, then, then, she would...

If there were a Supreme Being, He would have touched her and turned her to grave granite before this moment.

Emmett got up from his seat. "Don't be too long," he warned, eyebrows elevated. "If you want your *seeds*."

He left the kitchen.

Delphine called after him plaintively, futilely, "Be sure and wash up, Emmett...Emmett, please...Did you hear me?"

Isolated, she loitered in her cage. She visualized a

chalkboard at arm's length from herself and her mind scrawled one angry phrase after another.

He was just like his bulls. They always got what they want, too, even if they had to chase a cow into breathlessness, corner it in its pen and ride it without an ounce of love.

She was not one of his animals!

A moment of inevitability blossomed, then withered. Its rancid odor overpowered the scent of bread. A tide of revulsion washed away colorful visions of pansies in the thrusting hands of soft-spoken suitors. An impending command was x-ing out romantic words in her head.

"Delphine! Get you ass in here!" Emmett yelled from the bedroom.

On wooden legs, back stiffened, thinking herself the hapless innocent heroine who was approaching an executioner's block, she numbly stepped to the excited tune of his bellow.

The bedroom at the back of the farmhouse, shaded by an oak copse, was dim and gloomy. An illuminated clock tick-tocked, was as set and alarmed as she.

Emmett was anxiously posed on a worn matrimonial bed, a slumping square that one-sided passion had wearied into a maze of lumps and hollows.

She cursed the curtains, their slithering strip tease for the in-rushing wind. She damned the throw pillows that did not rise up in her defense after she had spent hours cross-stitching their complicated faces.

It consoled her not at all, the knowledge that it would all be over soon, that other women had been martyred this way for centuries.

When, she asked herself, *was "no" permissible?*

Away from him, her no and her yes would could for something.

Yes, yes, she could count her way through it.
1...2...3...

He complained, "What took you so long? The persuader already went flat twice."

"Sorry," she muttered, although she wasn't sorry. She posed timidly, "Did you wash up?" She shuddered when she saw that he hadn't. His faded denim overalls were smeared with barnyard offal.

"Prissy piece," he cussed, noticing her repugnance. "A little clean shit never hurt anyone."

With one raised hand, a symbol of degree, he began

the involved procedure Delphine laughingly called lovemaking. Nothing, not even the Devil himself, could hurry her. She would not rush at the spit where she would soon be turning, being grilled like a tasty morsel over a pit.

She carefully unbuttoned her clothes, folded them and placed them, with a loving pat, on a chair beside the bed. Within minutes, seconds, she knew, pounding persuasion would pin her against bumps and springs. His overall buttons would dig into her skin as he invaded her, this dry and emptied chamber he had purchased with their certificate of legitimacy, and the molecules confined to her veins would pummel each other, screaming rape-rape-rape, for sanctioning love was missing...was missing.

"Get your legs apart, for Chrissake," he ordered, working her into the position he liked. "Do I always have to do everything?"

On her belly, eyes skimming vines twined through faded roses on the wallpaper, she thought with precise reason.

Later, after he was finished, she would make a special trip into Bentonville and buy some seeds, ten, maybe eleven packets, yellow and blue pansies, and she would plant them tomorrow, early, so sunlight could begin its work...begin its...its...

Her fragile spirit slid beyond itself, as if on ice, skewed off the surface of the activities on the bed, and mentally babbled at him.

Someday when she had--had enough, when he had snatched from her that last crumb of something she had not yet named, she would--would--

She would! No one, not even that Being who supposedly watches over everyone--except women not worth watching over--not even her blind and sanctimonious neighbors who ignored her bruises and her withdrawl and her "female complaints," would silence her righteous scream.

As usual, she lost herself in inner arguments.

She took refuge in ideas about Lady-slippers. These unpicked flowers, growing unhampered in Minnesota's darkest woods, were protected by law, were more valued than she.

Something, with the softness and comfort of flannel, folded around her: Percy Dreamkeeper. *He was nearly hers,* she gasped.

The features of Percy's perfect face had come together. Her limp, malleable soul clung to his sharp cheekbones and revered the up and down curves of his mouth. And he valued her.

Fifteen minutes later, after Emmett and his fevered thievery were spent, after he equated his stamina with that of his best breeding bull, after he left her on the bed amid promises to repeat the pleasure after he "et a big supper--lots of meat and gravy," she waited for the air to cool around her, and waited for Percy Dreamkeeper's soothing hands to caress her and restore her sanity.

With deadly calm, she stripped the sheets off Emmett's bed--his! she claimed none of it--making sure no semen had soaked into the mattress where it might arise in the night, noxious and pungent, to assault her sense of smell.

After she got back from Bentonville, she decided with sudden, mad glee, she would paint her toenails red, curl her hair, and sew an extra row of ruffles around the hem of her new cotton sundress. Then she would hurry off to meet Percy, to sleep between the slippery satin sheets of *Passion Under the Pines*.

* * *

"Terrific, Ma," Delphine's older son said sarcastically. "The gravy's got lumps."

Such culinary imperfection was uncharacteristic of her and Delphine wondered at its cause. After she served Emmett, Frank and Mark, the two boys, she perched, like a rare endangered bird, on the edge of her chair, and she compared her life to the lumpy gravy.

How much beating into shape did life require?

She had no appetite. Earlier in the morning, before she had gotten through the second crate of pears she was canning, queasiness had overwhelmed her. The pears had floated in their salt water, impatient for the paring knife's approach, and she had likewise thought herself afloat in saline and waited to be sectioned, to be pickled.

Though the sensation was sixteen years old, she still recognized it. The Clodfelter breed was going to grow, around the end of March, by her figuring.

Maybe she would give birth to a girl this time, something pink she could call Violet or Fern or Marigold.

She sighed, no. No self-respecting Clodfelter wife would dare drop a girl into her husband's household.

Her eyes located small fists in her lap. She stared at her white knuckles; she stared at the balanced table she had set before Emmett and the boys and labeled everything else unbalanced, a lie.

The subject at the dinner table, as always, was breeding. Paragraphs ungrammatical, and unseemly for chaste ears, were being written in ether by dominant male voices.

"Screw bloodlines," Delphine's younger son preached. "What matters most in breeding is watchin' for incest in the breed, 'cuz, like man, crossbreeding close kin makes for f--kin' weakness."

Gutturally, Emmett laughed, "Heh, heh, heh." He leered at his wife over his can of Blatz. "Maybe that's where yours comes from, old lady."

Emmett had a way of making her envy an insect with a pin through its middle. While they complained, talked genetics, she squirmed, felt impaled on their pointed language.

"Christ, Ma," one boy said. "Is this the best meat we got?"

"Yeah, Ma," the other agreed, adding, "I thought we had a whole freezer of tenderloins from the stock we butchered last spring."

Se felt like a small clean feather drifting down into a room full of pollution. "we do. If you don't like this meat, I can--" she started to say.

Her man and her boys had slipped back into their bizarre chitchat and had effectively dismissed the importance of anything she had to say.

Emmett poured more gravy over his son's potatoes. "Eat 'em up, boy. Lumps'll make hair grow on your chest...and other places."

"Heh, heh, heh," the boys laughed, imitated in unison.

"You're a real card, Dad," the older boy said.

"You said it, Mark," the other boy seconded in admiration.

Delphine raised her hand and covered her ears. But she could still hear Emmett and the boys.

"Say, Pa," the older boy said. "I need the car tonight. I've got something on with Stephanie Brooks."

Emmett handed over the car keys, pausing a moment to jingle them and comment. "Ain't you had your fill of that little red-headed broad by now?"

"No fill yet, Pa," the boy replied.

Emmett hooted, released the keys into the boy's hand. "What you got that persuader for anyway, boy--stirrin' coffee?" He aimed a grubby finger at his other boy. "Remind m someday, I've gotta tell this crotch dead brother of your all I know about women."

All he knew about women, all he knew about...hurting women, pinching and whipping their spirit, hair-pulling, fanged, animalistic knowing, about to be delivered from his head-of-household pulpit to the babies she tucked in and called royal princes, had brought, hungry, to her breasts.

A scream, that was centered in her black interior and curled on itself like a snake, started to unloosen its coils.

She trembled, thinking, *The moment was here. Her last crumb was being snatched away, her children, her possibility, being warped and converted into the religion of generational breeding.*

"Been thinkin' about selling old mean Fritz to a rodeo," Emmett said.

Emmett slurped his beer.

The boys slurped their beer.

The scream moved up into her throat She swallowed, swallowed. Her throat was going to explode and eighteen years of swallowing the assault of sweat, excrement, semen, hearing bull talk, living bull, going to bed with bull--was straining to spew out.

"Good idea, Pa," the older boy said. "He's gored two cows to death already, and cost us f--king' money in the bank, man."

Her book people had deserted her and she was left on her own. Emotional dominoes started to fall. She came off her chair so fast that the chair was sent spinning across the kitchen floor.

She was bought,- brought like a thoroughbred cow to this farm, to be bred, to drudge,

to ask for nothing...

to be nothing...

to feel nothing...

to think nothing...

to come to nothing...nothing...nothing.

Nothingness swirled, echoed in her ears, pulled something inside her down on all fours. Heaven help her, but it crawled well, as if it were born to it.

She backed away from them, their puzzled looks, and backed full force--bam!--into the refrigerator behind her.

"Jesus, woman, take it easy on the furniture!" Emmett huffed. "I paid good money for this dinette. And old Vic had to do his duty three times before I had enuf stuffed in a sock for that refrig--"

A coyotelike wail was flooding the room.

Someone asked boyishly, "PMS, Ma?" but she didn't recognize his voice.

A second stranger said, "Give us a break, old lady. We've been out in the pens all day."

"Yeah, how's a guy supposed to finish a meal in this madhouse?" a third person, a boy, said, his Finish, Finish, Finish, a reverberation.

The second male added cryptically, "It's those damn books! I told her, 'that ain't real life, old lady,' It's crap, pure and simple. The sooner you see that, the better."

Eventually, her wailing died away, after it had passed like a wave through the room, after the fixative that kept her alive had been swept away on its crest.

Her offspring, lacking her dreams, and the spouse, defining what she lacked, took off for their usual Friday night trip into town. She was left with their jibes about "Getting herself together," and their semi-soft sympathizing --"You'll feel better tomorrow, Ma" and "You oughta come, too, old lady. Anybody'd think I had you shackled to this place. Heh, heh, heh"--and she was left with *her* usual: crushed beer cans, gristle and gnawed bones on diner plates, hopelessness exhibiting all its teeth, breeder pamphlets with the subtlety of knives and forks, but, also something, finally, all her own--purpose.

Bulging, red as any of his penile obscenities, her purpose had been scripted the day she stepped over the Clodfelter threshold and found a definition of hell even Webster's Third International Dictionary had overlooked.

Her book people, their arms wide enough to hold her, their flesh reconstructed before her eyes, repossessed her. A swelling yes-yes-yes rose from their ranks. Yes, yes, yes, they repeated. **Better off Dead.**

* * *

Some portion of Delphine's brain still lived, and it dimly told her that she was walking on an unfamiliar dirt road, that jagged rocks were cutting into her bare feet, that night breezes were sensual libertines playing underneath her flimsy peignoir. She lurches sideways, feeling the callused hand of exhaustion at her back, pushing her where it wanted her to go. Where *was* she going?

She smiled--*smiles for you, Percy Dreamkeeper*--kissed

the starry sky, and thought, *In this lively darkness, Percy was waiting. Percy was waiting to...*

Through a side door, a man's voice entered her darkness and either prefaced a command or extended an invitation with his, "Take it easy, little lady."

Delphine whirled around--thinking, *Percy was here--*clasping *Passion Under the Pines* to her breast. She was assaulted by the glare of a spotlight in her face, saw two police officers, one male, one female, cautiously approaching her.

"Take it easy, little lady," the blue male iterated. "What kinda shenanigans are we up to tonight?"

"Fight with your boyfriend?" the sweet blue female asked.

For a minute they talked *around* Delphine, not to her. Look at her, looks rattled, dazed, doesn't she? the blue female said, commenting, Not your run-of-the-mill weirdo, is she. What's that she's got dabbed all over her nightgown? the blue male asked, adding, and look, look, she seems to've been in a scuffle, a fight, the material in her nightgown is stretched, pulled.

Quietly, the man breathed, "Good God. Know what that is all over her? It's--"

Miss Velvet, Mr. Glass, Charlie Pendragon--all peered out from the dog-eared pages of Delphine's book, and hissed along with her, with her voice.,

Danger. Warning. Threat. Peril. Blue book thieves.

They would force her to go back, maybe even bring Emmett and spawns back to life...chant blue words over the deathly sleeping occupants of her home that wasn't.

Now the blue figures were eyeing her, their faces shocky and the drawstrings of their mouths slackening so their jaws could drop. What manner of amazement did they see in her?

From a safe distance, inside herself, Delphine listened in on their rapid-fire exchange.

The blue male said under his breath, "Dammit, Oleson, I know **blood** when I see it."

"Call in for help?" The panicky blue female asked softly. "Or do we take her in ourselves?"

The blue male's whisper dropped even lower. "Call it in. I'm telling you, Oleson, she's got crazy written all over her."

A thunderclap of reminiscence assailed Delphine, Emmett's injunction, recently, frantic, final.

GET RID OF THAT RIFLE, OLD LADY, OR I'LL GET UP OUT OF BED AND PERSUADE YOU TO GET RID OF IT!

Delphine hugged her precious book, said, "I was not persuaded." A cast of supporting characters squeezed out from between book pages and created a din of confirmation.

Better off dead, the destroyer.
Better off dead, the destroyed.
Oh, how vermin breeds if you let it.
Three shells of ruination, only three, none left for--

"Me," Delphine finished from her din. "There weren't enough shells for me."

"Crazy as a loon," the blue male repeated emphatically.

The blue man motioned frantically to Ms. Blue and she made a dash for the squad car, and the two-way radio.

"The loon is our state bird," a childlike Delphine informed the blue man.

Mr. Blue's suggestions, pieces of broken logic, bits she half understood, reached into her din. Would she care to...? The squad car was comfortable if she wanted to...An accident, had she been in an...? Did she want them to call...? A relative? A pastor? A friend? Her husband?

Delphine breathed her words as if they exhausted her, were to be the last ones she would speak on the sane side of the grave. "My husband doesn't speak to me anymore," she said with a faint smile.

The squad car's plastic seats were chilly and rigid.

She barely noticed.

Processing ink couldn't be removed from her fingertips.

She didn't care.

Blankets in Cell 20 were woolen and scratchy.

Her body hardly felt them

A paradigm of carnage, the photos she was shown of the crime scene, gruesome, but...

But not familiar, not disturbing.

The headline would read, **Three Slain. Suspect in Custody,** when in fact she was *missing.*

Who can be retrieved, when once bound up between the pages of a book?

Stretched out on her narrow cot, he jail greens and her fragile dreams tucked in around her, Delphine rested, rested out of the reach of persuasion.

Beaming heroes and lace-draped heroines circled about her. They jealously clutched her, one by one, to their celestial bodies.

"Promise me, promise me," Delphine begged thin air, "that you won't leave me again."

The crowd spoke to her with one voice.

"Lady-slipper, he comes, he comes...*he comes for you*," they vowed, stepping aside so man-dreamed-magnificent could approach her and reach out with gasping fingers and--

"What took you so long?" Percy asked, and a pinprick of conscience seized her:

Yesterday, someone said the same thing to her. Who? That breeder. He had cracked the protection she crawled under like a turtle.

Would Percy make her feel ugly, like Emmett?

Were there demons behind Percy's eyes, wolves of sightlessness ready to pounce?

Did even dreamed men think fists and feet instruments of love?

A shiver ran down the length of her body. "You won't hurt me, will you?"

Percy's answer had wings, flew at her, was like an avian rapture before and after life. There was a forever in this Avatar's, "Never."

Without an external ripple showing, she disappeared from the world's view, swam him like a river, doing the breast stroke. She took him ashore, calling him her beloved unicorn, her own breed, laid kisses unbruising over the hard membrane of the earth, and held his whisper in the palm of her hand,

"Here, here a Lady-slipper can grow."

That Particular Summer

Jeffrey M. Wilkes

First of all, I had just turned ten the summer I killed my great aunt Veneria--I was not twelve or thirteen as some of my more unsympathetic relations may have you believe. I remember because that was the summer of my father's trial. The trial was actually the reason I was staying with my aunt and uncle in the first place. My parents had heard the trial might be moved 200 miles away to Harlottsville to avoid some of the rather harsh publicity surrounding the case. Somehow my mother hit upon the idea for her and my father to spend several weeks camping in the drainage ditch adjacent to the Harlottsville county attorney's house, apparently in hopes of garnishing enough sympathy from the man to have the charges reduced from *Premeditated Fondling* to *Petty Rubbing*. I consequently was in need of a guardian for the duration, and as my older siblings were permitted their assortment of lame excuses--summer jobs, a ceaselessly unquenchable hatred toward me, total paralysis, etc.--I was unceremoniously deposited at the country home of my mother's elderly aunt and uncle.

Zostar Syphileski had inherited the sturdy frame house shortly after the Great War and immediately dug in and began ruining it. His predilection for short-cuts and saving time in maintenance and repairs had left the property in an almost surreal, yet highly delicate and somewhat dangerous condition. There were odd angles everywhere, plastic sheeting where was once glass, pipe cleaners where there was metal, and aluminum foil where was once roofing. *Why waste time looking for a tool when I can make one where I sit*, he'd remark, as he whiled away an entire afternoon fashioning a crude instrument out of bits of old toothbrushes and electrical tape, rather than make the five minute trek to the toolbox in the basement.

My aunt was on the whole a kindly woman who fancied herself a true lady in the finest traditional sense. She worked hard at having the speech, carriage, manners and general aura of a true gentlewoman, and apart from her unfortunate habit of punctuating most sentences with the crudest of obscenities, and her tendency to splay her legs wide whilst sitting in mixed company, I felt she would have made quite a go of it. All things considered, in a ten year old's eyes, her scrawny, age-spotted, pipe cleaner doll of a body represented the epitome of feminine refinement, grace and beauty. (Of course I had led somewhat of a sheltered life up until then. And I needed glasses.)

The afternoon I arrived my aunt led me into their tiny galley kitchen to show me her husband's latest domestic repair. Apparently their aged refrigerator had never sat completely level and was prone to rocking and wobbling when opened. This was, she explained, entirely due to the fact that my uncle had never bothered to adjust the front legs of the device. His final solution was to remove the front legs completely, and use a precisely sawed broomstick positioned under the door handle and braced in a carved notch on the floor to hold the machine upright.

"But how do you open it without it falling?" I inquired quite earnestly.

"Surprisingly I've become used to it," she said and demonstrating, she took aside the broomstick and opened the door in one smooth motion. Using her other hand to brace the top of the machine, she deftly snatched a bottle of soda from inside, let slam the door and replaced the stick without the refrigerator so much as leaving. "Saves electricity too!" she said as she placed the icy bottle between her sinewy thighs and yanked free the cap with her bony fingers. Her tone would almost have one believe she had some element of faith in her husband's sorry accomplishments, instead of her actual feeling of total embarrassment at even knowing the man.

Earlier that day, my aunt had dispatched him into town on another mindless errand in an effort to keep herself and me safe from another of his pointless monotone sermons on the cost effectiveness of flushing the commode only once weekly, or some such similar topic. This particular morning found him carrying a large cardboard box filled with every knife, saw, scissors and garden implements on the premises to Paulzie's Hardware to be sharpened. I was free, or so I thought, to glide idly on the tire swing, thinking about nothing, smelling the heavenly efforts of my aunt's baking. But that was before Clymidia showed up.

Clymidia wasn't exactly my friend. She didn't exactly have red hair. And I wasn't exactly sure why someone along the line hadn't beaten the living crap out of her. She certainly was not undeserving. However she was, as she cheerfully pointed out almost ten times a day--two months and four days older than me and about two inches taller. She being a girl, I was not allowed to strike her in any way, and as I had discovered the previous summer, drowning her was also forbidden. Out of sheer necessity and a total lack of other playmates, we were forced to mask our seething dislike for one another as best we could. I seemed to do a better job than she.

"Hey fartlips! You're looking stupider than last year. And I'm still taller!" she said shoving me off the swing while picking at the back of her dungarees with the fierce determination of one on the brink of discovery.

"Hi Clymidia," I monotoned, "how did you know I was here?"

"I saw your dumb old car leaving for the main road so I walked over. Besides I could smell your poop-breath ten miles away!" she laughed as though this was actually somehow funny. She dramatically slapped her knee with one hand and began inching her other down the back of her pants. I looked away and changed the subject.

"Let's play something!"

"What pus-face?" She paused and glanced back toward the garage. "Let's climb up to the car!"

The car in question was a moldy Model A truck my uncle had used years ago in his outhouse cleaning business. As far as I knew it was undrivable and the only remarkable thing about it was where it sat--atop a pair of homemade wooden ramps set against the garage facing the back of the house. They were almost seven feet high, and mildly resembled part of an old roller coaster. According to my aunt, almost ten years ago Uncle Zostar had been doing some minor repairs to the truck when his favorite little wooden stool with the swivel wheels gave way under him. One of the wheels had snapped off. He was faced with the choice of repairing the stool to accommodate the height of the car, or in his mind, the much simpler idea of raising the car to accommodate him. He left his tools where they lay and began building the ramps that afternoon. They took him the entire summer and most of the fall to complete, and as luck would have it, he consequently strained his back along the way and retired the next spring. He never touched the vehicle again.

My still-digging companion had already sprinted toward the truck.

"Aunt Venny'll kill us!"

"Ol' Slack Bags is probably baking something. She won't even leave the house. She'll never see us," she called back. "Besides...if you don't come with me, when you folks come back I'll tell them you showed me your weenis!"

I didn't have to consider this for long--she'd do it. Heck, now that she came up with the idea, she'd probably tell them that either way. I followed her to the ramp.

Within seconds we were at the top on each side of the old truck. It faced the garage so we'd have to keep a close watch on the mirrors for my aunt. On the way up I had noticed a chunk of wood wedged under each back tire--this helped me to relax a little, it was unlikely it could roll even if we pushed it. We climbed in and shut the doors.

"Let's pretend I'm Bonnie and you're Clyde and I'm telling you to drive me away from the cops!" she shrilled.

"Let's play like we're having a quiet drive in the country," I suggested, straining to watch the back door.

"Lemme drive then, Piss-breath!" Clymidia lunged for the door and then we heard the screen door. My aunt had stepped outside. Her filmy old eyes apparently hadn't noticed us so high.

She called out in a slightly nauseating sing-song way, "*Child-ren*...wherever you are...I'm going to bake some of my famous *Crum-ble* cake! With fresh *hon-ey*!" She turned without seeing us and started off towards their dog-eared old hive about forty yards to the side of the house. We sat motionless and silent until we were sure she was to the hive and out of earshot.

"Let's climb down while we can," I said opening the door.

"Oh, no you don't. She'll be back in the house in a few minutes and we can play!" For emphasis she whacked me in the arm with a small piece of wood.

"Where did you get those?!" I whispered.

"By the back tires. I grabbed them before we got in. We can pretend they're guns," she replied and presented me with one.

"You idiot! They're to keep the car from rolling! We gotta get out of here!"

"Even a girl knows the brakes are stopping us. These are just parts of the stupid old ramps."

I was carefully easing my way out when she violently yanked me back by one of my belt loops. I flew into my seat and heard a low squeak, not unlike that of wheels turning on rusty axles. The truck was moving.

We barely had time to glance at one another before we turned to watch the garage roof slip from view as the truck pointed skyward and began rolling earthward. I felt stomach acid in my mouth. Clymidia screamed. My only thought was--*we're going to smash the kitchen window--we're aimed right for it--I hate the sound of breaking glass.*

In my many years since that afternoon I have learned

to trust in Fate--she always provides. Unfortunately she is rather coarse and dim-witted at times and what she provides can often be considered pathetic. On that afternoon I would not have to hear the sound of that window shattering. Fate had provided a cushion for the plummeting mass of rusted iron and steel. My aunt.

We had stopped. The impact was much gentler than I expected. And quieter. Clymidia and I were obviously unscathed. I leaped from the car and landed right on a huge anthill. I ignored it and lurched to the back of the truck to see what we had hit. Clymidia didn't scream. I did. My playmate simply said, "You're in trouble."

We had caught my aunt on her return from the bee hive. The truck's bumper had her pinned at mid thigh against the house. She blinked slowly and her head lolled. "Take the honey for me, would you please, you rotten little prick," she said. Had this been anyone but my aunt I would have assumed she was showing anger towards me, however since this was her usual way of addressing me, I was gratified to know she was basically all right.

"Come on, Clymidia, let's push the truck back!" I started shoving the fender.

Clymidia, now fully composed, simply said, "We can't push it anywhere, Buttcrack lips! Look!"

I ran around to her side of the truck, deftly avoiding the ants. The front wheel, the one my uncle had apparently been fixing, had come completely off on impact and the front axle was shoved well into the dirt. "We gotta try", I said and we both pushed until I could feel what I thought were small vessels popping in my forehead. "You don't have a phone at your house either, do you?" She looked at me like I was asking her if a sperm whale could fit up my ass.

My aunt was muttering quietly and releasing noticeable amounts of drool. "You better get her to a hospital," my companion said matter-of-factly. "My parents are in town today so they can't help. We'll have to take her ourselves."

"How?!"

"Take an arm and pull!" On the count of three we yanked and merely succeeded in helping the old woman expel a rather large volume of unrecognizable chunks onto the back of the truck. "She's really stuck," Clymidia offered and resumed her earlier bout of posterior exploration.

After a pause my rust-haired companion looked thoughtful. "You know," she said slowly, "my dad told me about how some foxes get caught in traps and how to get away they chew their own legs off."

"You wanna CUT MY AUNTS LEGS OFF!"

"She's worth as much as some old fox isn't she? You love her more than some old fox don't you?" she yelled back.

This wasn't the reply I expected. Her twisted logic seemed to somehow make sense to me, and I suddenly had a vision of trying to explain to my mother why her favorite aunt had died. *Why didn't you just cut her legs off*, she was sobbing, as if I had ignored the obvious solution.

"You'll have to do it. I hate blood," I said simply.

"Okay sissy-slacks. Just find me a knife."

Had I then remembered the purpose of my uncle Zostar's errand, we could have saved considerable time. There wasn't a knife, saw, can opener or blade of any kind. After a twenty minute scavenger hunt, the best we could do was a small pair of pinking shears we found in the old lady's sewing drawer. "These should work," Clymidia announced finally, almost happily, "I'll just have to press harder." With no fanfare she knelt between the house and the bumper, rolled up the frayed hem of my aunt's cotton dress and began snipping.

For almost twenty minutes I sat on the old truck's running board listening to Clymidia slowly clipping through layers of my aunt's skin and tissue. Clymidia was silent except for an occasional "Yuck!" or "Eeew." My aunt was for the most part unresponsive to the whole exercise, and seemed content to moan incoherently. Her drooling had been replaced with a thick yellow froth. I began to worry.

My erstwhile playmate suddenly stood and brushed off her dirty knees. "I just reached the bone. I'm tired. It's your turn anyway." I thought of a dozen excuses but said nothing. I took the goo-caked implement she held out. "You're gonna have to use it as a saw now," she said.

Just pretend it's chicken, I told myself and reached toward the sloppy, multilayered wound. Thankfully the pressure of the bumper on her thigh had kept the bleeding to a minimum. Something was wrong. I sprang up.

"You were cutting BELOW the bumper! You were supposed to cut her legs off so we could take her away! She'd still be trapped, you IDIOT! Look how much time we wasted! She's almost dead now--we'll never have time!"

Confronted by her rather large mistake, Clymidia allowed herself to be flustered for only an instant. She quickly said, "You never told me were to cut, and you're the dope who couldn't find anything better than those stupid sewing scissors!"

"We should have just walked to town for help. Tie something around that cut and come on. We'll run. Maybe she'll be okay."

As Clymidia tied my aunt's ugly pink apron around her incision, another problem occurred to me. "It's gotta be almost ninety degrees out here."

"So?"

"She's facing right into the sun. She'll look like a fried tomato by the time we get back. We gotta find some lotion or something to put on her."

"These old people don't got any lotion. If they did they wouldn't look like an elephant's baggy butt."

"You're probably right," I said, "but we gotta do something."

"How about the honey? They'll keep her skin from frying."

"I suppose it couldn't hurt," I replied. We each stuck our fingers in the tiny bucket and began smearing the sweet goo on all the skin we could see. We stood back to admire our handiwork.

"She looks like she's made of gold," Clymidia said, "and if she wakes up and gets hungry she can lick herself."

Strangely enough that made some sense. My aunt somehow looked as if she'd never wake up. Under her sticky sunscreen she was even paler than her usual face powder white. We had wasted enough time. I nudged Clymidia and we took off down the dirt hill.

It had taken us almost an hour and a half to reach the tiny intersection that was downtown Spewdom. Apart from the two times Clymidia had to stop to check her head for wood ticks, and her mandatory stop for ice cream cones, we had ran almost the entire way. We soon found the doctor's shabby office and made our breathless explanations to him. In what seemed like minutes we were riding back towards my aunt's in the doctor's new Packard, Clymidia, the skinny old doctor, me and the mayor. The mayor turned out to be an extremely sweaty man in coveralls with a wet roll of fat on the back of his neck. He was smoking the thickest cigar I had ever seen and seemed to be looking at Clymidia in a not altogether wholesome way. Halfway back we caught up with my uncle and his box of knives. While the doctor repeated the unhappy story to my uncle, he just sat blinking his eyes in an artificially fast way. Clymidia was looking over the knives and saws in a regretful sort of way. The ride was short. We pulled into the dirt driveway my uncle had never quite finished and skidded to a stop. Clymidia and I were the first out and bolted to the old truck.

My first thought was *why did the honey turn black*. But honey doesn't move. Every square inch of what was left of my aunt's skin was covered several layers thick in huge black army ants. I jumped back to avoid vomiting on my own shoes. It got worse. She was alive. And awake. She opened her mouth to speak and a solid ball of ants fell out. Clymidia was screaming and vomiting simultaneously. My uncle Zostar was halfway to us when he made out what he was seeing. He threw his head back and collapsed forward onto the gleaming box of upturned knives he still carried. The doctor was brushing sticky insects from my aunt. The fat mayor was pushing the truck and drawing hard on his greasy cigar. My uncle rolled over and I could see he had somehow avoided actually stabbing himself. I helped him to his feet while the doctor and the mayor picked up my aunt.

"Open the door!" the skinny doctor said sharply. Clymidia held the door and my uncle hobbled in the first to clear the way. The two men carried my limp Aunt Veneria with Clymidia close behind.

When I attempted to follow, my playmate said in her most adult voice, "Don't you think you've caused enough trouble for one day?" and roughly pushed me back down the steps. I was almost thankful for the excuse not to have to witness the unpleasantness within, and turned back toward the tire swing. Less than a second later there was a flash and the loudest thunderclap I had ever heard slammed into the back of my head and sent me flying over the yard to land face flat on the leather roof of the Packard. I looked back to see huge orange flames shooting out of every window in my aunt's house. The roof was largely gone, and one of the side walls of the kitchen was puffed out like crumpled paper. For some time I just sat there motionless and watched the fire. The idea of entering the inferno in some sort of rescue attempt was squelched by the sight of a greasy fat forearm in the back of the Model A and a clump of singed red hair by the back step.

Things take time. It was over a week before my parents and I heard the cause of the explosion. They were shocked. I had to stifle a laugh. Apparently the impact of the truck had caused the broomstick supporting the fridge to pop out of place. The old refrigerator fell forward directly onto one of the knobs of the stove. For almost four hours, gas filled the tiny house until his Honor the Mayor and his fat cigar pulled the curtain, shall we say, on one of the more interesting acts of that particular summer.

Backfire

William Reichard

Viola knew the space of the night, the darkness, the forms of shadow and spilling moonlight that made up her bedroom once the sun had set. She knew the space of her bed, without a husband now, the island of black between bed and window, and the window's dull frame, moonlight struck sepia as it filtered through thick, brown curtains. She knew the sound of the refrigerator, humming softly, blending with crickets. Occasionally, a car passed by on the highway, rising up like a gust of wind, then falling away again into silence. In the distance, a dog might bark, once, and shatter the pattern. And the house would settle, beams and walls pushing at each other until the wood and plaster sang, adding their voices to the darkness.

Above her, the girls were moving, walking in their rooms on unquiet floors. She glanced at the clock: one a.m. She knew they were expecting something, to be staying up so late. She wanted them to turn out their lights and sleep, close off the beacons which called to the boys that passed in their cars, her daughters' friends. Their boyfriends. But she couldn't think about that. Not her girls. Jeannette was nineteen now, out of school and working. Rita was eighteen, ready to graduate. And Linda, her baby girl, seventeen; some days Viola wondered if Linda would ever graduate, this child who burned brighter than any she had known. Viola could see their faces. They all had the same smile. "Netty," she whispered, using the secret names for her daughters. "Reet. Lin."

Something in the house was vibrating, an energy flowing down through the floors from where the girls sat and waited. Her daughters were all life, all movement and sound. They had been quiet, before the frenzied pull of puberty took them just out of her reach. Their older sisters, married now with their own children, hadn't possessed that abundance of energy; they were never pulled away by longing, by the promise of sex, of desiring bodies.

Above, the girls were whispering. Their voices passed down to Viola as the sound of leaves in wind, indistinct, brushing against each other. Occasionally, a single decipherable would could be heard: "No!" or "Wait!" But through the floorboards, she couldn't guess whose voice it was. Giggles escaped their rooms, coming in dull waves for a moment, then replaced by a total silence, tensed bodies frozen with fingers to lips; Viola could see it all, as if the ceiling were made of glass.

In the distance, she heard the sound of a loud car; it had a hole in its muffler. It was firing through the dark and she wondered if it was coming for her girls. She tensed, willing the car to pass by the house.

The girls went out without her permission. At first, they had asked. When she said no, they had stayed home, sulking on the couch and rising sometimes to glance between the closed curtains to at least see the cars as they slowly passed by. Later, they still asked, but only as a formality. As the questions formed, the girls were reaching for their coats and shoes and moving toward the door. She had called after them, but they wouldn't come back. One day, they simply left, telling her they were going but not expecting or accepting any argument. Finally they left with no word, only the sound of their feet on the stairs, the closing of the heavy front door. She had stopped calling out. They wouldn't hear her voice.

The car was closer now. As it passed down the street, the echo of the slowing engine bounced off the walls of the few houses in the village. Viola knew the car was going to stop. It was the boys, Rita's boyfriend, and Jeannette's. Linda would ride along, waiting for her own chance.

As the car approached, the sounds from overhead increased. Feet played quickly across the floorboards and someone put on shoes, the heavy sound of the soles on wood. She heard an upstairs door open, slowly. They still tried to be quiet, but made too much noise, like a drunk trying to tiptoe through a sleeping house.

"Come on! Before they blow the horn!"

Pulling to a stop, the car sat idling in front of the house. Through the open window, Viola caught the muted sounds of the radio: fast, loud music. She prepared to call out. It came to her every time they did it, the urge to scream at them as they bounded down the stairs toward the door. She wanted to jump up, stop them, lock them in the house and wait for the insistent car to drive away. She had a right. They were too young to go out on their own. What they did with the boys was wrong, and too many Sunday mornings were too bright for them, sitting with the blinds drawn, their eyes squinting shit with a hangover as they sipped at glasses of 7-Up and swallowed aspirin.

Footsteps on the stairs. Viola prepared to move. She would get up this time. She put her hands to the top of the sheet. She would put on her housecoat and go. They were moving down. The dull thudding. The stairs were old, they creaked under anyone's weight, became a stream of sound. She would get up, would stop them. One reached the bottom, her shoes clacking the tile. The lock was undone, the door pulled open. The hinges cried out and the house was a sea of sounds, of uncoiled metal and dried wood. Two were down. One on the porch. "Come on!" A horn sounded, screaming out in the darkness; Viola felt the sound pass through her life electricity, pulling and pressing her back at the same time. "Cut it out! We're coming!" Jeannette's voice. She was out the screen door and moving down the cement steps, down the sidewalk. Viola didn't move. She heard Linda's bare feet on the tile; Linda who wouldn't wear shoes in the summer. Rita was out the door and Linda followed. As she left, she pulled the door shut as softly as she could. Viola heard the latch catch, and a moment later, a car door slammed, an engine gunned into high, and the car pushed away in a gust of music and laughter.

Viola lay in her bed, her hands still poised to push the sheet away, her eyes still on her housecoat. She was listening; slowly, the car faded from earshot, the quietness returned. They were gone. She didn't know how to bring them back.

* * *

Viola sat at the kitchen table, running her fingers along the hot lip of her coffee mug. She stared out the window at her summer garden, growing too wild with weeds.

"Mom!" The voice was slight, weak, edged with pain. "Ma, I don't feel good."

Linda stood in the doorway, her robe pulled close around her skinny body, her eyes dark, and she squinted in the brightness of the morning light. Viola glanced at her, then looked away, back to the garden.

"There's some 7-Up in the fridge," Viola said. "Just take half a glass."

The girl moved silently, slowly, to the cabinet, got a glass, and went to the refrigerator. "I don't feel good." She said again.

Viola arched her brow. Linda didn't feel good. That was too bad.

"Ma," she winced, "what can I take?"

Viola didn't want to hear it; she wanted Linda to be quiet.

"What time did you get in?" Viola asked, though she knew the answer. Four a.m. She had been pulled awake then by a dull sound in the distance, a popping, but lower, like the backfiring of a car. At the same moment, she had heard Jeannette retching in the bathroom. She couldn't sleep with that sound.

"I don't know," Linda answered, easing herself onto a chair. "Not that late. I really don't feel--"

"I know! You don't feel good!" Viola cut her off. "You drink, that's what you get! And you came in at four in the morning! I heard you! Four in the morning! Who gave you permission to go out, anyway?"

"Linda groaned and sipped her 7-Up. "You were asleep," she said. "We just went. We didn't want to wake you up. We were only out for a little while."

"Out all night," Viola muttered. "You'll make yourself sick."

"I am sick," Linda whispered, trying to breathe, but her lungs wouldn't work.

"What do you think? You can just stay out all night? What do you think will happen to you?"

"Nothing," the girl sputtered.

"I saw the news last night. Some girl in the city was murdered. She was probably out too late. Some man killed her."

Linda coughed once, a thick, hacking sound that bent her body over. She tried to breathe in again and another cough came, and another. Suddenly, she pushed herself away from the table and ran for the bathroom.

"Don't you throw up on the floor!" Viola shouted after her. "I won't clean that mess up! I won't clean it!"

Rita and Jeannette came down later, waiting their turn for the bathroom, pouring out their glasses of 7-Up. The three girls ended up in the living room, shades drawn to shut out the daylight, wearing their bathrobes and watching TV with the volume turned down. Viola made them soup for lunch, the way she did when they had the flu.

* * *

Viola was walking behind the tiller, churning the deep black soil up like dark foam, uprooting weeds from between rows of potatoes. The machine vibrated in her hands, lulling them to sleep so that she had to stop every ten or fifteen minutes to rest, to shake her tingling arms and hands awake. As she stood there, waiting for the dulled feeling to drain from her limbs, she looked at the country around her. The grass in the ditch nearby was pushing at itself, hissing in the wind. Beyond the ditch there was the space of fields, an occasional stand of trees and then, space. In the distance, a neighboring water tower stood silver against the pale sky. When her hands were rested and awake, she bent and pulled the tiller's starter rope, and the machine lurched ahead, pulling her along.

Walking the tiller through the garden, Viola's thoughts were scattered, jarred by the sound of the engine and the pull of the machine: this wasn't the city. The city was almost a hundred miles away, but the photograph of the dead girl on the news hung in front of her; she was only sixteen. Every night when her daughters left, she wondered who would bring them home. Always, it was the boys. The girls were always safe with their boyfriends. But she could see a night when it might not be the familiar boys who brought the girls home. She could see a night when they might not come back at all. The girl was sixteen. But her daughters couldn't be kept in. She had raised her children and maybe they were too wild, she could admit that. Maybe she had been too wild herself. But she had to let her children grow. She was a good mother. The older children had taught their sisters what they knew, a legacy of rebellion that saddened her, but she had to let them go. Too many children hated too many parents for pulling in too much, for holding on too tight. She couldn't let them hate her, her only family. And they lived in the country. There were no dead daughters here, no lost children. Following the pull of the tiller, allowing the sputtering engine scream up to her ears, Viola pushed the dead girl away; she didn't exist.

It was a siren. She had been tilling all afternoon and her ears were dimmed by the sound of the machine, but she knew she heard a siren. She reached down and switched the engine off. Looking down the highway, she saw the Janesville squad car, its red lights turning as the car approached and sped by. Viola left the tiller standing in the garden and headed for the house.

Jeannette was on the phone when Viola came into the kitchen. She was talking excitedly to someone about the police car; it didn't happen often, the police coming out with sirens. "I need to use the phone," Viola said. She wanted to call her elder daughter, Wanda, who was married and lived in Janesville. News passed quickly between the small towns, and Wanda would know what had happened, or know someone who knew.

"Jeannette, I need the phone."

The girl flashed angry eyes at her mother, then looked away. She had finally put on some clothes: tight, faded jeans and a halter top printed with strange, sixties graphics; fashion came slowly to the area. "I have to go," Jeannette said. "She wants to call someone. Do you want to talk to her before I hang up?" Jeannette paused, listening to the unseen speaker, then held the receiver out to her mother. "Ma, it's Wanda. She wants to talk to you."

Viola sat at the table, taking the phone from her daughter. As she spoke, she reached up to the counter top and grabbed her pack of Camels. "Hello?" She put a cigarette between her lips and reached for a match. She struck it, and as the match danced into flame, the air was filled with the stinging scent of burned sulfur and tobacco. "I saw it," Viola said. "What happened?"

"I just heard it from Bob," Wanda began. "He's up at the bar. Someone was driving down Highway 14 and they saw a body along the railroad tracks! It's only about half a mile from your place." Wanda paused, but Viola didn't respond. "It's some man," Wanda continued. "They don't know who yet. They said he was shot right through the head, maybe last night. Some woman was driving by today and saw his arm. He was under two old railroad ties. Bob said he was shot right through the back of the head!"

Wanda kept talking, relating the same story over and over in variations, but Viola was only half listening. She was dragging on her cigarette, stunned, trying to pull her mind and her memory back into a single piece as she drew in the smoke. Half a mile away...Wanda's voice faded back in.

"It's gonna be on the news," Wanda said. "At six. You should watch."

Viola asked quickly, "Did they catch the killer?"

Not yet. They're still questioning people. The County Sheriff is going around asking. Has he come out to the house yet?"

Viola started. "Why would he come out here?"

"To see if you heard anything last night. Did you hear any gunshots?"

Viola answered immediately. "No. I was sleeping."

Wanda said, "Oh," and paused. When Viola didn't offer anything, she continued. "Jeannette said that you were awake when they left and you were still awake when they came home."

"I was sleeping," Viola repeated. "I fell asleep right after they left. That was at one." The backfiring car. Suddenly she heard it. "I just heard..." she began without thinking, then stopped.

"What, Mom?"

"Nothing. I was asleep all night, except when those three left and came back." Viola paused, trying to push her thoughts into order. "I don't know what to do. I tell them no and they go anyway. I just can't make them stay." She felt her mind, her heart, folding and unfolding in confusion. The backfiring car that was not a car. She wanted to cry.

"I talked to Jeannette," Wanda said, her voice soft, a comfort to Viola. "The girls didn't mean to make you mad. You know how it is. They're wild like the rest of us were. You remember. We all went through it."

She would have to tell the police. It was right around four. Muffled, like a gunshot into a bale of straw. Half a mile away. "I don't want them out with those boys," she said suddenly. "They drink too much. You don't know what could happen." But Viola knew.

"I told Jeannette to keep it down," Wanda said. "She promised to stay in tonight. You know, they still haven't found that guy."

"Who?" Viola asked. She was distracted, and felt that she'd missed some part of the conversation.

"The killer," Wanda answered. "Whoever it is. Probably a man but you never know. I get so mad at Bob sometimes I could kill him." Wanda laughed then, but Viola said nothing for a moment.

"I saw on the news that they found a sixteen-year-old girl last night. Murdered in the city," Viola finally said. "Can you imagine? Sixteen and murdered?"

"I told the girls to stay in tonight," Wanda repeated. "I told them there was a curfew on until they get the killer. They'll stay in." Wanda was older than the three girls, and her marriage, her own children, gave her an air of authority, of credibility.

"Tell them to stay in every night," Viola said quietly. She looked around. She had held the burning cigarette in her fingers until it dissolved into a glowing orange stub, which she dropped into the ashtray. She'd lost track of time while she tilled the garden, and evening was setting in. Through the doorway into the living room, she could see the glow of the television.

"You know they won't do that, Mom," Wanda said.

"But they promised for tonight." Somewhere near Wanda, Viola heard a child begin to scream. "Ma, I gotta go. Timmy's up and it's dinner time."

Viola heard her voice, but faintly. She was watching the light fade from the room, stealing details away.

"Ma?" Wanda's voice pulled Viola back.

"You let me know if you hear anything more," Viola said. "I'll watch the news."

The child wailed again. "I gotta go, Ma. I'll see you later."

The sound of the dial tone, and Viola hung up the phone. She checked the clock. 5:30. She moved toward the stove, to start dinner before the news began.

* * *

"It said on TV that people should avoid going out until they find the killer," Viola said, buttering the bread crust that nobody else would eat. She used to tell the children that eating the crust would add curl to their straight hair, but now they passed it over.

"The killer probably isn't even around here anymore," Rita said. She was spooning another helping of potatoes onto her plate. "Anyway, the dead guy isn't from the area. The killer probably did it somewhere else and drove here to dump the body."

"It was only half a mile away," Viola said. "He could have walked right into this house."

Linda picked at her food; she ate little and ate slowly. "Good thing we weren't home then!" she laughed.

Viola shot her a glance, chewing silently on her buttered crust.

"Wanda said he was shot right through the back of the head!" Jeannette said. "I bet there are brains all over the railroad tracks!"

No way!" Rita was smothering her potatoes in butter. "And even if they were there, they have to be gone by now. The train went by twice today."

"Maybe the animals ate them," Linda said. "The crows or the squirrels."

"Squirrels don't eat meat!" Rita said.

"Maybe they eat brains, though."

Rita snorted. "They wouldn't eat your brains, in any case!"

Viola snapped. "All right! Shut up! This is the dinner table! A man is dead! What difference does it make how he died? There's a killer out there and I want you to stay in until he's caught!" The words fell like stones. The girls' faces twisted.

"Ma!" It was Jeannette. "The guys are coming to pick us up!"

"You let them pick you up some other night! I want you to stay in tonight. Besides, Wanda told me you said you would."

"They're already on their way out," Rita said. "We're going to the drive-in!"

"Me too," Linda added. She rose suddenly and started out of the kitchen. "I have to get ready."

"No!" Viola's voice demanded no argument. "You don't have to go out!"

There was a pause, and the girls looked at their mother with empty faces, faces that no longer knew how to react to such a situation. Then a cry rose up, the three voices at once.

"Ma!" "We want to go!" "We made plans!"

Viola exploded. "Why? Why? You go out every night and I don't try to stop you! Do I ever say no?"

Sometimes you say--" Linda began.

"I always let you go!"

"But we don't ask that much," Rita said, her voice a whine, nasal and sharp.

"You don't ask period! You never ask, you just go! If I'd tried that with my father, he'd have shipped me!"

"We don't have a father!" It was Jeannette, who had risen to stand by the window and watch for her boyfriend's car.

"You have one," Viola said flatly. "Go and live with him if I'm so mean."

There was silence.

"He's goofy," Linda said. "He left us," and her voice was edged with disbelieving laughter. Then she paused, became serious. "I have to get ready."

"You better just get ready for bed and go and stay there," Viola said. "I mean it. I'm sick of this running around. I want you to stay home tonight."

"Why now?" Rita asked. "Why all of a sudden?" She was finishing up her potatoes, reaching for a piece of bread.

"It's not all of a sudden," Viola answered, trying to control her anger. "You go out every night, drinking and I don't know what else. I can imagine." She paused. "I just want you to stay home tonight. Stay home and watch TV like you used to?"

"God, Mom, it's getting late," Linda whined, her voice sharp like Rita's, but not as strong. "Besides, there's nothing on TV."

"We just go riding around," Rita said. "What difference does it make?"

"It makes a lot of difference! To me. Things happen...out there, in the dark. They happen to anyone. It could be dangerous. You know what's out there?"

Jeannette started to laugh, but stifled it. "Out there?" she asked, pointing to the window. "This isn't a city. There's nothing out there."

"There is," Viola started. "There is so much--"

Suddenly, Jeannette turned from the window and moved toward the door. "The guys are here. I have to go."

"No!" Viola commanded.

"Me too," Rita said, moving from the table.

"You'll stay--"

"I'm going with them," said Linda, following her sisters out of the kitchen. "We're going to a dusk till dawn triple feature. All horror movies."

And they were gone. Three sets of feet pounded up the stairs and down; a car horn sounded; the front door opened and closed; and they were gone.

Viola sat at the abandoned dinner table. Rita's bread was half eaten, a peanut butter and jelly dropped into a pool of potatoes and butter. Linda had eaten almost nothing. Jeannette had left her milk. She hated milk. Viola was alone.

She rose, picking up the dinner dishes, scraping the leftovers into a dirty bowl. She thought about the murder, then glanced out the window; it was still light. The soft summer dusk made it hard to imagine. The trees all swept together in an ocean of green. The sun was setting; golden light pooled on the lawn, dappling the grass green then yellow. It was hard to imagine, a dead girl. "It's not here," she said out loud. But she saw the man again, the railroad tracks, the ties over his body. She heard that sound again, a shot into a bale of straw. Or maybe a car backfiring. Probably that. It happened all the time. She moved toward the sink to run the dishwater.

Golden Girl

Jane Cowgill

Mrs. Kingston lay curled in the fetal position, her long legs, bent knees toward chin, still as slim and graceful as a girl's, though she was now 76. In her youth, her "flapper" days, those legs had brought her, in a local way within her crowd, a certain fame, and there had been one young admirer who had composed an affectionately humorous tribute to her "elegant gams." She *had* been proud, not just of her legs, but of her whole body, its statuesque height, its power to attract men. The face, however, had never seemed acceptable. The nose was too large and presented an obstacle throughout her life to her sense of full possession of feminine beauty. Now she lay quite still, purposely, since she did not want anyone to know as yet that she was awake. She imagined the bones of her skeleton with the flesh fallen away--like carefully placed sticks--her legs and feet forming two parallel *z*'s, her nose reduced at last to only a small undulation on the skull. She sensed herself existing somewhere inside the desiccated shell of her body, still confined, but floating and indifferent to the flesh that had once been the glory and now was the regulator of her life.

Sounds of bustling efficiency filtered from distant rooms into Mrs. Kingston's consciousness. There was a certain luxury, she had to admit, in lying very calmly, sensing beyond closed eyelids the sun hovering outside the blinds, especially when others were up and about taking responsibility for the urgent demands of the day. Like being a pampered child, she thought. How often had she envied her own children their clinging to every last moment of sleep while she frantically prepared their breakfasts before their school and her work day began? Such sluggishness would not have been allowed her as a child, not by *her* mother who had definite ideas about the proper training of young ladies. Luxurious abandon was not a quality to be encouraged. Efficiency in household management and a cheerful disposition were the qualities Mrs. Kingston's mother had hoped to inculcate in her three daughters. Admirable qualities, really, yet even now Mrs. Kingston's heart withered at the memory of her own inability to measure up, to please...or was it a justifiable unwillingness? She had balked at her mother's restrictions; she had resisted willfully things to which her younger sisters had, apparently easily, accommodated themselves. Truth be known, she had been rebellious.

In adulthood, she had told her own adolescent daughters, Joanne and Helen, tales of this rebellious behavior as though it were a badge of honor and she an early and lone pioneer for freedoms they now took for granted. There was the incident of the underwear when she had abandoned the stiff corset her mother presented her for a shift-like undergarment she herself designed and sewed. Had she done this, as she told her own daughters, merely for the reasonable elimination of obvious discomfort, or, as she secretly feared, to antagonize her mother, to intentionally raise fears that her daughter was exhibiting early signs of licentiousness? Mrs. Kingston always recalled with shame and regret her mother's pained and angrily disappointed expression on discovering that she had bobbed her hair. In the retelling Mrs. Kingston had attempted to transform the event into something humorous. She exaggerated her mother's pitiful wail--that she would not be able to take her daughter back East to visit relatives because her beauty and femininity had been ruined. To *her* daughters, Mrs. Kingston emphasized the irony that in her day short hair was a sign of rebellion while in theirs long hair was. Drawing this ironic parallel helped her feel a certain solidarity with her daughters and reassured her that while her own mother had been remote and disapproving, she had done better, was understanding, even encouraged her daughters' explorations.

Actually, though, Mrs. Kingston knew in her heart of hearts that her attitude went beyond solidarity and encouragement. Secretly--because she would never admit this weakness to either of her girls, especially not to the older one, Joanne, who probably suspected it anyway--she had envied her daughters' long, straight locks, which still retained something of the golden luster of childhood blondeness, while her own short curly hair was fading to gray. And she had envied even more the unconcern with which both girls, children of the 60's, resisted social expectation, flaunted their glorious manes with abandon in an adult world which still prescribed for women hair spray, wire curlers, the bouffant, the beehive, and the flip.

Mrs. Kingston's attempt to explain her life to herself through tales told to her daughters had not entirely transformed the experiences, though. *She* had not been granted the easy gestures of resistance enjoyed by her daughters. The small ecstasies of her own rebellions were always tainted by the painful knowledge of her mother's disappointment. And there was still the shame of it all.

There had been the secret smoking, secret even after she returned as an adult from a year at college, and then there was Willard Hawkins, a man instantly disliked by her mother, and her mother had been right too, as it turned out, for that first marriage had lasted only a few years. How was it all to be understood? Was she or wasn't she responsible for the fact that, simply put, her mother disliked her? It seemed to Mrs. Kingston, an elderly but still graceful woman lying in an unfamiliar room with sun promising behind the blinds, an urgent and crucial question.

Mrs. Kingston would dearly have loved to shift her position in the bed. The flesh of her hip was going numb, and the smell of the medicines on the bedside table was beginning to depress and nauseate her, mingling as it did with the aroma of breakfast foods in the nearby kitchen. But as yet she was unwilling to declare herself present to the world, to allow into what had always been a deep sense of personal privacy the cheerful, competent, and well-meaning Mrs. Jarvis, or Maddie, as she asked her clients to call her. Maddie ran this establishment from her own home. Everyone involved in the decision to move Mrs. Kingston here, everyone, that is, except Mrs. Kingston herself, was delighted with Maddie. She was a treasure, the home a real home, the clients integrated into the life of Maddie's own family.

A wave, not of gratitude, but of resentment rose in Mrs. Kingston's breast, and she allowed her eyelids to flutter open to a squint so that she could surreptitiously observe the room. The imitation wood-grain paneling on the wall announced immediately the taste of the working class to which Maddie belonged, and it infuriated Mrs. Kingston. Not even the mahogany dresser and hand-carved mirror which she had been allowed to bring with her could subdue or obscure it. In fact, they were overwhelmed by the paneling's insistent, artificial flatness. Mrs. Kingston could not feel that her new surroundings reflected her own, unique personality. Her belongings were merely temporary punctuation marks in the larger narrative of Maddie's inept efforts at home improvement. Mrs. Kingston felt, somewhat ambivalently, that her anger was petty and ungrateful, that she was putting something essentially trivial, her good taste, above something important, the kindness of Maddie's soul. And yet, there was, wasn't there, a matter for legitimate annoyance--the obscuring of her own identity which she no longer had the physical mobility to assert? It had all been the same from the beginning of her life; it was the corset, the hair, the smoking, and even Willard all over again--or still, since, it seemed, one was obliged to assert one's independence continually in order to avoid being subsumed into the great mass of kindly, unoriginal, and submissive women.

Tears of frustration formed in Mrs. Kingston's eyes and rolled sideways across the bridge of her nose, her "beak" she had begun self-mockingly to call it as age slackened the skin of her cheeks and exaggerated the nose's prominence. Without attempting to quench her tears, Mrs. Kingston gazed at a watery view of her room. By the window she could pick out, just barely without her glasses, the flowers sent by her youngest sister, Kay. Annoyingly enough, Maddie had placed them on the stand by the easy-chair rather than on the dresser as Mrs. Kingston had instructed her to do. Set on the dresser in front of the hand-carved mirror, the flowers would have been reflected in the glass to create the illusion of abundance--to make a small bid for elegance. Couldn't Maddie see that when the blinds were open for the day the flowers set by the window would be lost in the background of the grass and trees outside? Perfectly obvious, but just like Maddie not to notice, or to think such refinements unimportant. Maddie had been too interested in babbling on about Kay's consideration to pay attention to Mrs. Kingston's attempt to make her wishes understood. Kay would have known how to handle this situation, though; she wouldn't have minded interrupting Maddie and insisting. Mrs. Kingston knew that she herself, even if she hadn't had the difficulties of speech she now had, would have been polite but resentful, and that the resentment would have grown until she practically choked on it.

Now she felt merely bitter, especially about Kay. Kay was her junior by ten years, but had always been able to negotiate the world better than Mrs. Kingston. Kay didn't seem to struggle so hard, and Kay had loved their mother, whom she described as gentle rather than remote, helpful rather than critical. Kay liked to recollect long afternoons the two spent sewing Kay's clothes for college, and Kay had turned out to be an excellent seamstress, too. None of this would have mattered to Mrs. Kingston if Kay had remained a homebody like their middle sister Marion, but Kay had lived independently and had even gone to New Guinea with the Red Cross during the war. Kay, in fact, was a thorn in Mrs. Kingston's side. She always seemed to want to deny Mrs. Kingston her legitimate outrage. Kay had said recently that Mrs. Kingston, for all her life, had always had something to prove.

The pillow under Mrs. Kingston's head was developing a wet spot where the tears were being absorbed. The dampness reminded her that her bladder was painfully full, and already she felt a corresponding dampness between her legs as she leaked slightly into her underwear. She was going to need some assistance. Not that she couldn't control her bladder. She knew what exercises to do for that problem, and she did them secretly and religiously because she dreaded the day she might be found lying in a pool of her own urine. Her balance, not her bladder control, had been affected by the stroke, so that she was unsteady on her feet, and her daughters had insisted she call Maddie for help in getting around her new room.

Mrs. Kingston reached out to the bedside table for the intercom. Holding the unfamiliar machine in both hands to steady it, and bringing it close to her face, she located the talk button which she pressed carefully with two thumbs. Putting her mouth right next to the speaker and concentrating on her enunciation, she called as noncommittally as possible so as to disguise her distress: "*Maddie.*" But, despite her deliberate efforts, Mrs. Kingston was frustrated by the difficulty of getting her tongue around the "d's" in Maddie's name, and she was disturbed by the sound she had produced, not like her own voice at all. The whole thing had sounded loud and indistinct, like the wail of a retarded child: "M..A..D..D..I..E." Mrs. Kingston shuddered but recoiled away from this alarming observation. What kind of name was Maddie, anyway? Any self-respecting young woman would have stayed with her lovely given name, Màdeline, and would not have allowed it to be corrupted into that ugly, common-sounding nickname, thought Mrs. Kingston, consoling herself.

By the time Maddie arrived, Mrs. Kingston had raised herself to a seated position on the edge of her bed. Under her feet she could feel the coarse strands of the yellow shag rug Maddie had just had installed. Won't last long, she thought, this cheap stuff, and a perfect gathering place for dust. Her own policy had always been to buy one quality item regardless of cost and to make it last. An unbidden image of the maple floors in Kay's co-op precipitated another wave of resentment and made her shoo away in disgust Maddie's efforts to take her elbow and help her to a standing position. She reached out to steady herself on the bedside table, and despite the rattling of the pills in the bottles as she pulled jerkily against it, Mrs. Kingston was determined to stand alone and certain that she could. After all, the agreement to call Maddie when she wished to walk around her own room had been forced on Mrs. Kingston by her daughters, particularly Joanne, who was, she thought, again with disgust, really just interested in her own peace of mind.

Invigorated by her anger, Mrs. Kingston propelled herself upward successfully, though one of the pill bottles fell over and rolled off the table and under the bed. She could hear Maddie making comforting noises, but she ignored them. What did she care if Maddie, whose salary Mrs. Kingston paid, had to crawl under the bed for the bottle? Concentrating carefully on the door to the bathroom, Mrs. Kingston crossed the room unsteadily and passed inside. She turned herself around and backed up slowly until she could feel the cold edge of the toilet bowl against the backs of her calves. She pulled up her nightgown and then lowered her underwear with one hand. She steadied herself with the other hand against the wall, lowered her body as far as she could until her legs gave out, and then allowed herself to fall heavily onto the toilet bowl. During this procedure, one edge of her nightgown had gotten caught under her bottom as she landed. She attempted to extricate it but couldn't manage before her over-full bladder let go, thoroughly wetting the edge of the gown. Mrs. Kingston knew that Maddie would have to become aware of this accident. Maddie was at the moment waiting politely but vigilantly outside the bathroom door--just as Mrs. Kingston had waited when her young daughters were learning to navigate in the bathroom for themselves. Now Maddie hovered outside like Mrs. Kingston's keeper as though some horrifying pitfalls awaited Mrs. Kingston between the bowl and the bed.

A sarcastic sneer pulled down the corners of Mrs. Kingston's mouth. If Maddie only knew the kinds of dangers Mrs. Kingston had courted in her life she wouldn't waste her time. Hadn't she, even recently, just before the stroke, disregarded the warnings of neighbors and friends at her summer place and sailed her catamaran out into the middle of the sound? In fact, Mrs. Kingston had an image of herself poised over and over again throughout her life at that existential moment between the fear of the unknown and retreat into comfort and security, and she had, she reflected in proud defiance, always chosen to leap. She remembered standing as a young girl in the prow of her father's anchored dinghy, bent to dive for the first time, hands clasped over her head, arms pressed against ears, hesitating in fear of finding her head enmeshed in the bottom weeds, her wet spindly body shivering so violently in the evening breeze that it shook the boat. But she had gone in, and her father had been surprised and pleased. She could remember similar moments of wavering in later years when, for example, she had first tentatively approached the expert slope at Aspen, but she had gone down without excuses. And now they all thought she needed an attendant. They were forcing her into the great undifferentiated class of the elderly who are all treated the same regardless of who they had been before they crossed the hellish portals into their declining years--the time of true democracy, she mused, when all persons are reduced to being equal.

Mrs. Kingston wanted to show them all--all being mostly just Maddie and the other clients who were as vague a presence to Mrs. Kingston as she was to them--who she really was, or at least had been, but she wasn't sure she could manage it. More practically, she wanted right at this moment just to get up off the toilet bowl by herself. But when she looked around for the wall handle specially designed for the handicapped she remembered that Maddie's husband had removed it so that it could be installed at a better position for her. In her haste, she had forgotten about it earlier; no wonder she had had problems lowering herself to the bowl. Now it lay gleaming its ugly stainless steel gleam, useless against the opposite wall. The only possible aid was the toilet paper dispenser which she grasped as tightly as she could with both hands.

The dispenser held firm as Mrs. Kingston heaved herself off the bowl to a standing position, her success a tribute to the good craftsmanship of Maddie's carpenter husband. But the roll of paper popped out of the metal pincers and clattered across the room trailing its white streamer over the floor, reminding Mrs. Kingston of the Halloween mischief of her youth in which she had egged on her younger sisters to drape the trees next door with toilet paper, excited by the possibility of adult annoyance or even anger. She felt a surge now of that illicit delight when she thought of the vigilant Maddie having to re-roll the paper and set things to rights, but her pleasure evaporated in Maddie's actual presence. Maddie had, of course, entered the bathroom at the sound of falling objects. Mrs. Kingston's perverse pleasure melted into impotent humiliation, the toilet paper roll a sign of her incompetence and ridiculous small act of defiance in trying to prove she could manage alone.

Self-disgust overwhelmed Mrs. Kingston as she saw Maddie tactfully observe both the toilet paper and her wet gown. She felt her energy dissipate, her shoulders sag, her very self wither into decrepitude. She allowed herself to be gently led to the bed, to be helped into her clothes and to be served her breakfast in the easy chair beside Kay's flowers, the breakfast on a special tray-table that rolled up under the chair. It was a good breakfast, too, even if she did have some trouble with swallowing since the stroke. Maddie was, Mrs. Kingston knew and admitted grudgingly, a good woman, she and her husband completely competent. Mrs. Kingston's last years could be made pleasant by their cheerful ministrations, their tactful help, their good food, their clean home. Mrs. Kingston wondered how her own mother would have behaved had she been in Mrs. Kingston's position. But her mother hadn't had to face this since she had died at home at a younger age of heart failure. Still, she knew her mother would have approved of Maddie, would have been grateful for her kindness and would, above all, have deplored Mrs. Kingston's own embarrassing behavior and attitude.

Mrs. Kingston felt ashamed, repentant, and defeated. She wanted to resolve to be good, as her mother would have been, to be cooperative, to assure her own daughters by her obedient behavior, reported to them through Maddie, that they need not worry about her well-being. While she slowly consumed Maddie's tasty breakfast of home-made muffins and eggs she felt capable of this heroic act of resignation. Bodily comfort and the day's early defeats conspired to produce passivity. And yet, when breakfast was cleared away and a day of incapacity stretched bleakly ahead of her, Mrs. Kingston felt the worm of resentment begin to uncoil again. How could they all expect this of her? Who would she be but just another of Maddie's lovely clients? Mrs. Kingston knew exactly how the elderly resigned looked: like mechanized dolls whose batteries had run low, the permanently expectant expressions of their painted faces a mockery of what they could ever hope to encounter in the remainder of their days.

Mrs. Kingston saw herself suspended between two alternatives: resignation or defiance. Resignation was terrifying, but defiance made everyone else uncomfortable. Besides, defiance could be pathetic as easily as could resignation. It was one thing to exhort people, as some poet had done, to "rage against the dying of the light," but rage in the elderly could easily lead to humiliation, as Mrs. Kingston's morning had shown. Mrs. Kingston stared at Kay's flowers which slowly melded into the background of trees outside the window. Her mouth sagged open as she distractedly contemplated not the flowers, but the murky landscape of her interior reality.

It was Maddie's entrance to clean away the breakfast things and to make the bed which recalled Mrs. Kingston to the outside world. As she bustled about the room, Maddie reminded Mrs. Kingston of the visit of her elder daughter Joanne, who was driving the three hours from home, leaving her kids with her husband for the day. How lucky Mrs. Kingston was, Maddie said, to have a loving family, a sister to remember you with flowers, and children to pay you visits. Mrs. Kingston agreed obediently to these platitudes, true as they probably were, but a new anxiety began to accumulate in her breast regarding her daughter. She wished it had been the younger one, Helen, instead of Joanne who was coming. Helen was easier to be with, more sympathetic and less critical, and Helen would confide in you. You didn't feel so self-conscious with her. Joanne was different; there was something watchful about her, some way in which from early childhood she would never commit herself wholeheartedly to Mrs. Kingston's energetic projects for fun. When, following her husband's death, Mrs. Kingston had taken up sailing, Joanne would go along for a ride but would never express pleasure in it or admiration for her mother's accomplishment. There was some part of herself that Joanne never revealed, and that reticence felt like criticism to Mrs. Kingston. She had told Joanne point blank on several occasions how proud she was of her, but her attempts at communication had not taken. Joanne remained a distant though dutiful daughter. And now Joanne would arrive and observe Mrs. Kingston in her quandary, would, in her silent way, judge Mrs. Kingston and imply mysteriously that there was something lacking.

As the tedious minutiae of the day flowed only partially noticed past Mrs. Kingston, images of her daughter consumed her attention. While Maddie vacuumed the room, Mrs. Kingston called up in anxious assemblage memories of Joanne as child and adult...Joanne standing mournfully outside the gate to her baby sister's room, barred from entering because of a cold; Joanne hiding in her closet with her stuffed animals, refusing to come out; Joanne the teenager disgusted and embarrassed by her mother's attempts to rock-and-roll dance in front of her high school friends; Joanne passionately attached to her father, though he hardly deserved it; Joanne always quietly pointing out errors in Mrs. Kingston's thinking about various matters. Really, it was hard to enjoy yourself or to rest secure in what you knew about the world with Joanne around; she could always deflate you.

Mrs. Kingston now focused on one particular memory of the days at the beach cottage, the days before they had moved, before everything had changed and they were unable to return. Those summers had seemed like the early days of Creation before the Fall. Every task had been a joy-- sweeping the sand out of the house in the early morning while the sun glittered blindingly off the water, hanging out laundry in the salt breeze, even cleaning up the dishes in the water heated just before washing by a quaint, old-fashioned gas heater in the kitchen. The kids had seemed effortlessly happy then, forever amused by just water and sand, two small golden-haired elves--"my little towheads" she called them--busily occupied with digging and splashing by the sea.

Now, as Mrs. Kingston sat distracted by her thoughts, her formerly statuesque form crumpled in her easy chair and her head sunken between her shoulders like the head of a vulture, she recalled one of those sparkling mornings of cheerful activity. She had lost her glasses and had searched everywhere. She had grown frustrated and irritable wanting to be done with the house and to go down to the sea. Just as she approached exasperation Joanne, then only about five or six years old, had materialized from somewhere outside, timidly offering to help. She had stood in the porch door with the sun glaring from the water behind her and illuminating her blond hair like a halo around her head. A lovely, momentary apparition, but, Mrs. Kingston had thought, just another frustration, really, for what could the child do that she hadn't already done herself? But Joanne had led her mother directly to the glasses which were lying in a little tunnel formed by logs in the wood pile near the fireplace. At that moment the bright expectations of the day clouded, for how could the child have produced the glasses unless she herself had secreted them there? What had possessed her? It seemed to Mrs. Kingston then and now that some unspeakable grudge had been smoldering in that childish will, and Mrs. Kingston had felt, she had to admit, her motherly sentiments recoil from the child. Remembering it now, slouched in her easy chair, Mrs.

Kingston shuddered as from some chill, even though Maddie considerately kept the rooms at seventy-two for the comfort of her ailing clients. Mrs. Kingston was alone in the world, and she knew it.

Just before 11:00 A.M. Maddie approached Mrs. Kingston to help her spruce up for Joanne's visit. She brought lipstick, comb, and mirror. Mrs. Kingston was able to manipulate these objects without too much difficulty, though she avoided a prolonged gaze in the mirror, fearing to see crooked lipstick under her prominent nose and the flattened, unattended hair which had given up its curl as she aged. She gathered herself, placed her feet firmly together in front of her, toes together but heels slightly rotated outward so that her knees would rest against each other and her legs would not fall slackly open in a moment of inattention. She straightened her clothing and folded her hands in her lap, the hand with the Indian ring made from petrified wood on top. Even Maddie had noticed how unusual that ring was. And so Mrs. Kingston was prepared when Joanne's car pulled into the drive right on time.

Right on time, that was Joanne through and through. You could never really fault her because she always did what was responsible and sensible. It was Joanne who had thought of the large-type newspaper subscription when Mrs. Kingston's eyes began to fail and of the tapes of novels to listen to. But Mrs. Kingston *did* want to fault Joanne because of her standoffishness, because, for Joanne, even a hug was an uncomfortable formality. Mrs. Kingston heard her daughter in the hallway exchanging muffled conversation with Maddie, and she imagined the two of them assessing her progress, or lack of it, like two scientists considering the condition of an experimental animal. And then Joanne was there, looming above Mrs. Kingston's chair, bearing gifts, helping her to her feet, proposing a walk across the lawn in the fresh air, concentrating intently on her mother's garbled expressions of welcome.

Mrs. Kingston regarded Joanne with a mixture of skepticism and trepidation. She approved of her daughter's still youthful and athletic body, her long straight hair falling in two curtains on each side of her face as she bent attentively over her. But Mrs. Kingston, even with her failing eyesight, could discern at this intimate distance the stress lines beginning to etch themselves into permanence under Joanne's eyes and around her mouth. Joanne was approaching middle age not altogether happily, she observed. But she didn't pity her or the incipient deterioration of her face because those lines also looked hard and because Joanne would never discuss with her mother their genesis, though Mrs. Kingston suspected it had something to do with that husband, and because Mrs. Kingston was afraid of her own daughter, of her opinion, and, most immediately, of her proposal for a walk.

Mrs. Kingston wasn't sure she could make it even once around the lawn, but she saw Joanne's proposal as a challenge, and she was determined to rise to it. With Maddie's help they made it down the front steps and onto the flat terrain of the lawn. Then Maddie left them and they were on their own--mother and daughter in an awkward embrace, Mrs. Kingston leaning heavily on Joanne's side, Joanne's arm circling her mother's waist. They clung to each other in a grotesque parody of easy, natural feeling.

Attraction and repulsion alternated in Mrs. Kingston's breast. How easy and what a relief it would really be to give in and allow this competent and dutiful daughter to support her in her weakness. But relief felt too much like defeat to Mrs. Kingston, and as she and Joanne progressed carefully across the lawn she grew annoyed at her dependence on her daughter. She abruptly pulled herself away from Joanne's side. She could see in a blur the lounge chairs on the far side of the lawn, the destination of their walk. The need to get to them on her own began to form itself pressingly in Mrs. Kingston's mind. She would *not* let this child who had so often silently rejected her have the satisfaction of feeling herself to be a good daughter. No! Because that would be a lie; because Joanne didn't really care, not in any way that mattered to Mrs. Kingston anyway; because Mrs. Kingston knew herself alone in her battle against decay and death; because if she had to be alone she would be defiantly alone even if she was terrified; because none of them wanted her to be who she was; because she hated them all, her mother, Maddie, *and* Joanne; and because she would not allow the living ones to participate in her moment of need and then congratulate themselves afterwards oblivious of how she had despised them.

Mrs. Kingston surged ahead of the unsuspecting Joanne, who momentarily lost hold of her mother. She tried to focus her concentration on placing one foot in front of the other so as to maintain her balance, but she had propelled herself forward so precipitously that her body catapulted ahead of her feet, and her momentum carried her not just forward but downward. She could see the individual blades of green grass as the ground surged up towards her and then felt a mighty wrench as Joanne grabbed her arm to slow her fall.

Mother and daughter, they fell together, Mrs. Kingston's uncontrolled body pulling Joanne's after. How slowly everything seemed to be happening. As she collided with the ground, Mrs. Kingston had a clear apprehension of her glasses balanced on her beak, her jacket ripped, her hands stinging. She wanted to roll onto her back to get her bearings, and she began to turn very slowly, fearful of having broken something. As Mrs. Kingston rotated, her daughter's distorted face loomed into view. Joanne was on her hands and knees hovering over her. And she was weeping, yes she really was, thought Mrs. Kingston in surprise. Real tears. In fact, she was sobbing and seemed strangely out of control.

Suddenly, Mrs. Kingston saw Joanne from an unfamiliar vantage point as though she, Mrs. Kingston, had been wafted out of her own body and was floating in the air above the two of them. Joanne on hands and knees no longer seemed so formidable; in fact, she seemed to be supplicating herself. And it was Joanne desperate, Joanne in pain, Joanne needing something from her mother that Mrs. Kingston saw now in her old age for the first time. Mrs. Kingston reached up with both hands and grasped the lapels of Joanne's blouse. She drew her daughter's face closer to her own, intent with the desperation of a woman on a sacred mission. In what she knew to be her very last effort at concentration she summoned her energies to enunciate carefully to Joanne:

"Mother never liked me...my fault...something wrong with me...wanted to be good to you...my little golden girl..."

And as she sank back exhausted, Joanne's broken sobs rolled over Mrs. Kingston like a blessing from heaven.

Flat on her back in the grass, Mrs. Kingston stared straight at the sun until its white-yellow brilliance exploded to black. No need to worry about the effects on her eyesight, now that she knew her own death to be near. She was not afraid but, rather, immensely satisfied that she had managed to keep herself alive long enough to do what she had been meaning to do all her life.

Covering Home

Joseph Maiolo

    Coach discovered Danny's arm when Danny's parents were splitting up at the beginning of the season. For a while it didn't seem that Danny would be playing at all, but Coach called him at home where he was staying with his father and told him he needed his "natural curve and pretty good heat," said he'd been watching him warm up with Pye, their big catcher, before practice. Danny had always played second, though secretly he'd rather be at short even before the mound. The problem has always been that his arm isn't strong enough for short, but when Coach pointed out that the rubber is closer to home than the hole is to first--Danny could never throw from deep in the hole--it made sense even though the rubber was still farther to home than most of his plays at second were to first. After Coach talked to Danny's father and then they both talked to him, Danny was convinced he was a born hurler.
    And after he popped Pye's mitt a couple times hard enough to make Pye shake his hand, he was hooked. Each time he throws he imagines the big mitt to be the face of somebody he hates. But he doesn't dislike enough people that he can change with each pitch, so he uses movie and TV criminals and assorted villains from board games and videos. He has taught himself to do it over and over, treating Pye's mitt like a face in a hole in a wall at the carnival. Works pretty well, too. They're in the play-offs.
    Danny knows he will not be pitching tomorrow; nobody will unless he wins today. So what he does now determines whether or not Ethan, the new kid, gets his chance. Danny and Ethan have been rotating between second and pitcher, but the guys don't work so good with Ethan on the mound. They say he thinks he's hot stuff. His father's always at practice, helping Coach and volunteering to drive the boys or take the equipment in his big van. Even mows the grass and fills in at the concession stand. No wonder Ethan plays every game. The only thing is, the guy's good. Danny has pointed this out, tactfully, on many occasions. Danny is glad to have old Pye, big as a backstop, behind the plate; Rufus on third, who scoops them up like a vacuum cleaner; Jo-Jo at short, with an arm like a rifle; and at first Dingleberry, who can stretch five feet for the throw. But Ethan's pulled Danny out of a few tight ones: with a backhander in the seventh against the A's, a

line-drive stab against the Yankees with two on, and a gorgeous double play against the Reds with Ethan doing two-thirds of it alone. But the guys still think Ethan's where he is just because of his old man.

Danny's parents haven't been coming to the games at the same time anymore the way they used to, back when he was on second without star status. After they split up they must have made it a rule to take turns because he has seen only one of them, if one, each game all season. He never talks about it with either one of them, but he can't see how they can work it out without talking to each other. All he knows is that there's never both of them congratulating him after he's won, not unless they *are* both there and just taking turns coming out on the field after it's all over, but then that would take some talking together, too. However they do it, it has worked out okay for them.

But today is different.

Earlier when Danny was getting ready in his room he heard his father, Jack Ferguson, come in, and then the tinkle of ice cubes in the kitchen. He didn't say anything, just kept putting on his uniform, and in a few minutes his father yelled through the hall, "That you, Dan?" Danny put his head out the door to show that it was, and Jack said he'd be at the game but probably a little late, he had to cancel a trip first.

Then in a little while, Cora came in--she'd moved in with them a few weeks ago--and Danny heard the tinkle again. By now he was dressed, but he stayed in his room until he could get out without seeing Cora.

"I don't even like baseball," Cora said.

"Ssshhh," Jack said. "That's not the point and you know it. This is something we have to do."

"I am not ready to face a crowd of people yet, Jack. And you know as well as I do that she may be there today."

"That's just it," Jack said. He sighed loud enough for Danny to hear that too. "If she can be there, why can't we?"

"Because she may not be there with her boyfriend."

"Oh, he'll be with her."

"Your horns are starting to show."

"Knock that off."

In the end Cora agreed, if Jack would let her take the time she needed to get ready. When Cora went to Jack's bedroom and Jack went back to the ice cubes, Danny walked quickly through the hall and out the front door.

Now Danny is in the dugout, his pitching arm in his

jacket sleeve. It is the top of the third, no score, Ethan at bat. Ethan's father, a large, imposing black man, sits inside with the score book; he is serious, energetic even when he is at rest. Danny is glad to have him there because Pye and Dingle and especially Rufus are not able to bad-mouth Ethan to Danny; Danny won't have to pretend to go along with it and even add something himself from time to time. When Ethan raps out a stand-up double, his father claps twice, enters it in the score book, and yells to Jo-Jo, coming up, to "Keep it goin'!"

Then Dingle moves on deck, Rufe in the hole, and Pye goes out for something at the concession stand. Danny takes the opportunity to say to Ethan's father, "Good hit, Mister Norris."

"Yeah," Ethan's father says. "Keep it goin'!" he yells out of the dugout.

Danny sees his father, followed by Cora, walking through the stands. Jack smiles at people he knows, turns to take Cora's hand, and sits with her at the bottom of the bleachers. The two of them stand out in the crowd of people mostly wearing jeans and short-sleeved shirts, sweat pants and tee shirts. Jack wears patent-leather shoes and a wide-lapeled suit; Cora, in a tight white blouse and tighter purple slacks, crosses her legs and sits straight, straining her breasts. Then Jack removes his jacket and places it across his lap, and in a moment he seeks out Danny and gives him a nod.

Jo-Jo then Dingle and Pye keep the rally going, scoring two, and then with two out Danny comes up. He feels self-conscious swinging two bats, knocking imagined mud from his rubber spikes, and after he swings at the first pitch and misses inches under it he hears from somewhere, "Sucker for a high one," and knows that he is. He just cannot help it: When they come in around his shoulders, it is as if somebody else's hands swing for him. He hopes the pitcher doesn't know, or that he won't be able to throw a high one whenever he wants if he does. Danny crouches and that helps some; at least it helps the way he feels about being there in front of everybody in the first place. But still he strikes out.

As he heads for the mound he smells something in the air that reminds him of his father's new after-shave lotion; maybe it is his father's. It's like that disinfectant used in the boy's room at school, and he cannot help thinking that his old man dresses like a TV preacher and smells like a urinal. Between warm-up pitches he glances toward the bleachers without appearing to and sees Jack and Cora talking and laughing with people behind them. Cora is turned so that her breasts seem larger than normal. Rufe has nicknamed her Unsinkable Cora. Pye and Jo-Jo call Danny's mother Barbie. They make it sound like a compliment, and he goes along with the joke because everybody in the infield except Ethan has split parents who are just plain *plain*. So he figures to get at least some status from his Ken-and-Barbie mom and dad and their "friends." They always call them that when introducing them. "Hey," Jo-Jo will say, referring to his mother, "I'd like you to meet my pal." "My chum," Pye will add. "My comrade," Rufe'll say. Jo-Jo will complete it: "My--oh, my!--my *friend*." Then they all crack up. Pye says his old man's got so many friends he can't keep up with them. "Friendly Fred: That's my old man. Big problem, huh?" Danny's folks only have a friend apiece, and now they are both--they are now all *four*--at the game.

While Danny waits in that awkward lull after the ump yells "Batter up!" and the infielders throw the ball around the horn, he sees Nikki, his mother, walking dangerously close to where Jack and Cora sit, her friend Cole beside her. After Danny gets the ball from Jo-Jo, he looks back to see Nikki see her mistake and veer off with Cole up the bleachers. Cole has on his running suit, and as usual Nikki is in impeccable black: slacks, blouse, ribbon around her throat. She is perfect: bleached-white hair, a mouth that seems always to be craving something, eyes that blink thick black lids slowly over violet contact lenses, and, as Pye puts it, "legs all the way up to here." Pye once said, when he and Danny were comparing homeliness, "Frig, how'd you ever come out of somebody like her?"

Everything about her that really counts is delectably tapered: legs, breasts, fingers. Her fingers count so much because she is so expressive with them. With long, deep-red nails she seems constantly to clutch at the air before she talks, as if the polish is never fully dry and she might as well use the occasion. Even her toenails are like a magazine ad. It has been some time since Danny has thought of her as Mother. She is Nikki Ferguson, who wears black so often she might in another time have been thought of as being in constant mourning.

Danny's imagination is virtually boundless this inning in replacing hated faces--all fictional--for Pye's big mitt. He and Pye have worked out a little system where Pye will squeeze the mitt several times, like a gulping mouth, and yell things like "Put it down his throat, Ferg!" Danny fans the first batter on three strikes down the gullets of Darth Vader, Lex Luthor, and Ivan Drago. From his *Monster Manual* he dredges up faces for various Dungeons-and-Dragons villains for the second man, taking him after several foul balls with a pop-up to Rufe. Then conjuring mouths from the limitless electronic ogres from his video storehouse, he has a three-up-and-three down inning going when he forgets on a pitch and sees the ball sail into the outfield, an in-the-park homer. He doesn't forget with the next batter, who grounds out to Ethan, and once again he is heading for the dugout, the warming jacket held out by Ethan's father. "Better keep this on, son," Mister Norris says. The man is too serious for the decent inning Danny has just had, and Danny suspects him of making too much of the gesture, deliberately showing Coach that Danny is tiring. Sure. He's hoping that Danny is, so Ethan can get a chance to show his stuff. Danny takes the jacket, then turns away, thinking the guys were right about those two.

At first Danny said he would divide his time between Jack and Nikki. He and his fifteen-year-old sister, Geraldine, were given their choice when Jack and Nikki sat with them at the dinner table and explained to them that they were splitting up, that Nikki was going to move out of the house into her own apartment. Jack and Nikki were very civil, very matter-of-fact, about it all. They didn't talk about not loving each other any more, nothing like that. They simply said what they were going to do and gave Danny and Geraldine their opportunity to say what they wanted to do. Nikki did add that her new apartment was small, that it might be better if only one of them at a time stayed with her, but she said that they could make out whenever both of them wanted to be together with her.

It was only after the family meeting, as Jack called it, that Jack and Nikki had a big argument and Geraldine left the house and Danny went to the family room and put on the headset. He sat listening to rock music for over an hour, and then Geraldine came back and they talked.

"I don't have anything against him," Geraldine said, "but I'm going to stay with her full time. I think you'd be better off here."

"Why?"

"Well, you've got all your stuff here--you know, your computer and records and stuff. You've got your room and everything."

"So do you."

"Yeah, but I can move easier than you can. Besides, I'm not going to be around much longer."

"Where are you going?"

"No place yet. But it won't be too long before I, you know, graduate and go off."

She went on to say that she didn't blame their father for anything; he was an okay guy in her book. It was just that, well, she hated to sound corny but a girl needed her mother. It was different with boys. Didn't he still want to do things with Dad?

"Like what?" Danny said.

"Well, hunting and fishing and all that stuff."

"Why, we don't do that much anymore."

"Well, just what do you want to do, Danny?"

He finally said he'd stay where he was for the time being.

He visited Geraldine and Nikki a few times, even stayed overnight on a weekend, but then everything changed when Nikki and Geraldine moved in with Cole. Cole has his son with him and Danny felt awkward going to an older boy's house to visit his own mother and sister. But then when Cora moved in with Jack, it was awkward, too. The best thing about it was that she didn't have any of her kids with her--that and the fact that Cora didn't try to act like a mother to Danny. She'd already had a bellyful of that.

Danny saw Geraldine only occasionally, since he was in junior high and she was a tenth-grader across town. But he heard about her from his friends who had older brothers and sisters who went to school with her. Pye said his oldest sister Barbara said Geraldine smoked dope at recess with a fast crowd; Jo-Jo said his brother Larry was bug-eyes over her. When Danny did see Geraldine the next time, she said everything was going pretty good. When Danny asked her if she wasn't--he couldn't think of the right word; he used crowded--if she wasn't crowded living with Cole's son Matthew, a senior, in the house, Geraldine said that she and Matt got along fine together; they just didn't get in each other's way. And when he pursued it further, asking her if she was ever going to come over to the house, she said she wasn't. "He's too strict," she said of Jack, and she wasn't about to go back to that sort of stuff. Besides, Nikki and Cole were fun, she said. They let her and her friends watch whatever they wanted on the VCR, and they had cable.

"With MTV?" Danny said.

"Of course." Then she went on to tell him how they

let her have private parties without always being right there trying to get in on the act, though every now and then they might show her friends how to really dance. "You ought to see them," she said. "I swear, Danny, they ought to be on *Star Search* together."

Danny told her he didn't think Jack was so strict.

"And how's that woman who moved in with him?"

"Cora? Okay, I guess. She don't bother me none. She brought over her own VCR for their bedroom, so I as good as got my own now."

"You mean he lets you watch it without making you feel like you're doing something wrong?"

"Sure. And as for cable, that was the first thing Cora said she had to have, but that's in their bedroom too."

"You mean they didn't hook you up?"

"Huh-uh. But I'm going to ask them to."

"Great!" Then she told him that Cole bought Nikki a new Mazda RX-7. Her face lit up, waiting for Danny to say something about that. When he didn't, she said, "And I get to drive it whenever Mommy isn't."

Then Danny began thinking about what he'd heard from his friends about her and he wanted to ask her about it, but didn't. Instead, he asked her if she ever got to drive Cole's new Camaro.

"Are you kidding me? Matt had a fit when Mommy asked Cole if I could. He's such a jerk anyway."

"I thought you said you two got along okay."

"I said we just stay out of each other's way. He's one of these new jocks. Super Sunday's bigger to him than Christmas. He thinks he's Brian Bosworth or something." She laughed. "He even started wearing an earring." She made a face. "You should've seen him when I lit up a cigarette in my room. I mean, Cole can't stand smoking but Matt's a fanatic."

"You mean you smoked in the house?"

"In my room. It's supposed to be my private space."

"Well, you never could at home."

"Yeah, I know. None of them smoke."

Then Danny didn't see Geraldine much after that. Pye said Barbara told their mother she knew guys were on the lookout for girls like Geraldine. Danny asked him what she meant by that, and Pye said he heard her tell their mother that there were guys who went after girls whose parents had just split up, that they were--. Pye couldn't think of the right word, something like vulnerable.

"What's it mean?" Danny said.

Pye punched him in the arm and laughed. "Means hot stuff, Frig."

It is the bottom of the seventh, Danny's team leading by one. He has exhausted the hate faces from movies and games, and since he never uses one twice in a ball game, believing that if he does it's a sure hit, he must rely upon the real thing. He also believes that if he uses a real one that is not an object of hate, that too will be a hit, and so he must avoid all the marginal villains. Even Cora and Cole are not sure things.

In the time of his uncertainty and since the last inning will not wait for him to make up his mind, he walks the first batter. Pye calls time out and waddles out to the mound. "What's the matter, Frig?" he says, doing his best to act big-league and casual at the same time. "Just settle down and we got 'em." He puts the ball in Danny's glove with a little plop, whispers some hate names, and lumbers back to squat behind the plate.

After a strike down the gut to Marcos, the next batter grounds out to first on a sinker to Baby Doc, the base-runner advancing to second. Dingle walks the ball over to Danny, pats him on the rump, and trots back.

"Put 'er in there, Dan, old boy!" It is Jo-Jo. Rufe and Dingle chime in, Ethan mumbles something grudgingly, the outfielders come alive, and then Pye is squeezing the mitt open and shut as a collective cheer comes from the stands. With a sizzler between the Ayotollah's evil eyes followed by another through Gaddafi's brilliantly evil teeth and two straight balls to Ethan and his ass-kissing daddy, Danny gets two-and-two on the next man, who then flies deep to right on an unconvincing curve to Gorbachev's genuine smile. The runner tags up and goes to third as Danny's right-fielder runs the ball in to Ethan, who looks the runner down and walks it to Danny.

"Time!" yells Coach, coming onto the field. He has his head down, his right hand slightly raised, his left in his back pocket--all sure signs from what Danny has seen of the majors that he will be jerked.

Ethan stays below the mound, surely licking his chops. The others complete the circle around Coach and Danny, and they stand there as if some solution to winning is about to descend.

"How's your arm?" Coach says.

Danny feels the blood in his face. He wants to give the ball to Ethan just to make this moment pass, for he cannot bear being at the center of their attention and everybody else's. He is looking down, his glove crooked with the ball at his breast, when Pye slips a chunk of unwrapped gum in his right hand, limp at his side. He puts it in his mouth and begins to chew, glancing at Coach as if to say, Well, what are you going to do?

"What do you say, Danny?"

"Come on, ma-a-a-n." It is Ethan, the cocky little bastard with his big, fat father behind him all the way, letting Coach know that Danny's had it. Then Danny hears: "You can do it, Dan-the-man!" And this is Ethan too, now patting Danny's back.

The others follow his lead, and before he knows it he is buoyed by their words, his eyes beginning to mist. He takes off his cap and wipes his head with the same hand, looking his guilt and remorse at Ethan, smiling, saying through the gum, spit bubbles forming at his lips, "Let me just get this last guy, Coach."

"You got him," Coach says, then explains quickly the old squeeze play. "Pye, you and Rufus move up at the first sign of a bunt. Danny, you cover home. Same for a passed ball. If the ball's hit in the infield, make the sure play at first. Got it?"

They all say that they do. Then they pat Danny here and there, Pye caresses his head with his big mitt, and they break up and trot back to where they came from, frantic with chatter, pounding their gloves. "Give it your best shot," Coach says, and he too trots away.

Danny sees Mister Norris at the door of the dugout, scanning the infield with a Camcorder. He shoots Danny, removes the camera from his face, and says seriously: "Come on, Danny-boy Just one more." Then he turns and goes into the dugout.

Danny is hot with shame, and he forgets about the hate faces.

"Ball one!"

"'At's okay, Dan-boy. Shake it off!"

Before he can come up with anything, he throws again.

"Ball two!"

The batter has not yet squared off for a bunt, but Danny is ready to charge the plate if he does. Only he has to pitch first. If he walks this man, he decides, he will ask to be taken out. He fixes on the face of a terrorist from the morning paper and lets go.

"Strike one!"

The fans in the bleachers are clapping and yelling, the

infield chatter constant. Pye too soon throws the ball back to Danny, who, still out of balance from the pitch, misses it. With his side sight he sees the runner start for home, but Ethan is there just behind the mound, the ball firmly in his right hand, daring the runner, one-third of the way, to take another step. The runner retreats; Ethan hands the ball to Danny.

"C'mon, Fergie-baby. C'mon, babe," and Ethan is back at second.

Again, Danny forgets and pitches.

"Ball three!"

"Don't lose him, Fergie-baby!"

He puts the mug of a convicted rapist onto Pye's mitt and throws.

"Strike two! Full count!" The ump puts up both fists and rotates them.

Danny looks up, high above the backstop. There is a big sign there: RONALD MASON MEMORIAL PARK. He thinks of a boy, drowned two summers back, someone he knew. He holds up his hand for time out and gets it, bending to tie his shoelace, squinting at the stands. But he can see nothing plainly, and the blood is in his head. He takes the resin bag and buys a little time with that. He know that if he wins, his parents will be out on the field, each one wanting to be first. He knows that they will not bring their friends with them but will have to come alone, together, that he will be embraced by each of them, between them. The thought sickens him as he turns briefly to see the calm of the outfield, wishing he were there. He is aware of the clipped grass of the infield, the packed red dirt of the baselines. The bags are hard and clean. He is the center of it.

But he is aware as well, for the first time, that he has nothing at all on the ball without his own illusion. With it, he has gripped with his forefinger and middle finger the space between the ball's seams and imagined its darting and breaking to the plate. That is now all gone, and he grips with all of his hand, all his fingers, as much of the ball as he can, pushing it tight into the weblike skin formed by his thumb and forefinger. Pye is squeezing the mitt and relaxing it; everybody--the other team, the other fans--everybody is yelling something...atta boy and little bingle and you can do it...and he bends for his wind-up, begins the rhythm, looking at the mitt looking back at him like an oversized mouth. He tries but cannot stop the face it takes on, his own, mocking back, as he pumps and winds and rears back for everything he's worth, then lets go.

Stupid Animals

Brian Batt

"You remind me of a dumb dog."

With a straight face, Juliana says this to me. I squint at her. She keeps her eyes fixed on her hair brush. Black, with white bristles. Strands of her hair are gnarled around the bristles. She picks some out, rolls it into a clump, flicks it onto the floor.

"All dogs are dumb," I say.

"Some are smarter than others. Like Labradors."

"They aren't any smarter. They just have a better capacity to learn."

"Don't start with me again."

"I'm not starting with you."

"See, Eliot. You have to disagree with everything I say."

"Okay. All right." I hold my arms up. Juliana's eyes stay on the brush. I let my arms flop onto my legs. "Tell me how I'm like a dumb dog."

"No. Just leave it. I don't want to talk if you're going to be an asshole."

"I won't."

"Just leave it, Eliot."

We sit at the kitchen table drinking beer. The sink is filled with empty cans. We're a couple of college students living in the basement of a small house downtown. Eb, the old man who owns the house, lives upstairs. The rent's cheap and it stays nice and cool down here on hot days.

"You remind me of a dog this kid that lived next door to me had." Juliana looks at me, then back at her brush. A ball of hair rolls off her fingers. "His name was Lonny. I think I was like seven then. He had this big brown mutt, one of those kinds with big sad eyes. He beat it all the time. This one time he chained it to a tree and whipped it with a clothes hanger until he drew blood. I watched it all from my bedroom window."

"Jesus," I say.

"After he whipped it for a while, he let the dog go. The dog just laid there bleeding, looking at him with those sad eyes. I was like, so sick, I couldn't even cry." Juliana puts the brush down. She pulls in her lower lip, lets it out. "Lonny started patting his knee, calling the dog. And that stupid dog went over to him, wagging its tail. Lonny petted it for a minute, and then the bastard kicked the poor dog in the guts. As hard as he could. I mean, I could feel it. And you know what that bastard did?" Juliana drags her middle finger over the bristles. She peers up at me. "He stood there, laughing. That bastard."

My stomach turns. Juliana shakes her head, slouches in her chair. She crosses her arms under her breasts and just stares into her lap.

I feel my heart being squeezed, seeing her this way.

It's the day after Juliana told me about her fling with Paul. One night a couple weeks ago. She was out with the girls at this bar near campus, having a few drinks, and one thing led to another. Nothing serious. Sure, I was upset by it. But what can a guy say? Things like this happen in college. People get drunk and lose control of themselves. The best thing to do is pretend it didn't happen. Don't dwell on it, don't let it drive you crazy.

"You feel all right?" I asked.

"Been better." Juliana feels her forehead. She's had a headache for the past few days. Guilt, she calls it.

Hangover is more like it.

"It only hurts when I think about it," she says.

"Don't think about it, then."

"Then quit asking me how I feel, Eliot."

"Sorry. I won't anymore."

She purses her lips and gives me that look.

"Okay, I will," I say. "Just give me a few days and I'll forget about it."

"No you won't." She runs the brush through her hair. "And neither will I."

"Yes you will."

"Will you quit trying to piss me off."

I take a drink and glance up at the clock. In an hour or so we have to meet my parents at a supper club near campus to celebrate their twenty-fifth wedding anniversary. Just the four of us. Nothing special.

But when you consider it, twenty-five years of sleeping together is something special. Juliana says it's impossible to even imagine. But I can see it happening. With us, I'm saying. We just have to weather this.

She and I are dressed and ready to roll. Her perfume is so strong I taste it every time I drink. Every now and then she sweeps the brush through her hair. She has beautiful straight red hair that highlights her pale, apple-shaped face and green eyes. She's so beautiful and pale that if you saw her walking down the sidewalk on a sunny day you'd want to run up to her and hold something over her head, anything, to shield her from the sun. I know I did the first time I saw her.

There's other things worth noticing about her too, things that turn guys' heads in bars and in the campus halls. I don't mind. In a way, it's kind of nice.

"So do you think I'm like Lonny's dog," I say.

She shrugs. "You both came crawling back to the person that hurt you."

"A dog always returns to its own vomit."

"Vomit? What the hell is that supposed to mean?"

"Nothing. It's just an old saying."

"So now I'm vomit." She exhales sharply through her nose. "Thanks, Eliot. I really appreciate that."

I open my mouth, think better of it.

"Let's just drop this. Okay?"

I watch her brush her hair. When it's up behind her ears, she looks like a child.

"Please, Eliot."

"All right." I cross a finger over my heart. "I promise not to talk about it anymore. Or you can stick a needle in my eye."

"I've done enough harm already." She finishes her beer with a sour face. "Get me another."

I raise my eyebrows.

"Just do it, Eliot."

I stand up and go to the fridge. It seems easier to move now, with a few beers in me.

"Why do your parents have to have their anniversary today?"

"Because it's the day they got married."

I hand her the beer. She cradles it in both hands, like it's a cup of hot chocolate.

"It's bad timing," she says. "It's like, everything we're not about." Her eyes widen. "Call them up and tell them we can't make it."

I take my empty can, put it upside down in the sink. A fly zips out. The window over the sink is level with the ground. There's three blackbirds walking stiff-legged and shiny through the wet grass. The sun glares off the white house next door.

"Maybe they haven't left yet," Juliana says. "Call them, Eliot. For me."

I sit down, grab her beer, open it. I take a big drink and hand it back. Foam bubbles onto the lid.

"I don't know," Juliana says. She shakes her head and makes a humming noise. "I don't know," she says again. "I don't think I'll be able to look your parents in the eyes, I feel so guilty. It will be like, every time they look at me I'll feel like they know."

"Knock it off."

But she keeps on shaking her head and humming.

Well I feel lousy, too. But this isn't doing us any good.

"And your mother will be thinking, 'What a tramp that Juliana is. Why does my son stay with a slut like her? He could do so much better.'" She wedges her palm under her chin, as if that's the only way to stop her head from moving. "Why do you?"

"Why do I what?"

"Eliot. Good God, Eliot. Does love make you deaf, too?"

"Quit it and drink."

"Go ahead and pretend like the macho man you aren't, Eliot. I know, I know that right here," she jabs her thumb between her breasts. Her nails are long and red and beautiful, like her hair. "Right here I know it's hurting you."

"I thought we weren't going to talk about it anymore."

"Shut up, Eliot. Just shut up."

She starts to brush her hair again. Hard, quick strokes followed by a grimace. I stand up, stretch. She drops the brush.

"Are you going to call them?"

I smile. Then I turn and grab the bulging garbage bag by the back door, swing it onto my back. It's heavy. The drawstrings dig into my shoulder.

"Finish your beer," I say. "We have to jet pretty soon."

"I don't want to go. I'm not going, Eliot. Tell them I don't feel well. You wouldn't be lying. I feel like hell. Really, Eliot, I do."

I shut the door behind me, go up the stairs and out onto the sidewalk behind the house. It's a warm, clear evening. Eb's dark green Dodge Dart is parked next to the dumpster, under the trees. Flecks of bird manure dot the roof and trunk. A couple hours ago it rained and the air smells musty like it always does after a downpour on a really hot day. There's worms writhing on the sidewalk.

Wet gravel scrapes under my shoes. I heave the garbage bag into the dumpster. Flies come shooting out, they way sparks do when you throw a log onto a fire. Something smells awful, like a dead animal that's been baking in the sun for a couple days.

I think of Lonny's dog, lash marks across its back. My stomach turns again. I hate Lonny, and I don't even know him.

The house door bangs. Eb limps out with a bucket in one hand and a fat sponge in the other. Soapy water slops over the bucket. Eb wears a golf shirt and white shorts. Masses of wrinkles hang from each of his hairy kneecaps. His arms are almost pink, with bulging veins.

"Hey, old timer," I say. "How you doing?"

"Fine, fine," he says. "Look at you, all spiffed up." He hobbles over to me. The limp is from a war wound on Iwo Jima. Mortar fragments. Every now and then he asks us up for drinks. If he gets enough brandy in him, he tells war stories. I've heard most of them five, six times.

Eb's wife died of breast cancer about eight years ago, so Juliana feels sorry for him. She thinks he's lonely. Whenever she cooks, which isn't often, she makes enough for three and takes him up a plate.

That's Juliana for you. A heart of gold.

Eb put the sponge under his nose, wrinkles his face up. "Judas Priest," he says. "You've been hitting the corn. You going on a toot tonight?"

"Nah. It's my parents' twenty-fifth wedding anniversary, so I'm taking them out to supper. Me and Juliana."

"The big silver." Eb nods, clicks his tongue "Twenty-five years. That's a long time."

"Longer that I've been around." I swat at a fly on my elbow, miss. There's flies everywhere. I can hear them swarming inside the dumpster.

"You tell them congratulations from me."

"I'll do that."

Eb looks at his car, then up into the trees. Baby birds are screeching. I can't see them, but they're making a racket.

"Damn birds." Eb points the sponge at the trees. "They must think my car is a toilet. Look how they shit all over it."

I look. A white glob slides down the back window.

Eb spits.

"Can't win for losing," he says. "Park under the trees to keep your car cool and the birds shit on it. Park away from the trees and the inside of your car roasts. Especially this heap, with its plastic seats."

He walks to the car, bends over and sets the bucket down by the tire. More water spills. It takes him a long time to straighten his back. He steps back, crosses his arms over his stomach, and squints at the trees.

"Gonna wash the car today, huh?" I say.

"I reckon. Don't know why I bother. The second I get her shiny, the birds open fire."

He keeps staring at the trees, but I can tell he isn't seeing them. He has that glazed look, the one he gets after a few brandies. I brace myself for a war story. Up in the trees, it's quiet.

"You ever been down to Ripley Park?" Eb says. "Along the river there."

"Sure. A few times."

He nods, drops the sponge into the bucket. It bobs on top of the water.

"I haven't been down there for ages," Eb says. "Last time I went was with Lucille. Not long after she found out she had cancer."

I grunt and look down.

"She'd just had her hair done that morning. We had a big day planned. Supper at a fancy restaurant, a movie later. The works." He waves a hand by his face. "Lucille fixed a picnic lunch and we ate it by the river. Peanut butter and cheese sandwiches." He looks at me from the corners of his eyes. "You like them?"

"Never tried one."

"You'll have to. The cheese makes it so the peanut butter don't stick to the roof of your mouth." He turns his gaze back to the trees. The sponge has started to sink in the bucket. "After we ate, Lucille said she wanted to take a walk through the park. To see the animals. So we bought some peanuts and threw them to the goats and ostriches."

He pauses, and I nod. What else can I do?

"And then we were looking at the prairie dogs. We were kneeled down by the cage there. It was a hot day and I was trying to call them dogs out of their burrows." He makes several smooching sounds. "Like that," he says. "So while I'm doing that, a flock of blackbirds passes over and one dumps on Lucille's head. Right here." He taps the top of his head. "And she'd just spent all that money getting her hair fixed."

"Jeez," I say. "That's some lousy luck."

"I'd say. You'd think most women would throw a conniption fit after that. But not Lucille. She feels her head, gets some crap on her fingers, and starts laughing, of all things." Eb smirks. "And get a load of this."

He stares right into my eyes. I hold his gaze for a second, then look at my feet.

"She says to me, 'Crap happens.' Can you beat that? With a good stick, can you? She couldn't even get mad enough to cuss." Eb's shoulder's shake a little. He leans over, spits into the bucket. The sponge is under water now. "There's one woman who was happy to be alive. Some women, if a bird shit in their hair, that would be the second coming. But not Lucille."

I force a smile, push gravel around with my shoe.

"God damn stupid animals." Eb reaches into the bucket, lifts the sponge out. I hear water meeting water. Eb steps up to his car, presses the sponge onto the roof, holds it there. Water trickles down over the window. "Every time I see a flock of birds go over, I think of that day in the park with Lucille."

He starts to scrub the roof. Slow, wide circles, leaving streaks of bubbles behind.

"Funny how a guy's mind works," he says. "You hear something, or see something, and suddenly you think of someone. The darndest things too. Like birds, or bird shit."

"Yeah." I draw a long breath, let it out. "Well, I should get going, Eb.- We gotta meet my parents pretty soon."

Eb turns to me and wrings the sponge out. Water splatters around his feet.

"I'll see you later," I say.

"Sure," he says. "Unless you go blind."

I go back inside. Juliana stands by the kitchen sink, rinsing out the empty beer cans. Steam rises from the faucet. I lean against the door with my right hand on the knob. I feel winded, as if I've just come in from a long jog.

"Was there a line at the dumpster?" Juliana says, not looking at me.

"I was talking to Eb."

"About what?"

"Nothing much." I shrug. "Things."
"Mmm." She turns the water off, wipes her hands on a towel. She drapes the towel over the faucet. Then she leans toward the window and rubs steam off the glass. She gets this look on her face. Like she sees something.
"What?" I say. "What is it?"
She squints harder out the window.
"What the hell is it?"
She doesn't seem to hear me. I stand there, watching. Then it hits me--she sees something that reminds her of Paul. Wet grass. Blackbirds. I don't know. But I can feel it, tightening around my lungs. I can feel her thinking about Paul. And for a second, I want to grab her by the back of the head and slam her face into the counter. Bash every thought of Paul out of her until all she'll ever be able to think of is me.
There's a rushing sound in my ears.

They Gathered at the River

Lawrence Owen

Ralph saw them first. He kept to high ground because he was afraid of falling into the river. From the high bank he saw a man and woman on the sandbar and he knew something was up. He went "Sssh" to his buddies, who were walking near the water and arguing about religion. They didn't hear him so he threw a clod at them. When they saw Ralph up there signaling with his finger on his lips, they thought he probably saw a deer or mink or fox. Ralph then began gesturing to them to climb up the bank to where he was. They climbed while Ralph kept keen eyes on the sandbar.

"What is it?"
"What's going on?"
"Sssh. Sssh. They're on our sandbar."
"Who's on our sandbar?"
"Sssh. Get up here so you can see. They may be fucking by the time you get up here."
"Deer aren't in rut this time of year."
"They're not deer."
Brian and Morris made it up without causing a ruckus.

After pulling their canoe up out of the river, the smoothed out a patch of sand, then spread a cream colored blanket. They drank from a wine jug, set the jug near the blanket, embraced, laughed, stripped off their clothes. She walked into the water, turned and splashed water on him, then he rushed in after her.

"Jesus Christ," Morris said. "Skinny dipping. Can you believe it?"
"Nothing to believe," Brian said. "We saw it. Belief has nothing to do with it."
Ralph said, "They may be doing it right there in the river right now. The way he's leaning and the way it looks like she's floating on her back, they're probably doing it right now."
"Would she get polluted if they're doing it? Those PCBs, and the farm chemicals from runoff. Will that stuff get in her and pollute her?" Morris stopped his questions. "Oh Judas H. Priest, they're coming out. Look at that."

The man and woman walked out of the river. They

toweled each other. She looped his towel behind her back and pulled her body toward his. They held each other in a tight wrap of towels and arms.

I don't believe it," Ralph said. "Don't believe it. Did you see the way they did that?"

"They're dancers," Brian said. "The whole thing. It's all choreographed. Wish we had a film of the whole thing. From when they pulled the canoe up onto the sand, to right now. It's all a dance."

Morris said, "Why call it something else? It's canoeing, then skinny dipping, and now it's going to be fucking. Why call it a dance? You got your eyeballs and your theories up here. Those people down there are down there in their bodies. There's nothing between you and them. Why do you want to get language between you and what's happening?"

"Would you guys shut that shit up and watch," Ralph said. "Brian will be calling it religion in a minute. Just wait."

"It is," Brian said. "That is a religious event happening right in front of your eyes, Ralph, and you can't see it. Morris thinks there's nothing there just because he can't see it."

The man folded the towels into a pillow. The woman lay down on the blanket, on her back, and rested her head on the pillow. The man lay down beside her, moved one leg over between he legs, then began kissing her.

"They're going to do it. Right out her in front of God and everybody."

"I need a drink," Ralph said.

The watchers stayed quiet. Ralph opened beers around. They sipped and watched the woman move from under the man to where she rested on her elbow and began looking down, kissing down. The watchers groaned when the woman's hand moved down the man's belly to his penis.

Morris turned from the lovers, leaned his back against a cottonwood tree, and chugged down his beer. "They really are going to do it aren't they? I'm not going to watch."

Brian said, "What are you afraid of Morris? You said yourself that there's no meaning down there. You said so yourself. Who is watching what a man and woman are doing any different from watching the sun set behind those plum trees? Haven't you ever watched human beings fuck?"

Ralph moved over to the cottonwood tree, rested his back against it, sat close to Morris. "I'm with Morris. I'm not going to watch. You go on Brian. You watch and tell us what they're doing."

Brian stood up, walked to the beer, handed beers around, then stood looking down at his two buddies. "I don't believe this. You two guys are afraid to watch a man and woman fuck."

"Looks to me like you'd rather preach at us than watch," Morris said.

"Are they doing it yet?" Ralph asked.

Brian positioned himself so that he could see both the lovers and his buddies. By moving only his eyes he could focus on either pair. Dusk had settled in, making it impossible for Ralph and Morris to know where Brian was looking.

"Yes, they are doing it."

"Which one's on top?"

"I never have seen it," Ralph said. "I'm forty-three years old and I've never seen it. Saw movies. Hard porn stuff. But you're right, Brian, I've never seen human beings mate. Heard my parents one night, but couldn't see anything.

"What did you hear?"

"My mother saying, 'Hurry up. Hurry up. Come on and hurry up.'"

Morris said, "Doesn't sound very romantic."

"It wasn't. She sounded just like she did when she had to wait for us to get ready to go to school. 'Hurry up. Hurry up.' It wasn't romantic. It was pitiful."

"I never have either," Morris said. "I've never seen it either. I'm just forty, but I've never seen it. Have you Brian?"

"I'm watching right now. And it's still a dance. Those two people are performers. They're playing parts they had nothing to do with. Her arms are spread and she is soaring. She can stay on the blanket, on her back, and still fly. He's holding her hands now and they're flying together."

Morris said, "Window peeping one night I thought we were going to get to see it. Saw all the foreplay. Then they turned the lights out."

"You didn't say, Brian. Have you ever seen it before?"

"I've never seen anything," Ralph said. "Haven't seen anyone die or make love or anything. Mary wanted me to be in the delivery room when she had Robin and Patrick. But I couldn't. I went in for Robin but didn't stay. I'm the same age as you two and I've never watched people die, or have babies, or fuck. Nothing. Hear them talk about it all the time but never see them do it."

"What are they doing now?" Morris asked.

"See for yourself. They're making love. You've seen those movies where the colors are filtered to create fuzzy, impressionistic, pastel scenes. That's what this is."

Ralph stood and turned toward the sandbar. "He's right Morris. It's beautiful. And there's just one. You can't tell there are two people."

Brain said, "This is the first time for me too. I've never seen people do it."

Morris stood beside his fishing friends. He could just barely see the man and woman down there. "They're through aren't they?"

"Dance is over."

"Church is over. If someone would say a benediction they'll leave."

"I may never get another chance to see it," Morris said.

Brain whispered, "Amen."

The three watchers kept to their high bank, looking down onto the darkening river. They could hear the man and woman laughing and slapping at mosquitoes. They could just barely see the canoe entering the river. Then, keeping perfectly quiet and still, they watched the silvery canoe come gliding beneath them. The woman sat in the bow, face forward, singing an old song about love, love, secret love. From the stern, the man guided the canoe. The river carried them away.

"Was she saying secret or sacred?"
"Secret, you jerk. Don't you know the song?"
"I think she was saying sacred."
"Aw, come on. Let's go fishing."
"No more beer until someone catches a fish."
"Carp don't count."
"Sheepshead either."

They fished until midnight, arguing all the while about how life in our time is different from the way it used to be.

Van Meter

Kent Cowgill

This is a story about killing things.

It happened in 1978, a long time ago--at least that's the way things appear to me now in this country. Back when you noticed if someone used an expression like "chemically dependent" and a motel room could be had for ten or twelve dollars a night. I was forty-three years old, a closet alcoholic, and president of the Merchants' Trust Bank in a little town not far from Duluth, Minnesota. This last hasn't changed--I'm still the bank president--but not much else in my life is the same as it was back then.

Like a lot of experiences in this part of the country, it started with a snowstorm, the year's first snowstorm, the one you never get used to no matter how long you've lived in the North. I'm not talking about the harshness of winter, or its length--the clichés that come to mind whenever most outsiders think of Minnesota. What stuns you is the *suddenness*--how fast it can come on. The storm hit on a Wednesday, in late October, at the end of a heart-searing Indian summer, and all I could see at that moment were the last few escape routes shutting down.

I fled.

It was the kind of act a man is capable of only when his life has quietly come apart but his mind hasn't acknowledged the reality. An act of impulse--its onset as sudden as an autumn blizzard but with none of the same power to shock. Today it's called denial. Back then, if I had been in a position to recognize it, I would probably have called it self-delusion. And I'd have been thinking of somebody else. I once screwed another man's wife in the laundry closet of a Minneapolis hotel fifteen minutes before chairing a panel discussion on the statistical probability of high-risk loans ending in bankruptcy. I was as incapable of seeing the irony as I was of dealing with that sudden winter storm.

When it hit I was in my office, at my desk, listening to a pair of newlyweds describe the antique store they wanted to open in a vacated creamery. I had heard the wind stirring, but I didn't turn to look until the woman gestured toward the window behind my chair. Blowing snow caked the building across the street--an abandoned shell that had once held the town's only butcher shop and a small ice-cream parlor and pharmacy. I turned back to my desk, answered their remaining questions about the loan application I knew we would have to deny for lack of collateral, and walked them to the door. Of the eight or ten other people in the bank, none was under fifty. One of my tellers was wearing the same blue suit he'd worn a decade earlier to my father's funeral. Outside my office, a kidney-shaped stain on the carpet was still visible where he had spilled coffee the year before he died.

A few minutes later I was gone. I had probably already had a couple of drinks--I don't remember, but it was early afternoon; it would have been a rare day back then if I hadn't--and I was desperate to get south of the storm if I could. I was flying. Driving the way for years I had secretly been living. A man in a car on a snow-packed highway on the outside edge of control.

I had stopped at home only long enough to leave a note for my wife, and to pick up a box of shells and my shotgun. My kids were in school. And there was obviously no problem leaving the bank--though I don't mean by that what most people do when they talk about "bankers' hours." Even back then, with all the drinking and the womanizing, I'd have matched my work week with anybody else's I knew. What you do have is some freedom--and the power to abuse it--and in that period of my life I was pushing both about as hard as you can.

I didn't have a destination, hadn't even taken the time to unkennel my dog, which will say more about my condition than words can to anyone who knows much about hunters. I was floating--fleeing--on a road to whatever I happened to stumble on that lay south of the snow.

It turned out to be the middle of Iowa. By then I was numb with exhaustion--I had driven until almost midnight--and I woke the owner of the first motel I happened on after following an exit off the Interstate. I didn't have a suitcase, but it wouldn't have mattered. I collapsed in bed leaving the uncased shotgun on the front seat of my car.

I didn't wake until almost ten the next morning. My body was so stiff it hurt to tie my shoes, and I hadn't eaten for close to twenty-four hours. But I had no thought of food. It was a beautiful day, clear and windless, and I'd woken with an almost *demonic* desire to go hunting. It's the only word I know that comes close to describing how I felt. I was alone, in a little town I didn't know the name of, with things deeper than hunger clawing at the inside of my chest. In the couple of minutes it took me to dress, I felt like an animal in a cage.

But it wasn't the animal feeling a hunter recognizes--takes for granted if he's grown used to hunting behind a good dog. I'm not quite sure how to convey this. Maybe one needs to have hunted in order to understand it--how different it felt those next three or four hours to be out there without Rip working the cover ahead. I had owned a dog for years, had always hunted behind one, which has a way of legitimizing the killing. Hunting comes to a bird dog so instinctively--it's so obviously a part of his nature--that it's easy for a man to feel it's a part of his nature too. But on this morning I was alone, dogless, forced to think about what it was I was doing. And what I was doing was hunting with a desperation, a *deeper* instinct, I'd never felt before. Just enough snow had fallen while I slept to knock down some of the cover, exposing the birds, yet it had also made them calmer, less flighty than usual. I'd seen it happen a few times before in the years I had hunted--that same sudden, inexplicable loss of caution--most often in a light mist or fog.

Since I hadn't taken time to buy a license, the hunting was illegal--*lawless*--which made my sense of being driven by some atavistic instinct even more acute. Pheasants kept flushing. I kept killing them. Then I moved to other fields and killed several more. When I finally stopped I had shot eight and found them all, even the cripples, following their tracks and their blood in the snow.

I stopped only because I needed a drink.

The bartender was the type you often find in small towns. Around thirty, bored and balding, so leached of energy he seemed barely capable of speaking--interest distilled to the slight lifting of an eyelid, the twitch of a toothpick in the corner of the mouth. This one had weightlifter's arms, pink and hairless, swelling from a sleeveless T-shirt. He turned away as I ordered a scotch.

The only other person in the room was an old man, perched on a barstool, clutching a beer. He was so short his legs dangled off the floor, like a little boy's, though his frame was so thin and bony he reminded me more of an oversized spider. I was into my second or third drink before he spoke.

"Ain't from around here, are you?"

I glanced at him, then turned back to the bar without answering--tried to deny even the little opening he could find in a hostile stare. He bore in anyway.

"So where you from?"

Seconds passed. The bartender had disappeared, was frying something on the grill in the kitchen. No one else had come in. The old man slid off his stool, crunched toward me across the bed of peanut shells that littered the scarred linoleum. He couldn't have been more than five-foot-one or five-two.

"Duluth."

"Minnesota?"

He waited for me to respond. When I didn't, he snorted dismissively, taking a slug from the bottle in his shrunken hand.

"Whatcha doin' here? Whyn'tcha stop in Des Moines?"

I turned and looked hard at him. Dark stains spotted his jacket. His eyes were bloodshot. A huge red mole flamed on his chin.

"You stop and see Van Meter?" he said.

"Who?"

"Not a who. A what. Van Meter. Next town up the road. You had to see the sign if you come in on I-80. Just after you passed Des Moines."

"I didn't see anything," I said.

"It's Bob Feller's home town. Where he's from."

I looked away, downing what was left of my drink, then headed for the door. He followed, his brown fingers tugging at my sleeve.

"Fastest pitcher that ever throwed a ball, don't let nobody never try to tell you no different. Those hotshots you see today, they couldn't hold a candle to him. Bullet Bobby. He could *throw* that goddamned ball!"

"Could he," I said, pulling away.

"Goddam right he could. I seen him once throw it through the goddam screen behind home plate--throw it right on through the chickenwire. That's how fast Bobby Feller was in his prime. Shit, people think he could throw hard when he got to the majors, but he was nothing like the same pitcher up there he'd been around here. He didn't have to be, playing against all them coons."

I was a step from the door when he grabbed my arm again, his beer sloshing on the floor. This time I knocked his hand away roughly, turned and glared at him. He was almost shouting now.

"I used to hit against him. He struck me out plenty, o' course, just like he did ever'body else, but there was days he couldn't get me out I don't give a damn what he tried to throw me. Once I hit two home runs off him, plus a single and a triple. He was so goddam mad he broke a bat when he got back to the dugout. We kicked his ass. I'll tell you that for sure. *We kicked Bobby Feller's ass!*"

I slammed the door and walked out into the street--a solitary drunk in an empty little town where nothing moved but the late afternoon shadows. It had gotten cold--the only clothes I'd brought were what hung on a peg by the gun rack--and my body was trembling as I got into the car. A welter of conflicting impulses surged through me: call my wife and ask her to forgive me; call the last woman I had been involved with; find a dead-end road and put a single shell in the gun.

I decided to keep hunting--which will seem unbelievable only if you're unacquainted with despair. An hour of daylight remained. I clung to it with the same desperation with which my hands clutched the steering wheel. You could call it a last resort, but that doesn't quite capture it. It was a more aggressive kind of desperation. I *wanted* to hunt.

The road led south of town, unbending, an arrow shaft into the heart of the heartland. Past Harvestores and cornfields and feedlots that smelled of manure. A black dog materialized from the ditch, snapping at my tires, then slowly vanished in the rearview mirror.

I don't know how far I drove. You drive until you see something, a patch of cover, and your foot lifts.

No hunter would have passed this farm. A weeded draw wound through a partly cut field of soybeans, itself choked with weeds--so overrun I could have hunted even the few acres that had somehow been harvested. It was the kind of place you rarely see today, but this was close to twenty years ago, when there were still a lot of bad farmers left in the country. Back then, even if you were a banker, you were just beginning to see what might come.

This was as bad as I had ever seen. The lane was a black ribbon of mud, narrow and rutted; the corn was stunted; the fence was nothing but a sagging strand or two of rusted barbed wire. I would have been sure the place was abandoned if it weren't for the tire tracks and the open mailbox, which was so bizarre I stared at it for a moment in disbelief. The box itself was in even sorrier shape than the fence--corroded, riddled with buckshot, anchored by a single bolt to a rotting stanchion--but a name had been painted on it in such bright green letters it might have been stolen from some suburban street. *THE JORGENSONS,* it read. *AXEL & GRACE.*

The place unnerved me, it was so incongruous--tapped into the despair I had carried out of the tavern. The alcohol had begun to wear off, but I was still drunk enough to hear the old man's croak, feel his spidery hand clutching at my arm.

And yet I was also conscious of how little daylight remained-- was clear-headed enough to recognize it was the kind of cover a hunter often goes several seasons without stumbling onto. After a last uneasy glance at the mailbox, I turned down the lane. It bent left through the bean field toward a two-story house partially concealed behind a grove of trees.

I drove past them and parked in the yard next to an old pickup, its axles raised on wooden blocks, the front bumper propped against a dead elm. There were no tires or wheels. A dirty rag fluttered through the shattered rear window. The broken teeth of a combine cutter bar and a tangle of rusty wire lay half-buried in the weeds.

I turned off the ignition and sat in the yard, staring at the house. A pair of muddy overshoes lay where they had been shucked off by the doorstep. Peeling paint curled under the porch eaves. Mismatched shingles patched the steeply pitched roof.

Leaning over the steering wheel, I thought I saw a curtain stir in an upstairs window, then go still again, but it might have been the sun glinting off the darkened pane. There were no cats or chickens, and no dog--which would have helped calm me a little even if it had been hostile. The only signs of life were the occasional clank of a hog feeder and the coo of a pigeon on the barn.

I had forgotten about the names on the mailbox. What I felt went beyond uneasiness, anxiety, the faint quiver in the stomach one occasionally experiences approaching a darkened house devoid of any sign of activity. It was something close to panic--a visceral fear.

They seem absurd in retrospect--the images my mind conjured in those next few moments of alcohol-fueled hallucination. Lampshades made of skin. Severed heads in wells. Naked bodies strung like butchered hogs in boarded-up outbuildings. I sat for some time, staring at the house, my knuckles tight on the wheel.

Walking to the door took an almost physical act of will--was possible only because I was more afraid of what might happen if I couldn't do it. Of where the self-loathing might lead if I drove away. Standing on the step, I peered through the screen into the shadowed porch--waited for my eyes to adjust in the slanting light. What I saw calmed me a little: old newspapers covered with dirt-crusted onions, a hooded sweatshirt, a muddy spade.

Finally I tapped on the door. When no one answered, I knocked again, louder. Again there was no response. The relieved sound of my own breath was so audible my lips tightened in shame.

I had turned to leave, my back to the house, when I heard the inside porch door creak open. I spun around, filled with dread, peering once more through the screen. An old woman in bedroom slippers and a worn housecoat shuffled toward me across the floor.

"Yes. What is it?"

Her voice was so soft, almost a whisper, I could barely hear.

"Hello," I said, one hand shading my eyes. "I'm awful sorry to bother you, ma'am." The words rang as false as my forced smile, the reflexive grease left by years of hunting. I leaned closer to the screen.

The woman wasn't helping. She had stopped in the middle of the porch, short of the door, hanging back in the shadows. And she had said nothing else--simply clutched the housecoat tighter to her body. I stumbled on.

"Out on the road I noticed that draw that winds east through your soybeans. I was just wondering, would you mind if I hunted it? Tried to kick up a pheasant or two?"

My face was only a few inches from the screen. We were close enough that I could hear her breathing. Yet still she didn't answer, was barely visible in the shadows. Half-blinded by the sunlight, I was suddenly irritated enough that the good-old-boy pose fell away.

"Look, lady," I said. "I'm not out here to steal your valuables, or hand you a copy of *The Watchtower*. I'm just what I told you I am, a bird hunter. I know how to handle a gun; I close gates; I don't shoot up stock tanks or knock down fences. If you know anything about outdoorsmen, you know the ones to worry about aren't the ones that stop to ask."

I was halfway to the car when she spoke.

"Wait," she said. "I'm sorry. I wasn't trying to be rude...My husband's gone...We've had some trouble with hunters...Some of them, shooting up the mailbox. Firing their guns too close to the house."

She stepped forward as she said it-- opened the screen door-- and for the first time I could see her clearly. Saw she wasn't nearly as old as I had thought--was in fact probably a few years younger than I was. Her hair was disheveled, as if she'd been sleeping. She brushed it from her eyes with a nervous flick of her hand.

I knew she'd left the privacy of the porch only because she thought *she* had been rude to me, had apologized out of that instinctive fear of offending that's almost genetic in native Midwesterners. Standing on the step, in the sunlight, she pulled the housecoat even tighter around her body. I could see the outline of her thighs.

You sometimes hear it said about homosexuals--that they recognize one another--can tell if another person is gay. I have no idea whether it's true or not. What I do believe is that it's true of desperate people--men and women on the edge--where both Grace Jorgenson and I were at that moment. You feel it in a woman--somehow sense it. And she picks up the same thing in a man.

I'm not talking about seduction. I've never doubted that what she told me later that night was true: it was the first time she'd ever been drunk, and she had never before cheated on her husband. I'm saying only that if you're vulnerable, you recognize vulnerability. Something flickers in the eyes. A finger stirs. As often as not it's not even that perceptible. We were two strangers staring at each other across a muddy barnyard. But I *knew*.

"Are you giving me permission to hunt?" I said.

I remember exactly how I felt as I said it, and of all the things I'm describing in this story, it's the moment I remain most ashamed of. For even as I said it I realized how much freight the words carried--flared with satisfaction at starting so many possibilities at so little risk to myself. Maybe if the question hadn't been so instinctive, had been premeditated--something I'd come up with during those few seconds the two of us stood there staring--I'd still be a hunter. But that wasn't the case. And when I finally had to deal with all of it, I knew it wasn't the case--could no longer deny it, even to myself. The words had come spontaneously, *naturally*, as free of conscious thought as a gunstock rises to the shoulder. And what I felt after I had spoken them, waiting for her to react, was exactly what I had felt two hours earlier as I watched the last pheasant fall dead in the snow.

What happened next is what you would expect to happen if you understand the relationship between a predator and prey. I'm aware of how sexist that sounds--what it seems to imply about the weakness of women--but in this case it's the truth. It wouldn't be true to say it about any of the other women I had affairs with. Their methods varied, but they were as much on the make as I was. Grace Jorgenson wasn't. And if what happened in those next few hours had ended her marriage, she could justly blame the gods for dropping a slob hunter on her doorstep at the one moment in her life when she was that vulnerable, that exposed.

I don't know if I actually repeated the question, or if it only seems so now because the words hung so long in the air between us--"*Are you giving me permission?*" And I don't remember how she finally answered it, or what either of us said next, or even how much longer we stood there in the fading light. What I remember is sitting in my car, waiting for her to dress, watching the sun set over that weedy bean field, wondering whether there would still be time to hunt if she lost her nerve.

I was surprised when she came out, not simply because she had, but at how pretty a woman she turned out to be. Her skirt danced above her knee when she stepped past the overshoes on the doorstep. She had thin ankles. Nice legs.

I probably never knew the name of the town we ended up in, or the steak house, or the bar on the corner across the street. But the motel was called The Flamingo, I remember that. She was staring at the sign above the office when I got back to the car.

I began this story committed to telling it honestly, which isn't hard when you're describing the past--things you've done that you know are behind you. It gets harder now. The truth is, I've never felt as close to a woman as I did that night. It's hard because I'd give almost anything for this not to be so. My wife has saved my life. She was there when I got out of Hazelden, there through all the rehab--is there still after everything I've put her through. But it's not the same.

I don't mean that our sex life is terrible, or infrequent, or even devoid of a certain intensity. I mean only that when you owe someone as much as I owe Lynn, when you've given someone the kind of burden I gave her to carry--I stop only because I don't know what else to say. Neither of us drinks anymore. We're no longer young. There are a number of explanations I would once have clung to. But they would only obscure the truth. Grace Jorgenson and I were desperate enough, and drunk enough, to obliterate the line between inhibition and total abandon. And when we crashed, inevitably, it was into a sea of loneliness and pain.

She told me she'd learned a day earlier that she was carrying a child.

I woke the next morning rigid with resentment, my teeth clenched in anger, staring at the woman I'd seen hanging in the shadows behind the fly-specked screen. Her eyes blinked open before I could look away, and she cringed beneath me, her swollen face a mirror of my own revulsion. It only made me angrier. Remembering it frightens me even now, knots my stomach--having to acknowledge how much violence a man can have inside him. I turned away, toward the curtained window, as her feet slapped across the tile and the lock clicked on the bathroom door.

She said nothing on the drive back to her farm. Told me only what road to take--where to turn in order to get there. I think of it now whenever I ride in a taxi. Two people in a car, staring through the windshield. A man and a woman with nothing more to say.

What little I knew of her I'd learned the night before, during dinner, and later on in the bar as we sat drinking. Most of it would become so recognizable to a small-town Midwest banker over the next few years it came to have the feel of cliché. She and her husband rented their land; he'd gone to Sioux City to try to borrow more money; their marriage had deteriorated as the debts mounted and her pleas to quit farming bumped against his stubborn insistence that they carry on.

I was prepared for it, could even have *predicted* it ten minutes after I met her, sitting there in the barnyard watching the sun set over that stunted field of beans. What I wasn't prepared for was the baby. I don't mean I didn't believe it. It was in fact the reason I *did* believe it-- believed all of it. She was the kind of woman who could do something as desperate as what she'd done only because she knew she couldn't do anything truly desperate--saw doors slamming shut forever in her face. Both of us were out on a road we'd never driven, but for her it promised to end forever back at that weed-choked farm.

We reached it about ten. As I slowed to turn down the muddy lane she put her hand on the door handle and told me to stop, whether out of fear her husband had returned early or because she couldn't stomach the sight of me even a few seconds longer I'm not sure. It was as awkward a moment as I've ever experienced--the kind that cried for closure, some parting words of acknowledgment, even though you know they'll only make a bad thing worse.

She had already climbed out of the car when I spoke. But she still stood on the road, had opened the mailbox--a gesture as incongruous under the circumstances as that absurdly lettered bonnet of rusting tin. She was checking the mail. It was the kind of reflexive act I recognized instantly--bred of the desperate need to re-attach to any reality one knows.

I wish I could tell you that what I said at that moment came from the tension, or the curiosity I in fact did feel, seeing her pause there beside that ludicrous hood of green-lettered metal. But I know that at bottom it was an impulsive act of petty revenge.

"Those names," I said. "Did you paint them?"

She froze, her hand still in the mailbox--looked at me for the first time since her eyes had fluttered open an hour before. There was pity, a hint of mockery, in her face.

"You don't understand any of this, do you?" she said.

It was almost two in the morning when I arrived home. Part of the Interstate had been closed by the storm, and I had to work my way north of the Twin Cities over a dead-ending network of back roads. I'm sure I told myself I was doing it because I couldn't handle another night in a motel room. But the real reason was fear of what my wife would do--might finally have done--for herself and the kids.

I don't mean to imply that she had put up with similar flights before. Lynn knew I had an alcohol problem, obviously--had been pressing me hard for months to deal with it--and several times had asked me point blank if I was having an affair. But I had always denied it--had been discreet enough to do nearly all my womanizing in the Twin Cities--and I was the kind of disciplined drunk people suspect without knowing for sure. *Co-dependent. Enabler.* Today's jargon describes the Lynn of that period pretty accurately. What she wasn't was a martyr--a woman who would take the kind of leap I had just made. My life had fallen apart the way a some fruits rot--slowly, from the inside, difficult to see until you cut it open. Right up to the nightmarish moments I'm about to describe, I'd have been shocked and humiliated to learn that either of my kids even suspected their father had a problem with booze.

I could see her Pinto through the closed door of the garage when I bumped over the last ridge of snow and pulled into my driveway, but for some time I simply sat there, motionless in the car. For the second time in less than forty-eight hours I found myself outside a darkened house, gathering myself, afraid to approach. The sidewalk had been shoveled, swept clean of snow, its stone surface gleaming hard in the moonlight. The thud of my boots when I finally opened the car door echoed like death in the frozen air.

The house was locked, the door bolted, and nothing I could say or do in those next terrible minutes would change that. My wife refused to answer me. It made no difference how much I pleaded. Promised to reform. Swore I had done nothing but take a spur-of-the-moment hunting trip to Iowa. I was sure she was inside only because of the car in the garage and because, near the end, my daughter cried out from her room upstairs.

It triggered some last, barbaric act of self-loathing in my frame.

I ripped the mailbox off the house and smashed it on the railing. I ran to my car and unlocked the trunk--reached for the pheasants--lifted them off the floor. They had been dead for almost two days, lay with grotesquely twisted heads and frozen bodies. One by one I began throwing them at the house, as hard as I could throw them, their spurs raking my wrists. One or two landed on the steps. The others bounced off the brick and buried in the snow alongside the sidewalk. When I had thrown all of them I threw what remained of the shells. And then I threw the gun.

When there was nothing left to throw, I got into the car, gunned the engine, and backed out of the driveway. As the headlights swept across the lawn, the tail feathers of dead pheasants rose like bayonets out of the snow.

I spent that night in my office at the bank. And the next night too, a Sunday. But I didn't drink. Whenever I would reach for a bottle in the cabinet, I heard my daughter. I could hear her voice as clearly as I had on the steps, pounding on the door--that frightened cry from her upstairs bedroom. The voice of my three-year-old daughter crying in the dark.

Time can heal a lot of things. Jenny is grown now, away at college out East, not far from her older brother. Lynn is teaching music, the job she gave up when Joshua was born. I believe that all four of us have gotten past most of it--are living in the present. That we're doing well.

I want to believe the same thing about Grace

Jorgenson. I put it that way only because I don't know, which is both a confession and an act of faith.

But it's not blind faith. I know where she lives, where her husband works--even that the two of them also have two children. I've even seen her once, for five or ten minutes, though she had no idea I was there.

I'm sure she would have been shocked and angry if she had known. I say that mostly because of her reaction the one time I did talk to her after all of it happened--a few seconds that did almost as much to shatter my cocoon of illusion as the few hours I had spent with her had ultimately done. It occurred a few weeks after I had got out of Hazelden, maybe four months after our night together--back when the tide of guilt had flooded me with the feeling that I should--that I *could*--"do something for her."

And so I phoned her.

At the time, it seemed the one way I could help, given what I knew--knew in part because of the things she had told me: the sorry state of their farm, the stress it had put on her marriage, her husband's deluded belief that a distant city bank would lend him what those in his own county had refused. I was a banker. And it wasn't a large amount of money, though perhaps enough to give them a fresh start in town. What I'd seen of Grace made me believe that someday they might actually be able to repay it. Part of the illusion, of course, is thinking you want them to.

When I told her who I was and why I was calling, she slammed the phone down so hard it rang in my ear.

After that I didn't learn anything more of her life for almost fifteen years, though it wasn't entirely by choice. Few things die harder than an illusion. I don't mean I tried to call again--thought she'd speak to me if I could get through to her--only that I would ask about them whenever I ran into someone from that part of the state. I wasn't actively pursuing it, told myself I simply wanted to know where she lived. Once I even called Des Moines information and asked the operator to check for any listings of an Axel or a Grace Jorgenson. I couldn't remember the name of the town I'd stayed in--knew only that it had to be somewhere not far from a place called "Van Meter." I wasn't going to call her. I just wanted to know if she still lived anywhere near.

What strikes me now is how much I must have believed in her to have kept trying. To have inquired about the two of them over so many years. It never occurred to me she might no longer have the same last name.

I finally located her through a chance acquaintance, another banker, while I was attending a debt consolidation seminar in Des Moines. As it turned out, they in fact didn't live very far from Van Meter. The man who told me about them knew both of them well. His bank held the mortgage on their house; her husband had turned out to be as good a mechanic as he'd been incompetent a farmer; Grace had started a day-care center as soon as her youngest daughter had started to school. He asked how I knew them. I told him I didn't--that I had been asked to inquire by a friend.

I was going to leave it at that. But a couple of hours later, I skipped out of the afternoon meeting and drove the hour or so it took to reach the town they lived in, a little town called Arbor Hill. I didn't have any trouble finding their place. The house looked exactly as the banker had described it to me--an old white clapboard that could have used a new roof But big--big and roomy, and well kept. It was early spring; the grass was just beginning to turn lush, and a lilac bush had started to bloom by their garden. The garden hadn't been planted yet, but a roto-tiller was parked by the garage, its blades muddy with soil. The back yard was huge, with a lot of playground equipment next to a freshly painted white fence.

I had parked a little way up the street, and for five or ten minutes I simply sat there, looking, taking it all in. I didn't need to see her. Had already turned on the car again, was ready to leave, when I saw the back door nudge open. A tiny child stood on the step, followed quickly by another, then several others who toddled past them trailing a small brown and white dog. Soon there were eight or nine kids running toward the swings, tumbling in the sandbox, squealing with delight as the dog scuttled around their knees. But the first one remained on the step, uncertain, looking back anxiously at the door.

I saw her then.. She had gained weight, but she looked good--light on her feet in jeans and a loose-fitting sweater. The dog had seen her too, and ran back toward her yipping with excitement. The little boy cried out in fear, clutching her legs, and I could hear her laughing as she bent down to reassure him. I sat there for a few more seconds, watching, then turned and drove back up the street.

Night Fishing

Patrick Martin

John pretends like he talks in his sleep. It's the only way he thinks he can get Kim, the wife, to listen without committing himself to dialogue.

He's a walleye fisherman, which says a lot, and casts his line in the water which has filled their bedroom, tugging a lure just inches beyond her grasp. Night fishing.

"Truth and beauty," he murmurs.

He feels her tense and knows he has her. Holding her breath, she's ready to strike bait. Then he jigs the lure, dropping hints in his monologue. Single words. Vague phrases dangling in the dark on eight pound test line.

He switches to live bait and casts the name "Terry" into the unforgiving night, knowing she will wonder, "What's a Terry?" Sweet ambiguity. Is he a she? Is she a he? Is it an ex or current lover? Or just a fishing buddy?

He pauses. Less is more. He strings her along, and it's almost art--minimalism. In the spaces between, he listens to her shallow breathing at the surface and the clang of windchimes in the dark.

Sometimes the bait is vaguely sexual, other times religious or philosophical. "And they nailed him to a cross," he mumbles.

His pitch never changes. His tone is linear and flat.

She poises but never strikes.

It's his third marriage.

* * *

She once believed marriage meant two people listening to Van Morrison records with the windows open while cooking pasta. But then she moved to a new state, met and married John, and found out otherwise. No Van Morrison. No open windows. No pasta. She would settle for pasta.

"Woman at a ball game," he murmurs. "I hit a home run."

She follows his bait but never strikes, so he does not set the #6 snelled hook. She follows, swimming naked and cold, a big fish hungry for his secrets, secrets swimming like schools of silver minnows in the shallows, secrets darting en-masse in the very liquid night she breathes.

"Who put the straw in strawberry?"

Turning the bare line of her well-defined clavicles, she listens to him hold his exhale and unknowingly does the same. The windchimes clang from the trees. The leaves rustle. Nothing more. Not even blank verse. So she rises to the surface and breathes. And the cycle repeats. He ties a fisherman's knot to a new lure. Another word, another cast.

What's a Terry?

She wonders.

Sometimes she says in the morning, "You talked in your sleep last night."

"I did? What'd I say?"

"I don't know. Some mumbo jumbo."

"Oh."

The subject falls into the water and drowns.

It's her first marriage.

* * *

He left his first wife because she was a child and his second because she'd wanted one.

He often gets away from his job as a baseball journalist to fish walleyes. And when he stares at himself in the mirrored waters of a fishing hole, he sees the stoic look of the Marlboro Man--a man among men, a fishing, drinking, existentialist who has come to terms with his existence. He doesn't even believe in the sort of romantic love that she does. He believes in the power of the pen and a stringer full of fresh-caught walleyes--"'eyes," as he calls them.

He can't reinvent himself. It's like what a famous sailor once said, "I yam what I yam and that's all that I yam."

He believes he is wisdom, and will, someday, be America's jaded savior. An Amer-Icon

Sometimes he thinks he is bullshit. But not often.

* * *

She hopes at least someday they'll have that sun-baked type of love. The kind we call "settled for." Love by concession. Give nothing and take even less. No deposit, no return.

* * *

John plans a three week fishing trip in the middle of baseball season, and it is to be the trip of all trips, flying into a Canadian lake that's never been fished by white men, where walleyes have never known the sting of a barbed hook, where a Cree guide will lead the men through swarms of black flies to the fish, and perhaps, even lead the fish to the men.

* * *

It is Sunday, the day before he leaves. He returns from an afternoon ball game and writes his last column, a biting commentary on the overpaid and underachieving home team.

Kim helps him pack, neatly arranging a box of Dutch Masters alongside wool socks.

"Where are you off to?" she asks as he grabs his jacket.

"The bar."

"The Clover?"

"No. It's closed Sundays."

"Really?" she asks. "I didn't know depression took a night off."

He grins and rolls his eyes. Then he's gone, leaving her to pack. She thinks of his buddies at the Clover, the men he is going to Canada with. Many divorced. Some out of work. Once they all got together and had a barbecue, inviting their significant and insignificant others. Kim had nothing to say. Even the women drank too much and talked hunting and fishing. One of them had been man enough to shoot a moose. Not her people at all. They were his friends, clearly.

She pauses, one sock in her hand, and thinks how she could pack his beach clothes. And he wouldn't know it until he opened his bags in Canada. She can almost hear him mutter, "Dumb bitch."

The thought makes her smile.

* * *

"Alcohol abuse!" He laughs at the ad campaign coming over his truck radio. It is 1:15, after bar close. Alcohol abuse, he decides, is a two way street. You can abuse the alcohol by, say, leaving a case of beer outside in the winter. The cans explode, and really, you didn't deserve them. That's abusing alcohol. Then there's that other kind, he thinks. Where the alcohol beats the snot out of you.

* * *

He comes in, drunk, and they make tedious love. He passes out, the job half-finished.

"It's the way they all are," Kim's mother once said with a grim smile. "Leave you high and dry in more ways than one."

And Kim feels odd, allowing her mother (or at least her words) into the marital bedroom. Her mother, who had run off with a woman. Half her age, too. Young enough to be Kim's sister. It makes Kim wonder if there are women who are predisposed and women who become.

And she thinks back to her brother. As a child, he and his friends cut up Playboys for trading cards--two brunettes for a blond, etc. Some were just body parts--two sets of breasts for a butt, three panting tongues for a crotch. It makes Kim feel taken apart, dissected. The sum of a woman's parts greater than the whole.

She lies awake, smelling the Jim Beam in her husband's lathered sweat, wishing for the strength to stop enabling, the strength to stop nurturing a man old enough to nurture himself.

He says nothing in his sleep. Too drunk.

* * *

John wakes before the wife does. It is dark. He listens to the meticulous rhythms of her breathing, incantations, the rise and fall of her breasts. Would he know that sound anywhere? No. She's just another person, breathing the same air he does.

* * *

She stands on tiptoes in the doorway and kisses him, partly for love, partly for her belief in love. He hurries out to the Ford Explorer honking in the street, three men inside. As he slides in, he says something funny and the guys share a laugh.

She stands on the front stoop, frozen in mid-wave,

wishing she had an idea what he would joke about.

* * *

He sits in a boat with the Cree guide, Simon. The other three men follow in a second boat, doing what Simon says. Simon says cast in those rocks. So they do. "No more trolling or drifting," Simon says. "We gotta do some jigging, still fishing." They drop anchor and cast. The water is clear and deep.

John thinks how he can't relate to the woman, She's pretty, sure, but that's about it. She is form following function. And she can't even clean fish. But maybe he could teach her. Would he want her that way, more rugged? Sleeping with a dip of Copenhagen in? Smoking cigars by the fire? Sharing rye whiskey in a tin cup at first light?

The black flies bite at his ears. The gnats burn in his eyes and throat as he waits for an answer, still fishing.

* * *

The only sound is the seductive clang of windchimes outside her window--odd shapes of glass spinning and smacking each other at random. A sound with texture.

It's strange, the nights no longer filled with John's sleep monologues. It's too damn silent, she thinks. No presence, only absence.

She turns on the light and looks at his half of the bed. Empty cases of imported beer serve as his nightstand. He calls it eclectic furniture and she calls it lots of things.

Well I ever know him?

She wonders.

She decides it is good she is patient. She will wait him out, win him over. She will try harder and harder, get less and less. The law of diminishing returns.

* * *

In a thick cloud of black flies, John cleans fish with the Cree guide Simon.

"We did pretty good," says John as he cuts away slabs of white walleye meat.

"We done all right," agrees Simon, gouging out cheek fillets.

"Damn, Simon, you're a real Cracker Jack of a

fisherman."

Simon laughs. "It's funny you say Cracker Jacks. I been reading up on stuff. It was us Indians that created Cracker Jacks--we grew peanuts and corn, and made our own caramel. It just took an enterprising white man to stick it all in a box with a prize."

They share a laugh, then John asks, "Say, Simon, you like bein' married?"

Simon is silent.

"Too personal?" asks John as he swats a fly on the back of his neck.

"No, I guess I never thought much about it. Sometimes I think we understand each other without speaking, me and her. Other times we don't understand each other at all. Course, my nearest neighbor is ten miles away, so we got to get along."

John grins and reaches for another walleye to clean.

* * *

Lying in bed, she wonders why, with John gone, she can no longer hear the silence in silence.

And she wonders if, one night holding her breath with him, she will somehow forget to breathe.

But mostly she wonders whether he's in the same tent as Terry, man or woman. The same sleeping bag.

* * *

He sleeps because the wife isn't there to night fish with. He sleeps, dreaming of women in leather and baseball games. Perhaps both.

* * *

She goes to the bar with four of her coworkers, all single women with soap-opera style relationships. They sit and man-watch, whispering like junior high girls.

A guy named Sandy asks Kim to dance a slow song. She peels her bare legs from black naugahyde and stands, rearranging her skirt. He is of slighter build than John. Shoulders narrow, like a woman's. And so they dance, bodies accepting one another. He buys her drinks.

At bar close their talk carries out into the parking lot. The co-workers follow with their Mace and rape-whistle key chains, but Kim assures them, "I'm fine."

"I bet you are," says one. The co-workers giggle and stumble off to their cars.

"This'll give them something to talk about around the coffeemaker," says Kim.

Sandy smiles.

Kim wonders about determinism and what if it had all been different. She asks a question, point blank; "Do you ever listen to Van Morrison with the windows open?"

"You mean that freaky rock singer from the Doors? No. I like country."

"Oh."

He looks into her concrete-gray eyes, and though they reveal nothing, says, "I feel like I know you, Kim."

"Is that really possible?" She turns away. "It seems more and more, at least to me, that we're all different, each of us, just like how snowflakes are different."

He grins. "You're a snowflake? When I was a kid I used to melt snowflakes on my tongue as they fell from the sky."

"I'm married," she reminds him.

"So am I."

* * *

The Canadian night wind whips cold. John warms himself with a slug of Kentucky straight bourbon. It goes down like kerosene. Hunched forward, he stares into the fire, wondering why he night fishes with the wife. Maybe it's the only point where their ragged lives really cross. A place like sunset where things merge then separate. Her listening, him word-dropping.

He thinks how good girls go to heaven and bad girls go everywhere; and how he marries the good girls but still likes the bad ones.

Then he thinks about fishing and why it's such a kick. Maybe it's a testosterone thing. He can't just sit there and have a good time unless he's catching the most fish, the biggest fish. Maybe it's that way with women--picking one with killer looks to mount on the wall like a trophy.

There has to be more, and if there is, he believes he is capable of it. Somehow.

The fire consumes in greedy pops and crackles. The cinders rise, glowing like hope, burning to charred ashes.

"Give me a bump," John says to his buddies. They

pass him the bottle. He takes a pull and holds it out to the guide. "Simon?"

"Nah. Your people been boozin' up my people since you came over from Europe."

"I didn't ask for a history recap," says John. "I just offered a drink."

"Well, it ain't in the cards, and I'm going to bed," Simon says as he crawls into a tent.

"This sure beats ice fishing on Mille Lacs," says one of John's buddies. "My shack sits out there with ten thousand others. Someday we're all gonna go through the ice, ya know. But at least the fishin's good."

"I wouldn't eat your Mille Lacs fish," says another. "I been up there with you, ya know--you shit through one hole and eat the fish that eat your shit through a hole ten feet away. It sorta shortens the loop in the food chain, don't it?"

They laugh, and then John tells a joke. The hook--"I got a piece of ass before I left."

"Oh yeah?"

The line and sinker--"Yeah. My finger poked through the toilet paper as I was wiping my butt."

Ha, ha. The men howl with laughter. One of John's buddies exclaims, "Women, you can't live with them, you can't kill them."

John and his buddies stay up laughing and drinking and bragging and storytelling, until they are each ten feet tall and bulletproof. Simon says shut up. But they laugh on into the night, as only men around a fire can.

* * *

Maybe the only way to find a matching snowflake is to give birth to one. She thinks this when she is nine days late.

* * *

In the morning, John is the first to rise. He swims alone. The water is cold and shocking. He swims out until his arms ache and then swims back. He stands naked in the choppy lake, water to his nipples, feeling cleansed.

* * *

"I'm pregnant," she says when John comes home with

a cooler full of walleyes. She feels charged. But still his pause makes her flinch, the way she does in the gaps of his sleep talk.

"You're what?"

"I know you don't want children, but it just happened."

"No 'How was fishing, honey?' Just a big fat 'I'm pregnant'?"

"Listen," she says, "I didn't ask for this either."

His tone rises. "I can't believe, I just can't..."

"You can handle this, can't you, John?"

He says nothing.

He wants me to terminate, she thinks. Or does he? The ambiguity of silence settles in. Silence is a lie by omission. She rehearses what she will say, how he's not the person he once was or believed himself to be, how if he doesn't want to be a father he can no longer be a husband, how she is strong enough to raise a child on her own.

But finally he asks, "What the hell are we gonna name it?"

They lie in bed and talk late into the night. And the dam between them breaks open, flooding the room. She confesses in the dark, "You know why I'm talking so much, John? Because I'm afraid I'll never know you." But by now he is asleep.

She wants to wake him and keep talking, but she's run out of things to say. What can a woman tell a man, anyway? Nothing he wants to hear, at least. "High and dry," just like her mother said. But Kim doesn't love women the way her mother does. She has John, he has her. No more, no less. Love by default.

She thinks of the rough fisherman's knot in her womb, the part of her that has mutated and broken off. It will grow within her, a part of her and yet apart from her, conscious of its presence, its separateness.

He is silent, holding his exhale, no longer casting in the night. And all he murmurs in his sleep is "Big walleyes," and it's sincere. But she isn't even listening. The water in which they both swim is now what it should be, just air.

And when you think about it, there's a sort of quiet dignity to that.

So they sleep. And nothing remains but the clang of windchimes in the night and the varied rhythms of their breathing, in and out and out and in and in.

A Hint of Things to Come

Matt Kruger

(Set in the Universtiy of Minnesota-Twin Cities, Minneapolis Campus, between the dates of March 11-17, 1995,-for anyone who thinks they really need to know)

Okay, so I was sitting by myself, or about as close to it as possible, in the O. Meredith Wilson Something or Other Library sifting though a mound of paperwork that consisted mostly of three quarters of a notebook worth of lecture notes from my Survey of English Literature class when I ran across something that caught my rather short span of attention. I didn't really remember it as being all that important when I scribbled it down some two months earlier, but then again if I took the trouble to put pen to paper, it must have been important. Perhaps I knew then in some subconscious way that the idea would return to me with a greater impact sometime in the future. I suppose that is why we take notes. (Duh). But I'm getting off the subject; digressing, so to speak. I tend to do that once in a while. I think sometimes my whole life up to this point has been one continuous digression. Even this confession is adding to my digression. (I don't know if I should have put that line in parentheses or not. Shit, this whole damn story should be in parentheses, so why the hell should I care?) Anyway, I've really got to stop from digressing too much. It tends to get me sidetracked.

So where was I? Ah, yes, the lecture notes. I suppose I should convey to the discerning reader just what the hell the point of all this is. Well, let's start with how this bit of information came to be written in my trusty all-purpose English class notebook. My professor was going off on a tangent about the heroic aspects of Satan in *Paradise Lost* and at the end of his spiel he summed it all up in one maxim: A hero must have absolute conviction even in the face of absolute defeat. Pretty catchy, huh? Anyway, I was so taken by this statement that I reread it, circled it, and read it yet again to convince myself that I had indeed been right in circling it.

Now I suppose I should tell the inquisitive reader exactly why I had been thumbing through all these notes in the first place. You see, it was finals week and I had to take this goddamn, two hour, write until your hand falls off and think until your brain explodes essay exam in a mere forty-six hours. God, that sucks. Your hand gets all cramped up and sweaty until you can't hold your writing utensil and..ahh fuck; I'm doing it again. I've really got to stop drifting off like that. It's getting annoying, I can tell.

As I was saying this test was going to kick my ass with steel-toed boots and I was trying to do anything to keep myself from thinking (dreading) about it. So I just sat there for an undetermined amount of time and let all my thoughts circle around my brain until some nugget settled out. I was panning for intellectual gold as it were, but all that came to me was sand. This idea of the ideology of the hero kept fru-fruing around the dance floor of the two-bit dive that is my mind and at the same time I also began to reflect upon a wonderful conversation I had with two of my friends during an invigorating constitutional around campus the previous weekend.

It was probably the nicest goddamn day of the year to this point weatherwise. It was extremely sunny and real warm and fuzzy and the birds were chirping and singing and all this other crap I don't want to go into because it makes me sick. I'll explain later. Actually, the fervor of my loathing of "beautiful" spring days has been satisfactorily brought to a boil, so I'll explain some of it now.

Any time the weather is the focal point of someone's day or of people's conversation, it pisses me off to no end. I mean, don't we have anything more important to talk about, for Christ's sake? And if the sole reason for someone's happiness is that the weather is nice, then to me that's pretty sad. But then again I've never been one to understand the quality of happiness and under what conditions it is deemed acceptable to be happy, so I guess I'm not the best judge of people's behavior. Yet I still feel the urge to speak out when I perceive something to be moronic, like what I've just written about.

Anyway, back to the story. What was the story? Oh, yeah..actually, there isn't much more to it than a conversation about the weather. We went around to all the bookstores, which were either closed or didn't have the right books for our respective classes. The three of us proceeded to collectively bitch about the state of bookstores, the post office (which was also closed, the bastards), the world at large (actually, I did most of the bitching on that subject), and invariably the weather.

Now, I'll give a sample, a smidgen, of our discourse. The cautious reader may notice that there are no descriptions of emotions or physical actions during this conversation. However, it should not be construed that this is a passionless work; quite the contrary. It's just that I, as the author, am employing my freedom of expression to omit such descriptions. I know my Creative Writing instructor(s) have informed me that this is not a sound approach, but to be perfectly honest, I really don't give a shit because I am 1) too lazy to take the trouble to paint the reader a crystal clear picture of the action (I mean, come on, use your imagination) and 2) the conversation really isn't all that exciting anyway. Any exclusion of dumb expressions on the faces of my friends is necessary because, in reality, you're not missing anything. Trust me.

Ok, here it goes:

Chico (that's me. Actually, it's my nickname. Don't ask me how I got it.): God I hate this fuckin' time of year.

Rick (my friend): Why's that, Chico?

Chico: I hate it. (pause)(I'm never real direct)

Rick: But why? Spring is coming. You're supposed to be happy.

Chico: That's just it. Everybody's outside having fun, soaking up all the sun, holding hands and all that other mamby-pamby bullshit. It makes me sick.

Rick: Not me. This is the time of year when all the chicks just come crawlin' out of the woodwork with their skimpy outfits. (Rick's never one to beat around the bush. If he thinks some girl is hot, he'll say "God, she's hot" every time. I swear, that's what he says every time. It's like it's his only thought sometimes).

Chico: Big deal. That shit doesn't really appeal to me.

Marv (my other friend...Well, I've got more friends than that, but he's the only other one that shows up in this story): What are you, some kind of freak or something?

Chico: No, I just don't like being reminded of what I can't have. I see that shit enough in the wintertime the way it is. It's like living in an earth-size museum. You can look, but you can't touch. What the hell is that?

Rick: Good enough for me.

Chico: Anyway, I like it when it's cloudy and rains sometimes; if there isn't any wind to blow my hat off, that is.

Marv: Why?

Chico: Because then all the people who scream "I love this weather!" when it's warm and sunny out piss and moan when it turns cold and it makes me laugh. I mean, you live in Minnesota for Christ's sake, it's supposed to be cold. If you can't handle it, then move your pansy ass out.

Marv: Are we a little bitter, Chico?

Chico: Not really. (everybody laughs) I'm serious. I mean, I know I don't feel very strongly about a lot of what most people think is important, but that shit just can't be tolerated. It's not going to change. A hundred years of meteorology can't do anything about it and neither is everybody complaining about it.

Marv: You're weird, Chico.

Chico: Fuck that. (my universal comeback line when I have nothing to say which is of further intelligence)

* * *

Well, that's the kind of stimulating rapport that can only be expected when you bring three great minds together. Oh, before I forget I should say something else about the structure of this last exchange. All you critics out there may have noticed that I kept using the characters' names in front of what they said, like it was a play or something. And maybe you were all getting a little annoyed with that particular tactic. Well, that's just too bad because in my experience with reading quotations, I always get screwed up trying to follow who said what all the time because I lose track of the quotation marks, and that annoys me. So once again, I am using creative license to get this thing done the way I want it. But enough nit-picking, back to the story.

I guess the thing to take away from this conversation other than that people are morons is the other truism that complaining doesn't get anything done. Everybody says it, but not a lot of people practice this maxim. But of course, these same people will no doubt buy a bumper sticker or some other shit with a different truism on it just to make them look prophetic to a bunch of people they'll never meet- I hate that. The last thing I need is to be reminded I've been living my life the wrong way by some asshole that's stupid enough to believe some bumper sticker that says "Carpe Diem" is going to change someone's life.

Anyway, that's the gist of the conversation. But, as hard as you may find it to believe, even after that hearty discourse, my mind was still starved for more. Not because I had such a great time on our little sojourn earlier, but in all reality I was bored as hell. Also, something had been weighing on my mind for some time and I needed to let it out. I just needed an opportunity to chat alone with Rick and when it came to me, I took it.

I entered his room and we exchanged pleasantries while I found a place to get comfortable on his futon. Yet another reason as to why I made this little neighborly visit was because it was 2:00 on a Saturday afternoon--and we all know what that means. PBA Bowling action at its finest! But, since Norm Duke (1994 PBA Player of the Year, I think, well at least he is in my opinion) wasn't playing, and since none of the also-rans who made it to the final round were bowling a perfect game (which is about the most exciting thing that can happen in any sport, except for a gutterball), I decided I would take the opportunity to tell Rick what I had been wanting to say for so long.

Chico: Hey, ya got anything to drink?
Rick: Don't you already have a can in your hand?
Chico: Oh, yeah.

Now don't get the wrong idea. That wasn't what I was going to tell him. I've said before I'm not real direct sometimes, especially when I have something of relative importance to say. I guess I was stalling for time, hoping the words would form right if I took a minute to keep my head from spinning, but I'll tell you in all honesty that this tactic rarely succeeds. Oh, by the way, Rick was right. I did already have a can of Coke in my hand which I had been sipping from for the last twenty minutes. I guess I forgot. I must have been really focused, but I was probably more confused than anything. I remember Rick's room being quite stuffy that afternoon. I think I was starting to sweat more than the lukewarm can of Coke I was clenching. Finally I resolved to attempt something resembling a conversation.

Chico: When do you guys have another show? ("You guys" in this context refers to this band Rick plays bass in.)
Rick: We don't know yet. We might play next month at Middlebrook. (That's a dorm here at school if you really need to know)
Chico: Oh, really. (My interest piqued)
Rick: You really think anybody will go? (By that he meant any of our mutual friends. I'll try to stop interjecting from now on.)
Chico: I'll go...and if it's at Middlebrook I'll bet I can convince Marv to go.
Rick: Why's that? He's never come before.
Chico: Trust me.

Rick: Whatever, he's not going to come and you know it.
Chico: Hey, if I tell him to come, he'll come.
Rick: Why? Does he follow you wherever you go? Does he do whatever you say? Do you have him tied to a little leash that says "Rover" and do you walk him around until he finds a fire hydrant and...
Chico: No. It's just that...just trust me, all right. (Now when I say "Trust me," I'm one of the number of ever-decreasing individuals remaining that can live up to that statement. So believe me, I'm not just throwing the phrase around.)
Rick: Whatever, Chico.
Chico: Fuck that.

There was a rather long pause as the wheels skidded around the muddy bog that is my mind. This was it. If I didn't tell him then...I guess I could tell him later, but it was too important for me to let this out. Of course it wouldn't just come out by itself, so I had to beat around the bush some more.

Chico: Maybe I could open for you guys. (That is, Rick's band.) (Oh, yeah...I play guitar, too. However, if I were to go into any detail as to exactly what I do with it or why I do it, I would need to write a fucking novel and I can't afford to get sidetracked again.)
Rick: Yeah, maybe...Is that why you think Marv would go?
Chico: No, I mean, it's a factor, but...(this is really hard for me to write and infinitely harder for me to say) um...(I mean it) there's another reason (you people are draining the lifeblood out of me!)
Rick: What? Does he know someone over there?'
Chico: Well, (I'm dying over here) we both sort of know someone.
Rick: Who? Is he in one of your classes? (He's not exactly catching on to my oh-so subtle hinting)
Chico: No, it's a girl.
Rick: Is *she* in one of your classes?
Chico: No. (real slow-like, kind of like "Nnnnoooooo," but that looks too goofy for my taste) (Finally I just broke down. I couldn't take any more of this kind of hide-and-go-seek type of interrogation.) She's this girl I've periodically seen on the bridge on my way to my West Bank classes. (You see, the Minneapolis campus of the University of Minnesota is divided in two by the Mississippi River and the only way to get from one

side to the other without getting extremely wet is to walk on the Washington Ave. bridge. I absolutely refuse to delve into this subject any further because for Christ's sake, I'm trying to tell a story here and this kind of background crap is only getting in the way. You'll just have to take my word for it that everything I've said is true. And if you still don't believe me, then you can find out for yourself. Then I'll find you and kick your ass for not trusting me. Back to the damn story)

Rick: Is she hot? (I told you that was all he ever thought about)

Chico: Well, yes. (I mean, duh) But I'd like to qualify that "yes" by saying that she doesn't look like she's hot all the time, but I think so. No, that's not saying it right. She just looks like someone you would want to get to know. You know what I'm talking about?

Rick: No. (Also real slow-like) Do you know who she is?

Chico: Well, that's the problem. I know what she looks like, so I know who *she* is; but I don't know anything else, so I don't know who she *is*. You know?

Rick: I guess. (pause) So what are you going to do?

Chico: I have no clue what to do. I really don't. Let's just say I'm screwed. I suppose I could just go up and introduce myself, but...

Rick: But what?

Chico: Well, I was all ready to go last fall, I mean, I came this close. (Ok, try to imagine a forefinger and thumb coming together to the point where they almost meet, where there may be just a tiny sliver of light streaming through the crack. I think that's a pretty good representation of how close I came) I know what I was going to say, all I had to do was say it, but I didn't--something stopped me.

Rick: What?

Chico: I don't know. Fear, I guess. Fear of rejection. I don't take rejection well, I really don't.

Rick: So do you have a plan now?

Chico: Well, I figure if she's not in any of my classes next quarter, and I have no reason to believe that she will be, I'll just try to do the same thing I couldn't do last fall.

Rick: What makes you think you'll do it this time?

Chico: I don't know. You think this is weird, don't you?

Rick: Well, I don't know if it's weird, maybe a little, I don't know.

Chico: Yeah, I guess so. I just don't know what to do. I have no clue about this kind of stuff. But I promised myself a long time ago that I was going to do this. That's why I told you about her. I figure the more people I tell, the more forced I'll feel to go through with it.
Rick: So who else knows?
Chico: Just you and Marv, and you gotta promise me you won't tell anybody else.
Rick: Uh, sure. But do you think me and Marv are enough?
Chico: I think it's going to have to be. I can't tell anybody else because they're all a bunch of bastards.
Rick: That's true.
Chico: You think I'm crazy, don't you.
Rick: I don't know. It just seems kind of direct, I don't know.
Chico: Yeah, I know. (Boy, we were really submerging ourselves into the heart of the situation, let me tell you.)
Rick: What are you going to do if it doesn't work, like if she has a boyfriend or something?
Chico: Um...I don't know. I mean, I'd certainly understand if she did, it's certainly a possibility. Fuck it, I'm screwed. I'm a dead man and that's all there is to it.
Rick: But you're going to do it, right?
Chico: I'm going to do everything in my power to make myself go through with this.
Rick: You suck! Oh, not you, Chico. The guy bowling just left like four pins standing.
Chico: Thanks for the update, Rick.

* * *

Anyway, that's the kind of stuff that was being tossed around in my brain just after the exact time that I circled the now-infamous passage in my notes. Then the rusty carousel that is my mind began to spin that hero shit around and around until something put the brakes on and everything came screeching to a halt. It was as if someone had lit a match in a dark cave or tunnel, allowing me to see my way back to the outside world. Actually, it was more like this place was filled with some kind of explosive gas (I apologize for not being able to name any specific gas--I'm not too good with all that scientific crap), which caused the box of oily rags that is my mind to be blown away when the spark ignited.

"A hero must have absolute conviction even in the face of absolute defeat." Yes--yes indeed. I resolved right then and there in my secluded seat at the library to be a hero. I said to myself "I want to be a hero. I want to be like Satan." [Oh, I guess that didn't come out right, but I do find it kind of amazing (well, not really amazing, maybe more amusing) that the philosophy I'm using to turn my life around came from the Prince of Darkness, but hey, you've got to play with the cards you're dealt.] Once the logic was in place, all I needed was a plan--and then it came to me.

Now forgive me for derailing the reader momentarily, but this is a necessary diversion, believe me. I must apologize to anyone who has read this story up to this point, because you've been reading, digesting, and analyzing it under slightly false pretenses. But don't despair, for I hope to clear your conscience with the following explanation. You see, I've been hiding something from everyone in the fact that I possess an ulterior, albeit secondary, motive for writing this. However, before I progress any farther with my confession, the (hopefully) forgiving reader must gain an understanding and appreciation of the sheer genius of my two-pronged plan.

A few days before my fruitful excursion to the library, I had been looking for a job for the summer. I wasn't having much luck in my search (and I'm still not having much luck), but one day I ran across a golden yellow sheet of paper stapled to a bulletin board near the English department office. Now printed on this sheet was something or other about short stories being needed from Minnesota writers for some collection or something like that and I said to myself, "Hey, this might be fun to try." Of course, my inner cynic immediately replied, "Hey, this might be hell to accomplish." That quick remark was based on the fact that I neither had nor could think of anything to write about. I didn't give the matter much further thought--until that flash of brilliance overtook me on the third floor of Wilson Library.

Soon I found myself picking and choosing what would go in and what would stay out of my story. Themes were running through my head. I quickly gathered some of this information and wrote down what I hoped to accomplish. Basically the goal is this: I will use this opportunity to make my first, best, and last attempt at a girl who, day by day, has become increasingly important to me. This story will also be used to get me started, or maybe finished, in a writing career. Since this is what I'm going to school for, I figure I might as well practice my craft at least once. Also, since I'm new at this and don't really know what to expect, I might as well give it a shot. The writing thing, I mean. The girl means everything.

Anyway, that's the scheme I had in mind at the library after having that seed of inspiration planted there by my Survey of English Literature class, one of my professors, Milton, and Satan. I planned to kill two birds with one stone. (I must confess that I was also excited about my plan because it had two parts, and I could say cool phrases like "kill two birds with one stone" and "two-prong plan." I've always wanted to say those things, and now I was writing them down. That rules.)

With this new mission at my disposal, I must say that I had a fire lit under me. I felt empowered to do anything. I walked, nay, *strode* across the Washington Ave. bridge like a man possessed. No, wait a minute...I was a man possessed. There was no like about this at all. Simile had no place in describing my new state of conviction. I was so impassioned that I marched straight back to my dorm room and watched TV for several mind-numbing hours before falling asleep. Sure, you may be laughing now, but read this carefully and make it stick: Never underestimate the power of the phrase "I'll do it tomorrow," which is precisely what I said and did. I'm a man of my word.

Since all this shit was taking place during finals week, and I didn't have the English test straight from the bowels of hell for a couple more days, I figured I'd think more in depth concerning my story. But before I could do any more serious mulling over on the subject, I had to get the goddamn address from that goddamn sheet of paper so I would know where to send my story. (That is, in case I ever finished it, but then again I had to in order to give it to what's her face. That's the beauty of the plan--it knows how to get things done)

So Rick had to go over to Pillsbury Hall in order to pick up some shit for his take-home final in one of his geology classes. I figured I would tag along since I knew the least I would get out of the experience was 1) an invigorating walk and 2) a trip to Taco Bell, probably the best place possible for a tortured soul to drown his sorrows in the form of free refills of Mountain Dew. Of course, I was right. The Bell was even better than I had imagined it would be, or could imagine.

However, Rick came with a whole bunch of his little geology friends and they all talked about subjects that I either had no interest in or were outside my expertise. (In case you were wondering, my expertise involves using the word "expertise" as often as possible to make myself appear to be learned.) They went back and forth about such things as requirements for graduate school and expected me to chime in with something profound to say on the subject matter. Christ, half the time I don't even know what I want to be doing within a few hours of a certain point in time, and if I do know, it's usually something like, "I want to take a nap this afternoon," not, "In two years from now, I'm going to attend graduate school at Putzville University and my best friends there will be named Larry and Margaret." I mean, really.

Then they moved on to batting around theories and formulas they've learned from their various geology courses in the past, and needless to say, I really got lost with this one. I like geology and all (I took it, as a matter of fact. Got an A in it, too), but to be perfectly honest, about the only geology I know is the difference between a rock and a lump of shit; and if the said shit is hardened or petrified in any way, it gets increasingly difficult for me to discern the difference. I already told you, I'm not too good with that kind of scientific crap.

Anyway, we finished our meal and were heading back to our dorm when I casually slipped it to Rick that I needed to swing by Lind Hall and the English Department office to find that damn bulletin board and write down that damn address. So I was standin' there looking like a big dork copying down this address and I knew all that time Rick was thinking to himself, "What the hell is he up to and why did he drag me along? I hope this doesn't have anything to do with what we talked about last weekend." Well, he probably wasn't thinking that, but that's exactly what I was up to. Of course, anyone who has been paying attention to the story up to this point would be aware of that; and if you haven't been paying attention, well, I don't exactly blame you, but let me go on to say that it gets better. Trust me.

START PAYING ATTENTION TO THE STORY FROM THIS POINT FORWARD.

There, now the attentive reader has been informed to focus on the upcoming conversation. But then again, it's probably no more stimulating or significant than any other section to be found previously in the story.

Rick: What was that for?

Chico: What was what for? (Real smooth, huh? Nothing to hide here.)

Rick: Why did we go to Lucky Lind?

Chico: Oh...I had to copy down an address.

Rick: An address for what? For a job or something? (Oh, God. Here we go again. More duck and cover, stick and move, bob and weave type conversation.)

Chico: No, not quite.

Rick: Then what's it for?

Chico: It's for a story. Actually, it's something for Minnesota writers and needing short stories from Minnesota writers and stuff.

Rick: Are you going to write a story for it?

Chico: Uhhh, yeah.

Rick: That's cool...What's it going to be about?

Chico: What's it going to be *about*?

Rick: Yeah.

Chico: Oh, I don't know. Actually it's going to be about this.

Rick: About what?

Chico: This whole thing. Our conversation from last weekend and now.

Rick: What did we talk about? (He was beginning to tick me off. Mr. Short Attention Span Theater wasn't quite catching on that we were surrounded by a large number of people and I didn't want to be blabbing my intentions so any jackass on the street could hear it. Finally, though, I just said "Fuck it" and humored his lack of observance.)

Chico: You know, about the girl I told you about and not knowing what to do and all that other shit.

Rick: Oh...yeah. Do you think they'll like it?

Chico: I hope so, but it's not so much a question of "them" liking it as "she" liking it.

Rick: Huh? What "she"? (Imagine a light bulb flickering for just an instant over a mystified, pumpkin-shaped head.) You don't mean that chick we were talking about before, do you?

Chico: The very same.

Rick: Wait a minute, I thought you were going to introduce yourself to her.

Chico: I intend to, but...

Just at the point where I was about to explain to Rick

exactly why I was writing a story as a means of introducing myself we ran into somebody he knew from one of his classes or some bullshit like that. They struck up a conversation about geology and other things for about five minutes or so and by the time they had finished I lost my train of thought. Isn't that always the way? It seems someone is always interrupting you right at the time you have the most important thing to say. That's why I write; because no one can interrupt me but myself. (Actually, that's probably reason #1008 on the Why I Write list, but that's for another time.)

If I may, I would like to indulge the reader by making a quick list of the major reasons as to why I'm writing this story as opposed to just introducing myself as I was prepared to do last fall:

1) First and foremost, **I'm guaranteed that I won't be interrupted.** I know that if I were talking to her out in public, one of my stupid friends would walk by and interrupt me just as I was trying to give her the most important speech of my life. I'm positive that they would do everything in their power to embarrass me in front of as many people as possible because, hey, what are friends for?

2) Secondly, this approach allows me **to get things right.** Nothing ever comes out right the first time I say it, or think it, unless it's a rapier-like, snapping, biting, witty one-liner rip on one of my friends. Otherwise, everything always comes out messed up. That is yet another reason why I write--because you can change what you say until it comes out right. Well, I shouldn't say that because it never turns out exactly right. But if you practice enough, you can make it better.

3) This format allows me **to tell the whole story**, to give the big picture. I mean, I clearly can't do as much as I could with a novel, but I wasn't asked to write a novel. Plus, it would take too goddamn long. But really, this way the girl in question can hopefully learn quite a bit about me in the relatively short amount of time it takes to read this story. With any luck, a hasty judgment can be avoided. Also, I can say everything I want to say without sounding phony. Because, really, how do you know someone is telling you the truth until you know how they operate?

Well, anyway, that's my list. Now I must say in

commenting on the previous passage that I hope she realizes that I *am* as I portray myself in this story. There is no window-dressing here; what you read is what you get. Hopefully, this way a rational judgment can be made, backed by sound reasoning. In other words, if I am to be rejected, I would rather the decision be based on a rejection of my thoughts or values than on the awkwardness of their presentation. I realize that appearances are relatively important in any potential relationship, but I also think that our society is too quick to place style over substance, and to me that seems a waste. I believe a great many people would be a great deal happier in the long run if they would simply choose what works over what they feel is "pretty" or "cute".

* * *

Now that I'm done philosophizing, I think I'll get back to telling the rest of the story. But before I can do that, I have to explain one more shortcoming about myself. You see, I was sitting back in my dorm room watching TV and thinking about my story when I came to the realization that it would be very difficult for me to finish this project even though it's probably the most important thing I've ever attempted. Why do I say that? Because I never finish anything, that's why. Every other endeavor I've ever started always gets about three-quarters of the way finished and then it either gets too hard to complete or I lose interest and move on to something else. In other words, I get sidetracked.

Like, right now,- I'm about three-quarters of the way done with telling this story, and I find myself perilously close to hanging up my pen for good, but I know in my heart of hearts that I can't. Because if I've learned anything though my wasting of life it's this: If you have a goal, you can't trip and stumble around all half-assed. In order to get to where you want to be, you have to grab hold of something (I don't really know what. Whatever's closest to you, I guess) and stay on track until you get there. (Christ, I'm using so many clichés and mixed metaphors that I'm starting to sound like some bullshit football coach, But it's true; it's really true.)

Just to further expand this theme and give the symbol-hungry reader something to chew on for a while, I think I'll provide another example of my uncanny ability, a God given gift really, to never finish anything. Don't worry, this isn't exhausting my resources, I've got a million of them. In fact, if I were to list all the projects I never finished, no, if I were to give you three-fourths of that list just to be more ironic (moronic), it would fill three-fourths of the goddamned notebook I'm writing in right now. And I can assure you this isn't some pansy-ass little journal, either. It's full size, narrow ruled, 100 sheets, front and back, of pure folly.

Well, before I digress too much on the subject, I should give you, the reader, the example I was going to present in the previous paragraph. The example being my ill-fated album, "Overkill." I told you before that I play guitar. Mostly, I just write my own songs because I don't really want to make the effort to learn anybody else's. Anyway, if I keep writing about this it'll go on forever, so I'm just going to say that I put a few songs together over the last year and a half or so and made an album. Or three-quarters of one, I should say. It's been stuck at that point for a good month or so.

Oh, did I tell you that "Overkill" has a story behind it? Can you guess what it's about? You got it. It's about this kid (me) who wants to introduce himself to some girl (yes, the same girl) along with the rest of the world, but he's too afraid to come out of his shell for fear of being rejected as he was in the past. So he sits on his ass for the longest time until finally he decides to do something (Can you guess what that is?), but inevitably he's too late and he loses everything. His love of life, faith in mankind, the whole bit. As much as all these things mirror each other (i.e. the story, the album, and the real life they're based on) I hope 1) That I finish and 2) That if and when I finish it won't be too late, but that's not for me to decide.

Okay, so let me re-set the scene for anyone who forgot. I was sitting back in my dorm room feeling none too confident in my storytelling faculties, realizing I could very well never finish this story. At that point I decided I would write a note. I figured that, for one, I could at least finish that, and if all else fails (which it invariably does) I could at least have something to give her. Also, I reasoned that this note would give me a chance to write down my true feelings, in as a concise and genuine manner as possible.

Now, since I've already established some pages earlier that I am trustworthy and don't embellish anything or blow things out of proportion like my friends do, then I hope every word and every feeling in this letter can be taken at face value.

So, without any further ado, I started on a few rough drafts that would capture the essence of the emotions I had been feeling for the last few months so I could finally free myself from the great burden I've been carrying for the last few years. Anyway so here it goes:

Hey baby,
How's about you and me gettin' together sometime...

Oops. Sorry. I shouldn't have done that. I'm a real bastard sometimes. I guess I just had to do that as a warm-up in order to get the mind and pen flowing together as a cohesive unit. Besides, I'm a sucker for a good joke. Let's try this again, shall we?

Dearest Beloved,
Of all the women, in all the world, in all my heart, you are...

God damn it! That's not it, either. I think I'm getting closer, however. This is harder than it looks, you know. It's easier said than done. Or course, everything is easier said than done; as long as you can speak, that is. Besides, I'm not real good with put-on romantic, dime-store greeting card drivel. I don't buy into that and I hope to God no one else does either. Because that means any phony asshole loser out there can do whatever he wants to someone and get away with it as long as he knows the right words to say and the right buttons to push. I definitely believe that's one of the major problems with society today. We hear what we want to hear, even (and especially) if it's not the truth. But before I pontificate any further, please allow me to show you the real letter once and for all.

Dear whoever you are, To whom it may concern, and such and such:

You may think this strange, or think me strange, since I don't know who you are or even what your name is, that I could be in love with you. It's true. Every time I see you (which is pretty rare), even if it's only for a second, I feel ten times more alive than I have in any other time of my wasted life. I spend half my time wondering what you're doing, who you're doing it with, what you're thinking, what you'd think of me, and on and on. I guess what I'm trying to say is that I want that wondering to stop. I need it to stop, or I think I'll go crazy.

Now if you think that I'm crazy for doing this and that I'm making the biggest mistake of my life, you may be right. But on the other hand, win or lose, it could be the best thing I've possibly ever done, I don't know--yet. As much reason as these is to be afraid of the wrong answer, I have to know, or it will kill me. You see, as much reason as I have to be happy and content, I always feel like there is something missing. I'm hoping, hoping to God, that someday, someone will come along to fill the gaps and cracks in my life that are currently occupied by self-doubt and fear. Now that person may not be you, but since I wrote a story and an album about you, I have to give you a chance, just as I hope you will give me a chance to do the same.

Ever since I first saw you, I've been wanting to meet you. For months I've been agonizing over just what would be the right approach, but I never really figured one out. Finally, I just gave up and decided to write this, because I was making myself crazy.

I realize you may already have a boyfriend or whatever, and you may be ignoring this because you think you'll never be in my situation, but I must say if you ever, ever find yourself half as lonely as I have been, try to find me. I know I'd drop everything, which will probably be nothing, to find you.

I guess all I can really say on my behalf is that if you were to give me a chance to be with you, I swear to God or anything else that I'd do everything in my power to keep you from regretting that decision. Now I know I've felt this before and I've meant it before, but I've never written it down or expressed my feelings for anyone else in this way, and I know I will not after. There's nothing more that I can say about this, it's all up to you now.

In all sincerity, respect, and love,

Matt Kruger

* * *

It took me about five minutes to write it. That may not seem like much to all you literary giants out there, but first you must realize that a lot of the letter consisted of leftovers from the speech I was prepared to give in the fall, not to mention that much of it had been revised and reworked in my head over the last five months. So, as you can see, it's a much more complicated process than it first seems.

Anyway, as one of my friends argued to me some years ago, if you think about it, you can do a lot in five minutes. It's true. I suppose now you jackals think you need an example to back this up. Well, I should just leave you to try to think of one yourselves, but I'll indulge your curiosity anyway just to show you how benevolent I am. Fuck, you could usually listen to your favorite song in about five minutes or less. Unless you're like me and your favorite song is twice as long ("La Villa Strangiato"--Rush; in case you were wondering) I know what you're thinking. Who? Rush? What? Well, you're just going to have to trust me on this one. In fact, I plan on listening to it within the next hour or so, but that's irrelevant because I know that you know you want more examples. Everybody always wants more, that's another problem with society today.

Even though this goes against everything I believe, I'll give you yet another example. This whole passage from the end of the letter on was composed (roughly, in every sense of the word) in five minutes. No, that example's too vague. I'll try another. Oh, I know. On a slow day at Taco Bell you can go there, order two soft shell tacos and a beverage of some sort, get the said food and eat it in right around five minutes, if you're really hungry. But, hey, you're always at least a little hungry when you go to the Bell.

There it is. One of the most pleasing experiences a person can have and it only takes five minutes. About the only thing that can top that would be going to White Castle and doing the same thing. Which finally brings us back to the story. A short time after I composed my note, I had another sudden flash of brilliance. I saw a commercial for White Castle and right there with my mouth hung wide open and drooling, I knew that the Castle and I had a date with destiny. The only problem was I needed a car to get over there, even though I felt I could float to my destination on a cloud of steam-grilled goodness. Needles to say I teleported to Rick's door as fast as the laws of physics would carry me and started pounding.

Chico: Hey hey, Rick! We need a car.
Rick: Why, dude?

Chico: For going to the Castle.
Rick: Yes! Fa-doosh! (The international response to something, often an idea or suggestion, that kicks total ass, usually accompanied by a clenched fist and a wild pumping of the right arm.)

Well, that was about all the conversation that was required for the subject. Everything was sacrificed for the sake of securing a vehicle to make the trek. Through some swift negotiations, Rick was able to persuade his girlfriend to give up her car for an hour and we were all set to go. I must confess, there was yet another ulterior motive in my desire to make the trip. I needed more material, you know, for the story and all. Once I had composed the rough draft of the note I regained my writing fervor and resolved to go ahead and write my story to frame the letter. And on top of that, it was a rather exciting and eventful day up to that point and I was not about to let the rest of it become a wasted opportunity.

We were planning to embark on our quest right after one of the NCAA tournament games finished and I was plotting strategies in my head, ready to convey to Rick what my plan was with the attention to detail that it deserved, but then the damn game had to go triple fucking overtime. Can you believe it? But it turns out, it was kind of a blessing in disguise since the extra time afforded me the opportunity to further explore the situation and distinguish exactly what I wanted to tell him.

So, after much posturing on Rick's part, once the game was over we headed to White Castle to down some food and have a friendly chat. We started off discussing little things like the game, quoting entire episodes from The Simpsons line for line, stuff like that. Of course, being the ever-subtle person I am, I let this kind of stimulating chit-chat continue for almost the entire dining experience. I guess I kept waiting for him to bring the subject up, but I finally came to the realization that that wasn't going to happen on its own, so I took the initiative.

Rick: God, these things rule. (Oh...sorry. I think I cut in a line too soon. I believe he was referring to the apparent quality of the White Castle burgers, or maybe it was the fries. I can never be too sure with him.)
Chico: Hey, you remember that conversation we had this afternoon about the conversation we had over the weekend?
Rick: I think so. What'd you want to say, Chico?

Chico: Well, about writing the story and all that. I never got to tell you what it's all about.

Rick: Well, go ahead.

Chico: Okay, anyway, aaaah shit! Now I don't remember what I was going to say.

Rick: Well, I'll give you a minute. (I think if the reader hums the theme to Final Jeopardy about one and a half times through, this will give an idea as to how long the silence lasted while I contemplated a new way of expressing my thoughts.)

Chico: Okay, you know, about it, being sort of direct and stuff.

Rick: Yeah.

Chico: Well, wait. Let me back up a minute. I want to get this right (I cut him off before he could acknowledge me. The clogged drain that is my mind was finally starting to flow.) A lot of things have been going through my mind since I've started thinking of this story and I've been mulling them over and everything and I've kind of reasoned my way around the holes in the plan.

Rick: Like what? (I went on to tell him the reasons for choosing to write a story instead of just introducing myself which I've already explained some pages earlier and will not go through again. This way I hope I don't bore the fickle reader with a re-run of something they can go back and reference anytime they want. After about five minutes of explanation and many acknowledgments that I was correct in my reasoning from Rick, I changed the topic.)

Chico: Now, let me ask you something, Rick. Do you think this approach seems crazy? Because I've been thinking about it and I'm starting to believe it isn't so crazy. It's unique I'd say...

Rick: Yeah

Chico: Unorthodox in some ways...

Rick: Yeah.

Chico: I mean, most people don't just go up to someone and introduce themselves and tell them their feelings for that person and I've never heard of anyone writing a story to someone, although I'm sure that someone, or many someones, have.

Rick: Yeah.

Chico: But, I think maybe this is the way it should be done.

Rick: How so?

Chico: Well, it just should. I mean, if you have a feeling or idea, you should just go with it sometimes, within reason, of course.
Rick: Of course.
Chico: I mean, (I say that a lot, don't I?) like now, I'm just sittin' here, right? If somebody just came up to me out of nowhere and asked me some questions, even if they were personal-type questions, I'd answer them. At least I think I would. I suppose it depends on who's asking. But if that person were polite and everything and didn't bother me too long, I'm sure I'd oblige them.
Rick: Well, so would I.
Chico: So would anybody, I'm sure, but would you think that person crazy?
Rick: No, not at all.
Chico: Would you be bothered by it in any way?
Rick: Not really, as long as the person didn't bug me all night or anything.
Chico: Do you think that most people hold the same opinion as us?
Rick: I would have to say yes.
Chico: Exactly...But it seems that being direct gets frowned upon nowadays. Like if you go up and just ask someone a question, you'll get arrested for it. That's the way I feel anyways.
Rick: What's your point?
Chico: Well, it's just that usually it's expected that everybody plays these games when it comes to meeting somebody. You're supposed to deny your feelings for someone until you feel some sense of security about the other person, but I can't deny that I have these feelings, I can't play those games, because I never learned how. I can't not be myself. I've become a prisoner of circumstance, waiting for some miracle that's never going to happen on its own. All I know is, if I go on living the way I have been, I think I'll die.
Rick: You think so?
Chico: I'm pretty positive about it, yeah. (About the time I made my last remark, I glanced around the confines of White Castle and for the first time I saw just how dreary a place can be at eleven o'clock on a lonely Friday night when you're contemplating a new direction and you realize you've been living the wrong way for a large portion of your life. I saw the blank,

lifeless expressions on the other people's faces and how I had that same aura about me for far too long. I said to myself, "You know, I don't want to end up like this." I started thinking about the hero quote again and I decided to finally come clean with Rick and tell him everything.)

Rick: So you about ready to go, Chico?

Chico: Not yet. I have something to tell you.

Rick: What? (He didn't seem real enthused to hear it, I think he wanted to leave quite a while before.)

Chico: Well, I didn't quite tell you everything about my reasons for writing the story.

Rick: Why? What'd you leave out?

Chico: (I tried to stall, but found I no longer could hold anything back) Umm. Well, this may seem weird, but I want to be a great man.

Rick: Who doesn't?

Chico: Well, yeah. But I don't feel like I'm going to get there--ever. I mean, I can't be like this anymore. There has to be something more. Because half the time, I don't even feel like I'm alive, I'm just going through the motions. I figured I should try at least once in my life to do something to justify my existence. I mean, if you're not doing everything you can, then you're wasting your time and you start thinking, "What the hell am I doing here?" That's the way I've been feeling lately and, well, I don't want to feel that way anymore. If I'm going to be the person I know I should be, I can't be cowering in the corner anymore. I thought I was ready last fall, but...

Rick: But what?

Chico: Well, I guess I know why I didn't go through with it, but I can't face it. You see, back then I gave into a false sense of security. I gave in to my fears and traded my chance at greater happiness for the security of being with my friends and living a "normal" life. But the problem is I'm more insecure now than ever. I can't sleep at night, I can't really talk to anyone or be as open as I used to--I'm a wreck. I can't stop thinking about the "What ifs?", when I should be realizing that in life there is only "What is".

Rick: Yeah, but the question remains. Are you going to do it?

Chico: I already told you, I'm going to do everything in my power to make myself go through with this.

Rick: Even if you fail in everything?

Chico: What do you mean "if"? (I can be a real optimist sometimes when I want to be.)
Rick: Well, I think that's a pretty good attitude.
Chico: Yeah, I'm starting to feel that no matter what happens, win or lose, things will be all right. I don't want to lose that feeling, dude. Even thinking about doing this makes me feel like I'm doing the right thing...(Just then Rick 'tore one off', if you know what I mean, if you catch my drift, so to speak. He 'let one fly' in other words.) Yeah, I think my parents would be proud.
Rick: Of that? (Referring to one of the nastiest smelling farts this side of, well, raw sewage. Of course, I hope the reader knows what I was really talking about, unless they haven't been reading the last twenty pages. All I could say in response was:)
Chico: Uhhh...yeah, Rick

* * *

So, anyway, that's what's been happening the last few days. And now, as I try to sum up all my thoughts and I have doubts and fears such as: "What the fuck am I doing writing a story about a story which happens to be the same story? The level of verisimilitude is so high, it's staggering! I can't tell what's real or imagined anymore. I'm so screwed up now that I might have to start over or throw in the towel..." I can't just say "Fuck it," because I want to follow through with this to the end. I HAVE TO GO THROUGH WITH THIS. There, that reminds both me and the reader of just how important doing "this" really is, in case anybody forgets what I've been writing about for the last twenty-five pages.

While I've been thinking of a conclusion, I had a flashback to a lecture my oceanography professor gave to our class about the greenhouse effect a couple of weeks before the setting of this story. He did something that I feel is pretty rare for people in certain positions and with certain ideas to do--he told the truth. He said that nobody really knows what's going to happen and no amount of money or experts or superstition was going to tell us about the future. It could happen, it might not--we don't know. I guess the question I have to answer and the question we all have to answer is the question he put to our class--Are we willing to go through with the experiment? Are we willing to find out the answers, even if we may not particularly like the results?

I hope now that I know what my answer is to that question and I also hope that everyone who reads this is able to give an honest response to the question in their own hearts and minds.

Well, since I've said pretty much everything I wanted to say, and I have other pressing business to deal with, I'll give the insatiable reader one more relation of theme to the work itself, because I know if I don't, somebody's going to bitch about it, so here it goes. The title of this story is "*A Hint of Things to Come*" (I wasn't sure if I was supposed to italicize a short story or put it in quotation marks, so I did both just to be sure. You may think me a poor literary scholar for not knowing, but I've seen it both ways, I swear to God.), and maybe it's not the most appropriate title, but I'll try to give it more relevance by saying this: I don't know what's to come, the love interest of the story doesn't know what's coming, and you, the reader, doesn't know what's to come, although you may have an inkling about it according to what you think of me through my story.

I guess, all along, in my heart of hearts, I know that this won't work somehow; something will happen to make it fail, but I know that that something will not be my fear, and that makes me feel vindicated. I guess all I can really say in conclusion is that absolute defeat is a given, it's always around, but absolute conviction is a rare thing to run across and if and when you do find it, you really will feel like a hero. Trust me.

Into the Eyes of Sorrow

Ethan Wells

The door was open just enough for one to see the small room, with its cluttered desk by the window and its lone chair at the side of the unmade bed. The light from the window accentuated the darkness of the chamber, hiding the faces of its two inhabitants. No one spoke, and all listened to the perpetual ticking of the merciless clock that hung on the wall, as it had for so many generations before, and would for so many generations after, as the sole witness of the times. The colorless room cried with the despair that can only be felt by the ones that have already lost all hope of happiness, and the anguish of those in the room struck the body like a cold wind, forcing a shiver through the heart.

His eyes were empty of the resilient hope that is found in most men's eyes, and his haggard face had fallen, both in reality and in appearance, so that it resembled that of a man closer to sixty than to forty. The growth of a week-old beard shadowed his face, hiding the scars of a wounded soul. His tie hung loosely from his unbuttoned shirt, and his rolled up sleeves revealed the strong arms of a man who had known nature well. His singular regard rested perpetually on the pale figure in the slightly ruffled bed whose blankets rose calmly with every hard-fought breath, like a minuscule wave that breaks the surface of a calm sea. Her body was so gaunt that it seemed to be merely a ripple in the fabric of the white sheets that hugged the mattress relentlessly. Her pale face seemed a part of the colorless pillow that cushioned her now bony head, and her sunken-eyes, when they were open, awaited their final closure. There was no hope. All that remained was time; time to wait; time to despair; time to panic; but not enough time to express all the emotions that reigned in both their hearts.

As he looked into her sullen face, he saw the woman that had broken the solitude of his life. They had been so wonderful together. Their love was so spiritual, so deeply born from the very essence of their beings, that her death was his death as well, They both had viewed the world in the same pessimistic way and had been lost to a hopelessness that had encompassed their lives. And then they had met each other. And they had dared to dream, to hope, to see a future that was not dictated by loneliness and despair. Those days, those marvelous few days that now were the cause of his utter loss of hope, had seemed to give his life a meaning. Yet, even then, they knew that they were deceiving themselves when they began to forget their loneliness. That is why he had not wanted a child. She had been so adamant in her desire to bring another soul into the world, another lonely soul. He had argued that the world was too lonely for any person, and life was too hopeless for an innocent child to endure. But, in the end, he had given in, partly for her, and partly in the hope that he was wrong in his beliefs. But he was not wrong.

* * *

Nine months before had been the happiest day of her bedeviled life. He remembered it well. She had been sick the past few days, and, although she had not thought it serious, she had decided to visit the doctor so that he could give her some medicines to help her sleep through the nights. The doctor had examined her with a quiet confidence that comes with life-long experience and had left the room to consult with his colleague in life and death. When he returned, he wore a smile and, with his words, overcame the loneliness that can be overcome in any woman's heart by the news of impending motherhood. Further test would have to be done, he had said, but he didn't expect any complications. After a blood sample was taken, an appointment was set for the first Monday of the next month, and, for the first time since the demise of their childhood illusions, they felt hope.

The trip home from the hospital that day lived in his memory like a dream. They both had rambled endlessly on such inanities as what they would name their child, where her room would be, whether she would be an only child or, a few years later, be accompanied by a little brother. These questions had seemed so important that they couldn't be pondered during the inevitable nine month waiting period, but had to be responded to immediately. He laughed sardonically in his head as he remembered these questions without importance and answers without meaning. Yet he couldn't help dwelling on that first night home, when they had thought that they would be parents. He had dared to think that he was capable of defeating loneliness through fatherhood, and now, as omnipotent loneliness crept back into his hear with every dying breath of its conqueror, he watched the harsh results of this folly.

* * *

    The first Monday of the following month had been anticipated anxiously with the same impatience of a child waiting to open the birthday presents of Christ. They both had awakened early, while the dawn was still hidden behind a shade of darkness, and, throughout their hurried breakfast, the questions of parenthood had lingered unspoken, hidden under a mask of empty words. She wore her finest dress with a ribbon in her hair, looking like a child trying to be an adult by wearing her mother's clothes. He had shaved twice that morning, and would have shaven a third time if his wife hadn't asked him whether he hoped to peel off his skin and uncover his hard skull. Of course he was nervous. He couldn't even tie his tie. He was going to be a father, for God's sake! He spoke these words to her, and, in the wave of absolute happiness that embraced both of them, he lifted her up off the harsh ground, and, staring into her smiling face, swung her around the spinning world, challenging the indifferent laws of nature to overcome their joy.
    They arrived at the hospital twenty minutes early and sat down in the waiting room next to a freshly blooming white rose. They exchanged nervous glances with each other, and, as if they were again adolescents experiencing for the first time the crushing powers of love, their glances darted from each other's faces as soon as eye contact was made, and then slowly returned until they were forced to flee again. Her doctor had come in and out of the waiting-room a few times, but, for some reason, he had not noticed them. He remembered thinking that the doctor was probably very busy, preoccupied with the state of a less lucky patient, and that it didn't matter, because they were on top of the world, on top of their less lonely world!
    The doctor's eyes evaded their every glance as they approached his office. With a very unusual formality, he invited them in, and their nervous jokes were dismissed with a polite laugh if anything at all. But they drew strength from each other, even as he was saying there was a problem, a serious problem. They had conquered loneliness, how could any problem, no matter how serious, compare to this miraculous feat? But soon they realized that their victory had been less than complete. They must

decide, the doctor had said, between parenthood and a mother's death, because they couldn't have both. Her life would be lost, or the baby's. There was no hope of a compromise.

She had cried in his arms that night, from despair, from hopelessness, from the force of unconquerable solitude. She would die, she said, so that their child could live. There was no other choice. The child was her passage-way to happiness, and just the knowledge that she would be born was enough to ensure herself of a haven from quiet loneliness. He had argued, he had begged that she not condemn him to this frightful existence without her, this existence dominated by her death and his aloneness. But she had already given up hope, and she could no longer hide the cold reality of life from her eyes. And, as he looked into her eyes, he saw this reality too, and was overcome by it. His life would be a painful one. Neither of them had a choice. The meanings of their lives were clear: hers was to die, and his to suffer. They had realized that the world was hopeless. They had known it before the child had come into their lives, but, for a brief epoch, they had hidden this harsh truth from themselves. It had lingered under their happiness, and now it overcame both their souls to make them resigned to their bleak futures.

He thought about it all the time. It invaded his every word, conquered his dreams, dismantled his consciousness. Ever since he was sixteen years old, he had been acutely aware of death and its cold finality. He remembered running throughout his house, screaming, as he tried to run away from death. He had soon realized that he couldn't run away from it, so he controlled his panic, letting it slowly consume his happiness. By the time he was twenty, all the sprouts of hope in his life had been suffocated by the utter realization of his own mortality, and he walked his path through the world with neither hope nor despair; only a quiet resignation to helplessness. And then he had met her, and, slowly, hope had sneaked back into his life, only to be extinguished cruelly by this tragedy that had encompassed his being. He could no longer believe in God, and he had no hope of life after death. He would lie in bed for a dozen nights straight, imagining the moment when death would overtake him, and the end of his existence. And the panic that he had not felt since he had been sixteen would rush through his veins, and he wanted to find his parents so that they could tell him there was a God, that death was not the end of life, that everything would be okay. Of course, his parents were no longer an active part of his life, and there were no more illusions that he would use to protect himself from reality. He would become angry with himself for letting fear so encompass him when it was his wife who was facing the unblinking stare of her own mortality. Yet he had long since stopped trying to control his thoughts, and they flowed freely through him. He would imagine her death, and the wave of solitude that would encompass him in its wake, and then he would feel ashamed of his narcissism. He even imagined the child, although he could not imagine loving it. His love, his entire being, was dying with his wife, and all that would remain would be an emptiness that would monopolize his soul. He hated himself for thinking of his baby as an "it", for being so loveless, for feeling so much that he felt nothing. Yet it was who he was, and it had been too late to change that even when he was sixteen years old.

She too felt the panic of incumbent death. She would wake up in the night, her heart beating faster and her mind pondering the most terrifying of futures, and she would scream. She would beg him to make it stop, yet he could do nothing. He would have accepted all the human suffering in the world to relieve her of the tragic realization of her impending death, but her suffering was not given for him to take. He tried to comfort her with empty words about a Heaven he didn't believe in and a God he couldn't believe in, but she understood the world too well to fool herself with these idle hopes. She learned to govern her fear and to bottle up her panic until life became a controlled wait for the inevitable.

They shared their tragedy with no one. No one could say anything or do anything to end their infernal suffering, and the unwanted pity of those who had no idea of life's horrors or death's inevitability would be misplaced on them. This was their tragedy. They were lucky; they were not completely alone in it; they had each other. Most people face the tragedy of a foretold and inevitable death alone, leaving the solitude of death to overcome their entire beings. But he and she talked about the upcoming death, the upcoming birth, the upcoming loneliness. They cried in each other's arms, and they comforted each other as much as another person can, conquering the walls that divide a person from the world he inhabits and the separate lives of those around him. And the only reality that they knew was the reality of their love for each other.

In his chest, his heart pounded as the sea pounds the shore, approaching it slowly, while gradually building up speed, until it explodes against the rocky beach and then retreats in a flash for its next attack. Watching her broken body wasting away in the confines of an empty bed, as his mind would soon be wasting away in the confines of an empty world, a world without her, he fell into the despair that is born from the awful revelation that we all walk through life alone, and that when our paths do cross, even temporarily, it often serves only to augment this utter solitude. He saw his wife overcome by the solitude that accompanies death hand in hand like a father accompanying his daughter to her wedding, and he realized that even he could not break that hollow loneliness that marked a dying soul. The act of dying is a solitary one. The clock ticked with its hateful precision, an incessant reminder of how short man's time in life actually is. The sun penetrated deeper into the room, animating the inanimate body in the bed. Birds sang in the trees. And the silence of the room, the peace of the entire world, was broken by the screams of helplessness that overtook his mind.

* * *

She had decided not to choose her death clothes or buy the lodgings that would become her sole home for eternity. She had not wanted to concern herself with meaningless tasks such as these, tasks that would have no effect on her life and could not serve to make death more comfortable. No, for her, to live life was to think of the future; to contemplate her upcoming death and to be overcome by the enormous fear that accompanies thoughts of death; to find relief in the fact that she still felt this fear, this fear that meant that she was still alive. He understood these thoughts and subjected himself to the same horror, although his fear was so intense that it often left him shaking, draining his gray eyes of all their liveliness. Their faces carried the lost look of those who have stared death in the eyes and have been devoured by its limitlessness. They shared their panic with each other when it became too great for them to control single-handedly, and together, they looked into the eyes of eternity, alone.

Months had passed since the doctor's unforgiving sentence, and, with the death of each day, he thought of the impending future, moving closer with every subtle movement of the largest hand of the clock. He watched the clock every day, staring at it until he no longer saw it, amazed at its indifferent attitude. It was a constant memento of the reality of man's vain existence in life, a reality that he could not banish from his mind. This, and his horrifying death dreams, which had conquered even his waking hours, reminded him always that death lies on the horizon of life.

Eight months had passed, and the first ray of sunshine, which brought death to the darkness of the night even as it brought life to the dawning of a new day, was a constant reminder that the end was coming, marching indifferently towards its helpless victims. They had stopped talking about the future. They had said all that could be said. Now they could just wait without any hope of a happy ending and tortured by their knowledge of the upcoming reality. They were like the crew of a sinking ship in the middle of an empty sea. They kept busy doing meaningless tasks while they waited for that one final wave to swallow their existences in its indifferent dive. The stress of this wait for the inevitable took its toll on their appearances. The bones in her face were accentuated by the skin that tightened around them, and her paleness seemed to make the hazel-blue color of her eyes dull. Her arms seemed to hang at her side due to the lack of strength, or will, to hold them up, and her legs accomplished small miracles every day when they managed to carry her wasting body from place to place. Her stomach had grown in its size, as its sole inhabitant had conquered its vastness. With each growth of the one inside her, with each turn of its minuscule head, with each reach of its tiny fingers, she felt the awful pains of her upcoming death. Yet she loved the murderer that lived inside of her. That was the difference between him and her. He felt nothing towards the world. But he could not control his feelings, nor would he be controlled by them. He too displayed the wounds of the impossible battled they were fighting. His face had grown pale from the constant realization of man's mortality, his eyes had lost their vigor, his body had lost its strength. The beginnings of a beard, which grew due to neglect, could not hide these injuries. With the impending arrival of death and his child, he reflected constantly on what he was going to do with his wife's innocent murderer, and what he was going to do as he waited for his own vacant existence to be extinguished by cold death's appearance. He realized that, if he brought up the child, that child would be condemned to the same realization of man's lonely existence in the world that he had, the realization that had doomed his life to solitude and despair. Everything in him cried at the horror of bringing a person into the world to be condemned to suffer in this way. Yet the baby was her escape from this lonely world.

His eyes were staring at the dark ceiling as he lay next to his sleeping wife in bed. He was fighting to keep his mind empty of the painful thoughts that were waiting impatiently to dominate, again, his entire being. It was then that she screamed.

* * *

He did not even turn his head, but merely shifted his eyes to regard the agonized expression of her distorted face. He could tell from the nature of the scream that it was caused by the cold hands of death slowly grasping at the remnants of her life. The baby was coming. He pulled himself out of bed, and, unable to find anything to say, he said nothing. He put his arms around her quivering body and he held her until her screams stopped breaking the quiet of the morning. The sadness of their eyes announced the birth of utter desolation that would rule his life even as it destroyed her own.

He tightened the tie that, like a noose worn by a condemned man, hung ominously around his neck. She grabbed her clothes without thought, preoccupied by the arrival of death at the doorstep of life. And, together, they approached the battle-field where her life would be lost, his forgotten, and the baby's begun.

The doctor greeted them with an expression of utter pity and horror. He was the only other person in the world who was touched by their tragedy, and he showed his heartfelt sympathy with every nod of the head that replaced the unspoken word. His arms gently explored the confines of her body, whose sole purpose had become to bring a child into the world. If any of them had been able to remove themselves from the pain of the situation, they would have noticed the incredible nobility of a mother giving all she had for a child, a father losing all he had for his wife, a doctor trying the best he could to comfort the one dying while sustaining the ones that must live on. But the cries of the mother prevented such insight. Her cries, which introduced the birth of three new days, carried with them cries of helplessness, loneliness, and fear, while expressing the incredible pain that was taking her broken body hostage. Yet, even as she begged that death take her just so the agony of continuing life would stop, she refused to let them relieve the pain with medicines that would prevent her from seeing her child into the world. He cried as he watched his wife's tears running down her screaming face, and he begged God not to leave him alone in this world. The doctor fought back his own tears, keeping his emotions hidden so that he could bring one life through this tragedy. The whiteness of the room, amplified by the fluorescent lights, seemed to sustain the movements of its inhabitants, while the hard walls reflected the sound of her screams. Her crimson blood was the only color in the room, and her excruciating cries conquered its silence as light conquers darkness. And he, looking through the small, rectangular window in the door that separated him from her, watched the sustained suffering of his tormented wife. Then, at last, there was a chorus of cries inside this tragic room, and the doctor held up his screaming baby. But he didn't even look at the baby. He looked at his wife. He watched her as she reached out towards her child, using all her remaining strength to bring her child to her mouth, kissing gently the forehead of the one who had given her life a cause. The nurse came and took the baby away, and, once the baby had left her sight, she closed her eyes and waited for the inevitable.

* * *

The door was open just enough for one to see the small room, with its cluttered desk by the window and its lone chair at the side of the unmade bed. The light from the window accentuated the darkness of the chamber, hiding the faces of its two inhabitants. No one spoke, and all listened to the perpetual ticking of the merciless clock that hung on the wall, as it had for so many generations before, and would for so many generations after, as the sole witness of the times. The colorless room cried with the despair that can only be felt by the ones that have already lost all hope of happiness, and the anguish of those in the room struck the body like a cold wind, forcing a shiver through the heart.

He had stayed by her side throughout it all. He had not even looked at his baby, his daughter, after they had taken her away from her dying mother. He had taken his wife's hand in his own, and, as they moved her to another room, the doctor's office, so that she could die alone and with dignity, he had never taken his eyes off her calm face. He sat through the night in the small dull room with his eyes fixed on the serene figure of his lost wife, listening to the clock, despairing over the hopelessness of life. She had not regained consciousness since they had taken the baby from her arms, and she seemed to hang on to the final seconds of life with a deceptively staunch grip. He never once shifted his gaze from her closed eyes, as if he was inspired by the hope that the weight of his stare would arouse her from this final sleep. She drew a breath with every tick of the clock, and then exhaled with every tock. Tick. Tock. Tick. Tock. Tick. Tock. And then, with the chimes that marked the seventh hour of the morning, her breath stopped coming, her heart stopped ticking, and her mind escaped the prison of her empty body. His eyes never left hers until the doctor separated their visual connection with a blanket that closed the door between life and death. And it was at that moment, when his eyes no longer found hers, that he realized that he was alone.

His life was over. Happiness had never been a reality in his life. Yet the hope of finding happiness had motivated his existence; the hope that, someday, he could see the world and not be terrified by what he saw. The death of his wife, his sole haven from complete solitude, destroyed this hope as the blink of an eye destroys a dream. And now he was alone, with a young daughter who would have no hope of happiness if she was brought up by him. How could he hide his hopelessness from her when he could not even hide it from himself? He could not condemn her to live a life like his, a life overcome by the fear of death, by the loneliness of life, and by the limits of one's own consciousness. Yet he could not abandon his wife's only hope.

*　*　*

The dullness of the sky underscored the iciness of the rain against her face. The drab green of the grass clashed with the pale coldness of the surrounding tombstones, and the wind seemed to dance through this forgotten battle-field in a quiet, woeful manner. Her father was dead. His dying screams dominated her mind, and his last request, that he be allowed to die as he lived, alone, haunted her soul with relentless fury. She saw his vacant eyes before her own, and, as she looked deeper into those solemn mirrors of life's emptiness, she saw the loneliness of existence.

The stone that marked the pointless existence of her mother's life almost touched that of her tragic husband's, yet the few feet of cold earth that separated them in death were as insurmountable as the desert that separated their minds in life. Their graves exemplified the solitude that had marked their existences, and the company of mortals around them was as isolated in the world as they were in their coffins.

She was alone; alone in the cemetery and alone in the world. Death was not the cause of this aloneness, just the means of realizing it. The kindness in her father's eyes had never successfully shielded the hopelessness that dominated those gray worlds, and now there was nothing to stop that hopelessness from dominating her own gray world. There was nothing left in her soul; no love, no hope, and no reason for living.

Designated Drivers

Melanie Mallon

[1]**Absinthe** /ab-sinthe/ *noun* (1994) 1: The night she leaves her boyfriend Chisisi, Abby dyes her hair bright orange. The color is unnatural, but that's what she like about it. It's better than a real hair color. She looks like a completely different person, a criminal on the run, maybe, a master of disguise She pictures her wallet full of fake drivers' licenses with names like Sonja and Catalina printed on them, names that sound mysterious, secretive. She throws her clothes into bags as if the FBI are about to knock down the door any minute, and she imagines her narrow escape by stealing and then abandoning cars along the road to throw them off her trail.

When she walks into the kitchen and sees the crumpled balls of paper on the table, her fugitive fancy gives way to reality. She still hasn't thought of what to write in the note for him, but she knows she has to give him some explanation. *You knew too much,* she scrawls in her best jagged, maniac handwriting. Then she thinks about cutting letters out of a newspaper and pasting the words together, her criminal fantasy returning to her mind. A ransom note, yes, or something to do with the witness protection program, perhaps. But then the truth of the written words sweeps her thoughts into a funnel, picking up debris from her past, her present, her future. Tears pool in her eyes as she looks around the kitchen, her mind bombarded by the memories hidden in the toaster oven, in the egg stain on the table. She scribbles something down on the note and grabs her stuff. She has to get out. As she moves, the need to cry begins to disappear.

Abby disappears.

[2]**Absinthe** /ab-sinthe/ *verb* (1994) 1: Absinthe drives through Minneapolis, past familiar buildings, the places where throughout her twenty-four years she had eaten, lived, shoplifted, worked. But it hadn't really been her. "Absinthe" had meant something completely different then. She knows that much. Now, she's a blank page in a coloring book, an outline. She has no idea where she is going but she is certain she'll know when she gets there.

It's not until she hits Iowa that she begins to see the

cars on the side of the road.

At first they are hazy, indistinct. They disappear by the time she looks over her shoulder. She sees no color, cannot distinguish the makes of the cars, but she can tell they are undamaged, empty, as if the passengers had seen something so incredible that they abandoned their cars just to get at it. She wonders what they could have seen, who they were. Maybe the cars are there for her to find, left by some alternate Absinthe just over the horizon, hazy like the cars, waiting for definition.

Maybe she's lost a little too much sleep.

She sticks her head out of the window and lets the cool wind peel her face back. It's just a trick of the eye, she decides, created by a billboard shadow, or a lump of grass, like when you see a man crouched in the corner of the room that, with the light on, is actually a coat bunched up on the floor.

But when she looks back, she doesn't see a billboard, she doesn't see a lump of grass. Surrounding her from every angle are long flat stretches of land. She pulls her head back in and turns up the radio, tuning the dial with one long press-on fingernail.

"...so you see," a voice that sounds like burning paper fills the car, crackling, hissing. "This creature has adapted so that its color is identical to the poisonous monarch. Thus, predators are fooled and the Viceroy survives." She quickly changes the station to a radio mystery but the Viceroy continues to flutter at the edge of her mind.

Ahead of her on the road is a Ford Ranger truck. The "R" is missing from the "Ranger" and she's fascinated by this. She's fascinated in general by what something can become with a little piece missing. She follows the truck west and takes the same exit. She hasn't eaten for hours and didn't sleep the night before. *I'm gonna start seeing hamburgers hula dancing next to the cars if I don't get something to eat,* she thinks. The familiar sound of voices, the concrete feel of food in her stomach will break this strange mood, will make the cars disappear.

The truck turns down a side street but she continues into town, scanning the craft stores, the bars, and the gas station that looks as if it caters to ghosts, the broken chunks of concrete lifted by something crawling beneath the earth.

"Gawd!" she mutters, feeling creepy, wondering if she shouldn't have stayed on the highway. Even though a part of her is excited by the idea of confronting some sort of spirit, she is too tired and too hungry to fight back and live to tell about it. And without the telling, of course, the whole ordeal would be pointless.

She starts to circle the block, to head back to the highway when she sees it, like a lost relative whose face she'd forgotten until seeing it again. The marquee lights are blinking at her and she feels as if it's been waiting. She pulls into the movie theater parking lot.

[3]**Absinthe** /ab-sinthe/ *adjective* 1: Absinthe had always felt that a movie isn't complete until she gets there. In the darkness of the theater she disappears. Her mind projects itself and she is in the movie, escaping from the psychotic axe-and-blender-wielding Thelma who wants to grind her bones into human dishware. Or, she's in the Amazon, deftly saving her fellow travelers from the flying piranhas. She knows the part of the story they don't show on the screen. The part when she returns home after surviving a plane crash in the Himalayas and is looked upon with both awe and envy as she tells friends about how she had to stitch her hand back on with dental floss, how she ran from the rest of the survivors when they started asking her how much she weighed, moving closer to her with their thin bodies like the sticks they would burn to cook her on. Everyone would understand when she broke into hysterical fits, throwing things and screaming. *After everything she's been through,* they'd say, *It's a wonder she can keep herself together at all.*

Now, she walks into the theater just as the earthquake is beginning. People in business suits are screaming and ducking under tables. They're trapped under this forty story building with no food and the only water from the toilet that's been thrown through the wall. She sits in the third row, jumbo popcorn between her thighs, and scans the theater. The familiar sight of shadowy seats is comforting to her. She could be anywhere, in any theater in the world. She stares at a woman sitting across the aisle, watches the movie flickering across her face, multicolored lights painting life and movement on her pudding-like skin. The woman notices her staring and retreats to the back of the theater. Absinthe laughs and turns back to the movie.

She thinks about what Chisisi would do if he found out she'd died in an earthquake. The pink line above his lip would quiver and his skin would change from brown to a sort of greenish color like it had when he'd found out his father had been shot in the back of the head while driving his cab. Abby liked to believe it was coincidence that she had fallen in love with him after this, but there was a part of her that knew she was drawn to the tragedy, was secretly depressed when Chisisi began to put it behind him and move on. When discussing the accident with others, her voice was almost boastful.

"His dad was robbed," she'd say, closing her eyes as if holding back tears, "and shot point blank." But she might as well have been saying, "Your problems are nothing compared to this, you can't imagine the pain."

And when friends, coworkers, asked her what was wrong when they saw her face wrench into an expression of torment, she would simply shake her head and whisper, "It's Chis, his father," and then she'd let her eyes go blank as if she was lost in hopelessness, unable to keep up the strength it would take to stop Chisisi from leaping off the roof, to get him out of this listless funk he'd been in. Sometimes she became so absorbed that tears trickled lines into her blush and her hands shook. It was on an occasion such as this, about two years after his father died, that Chisisi came strolling into the Embers kitchen where she was surrounded by cooing co-workers. She had just been telling them that he hadn't left his room for a month and that he refused to say anything but the word "orange," like in that movie "The Last Days of Laura O." When he'd walked towards her, he ignored the horrified expression and wrapped her in his arms.

"We are going out tonight, mm-hmm." He bobbed his head as he spoke, smiling with one side of his mouth. "I got the job. You can stop all that worrying you been doing, 'cause I am now an official representative of Delta airlines." He stretched his arms out and bowed, first to the cooks and then to the servers. He began playing with the salad bar, making the carrot sticks dance and sing in different accents, running them up and down her arm that hung limp as she avoided the eyes of her co-workers. This was obviously not a man about to dive off a building. No one said a word to Abby about it but their attitudes changed toward her. When she spoke, they raised their eyebrows, pursed their lips. They refused to help her when her section was full, leaving her to spill coffee and let eggs slide off her tray into customers' laps. She was familiar with all of their reactions. She came to expect them, in fact, in some form or another. No one ever confronted her directly. It was if they were afraid of what she would do.

On the day that she quit, she'd managed to serve three orders to the floor, shatter a bottle of ketchup all over and inside the ice machine, and leave four orders in the window until the cooks themselves brought them out to the customers. As a man yelled at her to *get me a new burger, not this cold ass piece of flesh reheated*, she burst into tears in the middle of the dining room. Servers continued to swarm around her with trays in hand, as if she was just a decorative fountain. Finally, a customer from someone else's section got up to ask her if she was okay.

"Oh," she said, "It's just the tumor. I get a little crazy sometimes, you know?"

She walked into the kitchen, her hands trembling as if they contained earthquakes. She felt her body rupture and dismember itself, sending fingers flying into the creamy Italian, legs soaring along a fluorescent light runway.

The kitchen was filled with the smell of onion and the voice of a cook singing "The Hustle." A spatula scraped against the grill and plates clanked onto the metal counter of the cook's window.

"This one's Abby's" the singing cook said, and the other answered, "If that's her real name." And they both laughed while Abby slipped quietly out of the kitchen and out of the restaurant forever.

The theater lights come on and Absinthe is jolted back into reality. She is suddenly aware of the tiny size of the theater, the torn and unraveling condition of the seats, the veiny, potato-white color of her legs. For a moment, she thinks she can smell onion but then realizes the smell is vomit. She is instantly ashamed of the morning sickness she faked yesterday morning. Now, she really does feel sick. She feels like there are a million teeth inside of her, chomping on bits of aluminum. Her eyes close tightly, her hands grip the armrests.

"Excuse me? You all right?"

She dumps the tub of popcorn on the floor. An usher, a stocky teenager with the number 6 shaved into the side of his head, is standing next to her, his eyes moving from her, to the popcorn, and back to her.

"Um, my boyfriend--" she stops, unsure whether to tell the kid the truth or just make up something and get out of there. "My boyfriend saw the neighbor kill his wife through his apartment window and, you gotta promise not to say nothing, now, and I just--"

"*Rear Window*, 1954," the boy sneers the way only a

teenager can sneer. "What? You think I don't watch movies? You're no Grace Kelly, babe."

Absinthe feels her skin heat up and she looks down at her hands. She's slightly embarrassed until she realizes how ridiculous this is. She doesn't know this kid. He's a complete stranger. She could just walk on out of there and never see him again.

And she does.

As she drives, a plan develops in her mind, a purpose. There are millions of movie theaters in this country just as there are millions of strangers, people who don't know anything about her. When she starts seeing the cars again, she feels exalted, certain that they will lead her to the place she should have been all along, the place where the other Absinthe is waiting for her, with stories to tell.

See also: *Alive, Tremors, Airport 77, Friday the Thirteenth, Rosemary's Baby*

[4]**Absinthe**/ab-sinthe/ *noun* (1979) 2 *archaic*: Abby doesn't remember the first lie she ever told. So many of them have blended in with reality, have become mere stretches on an actual central truth. Sure, she had once sung on television in fourth grade, but it wasn't a national tour, it wasn't with Frank Sinatra, she wasn't featured on the cover of *Life* as the next Shirley Temple. Actually, she had gulped a Shirley Temple while waiting in the wings of a telethon with the rest of her church choir. Actually, it was Bob from Sesame Street who sang with them while Abby stared frozen at the lights, too stunned to sing, too stunned to make any sound until the song was replaced with silence and the Shirley Temple rose from her stomach and out of her lips into a resounding belch. The rest of the choir had been so furious with her for embarrassing them on national television (*syn*: cable access) that they'd voted to kick her out, to drive her out with the only power kids have: cruelty. The vote changed, of course, when Absinthe let them know about her terminal stomach condition. No one seemed to remember or notice when she didn't die.

[5]**Absinthe** /ab-sinthe/ *synonym* (1994) 1: The day Absinthe quit Ember's, she had a feeling that she would never be the same person again. She wasn't even sure of who she had been, her real self was so tangled up with who she wanted to be, left behind her now, discarded along with her apron in the Ember's parking lot. When she got home,

Chisisi was lying on the couch, half asleep. He sat up when he saw her, still wrapped in the blanket like an infant.

"God, Ab. What's wrong?" He asked her, his eyes examining the food collage on her apron.

"I just--" her throat caught. "I had a real screwed up day, Chis."

Chisisi stood up and walked towards her, letting the blanket fall to the floor, his body naked. Abby didn't notice. She was staring past him as he folded his arms and sucked in his breath, and she didn't notice his fingernails digging into his arms as if attempting to gouge out and release something that lay just below the surface of his skin.

"What happened?" He asked her, and she felt the edge in his voice.

"I, well, I don't know, Chis, nothing, I guess."

He stepped back from her, his eyes the color and expression of raw meat. "Nothing, huh? Fuck, Ab." He turned away from her and sat on the couch. "I'm not in the mood for your shit." He picked up the remote and began flipping through channels, stopping on the movie *Body Snatchers*.

"You're never in the mood for my shit!" Absinthe yelled and walked into the bedroom. She began to throwing pillows at the dresser, knocking off action figures and long, plastic necklaces. *Bastard!* She thought. *He'd rather hear a lie.*

"You never listen!" She screamed and grabbed the picture of her that hung on the wall near Chisisi's side of the bed. She threw it to the floor, shattering the glass, liking the loud clinking, the fragments getting caught in her hair. Chisisi walked in just as she was tearing her picture into severed arms, legs, head.

"What are you doing?" He grabbed what was left of the picture and her hands hung limp, lifeless.

She didn't answer him, but stared down at a dirty sock that lay at her feet. She could smell his sweat and the faint odor of cat urine from the people who had lived in the apartment before them. Who are you? She wanted to ask him. A *Twilight Zone* episode flashed across her mind in which a woman ends up in a parallel universe where everything is familiar but not quite right. For a brief moment, she entertained the fantasy that she was dead, empty, waiting for a new body to be born, waiting for a new name.

"I'm pregnant," she whispered, feeling a surge go

through her as her lips created the words, feeling the lie take shape, solidify.

Chisisi let a gush of air escape from his lips. "Whoa. When did you find out?"

"Today, stupid."

"And this is what you're crazy over? What? You afraid the kid will look like me?" He crossed his eyes, and stretched his lips into a lizard face, darting his tongue in and out of his mouth.

"No," she smiled at him, "I'm afraid it's gonna look like one of the cooks."

"Bitch! You been messing around when you got a body like this to call your own?" Chisisi stood up and began posing his naked body, rotating his thin hips like a hula dancer and moving his splayed fingers across eyes that held an exaggerated look of allure.

"I've been messing around *because* I got a body like that to call my own." She lifted his penis on one finger and let it flop, her eyebrow raised.

Chisisi picked her up, threw her back down on the bed and ran out of the room. They chased each other through the apartment, pretending to fight. They ended up on the couch, Absinthe straddling his waist with her legs, pretending to hold a knife, screeching "eee!-eee!-eee!" with every thrust of her hand.

Chisisi grabbed her wrist. "Hey, I think we're forgetting someone."

"Chis, if I've told you once, I've told you a thousand times, there is not a little man living in the toaster oven."

Chisisi began talking to Absinthe's stomach. "Don't listen to her, baby, she's been eating Ember's food, she's mad, I tell you, MAD! Boowahahahaha!" He looked up at Absinthe but she wasn't laughing. "What?"

"I lost my job, today. I-I sort of walked out."

He froze and for the first time Absinthe thought she could see his mind working, running its fingers along his options, selecting the easiest reaction, the lightest, the reaction most likely to keep her from freaking out.

"That's okay," he said. "We'll find it." Then he went back to talking to her stomach. "See? Mama's always losing things. First her keys, then her mind, and now her dream job. You better not let them cut that cord, kid or she'll be..."

His words faded from her mind into a low background noise. She was imagining the clothes she would buy for the baby, sleepers and overalls, and those tiny hooded sweatshirts, all in bright colors. Colors that reach out and suck you in. Colors that aren't found in nature.

⁶**Absinthe** /ab-sinthe/ *verb* (1994) 2: At night, the drive feels magical, like time travel. She's moving west, backwards in time, the future behind her, approaching in the unrisen sun. Chisisi, Embers, Minneapolis are all part of a hazy future, an elaborate prophecy that, once known, can be avoided. She wonders if this is how people feel when they've survived some horrible threat to their lives, as if they've been shown the person they were supposed to be all along, like finding out you were switched at birth and you are really the child of a soup label designer from Armenia.

As she makes her way across Nebraska, Abby stops to test drive her lies on strangers, to see how they stand up against sudden sharp turns, bumpy terrain. She chooses people with plain faces, unsuspecting faces, faces like the open road.

"He's been following me for miles," she tells a waitress in the Truck Stops Here Cafe. "He thinks I have the secret ingredients to a biological warfare gas."

She thinks the waitress is buying it until she sees her reacting in the same manner to another customer who is telling her that his hash browns are singing Spanish lullabies.

"Omigod, there he is!" Absinthe grabs her toast and runs out of the restaurant, using her lie as a way to evade her bill. It's three in the morning and no one in the restaurant cares enough to chase her down.

In Shelton, she tells a farmer that her husband was killed on their wedding day.

"It was the freakiest accident!" She says, unable to take her eyes off the farmer's left hand. There are two fingers missing. "We're at the altar and this overhead fan comes crashing down on him. Instant death. I ran and I've been running ever since."

But the farmer says nothing. He just taps his fingers across his knee, the stumps tapping as well, and stares at her through squinting eyes.

In Broadwater, she manages to get thirty dollars out of the drugstore register while the clerk is getting her candy bars to keep her from slipping into a diabetic coma. This tactic fails, however, at a 76 station in Scottsbluff. She barely escapes getting taken to the police station by telling the attendant, a pale teenager in coveralls three sizes too big for him, that she is from the corporate office and that she's just testing him. She laughs out loud once she gets into the car, wondering at the things people will believe. To the lawn man in North Platte, she's a mail-order bride. In the Fried Peacock Bar in Odessa, some know her as half of a trapeze duo, specializing in making peanut butter and banana sandwiches in mid-air. But there is always something unexpected, something not quite right about the people, the places. In every face she's lied to, she's searched for signs of herself, for the right reactions, for something to indicate that she's found the right place to stay, the place where she can stop seeing the ugly veins in people's faces, stop smelling their lunch on their breath, stop feeling the pure reality of them clinging to her once she's back in the car like the gray filmy cocoon of the Viceroy that keeps slipping into her thoughts and beating up against her brain, a meaningless cadence.

When she gets tired, she pulls her long, beige car over to the side of the road and sleeps with her feet sticking out the window, staring at the colorful stars she had glued to her toenails like a miniature Hollywood Boulevard, making the real stars, boring black and white, fade into a blur in the background. She dreams of babies: purple ones, green ones, orange ones, coming out of her mouth with pieces of her body in their chubby fingers. Her liver, her ribs, her heart, until there's nothing left of her but the lips that gave them life.

[7]**Absinthe** /ab-sinthe/ *noun* (1983) <an ~ of explanation>

usage Absinthe doesn't remember when the lies she told started to become more true to her than the reality surrounding her. It was sometime after her moods took on a life of their own, forcing tears from her eyes for no reason, tears like black and white film, filtering the world into shades of gray, shadows that crept around, laughing at her until she gave them names, gave them color, made them into people with tragic lives, made the tragic lives her own. *This lying must have started when your mother left,* the school councelor told her, her friends told her, her father told her. *You feel rejected, unloved.* So Absinthe embellished the memory of her mother, conjured tears when she pictured her shadow in front of the TV, picking her up and carrying her to bed, when she imagined her mother's smell of vanilla mixed with grease from the appliance factory where she'd worked. She tried to feel what she was supposed to feel by staring for hours at the oil slick her mother's car had left in the garage. *The only evidence that she was ever here,* she told her father, her friends, liking the dramatic impact of the words, the tears welling up in her eyes in response to the pity she saw in others.

But these words were false. Her mother sent evidence twice a year, on Christmas and her birthday, in brown paper packages with the same Montana return address. Absinthe kept the birthday cards handy for when friends came over, friends with abusive parents, siblings with drug problems, fathers in jail. To combat the envy she felt of these people who she thought had real reasons to be upset, she would bring out the card and stare at the "Happy Birthday, Love Mom" as if it meant something more to her than the cards that read, "Happy Birthday From Park Green Dental." She wished she had her mother's good-bye note, she even tried to fake one once, but was caught when she spelled her mother's name wrong.

[8]**Absinthe** /ab-sinthe/ *verb* (1994) 3: Halfway between Evansville and Powder River, Wyoming, the cars begin to solidify. They are colorful now, and every detail is distinct: the rust along the floorboards, the dents in the fenders, the hats and books in the back windows. She hopes this is a sign that she's getting closer because she just spent the last of her money on gas and she's beginning to wonder if she'll ever find the right lie, the right reaction, the right place to stop for good.

She passes a red station wagon, its nose down in a ditch as if trying to drive to the center of the earth. She whips the car onto the shoulder and stumbles out in her haste to catch the car before it--

disappears. It's gone. She sinks to her knees into the ditch grass and sits on her heels, her eyes searching for tire marks, broken glass, a spot of oil--some sort of evidence that the car had ever been there. The wind is blowing fiercely and her hair is an orange storm cloud, billowing around her head.

"Chisisi was right," she mutters, "I am a psycho."

A cattle truck passes her on the road, she can smell the pungent odor of it, the snarl of its motor draws her eyes up. It is then that she sees the headstones on the top of the hill across the highway. She gets back into her car and pulls into the long drive that leads up to the graveyard, stopping when she sees a trailer with a hand painted sign above the door: Mendell Stone Shop and Cemetery.

Absinthe gets out of the car and leans against the door. A woman comes out of the trailer and calls, "Can I help you?"

Absinthe watches her approach, a feeling of excitement beginning to grow within her. The solid cars, the graveyard--they all lead to this place.

"Yeah I--" Abby starts but the words won't come. Her mind is in park, revving but going nowhere.

"Are you okay?" The woman peers into Abby's face which looks as if it's about to slide off her head and collapse to the ground in a heap.

"I just need to eat something. I'll pay you." That's as big of a lie as Abby can muster. She puts her hand in her pocket and runs the movie stubs and pennies through her fingers.

"Don't be silly. I was about to eat some lunch. Come on up." As she speaks, the woman's head lowers so that she is looking at Abby from under her eyebrows. Her voice sounds scratchy. Abby suddenly wonders what sort of woman would sell graves for a living. She watches her walk up to the trailer but doesn't move.

The woman opens the screen door and turns back to her. "Chicken fingers all right?"

Abby's stomach clenches. She nods and follows her into the house, hands in her pockets.

"I'm Eileen, by the way," the woman introduces herself as she spreads frozen chicken strips on a cookie sheet.

Abby sits at the kitchen table in the only chair, sipping coffee and watching Eileen's hair swish back and forth as she moves. "Eileen, huh? That means 'light', you know."

"I bet you believe every word of your horoscope," Eileen replies.

Abby recognizes the tone. In her mind she hears Chisisi's voice. *You reading that crap again?* She sees him running his hand across his shaven head, smoothing down the hair he doesn't have, talking about the things he never said. She rests her head on the table and gives in to the memories that have been dancing out of the corner of her eye, waving their arms and trying to get her attention.

"Of course not," she lies. She used to read both hers

and Chisisi's horoscope every morning when he came home from working the graveyard shift at the airport. Or, if not turned to the horoscope section, the newspaper would be folded so that it covered everything but the first vertical column of letters down the page. On late night TV, she had watched a movie in which a hostage, forced to write a ransom note, had written their location vertically, using the first letters of the paragraph. She was sitting at the table, scanning down the column, hoping to find some sort of message there when Chisisi walked in, speaking to her as if they had been having a conversation for hours.

"This guy comes up, right? And he's got on this cheap ass yellow shirt and a pink tie," Chisisi wrinkled his nose and sat across the table from Absinthe. "And he asks for smoking, see, which we ain't got."

"The nerve." Abby saw the word "blood" in the column. She let go of the page.

"So I tell him," He deepens his voice. "*Sir, I'm afraid we are a non-smoking airline.*"

Abby lit a cigarette, leaned back and squinted at him.

"And this fucking guy starts pulling an attitude with me--hey! put that out, you know you can't be doing that shit--this guy lifts his little weasel nose and says--"

"One cigarette won't do any harm, Chis."

"'*What are they gonna do if I smoke? Kick me out?*' And then he laughs like he's not the hundredth person to say that to me." He reached across and tried unsuccessfully to grab the cigarette out of her hand. "Come on, what are you doing? You're gonna hurt the baby."

Abby took one last drag, put it out and looked down again at the paper. "So what did you say?"

"Huh? Oh, the guy, I told him that if I was on the plane, I'd put the cigarette out in that ugly ass tie."

"You did not!"

"No. I just gave him a seat next to one of those Amway guys," Chisisi chuckled. "He'll be wanting a smoke so bad."

"Whoa, listen to this," Abby tapped a finger on his horoscope. "It says 'you will be spending a lot of time with a stranger. Be careful of the words you choose.' A stranger, eh? Who is she? Huh?"

Chisisi didn't answer her. He was looking at the book that lay on the table. Absinthe reached across and grabbed it. "Check this out. I was thinking up names for the baby and this book's got all these--Here!" She held the book open. "If we name her Mabel, she'll be beautiful and happy."

Chisisi stood up and began to scratch, looking up at the ceiling. "We need to paint over those nasty blotches of-- what is that shit?"

"Irving means beautiful, too."

Chisisi made a face and lowered his arms. "Irving? Mabel? Girl, you are so white."

Abby lit up another cigarette and blew the smoke in his face as he walked past her. "You got a better idea? Come on, let's have it."

"Roast beef."

"What? You wanna name our kid Roast Beef?" Abby twisted her head around to see him searching the refrigerator. "There's some tuna helper stuff in there from yesterday."

"I'd rather eat my own stomach."

Abby laughed and grabbed at his stomach but he slid out of her reach and folded himself into a chair across from her.

"Don't be bitching to me," she said. "You're the one who keeps making it."

They sat in silence for awhile, Abby reading her book, Chisisi rubbing the back of his neck.

"Actually," Chisisi spoke, looking up at the ceiling. "if it's a boy, I'd like to name him Taye, after my grandfather. You know..."

Abby didn't know. This was the first time she'd ever heard of a grandfather named Taye. The name didn't sound real. It occurred to her that there was a lot she didn't know about him. He was sitting across the table, slouched in his chair so that the shoulders of his green blazer went up past his ears. His chin nestled into the collar of his shirt and his teeth nibbled lightly at the top button. He had that look on his face that had drawn her to him in the first place. It was as if he was about to tell her something so incredible that she would be rooted forever in her chair just thinking about it. This look was always followed by a laugh, tumbling from his lips, resonant and jarring like the sound of a heavy bureau falling down stairs. In the past, she had laughed with him but now she glared, watching his face behind the wavering smoke from the ashtray.

"So, what does 'Absinthe' mean?" He asked her, leaning across the table and spreading his hands flat.

"You know damn well what it means. Liqueur. It

means my mother was too much of a drunk to bother naming me Barbie." She wanted to suck the words right back into her mouth but it was too late. He was looking at her from under his brows and the look told her he knew that her mother wasn't a drunk. No, and her father didn't beat her, a tornado never destroyed their home, and she was never kidnapped by three cult members who made her eat entire tubs of mustard while singing "Yellow Submarine." He had heard them all from her and, in the past, the lies that failed were added to their repertoire of inside jokes, their secret language, the language Absinthe used to gauge how close they were. But there were no words in that language for anything remotely serious, no words for pain. Not real pain anyway. She looked at him now and wondered if he knew as much about her as she didn't know about him.

"What does your name mean?" She asked him, tapping the name book on the table, trying to draw his attention away from what she'd just said.

Still leaning onto the table, he lifted his head and smiled at her.

"It's a secret," he said.

She threw the book at his head.

⁹**Absinthe** /ab-sinthe/ *indefinite pronoun* (1994) 1: "Abby?" Eileen is wiggling her fingers in front of Abby's face. "Honey, you've got the attention span of a rotating fan."

"You say something?" Abby asks, still thinking about Chisisi, about the baby. Now, she wonders fleetingly if she had really wanted a baby or if she'd just wanted something to name.

"I was asking where you were headed."

Abby says the first state that pops into her head. "California."

Eileen groans and turns back to the oven. "You've got to be kidding. What is this obsession people have with Califonia? I suppose you're going to be a movie star, huh?"

Abby slams her mug on the table, spilling lukewarm coffee on her hand. "If you really must know, I'm going to the place where my boyfriend died." The coffee begins trickling down her arm. Abby imagines it's blood.

Eileen turns and leans against the counter, her face as blank as rice, her cold gravy hair dripping down the sides. "When did he die?"

Abby focuses her attention on the hallway that

stretches beyond the kitchen. On the walls hang two certificates that look like degrees, but she can't quite make them out. Probably awards for high speed grave digging, she laughs to herself. At the end of the hall is a bathroom with the door partially closed. She can see the sink and a little bit of the toilet.

"About five years ago," she finally answers. "Remember that earthquake in San Francisco? He was there for a convention and the building collapsed, trapping him."

Eileen's face is the color and expression of a corpse. Abby bites off a large piece of skin from her lip. She's determined to provoke a reaction.

"They say he was alive for weeks with about ten other people. The rest of the bodies were found crushed and some..." Abby pauses and leans toward Eileen. "Some were found half-eaten."

Eileen picks at a fingernail and Abby feels a twinge of victory when she sees Eileen's brow cave in. Neither one of them speaks until Eileen raises her head and looks Abby directly in the eye.

"That's odd," she says. "They were trapped for how long?"

"Damn!" Abby displays her sleeve for Eileen to see. "I'm so shook up, I spilled on myself." Then she gets up and grabs a dishcloth from the kitchen sink, avoiding Eileen's drilling eyes. She scrubs her sleeve with quick strokes and stares down at a Raggedy Ann plate and matching mug on the counter next to the sink. They are coated with a layer of dust. Now that she thinks about it, the entire kitchen appears to be covered with a layer of dust, as if no one has lived there for years. On the wall to her right hangs a calendar from 1978. She looks out the window at the cemetery. God, she thinks, all those names.

"Can I look at your cemetery?" She turns to Eileen who just nods and stares after her as she goes out the door.

The plot holds twenty to thirty graves. Abby pauses in front of each one, reading the name aloud and trying to remember what they mean. Each headstone is a different shape and color; some have smooth, simple surfaces and edges like grey teeth while others are intricately carved into designs of flowers, angels, faces or pictureless designs that swirl and dip like tendrils of hair.

She hears Eileen's swishing through the grass behind her. Without turning, she asks if she did all the carving.

"Yes," Eileen answers, "A long time ago."

"They're really beautiful." Abby crouches down before one and reads the inscription. *Vivian Mendell 1976-1977.*

"Wow. What happened to this little girl?"

"That's my niece. She died with my brother in a car accident."

Abby searches Eileen's face for some sort of sorrow, some sort of feeling but she finds none and this frightens her.

"I'm sor--" Abby begins but Eileen cuts her off.

"Don't be. It was a long time ago."

Abby doesn't know what to say to this. How can this woman just brush it away like that, like these people existed only to be a part of her life? As if there's nothing missing from her now that they're gone. She studies Eileen's face. She knows it. It occurs to her that she used to wait on Eileens at Ember's, serving them herbal tea with nothing in it, and a dry English muffin. They'd sit in a corner, reading or staring off with empty crater eyes. And they were always alone. Always.

"I think the fingers are burning." Eileen starts back towards the trailer, throwing a smile over her shoulder. Abby pauses for a moment, trying to reconcile the smile with the flat voice that accompanies it. Then, she shrugs, thinking it's about time she stopped reading so much into things. Look where it got me so far, she thinks. A fucking graveyard in the middle of nowhere.

While Abby eats, she pages through a book lying on the table, *The Stranger*, by some Camus person. When she reaches the place where Eileen had bent a page down, the paper triangle comes off in her hand, brittle.

Abby looks up at Eileen, who is sitting on the kitchen counter. "Do you wonder why? Ever?"

Eileen keeps chewing.

"I mean, about the accident. Vivian, your brother and all that."

"I once believed, was absolutely positive, that there was a fault in the brake line. I called the factory every day, sent threatening letters--a bomb threat." She closes her eyes tightly, as if not seeing the memory will make it go away. "God, I can't believe I ever did that!"

Abby starts laughing. A bomb. What a great idea. "What happened?"

"I moved back here, took a good look at the car..." She drifts off again.

"You know a lot about cars?"

"No. Not really. I wasn't thinking straight. Everything was so sudden. I had all kinds of explanations, you know. I thought, maybe they were being saved from something really awful that would have happened to them later. I thought I could see signs of their ghosts all over the house. Voices coming from the blender, faces in the--"

"I used to see faces in my bedroom door."

"Yeah, I know what you mean. In the grain." Eileen nods. "I saw my brother on TV, once. In some sitcom, tripping over a plant."

Abby never met anyone quite like Eileen. She has a sudden urge to tell her everything, to let it all go. The truth. She thinks of the Viceroy and wonders if the eerie feeling Eileen gave her earlier was just a disguise. If maybe she was meant to hear the radio program, maybe it was all part of the clue, like the cars, like finding the word "blood" in the newspaper.

"Nobody said anything?" she asks her.

"Nobody really around to say anything. I was never very popular around here because--" she stops.

"Why?" Abby asks.

"I'm that *creepy graveyard lady*."

Abby studies the woman's deadpan face. She wonders if Eileen is lying about the reason people don't like her. "So, do you still see things?" she asks.

"No. I spent all that time trying to find some meaning to their death, not wanting to believe that they were completely gone. Dead."

"And?"

"They were. They are."

"Well, yeah, but there has to be--" Abby begins.

"No. There doesn't have to be anything. I mean, it would be so easy, wouldn't it? If everything had a nice, neat explanation?" Eileen's voice is so forceful, so bitter, her words seem to become solid outside of her mouth before falling to the floor with a heavy thud. "Hell, we can give the world all the meaning we want but it's just what we want to give it. They're gone. That's all that's real."

Abby suddenly realizes she's made a horrible mistake. She should never have stopped here. *Dead.* She should never have let herself like this woman. *That's all that's real.* She stares at the huge birthmark on Eileen's elbow and wonders why she didn't notice it before. Her thoughts seem to be coming from the heads of everyone in the world, all at once, expanding through her body, until she feels like she is completely composed of everyone else's words, the living and the dead. She doesn't recognize her own voice when she tells Eileen she has to go. She doesn't feel her body shaking, as if all the voices are singing vibrato. She doesn't stop moving until she grabs the door handle of her car.

"Wait!" Eileen weaves through the headstones towards her. "I'm not the creepy graveyard lady! Really. I'm not." She's laughing.

Abby stares at this woman who let the people she loved just die, who shed them and left them forgotten. Meaningless. She was wrong about the butterfly. Eileen is poisonous.

"No." Abby says, staring at Vivian's headstone. "You're just dead."

Eileen stops, her face expressionless except for the thin white line of her lips pressed together. Abby wraps her arms around herself and the two women stare at each other, as if waiting for the headstone teeth to swallow them whole.

[10]**Absinthe** /ab-sinthe/ *conjunction* 1: In the car, Absinthe cries, her tears knocking loose a false eyelash like a person knocked off their roof during a flood. She tries to light a cigarette but drops it between the seats. There's no space between the cars now, they're all lined up along the road, bumper to bumper, like a funeral procession on pause. She begins to wonder if Eileen had ever existed.

Her mind spins around and she sees Chisisi in a waitress uniform at The Truck Stops Here Cafe, she sees Eileen spitting tobacco and waving her finger stumps in the air. She sees her baby driving a Ford Ranger, the steering wheel in her mouth like a giant teething ring. She scratches her arm, drawing blood. Real blood. The pain is all that's real. A press-on splinters and hangs off her finger, both nails, real and fake, are side by side. Both are somehow incomplete.

"Fuck! Fuck! Fuck!" Abby pounds the dashboard, thinking about the baby. Everything had been working out so well, until Chisisi walked in on her in the bathroom. He had accused her of using him.

"How can you say that? I love you," she told him.

"Why?" he'd asked, leaning against the bathroom wall.

She had stared past him and at him simultaneously, trying unsuccessfully to blur his face with the white tile behind him.

"Why, Abby? Huh? Cause I make you laugh? Is that

it? Hmm?" His words felt like abrupt, forceful pushes. She backed up, placing the toilet between them.

"Or," he continued, his hand raised as if about to karate chop the sink. "Or is it because I make you cry?"

"You are funny, Chis. I do love your sense of humor, and I--" She stopped as she saw him look up at the ceiling, shaking his head.

"I'm so thrilled that you find me entertaining, Absinthe." He spoke to the ceiling until he said her name. Then, he looked directly at her and she felt more exposed than when he'd first gaped at the tampon in her hand. In her mind appeared the vertical letters of the newspaper.

"I don't get it," she looked away from his gaze and down at her fingers. "What does this have to do with the baby?" she asked her fingers and then the word "baby" ht her with an idea. "Look, Chis, I was pregnant. I miscarried and I was scared to tell--"

"You're psycho." Chisisi told her and she looked at his calm face, not quite understanding the words. He continued, "You just chop little pieces off of people, like nobody's gonna miss them and you replace them with these--"

"What are you talking about? I miscarried, I--"

"--Fake fingers, fake arms, until this person is someone completely different, until their lives are yours, are what you want them to be. You think everybody's fooled because you are, you think--"

"I *was* pregnant! The baby's gone! You don't care!" Abby was screaming now, not so much to be heard as to not hear. Chisisi continued as if she were invisible. The words came out of his mouth as if he'd said them a hundred times before.

"--your phony parts look like the real thing." He paused and took a few steps towards her, his hands shaking at his sides. "You're psycho 'cause that baby is real. That baby's as real to you as I am." He turned and walked out of the bedroom.

Abby stared at the toilet and then at the sink. Curly black hairs stuck to the porcelain, dried toothpaste streaked the rim. Her eyes traveled up the mirror without looking into it and she stared at the fluorescent light, she stared at the black dirt and what looked like bugs underneath the plastic casing of the light. It all looked so real, so real and so ugly to her.

[11]**Absinthe** /ab-sinthe/ *noun plural* (1994) 1: The cars

begin to appear again only this time she is starting to see people in them. She gives names to each face, the names from the headstones, from the carved headstones that had flowers and dead grass leading up to them. Lucy, Eliot, Andrew, Gladys. All except Vivian. She never sees Vivian.

In Shoshoni, she starts to head north, towards Montana. But then she sees the first empty car she's seen since she'd been at Eileen's and it occurs to her suddenly, unexpectedly like a hurricane in downtown Minneapolis: Eileen was lying. She was lying and she didn't even realize it. She believed every word she said. Absinthe pulls over quickly and walks towards the car, refusing to move her eyes, refusing to give it a chance to slip away. She opens the car door and finds the keys in the ignition. She fires up the engine and heads down the highway.

Weeks, months, or maybe only hours, minutes later, she is waitressing in a truck stop, serving and speaking to an endless array of strangers. She listens to them intently, her eyelids spread wide open, her pinkie, maybe, in the corner of her mouth as each word enters her. When a new person arrives, she adds her own words, her own body to the stories that come out of her lips, crying, kicking, and screaming in pain, nestling in memories, perhaps retold somewhere halfway across the world. Perhaps altered, embellished, completely changed. It doesn't matter. They are still alive.

Absinthe leans over the counter, talking to a man in a leather vest. Her movements are graceful, controlled, even powerful. She gazes at her reflection in a cup of coffee, watching her own reactions with watery eyes as she tells him about the car crash. About Vivian.

The Guest Conductor

Roger Sheffer

You all look terrible. No wonder you can't sing. If you looked right, you would sound right. Really. Looking right is ninety percent of the battle.

From the way you look, I would guess that you people spend most of your time in a cave, stooped over, afraid you'll bump your heads. I have a cure for that. Watch and listen. First, I want you to pretend that you are outside on a beautiful day, picking fruit. You must *stand* first! That's good. Now rise up on your toes and stretch your arms as high as possible. Don't just settle for the fruit on the lower branches. Some of you are not reaching any higher than the shoulders. And that is cheating. The person who owns this orchard trusts you to pick even the highest fruit. The highest fruit is the best fruit.

Stretch! Higher! All right, that looks a little better, although I think you will lose your height before concert. I think you are all basically lazy people.

I want to tell you about my childhood, just a brief story, and then we'll do some singing. In late summer, I picked apples to earn money, but I was a lazy boy, and I took some of the apples that had fallen off the tree and were lying on the ground. I placed them in the box and finished off the top layer with fruit that I had picked from the tree. I was fired from that job. But even if I had not been fired, and even if they had not inspected my work, I would have felt terrible about my actions. Those apples that had fallen on the ground were bruised, worm-eaten. In fact, they were good for nothing but applesauce and cider. I should have followed orders. But I was a lowly creature, scuttling along the ground, satisfied with mediocrity, or worse. I should have been an angel, hovering about the highest branches. And so, you cannot sing beautifully unless you assume the posture of an angel reaching for the highest branches of the apple tree. You were born to sing like angels, but life has caused you to abuse your bodies, live in caves, and crawl about like vermin, which accounts for your terrible posture. Stretch again!

The upward motion along the vertical axis is what separates humans from animals. It is what represents the basic direction of man's being, for everything that strives upward, according to Herder, belongs to the unique nature of man (in contrast to the earth-directed posture of animals). Unlike the animals, we are oriented on a vertical line towards heaven. That we even *have* bodies is a mere inconvenience, a vestige of our evolutionary history. That we are subject to *gravity* is only a temporary burden--as I myself know from long personal experience--and when we sing, ladies and gentlemen, we should imagine that we have gone beyond our present state, that we have unlocked our voices from their dark cages and that they are free now. Raise your arms! Pretend that I am about to shoot you! Your money or your life! Ha, ha!

All of you must really believe what I am saying in order to sing well. You smile. You think I am amusing. You are thinking, "He will only be with us a little while. Two hours."

I have friends whose bodies have withered almost to nothing, but they sing beautifully, because their technique is so perfect. I know people who have sung even after their bodies have died. I once attended a funeral in London where a singing voice came out of the coffin.

Please stop talking for a minute. It hurts for me to shout over the noise. You sound like insects buzzing, a swarm of nasty bees.

We must work on the breathing, an important factor in concert performance--your failure or success. This is where the body really matters. Some of you have an advantage over the others, which I notice as I evaluate your body types. As a matter of fact, the Greeks considered the broad-hipped body as the ideal human form, which is accomplished by proper deep breathing. This results in the "breath ring" which the Greeks considered one of the seven bodily graces and whose aesthetic appeal they held in the highest sacred regard. You seem puzzled. You did not know that? Let me tell you. Every youth strove to attain this physical ideal by means of mental contemplation and physical gymnastics. Thus, the Greek concept of the ideal human form matches the form which nature bestows upon us at birth. We should all be adult-sized babies. The baby has hips that are curved outward, and this form guarantees firm support to his crying, which is necessary to survival! Crying and singing--no difference. It is not right, therefore, for you women--and some of the men, also, who look so undernourished--it is not right for you to go on a diet, or exercise too much, and become so slim-hipped that you cannot support your singing tone, for then you will never survive, musically. And when you die, your voice will already have died before you, long before, and gone to hell. I know that some of you are metabolically doomed to be slim-hipped. You should eat plenty of red meat and desserts with heavy cream. *Mit schlag,* we always used to say.

Here's a pathetic story. We'll sing in a minute. I knew a young woman who desired to become a great singer, and it was true, she did have a very musical *mind.* I believe she had perfect pitch, and she had mastered the musical terminology. She certainly could read music, and she played the piano well, in a mechanical sort of way. This young woman was an accompanist to a choir I conducted in the early part of my career. She traveled with us. When we arrived at a place that had no piano, it was her responsibility to give us our notes vocally. This she did, in a thin, reedy tone, as if her head were detached from her body, as if her head were kept alive in a jar. That poor woman consisted of nothing but skin and bones. When she inhaled, she lifted her shoulders, and you could hear the bones crack. When she exhaled, she let out the full capacity of her lungs--perhaps one cup of air. She could not sustain her singing tone more than five seconds.

And yet she desired to become a great singer. She confessed this to me after rehearsal one day. We were visiting the north of England, one of the lesser known cathedrals. She told me that she pictured herself as having Wagnerian proportions, and she often dreamed of performing opera and so forth. At eighty pounds! I told her the first thing she had to do by way of achieving her goal was to double her weight. Remember Maria Callas? A wonderful voice, when she was fat. But then, sometime during the early Sixties, when she wanted Aristotle Onassis to fall in love with her, she lost half her body weight, and her voice became a thin shadow of its former self. I think that poor woman would have lived longer if she had stayed fat. My young protegée would not listen to my advice. She ate meat, that is true, but she jogged every day. She ran in marathons, and she destroyed her femininity. Her voice dropped an octave and became very raspy. She had very small breasts to begin with. And now her hips completely disappeared. She cut her hair in a short boy style, which revealed how small her head was. A tragedy. I believe that if, in her mind, she had really wanted to be a beautiful singer, she should have let her body become that of a beautiful singer, and it would have. Instead, she had some other sick notion of herself that prevailed.

I would hate to see her now. By now, she is an old man, or a skeleton. I used to think she was quite pretty.

I hear your voices buzzing. I do not like them. Shut up.

In our exercises, we must do something about speech inertia. There is something about the northern latitudes that makes it difficult for singers to articulate properly. These northern people turn all their vowels into sounds resembling either *ah* or *ee*. They form these vowels with the same embouchure, and every expression of language, whether joyous or sad in character, they speak with the same lack of facial expression. Such people wear one mask through which all words are drawled so thoughtlessly that their mouths and hearts often have no recollection or impression of the words which the lips have spoken. A tragedy! Let me see the hands of those of you who have had an operation to destroy the nerves and muscles in your face. Nobody? Well, I hope that is true, because you will need all those nerves and muscles in the vocal warm-up.

You are so lucky. A colleague of mine, a really wonderful tenor who might have become a major star, had to have his larynx removed, a far more serious operation, and a far more serious loss for the singer, than having one's facial nerves detached. Some years after his operation, this tenor called me on the phone. I had not even known of the loss, because I was completely involved with my choir--on tour in Europe, Asia, and so forth. I really wish he had paid me a visit, face to face. After all, we were living in the same city. Well, to speed things up a bit, I picked up the phone and said hello, and the voice on the other end said hello, but it was a mechanical voice, produced by a vibrator which one places against the neck, like this. I believe that researchers have made great progress since then with this artificial larynx, but what I heard over the phone was completely toneless--or all on one note, I should say. Like some creature from outer space, a crude imitation of human speech. "Hello," it said. "Please don't be alarmed. I'm a real person."

Don't laugh. It was very tragic.

All the phonetic components of human speech were there, but in simplified form. I think my tenor friend aspirated the H in a normal way. But the machine produced ugly vowels. This is what I'm getting at. In your faces, you have a much more sophisticated machine for producing vowels. Only you must *use* it. You must learn *how* to use it. You must *un*-learn all your bad habits. Press your fingers against your cheek as I am doing. Pay attention. Now, ladies, you mustn't worry about disturbing your make-up. Really press now. And as we go through all the vowel sounds, I want you to notice the changes in pressure, the changes in position, and I am asking you to exaggerate them, so that you will always be aware of these things, and that you will be grateful for them, and for the fact that you have not been reduced to a machine.

Let me hear an AHHH on this note. Now go from AHHH to OHHHH.

Do it again!

Nothing? No sounds at all? You are embarrassed? You should be embarrassed by the terrible sounds that will come out if you don't learn how to activate the facial muscles when you sing.

Please give me your complete attention. You are all milling about, wasting vital energy. We have only a few minutes before we go on stage, and I must arrange the way that you will stand during the concert. And please don't complain if I should move you next to somebody different, perhaps a stranger to you, an enemy, though it is inconceivable that two members of the same singing group should be strangers or enemies. I believe that a choir is a community, and it is a shame that this cannot always be so, that you cannot live together in a community, like the Shakers or the monks of old. It is a shame that all of you come together only once a week, and various people are absent every time, with the unfortunate result that the group does not cohere. If I were your permanent conductor, I would forbid that any member of the group be absent from rehearsal except in the case of death.

But the singing, is that not our highest priority? And *not* our own convenience, our own needs? Why call yourselves a singing group if you cannot come together and harmonize and work for many hours towards that goal? Certain musical organizations exist merely in the same way that stamp clubs and garden clubs exist, as a way for lonely people to socialize. That would be all right if the singers only performed for themselves and never sang for the public or expected the public to pay to hear them. Is that what you all want to be? I hardly think so, not if you hired me as your guest conductor. So at least while I am in charge, you will be something different. You will perform as though this singing were your entire life, as though you had sacrificed your families and your homes and your jobs. As if you had killed your husband when he said you were spending too much time with the choir, and music were all you had left in the world. Then the public would marvel and believe that your voices were a miracle from heaven. You have heard singing like that, other groups. Perhaps you have sung that way in the past. I wouldn't know. I have never heard recordings of your concerts. I chose not to listen to the tapes that were sent to me, because then I would have prejudged you as a choir.

And really, how you sounded before I took over is essentially irrelevant to how you will sound under my direction. It will be a projection of *my desires*, not of your individual habits and quirks, of some kind of "music" you have become accustomed to making simply because of lack of energy or poor technique or both. Now, for just a few minutes, before I arrange where you will stand, I must tell you about a choir, not so long ago, in a place much like this. The singers always arrived an hour late. They failed to acknowledge my presence in the room. They chatted among themselves, but not about music. Some drank whiskey out of thermos bottles, others were taking too many pills. Several young men chewed gum, but I put a stop to that. I said, "Spit that garbage into your hand this minute." They resisted. They claimed that chewing loosened their jaw muscles. Their old director had let them do it. I said, "Spit it out. Now!" They called me a "fascist" and then ran out the door. There was complete silence. The rest of the choir waited for me to speak. And I finally said, "They're right. I am a fascist. Now let's sing." I like to give the impression that I carry a loaded weapon.

There is no use in hanging on to old theories when a new conductor arrives on the scene. But that other choir quickly forgot who I was, how dangerous I could be. They would get up and leave the room to make personal phone calls. They discussed business, and family life. They wanted to use *my* time to plan a bake sale, or some other nonsense. I would have none of it. I put on my coat and walked to the door. I cleared my throat and told them that I was leaving. "You don't really want me," I said. "So you can't have me." They would sing without a conductor. In medieval times, by the way, choirs sang that way--but I am talking about a time in history when people really knew how to sing, when their lives weren't cluttered with other affairs. They were *singers*, before everything else.

So, as I put on my black leather gloves and buttoned my coat, the room became completely silent. They knew they could not survive without me, and so they capitulated. They said, "We give up." And I smiled. They were mine now. And from then on, I was like an organist, pulling all the stops. The pipes don't play themselves, I told them. The pipes do not operate according to their own will. They have no will. They have no other life, than making music. And so, having bowed to my will, the choir made real music. As you and I will do in just a minute, if you will take off your masks, and unleash your bodies as I have instructed. What is this resistance I am feeling in the air? What are these skeptical glances? Do you think I have been lying to you? What if I made this up out of nothing? Does that really matter? What if I am an actor only posing as a conductor? I know such things have happened.

It happened to me, in fact, when I was very young, singing *alto* in a community choir, under a guest conductor whom we had never met before. Our regular conductor had been suddenly called out of town on an emergency, we were told, and this new person, a dignified older man, tall gray-bearded--much the way I look now, I must admit--stepped in as his substitute. Who were we to doubt his credentials? He took us through an amazing set of warm-up exercises. All burdens were lifted. We went into our concert completely relaxed. We sang beautifully. Our worn-out bodies had nothing to do with the music. At the end of the concert, our guest conductor was escorted from the podium, handcuffed, wrestled into a van, and taken back to the insane asylum from which he had escaped. That should give all of you a sense of anticipation today as you sing better than you have ever sung before.

Clair

Julia Klatt Singer

Clair shut off the alarm and watched as the 5:59 flipped to 6:00. She rubbed her eyes, then surveyed the room that had been hers for her entire sixteen years. Standing by the door were two suitcases she'd borrowed from Bea, the cleaning lady at Sears. Her red velvet purse with the purple and blue rhinestones in the shape of a unicorn was hanging on the doorknob. They contained everything Clair owned. Sitting in the corner opposite the door was a crumpled up Kleenex and an orange plastic barrette shaped like a duck. That was it, and a penny dated 1963, on the floor by the window. Clair had had Goodwill come by yesterday afternoon to pick up her pink and white dresser and her purple bunk beds while her mom was at the beauty shop getting a perm, even though she knew her mother wouldn't notice. It had been years since her mom had stepped foot in her room. Clair rubbed her eyes, and then the wrinkles out of her light blue cotton shirt, and rose from the carpet. After checking her alarm clock to make sure she had enough time, she unplugged it and threw it in her purse along with the other things she'd need on the trip. Sunglasses, sleeping pills, ear plugs, and three paperbacks with missing covers--*On the Road* by Jack Kerouc, *The 1992 Wedding Planner*, and a Harlequin Romance--*Forbidden Love*. She also had three or four little packages of crackers, taco sauce, salts, and peppers she had save from various restaurants, the one-way bus ticket, two dried squirrel skulls carefully wrapped in a tissue, the scrap of paper with Doug's phone number on it, and his softball team picture cut out of the Portland paper.

When she picked up her bags, she felt the strain in her back from sleeping on the floor, even if it had only been four hours. Clair negotiated her way down the dark stairway. Pausing for a moment to get a better grip, she watched a mouse watching her. "You think I'll be back, don't you? I'm leaving, and I'm in love. You're wrong about me, I'm not like my mother. Besides, if I was, I would have killed you by now." The mouse scampered away as her foot pounded the next step. Quietly closing the screen door behind her, Clair placed the note she had written to her mom in the crack of the door. Clair had two blocks to carry the suitcases to catch the city bus. It was a beautiful Tuesday morning.

She had walked this path to the bus every day to go to

work at Sears downtown, but never this early, and never with all her things, yet it all felt so normal. The sun was just coming up, breaking through the trees thick with mist. The ground came alive as she touched it. Glass blades bent from the weight of the dew swayed up to meet the sun as she passed them.

Clair didn't own a watch anymore. Her grandmother had given Clair hers for her fourteenth birthday, her golden birthday. It was too big, but she'd loved the way it had made her arm look, thin and sophisticated. This new-found sophistication had gotten Clair into more trouble than she could ever confess to. It started with Eddie. He was a sophomore and very mature. On their first date they didn't even make it to the drive-in. About a mile away from Clair's house, when it was still light out, he pulled over into a ditch, reached for her breast with his left hand and unzipped his pants with his right. Clair told him she didn't want to do it in the car so he carried her to the woods where they played Adam and Eve. It was great fun until Clair realized that in all the moving around she had lost her grandmother's watch. Eddie laugh, and complimented her on her ability to lose things.

Not having a watch--her grandmother's watch, got her in more trouble all the time. She was always late for her after-school job at Sears, tardy to classes, and late for dinner. Grandmother would ask to see the watch, to see if it was set right, and Clair would have to lie to avoid showing it to her. Clair was so ashamed she had lost it with Eddie.

That was a year ago. A lot had changed since then. Her grandmother had died suddenly of lung cancer last fall. Her mother was dating a guy named Ray now, an exterminator who was always spraying the kitchen and basement. It was a good excuse to stay out of the house. Her mom was between jobs. She had quit the 1-900 number job right after she'd met Ray. He didn't like coming over and having the phone ring late at night so she could talk dirty to some other guy. She was looking for a waitress job somewhere in town, but the only place hiring was the Brass Rail, and that's where Leroy, her ex, worked.

As Clair reached the end of the path, she paused to look at her damp Converse high tops. She wiggled her toes and noticed a group of sparrows chirping and singing, flitting and flying from tree to tree. The world hadn't looked or sounded so good in a long time. How long had it been? Clair wondered. Probably since before Eddie.

The loud rumble of the bus caused the sparrows to fly away, and it took Clair a second to realize what had just happened.

"Shit! Wait!" She ran to the corner swinging her suitcases, trying to get the bus driver's attention.

"You're all blind! Every damn one of you can't see worth shit. I don't know how you passed your god damn driving test!"

Clair knew if she didn't make it to the Greyhound station by 7:00 a.m. she'd miss her bus to Minneapolis and would never make her connection to Portland. It was at least a fifteen minute ride from here by city bus. She'd never make it walking. Clair had eight hundred and sixty dollars and eighty-eight cents to her name and it was all in her wallet, except the eighty-eight cents that was jingling in the front pocket of her jeans as she stumbled down the street. Carrying her purse over her right shoulder, a suitcase in each hand swinging her off balance with each stride, Clair shuffled along, trying to catch up with the bus.

As Clair stumbled down the next street, a car pulled up next to her and a woman with an overnight bag got out of the back seat. Like a relay team passing a baton Clair jumped in before the woman closed the door, banging her knee with one of the suitcases, and the car door with the other.

"Hello mister. Sorry to barge in, but I need you to take me to the Greyhound station. Do you know where the bus station is on the east side of town--oh of course you do--I need to get there by 7 am.!"

"Who do you think you are young lady? You nearly knocked me over with that suitcase!" The woman planted her feet, hands on her hips.

The man hesitantly motioned for Clair to stay.

"You're o.k. darling? I'll see you later?" He leaned out the passenger seat window. The woman dropped her hands from her hips and turned to walk away.

"I'm not usually this pushy, it's just that I'm late, I'm always late, and I'm in a hurry. I missed the bus to the station just two blocks back. See, I'm in love and running away from home and I have to catch the bus to Minneapolis." Clair took a deep breath.

"In love? And running away?" He drove steadily, like a dad, using a blinker and driving just a little under the speed limit.

"Ya, I'm running away. Leaving this hell hole. Can't quite believe it myself. Moving to Portland, you know where that is? Got me a man, one that wants to marry me. We met over the phone about two months ago. I work, I mean worked, at the returns department of Sears downtown, part-time after school, and one day I got this call from a guy who lived in Portland. Somehow they had given him our number here in Brainerd. So we ended up chatting awhile trying to figure out what his problem was, and how I could help him, when he asked me if I'd ever had phone sex while I was at work. I told the guy he was crazy, and I was just about to hang up when he started saying the sweetest things." Clair crossed her legs, rolling her hips a little to the right and then the left, letting her blue cotton shirt fall off her shoulder.

The driver was watching her in the rear view mirror. She could only see his eyes, so wasn't sure what kind of expression he had on his face, but his eyes looked interested. So she went on.

"It was crazy! He was just saying stuff like, from the sound of your voice, I can tell you are a pretty thing, with big tits and I bet your nipples are getting hard right now. I asked him how he knew they were--because they are--were, I mean, and then he said 'because girl's like you can't stay away from a guy like me. You find me like shit finds the fan, like a fly finds flypaper. It's fate.' That was what he said. I remember it word for word, because I wasn't sure what fate was, but I'm going to look it up in the encyclopedia as soon as I get a chance. Well, anyway, he's been calling twice a week since then, and two days ago he asked me to marry him. So I'm going to Portland to get married today. Actually I won't get there until tomorrow, but then we're going straight to the justice's office and getting married," Clair raised her chin, feeling proud.

"You've never seen him? How old are you, anyway?" The driver's voice sounded far away, weak, like somebody talking into a microphone that hasn't been turned on.

"Not in person, but he sent me a picture last week from the newspaper. He's very cute. From the picture I'd guess he's maybe twenty or thirty. It was one of those softball team pictures they put in the newspaper where everybody is about the size of a pencil eraser, so it was hard to tell. Hey, there's the station. I'm sixteen. My mom says I'm an old sixteen though. You don't know my mom, do you? No, you're not her type. Too normal. Nothing personal. Do you happen to know what time it is?"

"6:45."

"Thanks. I can pay you..." Clair dug in her purse for

her wallet as the car came to a stop.

"Ah, Hon, that's o.k. You keep your money. You'll need it once you get married."

"No, I don't feel right busting in here, not even paying for gas..." Clair pulled out a five dollar bill.

"Just promise me that you'll be happily married? The man said this to the empty passenger's seat, not Clair.

"Promise."

He helped Clair with her bags and she met the bus to Minneapolis with two minutes to spare. It was about now that her mother would be waking up, heading for the front door to pick up the paper, and finding her note. Clair felt a ball of sweat run down her side. It soaked into her bra as she boarded the bus.

The bus was practically empty. Only a few heads with faces hidden in newspapers were visible as Clair walked through the narrow aisle. This was the first bus to Minneapolis, one of three each day. A perm haired lady scowled at Clair as she bumped her with her purse, spilling the salts and peppers and a taco sauce on the woman's lap. "Wife hair" thought Clair as she took the seat a few rows back. The driver had stowed her large suitcases below and was now turning over the engine.

As they drove through downtown Brainerd Clair felt like a rabbit caught in a clearing by the road. Afraid to move for her motion might give her away, but aware that she was visible. Anyone might recognize her strawberry blond hair pulled back in a pony tail on the top of her head. Even a reflection in the window of her hand, with her long fingers covered with rings and her thin wrist, was undeniably hers. Feeling self conscious, Clair put on her sunglasses and watched as the town rolled by. The bus passed the bakery, Super America, Piggly Wiggly where her mom did all her shopping (unless she was short on cash and then she shopped at Super America where they took credit cards). They passed the Post Office, the vet, "Nails by Gails" (a hardware store run by two windowed sisters-in-laws with the same name), and the Brass Rail. They were nearing the highway. A bump and a swing and they were heading south on 371. It was a little over two hours to Minneapolis. Clair slid her sunglasses to the top of her head and closed her eyes. Shifting her hips forward, she put her knees against the back of the seat in front of her, and fell asleep.

The sound of passing cars woke Clair. She could see the Minneapolis skyline in the distance, the I.D.S. and other glass towers reaching to the sun. As the bus pulled into the Greyhound station Clair was amazed at how low and square the station was. She remembered it being so big when she and her mom came to Minneapolis to do some Christmas shopping when she was a kid. The lobby had been full of people going every possible direction, with line and suitcases and packages everywhere. The lobby now had only thirty or forty seats, about a third of them taken, and just three vending machines. There was one person working behind the ticket counter, and two people waiting in line. Digging for two one dollar bills out of the wad of money in her wallet, Clair stood a few feet away from the machines, trying to be discrete. Talk to yourself, thought Clair. That's what your mother always did to keep weirdos away. Strange how weirdos will talk to anybody, everybody but other weirdos. Clair surveyed the machines. The plexiglass was coated with a film of smoke, giving the candy bars and chips a hazy color. Two Snickers bars and a hot chocolate. $1.45 spent--not counting the $89 she had given to Bea to buy the bus ticket to Portland the day before.

Clair flipped through the Wedding Planner as she ate her breakfast. Lots of good ideas about hair and nails and which bra to wear under one's dress, tips she would try to remember. Clair hadn't even thought about what she would wear to the wedding. Perhaps Doug would take her shopping when she got to Portland, or maybe he had already bought her a wedding gown. When boarding for Portland was announced, a line of people formed at the first door. Clair surveyed the line and felt her stomach tighten.

Clair had ridden the bus before, with her mom, and she always picked a seat about one third of the way back. Clair knew what kind of people rode the bus. The back filled up with the loud, smoking crowd, even though they weren't supposed to smoke, and the front seats smelled like lavender and moth balls from the old ladies who, after cleaning out their attics, were taking old, dusty stuff to their kids' kids. They always needed two seats because they had their carry-on bags filled with macadamia nuts, plastic rain hats, extra underwear--as if they had any place to change--and a pile of photographs to show to whomever ended up sitting near them. Always about a quarter of them were really fat. They needed a seat and a half at least they were so well padded. Clair thought the carry-on was a cover-up, so they didn't have to say, "I can't fit my fat ass in one seat", although they would phrase it more politely than that.

Anyway, Clair's mom always sat in the middle of the

bus, closer to the old ladies than to the rowdies in the back, so that's where Clair sat. She chose the window seat so she could watch the world go by. She had never traveled any further than Minneapolis before. The bus engine started up, and Clair relaxed a little. She was alone, leaving, really doing this.

"Excuse me miss, is this seat taken?" The voice sounded like molasses, thick and slow and very sweet.

Looking up, Clair saw an older woman, ancient in fact, with thin white hair pulled back from her temples gently streaming into a coil on the top of her round head. Her face was tan, her eyes like olives, her nose straight and dignified, and her lips the color of cranberry juice. She was beautiful. She was wearing a burgundy wool sweater, buttoned up the front, and a khaki skirt. Her legs were bare, tan and freckled. She wore burgundy socks and a pair of practical shoes, brown leather with ties. She had a carry-on, a small cream canvas bag that looked like it had two or three books in it, that was all.

"Ya, that seat is open." Clair was suddenly conscious of how messy and cheap she must have looked to this older woman, dressed in her tight jeans, her fake jewel rings, and the faded blue shirt she wore unbuttoned just far enough to show off her nicely shaped breasts. Make sure they know what your assets are up front, that's what her mom always said.

"I just hate sitting up front, all those older women nattering on and on about their children, their dead husbands, and everybody else on this earth or in heaven, you don't know, and will never want to know after hearing about them. I prefer sitting here in the middle of the bus, between the two worlds." The older woman slid gracefully into her seat as she spoke.

"I know what you mean. Those old ladies up front give me an upset stomach. They smell like church potlucks--tatter-tot hotdishes and powdered doughnuts."

"And so much more. Layers of doctrine and death and dogma are right below the hotdishes and burnt cookies, waiting to ambush you. Old men are different. They smell like their hobbies, not their fears." The older woman held her eyes squarely on Clair's.

Clair wasn't sure what the older woman had just said to her, but she was sure it was true. Clair tried to think of something to say, but she could only look at her broken finger nails with the purple nail polish chipping off. She wanted to look at the older woman's hands, for she knew they would be beautiful, strong and dignified. Clair could picture the perfect nails with a half moon rising at each cuticle. Just like the women in the ads in *Vogue*. No polish. No peeling skin.

"My name is Amanda Walker. What's yours?" Amanda offered her hand to Clair as she spoke, and she noticed that Clair's hand looked older than the rest of her. Like a hand on a forty-year-old waitress. She wondered what had aged this girl's hands prematurely.

"I'm Clair. Clair Broman. Where are you going? To visit you grandkids?"

"No. They spend part of their summers with me, and that's plenty. No, I'm going to Portland." Amanda said, still looking at Clair's hands.

"Hey, me too. I'm going to meet my...boyfriend there, and getting married." Feeling self conscious, Clair rolled her hands in the hem of her shirt, hiding the chipped polish, the peeling skin and dirty cuticles.

"Really? Sounds very romantic. Getting married...I'm visiting the farm where I spent my childhood summers. Later, if I have the time, I may go back to the island my father was born on," Amanda said.

"That sounds more romantic to me." Clair knew she would never want to go back to her mother's childhood home, but an island...

"Really? More romantic than marriage? I may be forgetting what it was really like, but marrying Harold was the most fun. We eloped. He was such a kidder, no one believed we actually did it." Amanda looked past Clair, not out the window exactly, more like at the space at the end of Clair's nose.

"I think getting married will be romantic and all, it's just that this isn't exactly the way I planned. Who am I kidding? I've never planned anything in my life..."

Amanda smiled at Clair, and patted her leg the way her grandmother used to. Just one, two, three little light taps. Amanda then opened her carry-on bag and took out a book.

"What-cha reading?" Clair looked for the title on the cover of the book.

All Passion Spent, by Vita Sackville West. Have you ever read it?"

"I might have-Is it a Harlequin?"

"Most certainly not. It's about passion, not sex. It's set in England and the main character is an older woman, recently widowed."

Clair wished she knew words better. Just what was the difference between sex and passion? Had she ever felt passion? Were they interchangeable? Could she have one without having the other? She opened her mouth to ask, but before the words came out she noticed that Amanda had already started reading. Clair turned toward the window and watched the landscape of small towns, railroad crossings, strip malls and McDonald's roll by. Clair thought about home.

Home was kind of like this trip. Her grandmother was like the rest stops, temporary little breaks from the trip. Her granddad was more like a scenic overlook, rare, but interesting. It had basically just been her and her mom, Betty, but men came and went like the small towns and strip malls. Clair mused about the names of the passing small towns. Hector, Spencer, Westfield, and Austin. Names of her mom's boyfriends were never so proper. Harry, Fred, Dil, Wayne, Curt, and Leroy.

Leroy was the first one Clair remembered. He was only around for a few years, but somehow it felt like all of elementary school. Probably because he kept dropping in for a couple years after they split. Leroy was okay at first. He worked at the Maytag factory in town and made pretty good money. When he first started living with them he used to bring Clair a present every payday. This made her mom a little angry--jealous really--and she would always question Leroy, "So who ya courting, me or my seven-year-old?" Leroy would blush from the neck up bright red, but he never answered the question.

After awhile he stopped bringing a present. He forgot Clair's eighth birthday altogether, which really pissed off her mom. That night Leroy and Betty had a huge fight. It started as Betty was making dinner, spaghetti and meatballs. Clair sat in the livingroom watching Gilligan's Island.

She could hear their talk over the canned laughter.

"Come on Betty baby, what's wrong this time?"

Just the sound of a spoon hitting the side of a tin saucepan.

"Hell woman, I try and try to please you, but what ever I do I should have done the exact opposite."

The sound of spitting grease.

"Well, I'm not gonna just stand here talking to myself. There is plenty of women who would like to talk to me and help me spend my money. If you want me, you know where to find me...but don't wait too long or you're gonna have to get in line."

Leroy picked up his jacket and walked without picking up his feet through the livingroom, pausing for a second in front of the TV.

Betty stepped into the doorway, the saucepan in one hand and the spoon in the other. "What the hell are you doing? I thought you said you were leaving...get away from my daughter. Even *she's* a little young for you."

"Come on Betty, I'm not doing anything, I ..."

"I knew from the beginning at was Clair you wanted. Just waiting for her to get old enough, huh? Why not take the younger version of the old hag."

"Betty, I don't even like kids--come on--Clair has nothing to do with this. This is between you and me." Leroy's arms hung limp at his sides. His eyebrows jumped like a fish just hooked lying in the bottom of the boat.

Clair pulled the afgan up around her feet, tucking it underneath them. She tried to look only at the TV. To listen only to Gilligan and the Skipper.

Betty's voice got high and tight as she tried to say something, but a commercial came on that caught Leroy's attention. Out of the corner of Clair's left eye she saw it happen. The pan and the spoon and the sauce moved in slow motion through the air. It was like the air was as thick as marshmallow and the sauce and the pan and the spoon had to work really hard to get through it. Leroy kept watching the commercial for Mountain Dew. "Give me a mountain...give me..." He never saw it coming. The screen flickered black and it was then that Leroy turned his head back towards Betty. The pan and the spoon and sauce hit him in the face. Shoulder. Chest. The pot and spoon clunked to the shag carpet floor. He seemed to shrink from the heat. He was over six feet tall, but now looked like the wicked witch of the West during her death scene. A low, small scream came out, but it didn't sound like his voice at all--more like his pores screaming as the sauce soaked in.

"You bitch," slid from his curled lips. With the sauce streaming like blood down his face and shirt, he folded his jacket over his messy arm and left, footprints of red sauce marked his path to the door.

Clair kept her eyes on the TV after the door slammed shut. Betty walked to the center of the room, bent over and picked up the pan and the spoon.

"This is all your fault, you know."

Clair nodded "yes" and waited for the show to come back on.

Leroy wasn't the first or the last man to leave her mom. There was Fred, who was quite a bit older, a truck driver, and Harry, who worked at the gas station, often fixing their car for free, and Wayne, who was Betty's third cousin. They got together at a family reunion a few years back.

The bus slowed down. Outside the window Clair could see the flat green prairie dotted with houses and barns and silos, fences cutting the land into neat squares and rectangles. They seem to be nearing a small town. The bus passed an elementary school, the fire hall, two barber shops, a Hy-Vee market, an Amoco station, three beauty parlors, a butcher shop, and a few bars and supper clubs. The bus pulled over, driving up the curb, bouncing Clair's purse to the floor. The sleeping pills spilled, sliding under the seats in front of them like hockey pucks on ice. The face of her alarm clock cracked. Lots of "oh mys" could be heard from up front, a few "what the hells", from the back. Between Fluffy's Bar and the post office sat the Greyhound station.

Clair found the pay phone in the corner of the cafe, near the restrooms. Reading the directions twice, Clair dropped in a few quarters and dialed the number scribbled on a page from a Sears catalog.

"PLEASE DEPOSIT 50 CENTS TO COMPLETE THIS CALL."

"Ok, ok." Clair dropped in two more quarters, glad Amanda had given her the roll of quarters so she wasn't messing around counting nickels and dimes.

Rinnng...Rinnng...Rinnng..."Hi. You've reached Doug's Sex Shop. I'm busy now, if you know what I mean, so call back in fifteen minutes or leave me a message at the beep." BEEP.

"Hi Doug. This is Clair. Clair Broman from Sears. You know, the Sears in Brainerd, Minnesota. Just calling to tell you I'm coming, I mean, I'm on my way. I'm in some town called Prairie Chicken or something like that. Nowhere in the midwest, believe me. I'm due into Portland at 10 a.m. Tomorrow that is. Meet me at the station?" BEEP.

Clair boarded the bus and found her seat.

"Did you get through to...your boyfriend?" Amanda sat down, placing her carry-on under the seat in front of her.

"Well yes and no. I got his machine."

"Here. I got you this. It's a tuna sandwich and an apple. Eat." Amanda handed Clair the things wrapped in a napkin. As she took the food, Clair wanted to cry. It had been years since her mom had even made a sandwich, much less handed it to her wrapped in a napkin. Taking a bit out of the sandwich, she thanked Amanda, and ate the rest of it looking out the window. Amanda ate her sandwich in small bites, folded up her napkin into a little square, and returned to her book.

Clair could have had three or four little brothers or sisters, at least that's what her mom told her. But Clair was enough trouble (that's what her mom said) so Betty went to the clinic in Moorhead every now and then. Betty never told Clair when she was going, but Clair could always tell. Betty acted differently when she got home. She would make herself a rum and coke as soon as she returned, no matter what time of day it was. And she was nice to Clair. She wanted to talk, to play Risk or Scrabble, to be friends. By nightfall she would be drunk and would fight with whatever man happened to be spending the evening.

On one of those nights Clair first went out with Eddie. They were going to go to the drive-in. Eddie was a savior. He whisked Clair away two or three times a week, her knight in shining armor. He never called first, just a honk of the truck's horn in front of her house, the engine revving.

At first Eddie was great. He didn't like to talk much, but he did tell Clair how nice she looked, what beautiful eyes she had, or how much he liked her Van Halen T-shirt. Then they found a place to do it. Sex was real with Eddie, like raw hamburger. No frills, no awkwardness, just straightforward hip grinding sex. But as the weeks passed, Eddie honked less and less. Clair was pretty sure what was happening--she'd seen it happen enough times with her mother--but she didn't know what to do about it. The last time Eddie honked, she wanted to say no, but when she saw him sitting there behind the wheel, she was happy he had come. They only drove to the end of the block this time. It was dusk. She wanted to say no and yes at the same time, and wound up saying nothing. She would go anywhere with Eddie. He didn't even have to ask.

"Something's wrong with your tits, Clair. They're bigger and harder than they used to be." Eddie rolled her breast in his hand.

"Maybe. Careful that hurts."

"You've been keeping track of the days, haven't you? So you don't get pregnant?" He kept pushing himself in and out as he questioned her. Eddie never talked when they did it.

"Of course I've been counting. I wouldn't lie to you." Claire *had* been counting, but she wasn't really sure what she was counting to.

After Eddie had zipped up, he told Clair he wouldn't be dropping by anymore. He was seeing a senior now, a friend of the family's, and well, he couldn't do two girls at the same time. He wasn't that kind of guy.

Clair counted the days after Eddie left. Neither he, nor her period showed. It was five weeks later, in history class, that she finally bled. It was dark and heavy. Enough to make her feel like getting sick. She missed school for two days, the bleeding was so painful. Her friend Nora called to tell her that she heard Eddie had broken up with the senior because she was a prude. A week later Eddie honked in front of her house. Clair flattened herself on her bed, hiding her head under her pillow until the honking stopped and she heard him drive away.

The bus slowed down, making a turn to another small midwestern town.

"What did that sign say?" Clair's body mimicking the brakes, bouncing awake at an irregular beat.

"Baker or Barker. I couldn't quite read it." Amanda adjusted her glasses.

"Hey, Mrs. Walker, look at that man there--on the front steps of the church. What a face!"

"Like a road map. You can see where he's been. Each line and scar is like a road he's traveled down, each town he's slept in, probably for each woman who's broken his heart."

"Guess my mom's lucky. If she had a line for every man she's been dumped by..." Clair thought about her mom, and how afraid she was of getting wrinkles. "Well, like my grandmother used to say, she'd have more lines than a drunk horny sailor."

Amanda tried to picture Clair's mother and grandmother. The only image that came to mind was of her own mother, standing and ironing, the tea kettle in one hand, the iron in the other.

"Amanda, is this where you thought you'd be, I mean when you were growing up, did you think you'd end up here?"

"Riding the Greyhound bus to Portland? No. I didn't expect to end up an eighty-year-old widow, living alone in the midwest, riding the bus for adventure. But I honestly can't remember what I thought about at your age. I guess the usual things...boys and clothes and s.e.x." Amanda spelled out the word in a whisper. "I guess that's why I'm going back east. I need to get all the people I've known and the places I've been together somehow--"

"And have a party?" Clair asked.

"What a great idea, Clair. I could have a dinner party. I was considering writing about them, and finding a photo to go with each one, but a party sounds like much more fun. Sort of spontaneous and wild.

"You could send invitations to the living, and have a seance to invite the dead. I saw that one time on a movie on cable."

"Yes. I'd love to see my mother and my granddaughter chatting over a glass of wine. My granddaughter is extremely liberal, and very outspoken. She'd leave my mother speechless. All her talk about women's right, birth control and the bra--the symbol of women's oppression. My mother never went anywhere without her bra on. Swam in it, slept in it, too afraid that if she took it off for a minute she would start to sag."

"My mom would probably leave your mother speechless too. Especially if she started hitting on both your father and your brother at the same time. That's one of my mom's specialties."

"Really?"

"One time, at a church picnic, my mom started flirting with this guy in his fifties. She was in her thirties at the time. I was about twelve. Mom sent me to play softball, and an hour or so later I went looking for her because I had skinned my knee and needed a band-aid. I found them in the basement of the church in a Sunday school room. Mom was lying on the table and he was on top of her, grunting, the metal table legs wobbling and squeaking. When Mom saw me she straightened her hair and pulled down her skirt and then helped me find a bandage in the glove compartment of the man's car. That was when the son came over. He was probably seventeen or eighteen--still in high school. Mom stared at him and made comments about what a big boy he was, and how he looked like a chip off the old block. So a little while later Mom and I got a ride home from the son. She took me upstairs and made me take a bath. I ran the water, but didn't get in. Instead I snuck out into the hallway, careful not to make the floor squeak, and watched from the top step. I could see Mom and the son on the couch. He was pushing and pulling, and Mom was grabbing him by the ears, pulling his head away from her chest, trying to get him to listen to her. For about a month after that the son came over on Friday afternoons when he got done with school, and she would go out to dinner with his dad that night. I wonder if they ever figured it out..."

"The way fathers and sons talk. I doubt it."

At Taco Heaven Clair ate two beef tacos with extra cheese for dinner. She was glad she had the extra taco sauce in her purse--they needed it. Amanda had a chef salad and a cup of black coffee from the cafeteria in the bus station in Twin Falls. After dinner, Clair fell asleep. It seemed like she had just closed her eyes for a few minutes, but when she woke up, the little bulb lights were on in the bus and it was definitely night.

"You slept a long time. You must have been very tired." Amanda said, patting Clair's leg.

"Ya, I was tired. God, I can't believe it's dark out. What time is it?" Clair checked her wrist, forgetting for a moment that she no longer owned a watch.

"It's 9:30 p.m., we're just approaching Columbus."

"Wow, Columbus already...Are we stopping here?"

"Certainly. Columbus is a pretty large city. According to the timetable we have a forty-five minute wait here. Are you going to try calling your boyfriend again? You know, you don't say very much about him."

"There's not much to say."

"Oh?"

"See, we haven't exactly met yet. Just talked on the phone. You must think I'm crazy or desperate or real horny. Maybe I am. I don't know how old he really is, or what he looks like. But opportunity only knocks once, right? He really wants me, I think, at least that's what he says. It's sort of strange."

Amanda listened. She didn't yell, or scold, or offer any advice. When Clair finished speaking Amanda nodded her head and said, "You'll make the right choice. I think you already know what to do." She then opened her bag and took out her book and began reading.

When the bus finally stopped at the station in Columbus, Amanda offered to pick up a little snack for them at the cafeteria in station. Clair went to use the phone. Digging through her purse for the number, she came across the two painted squirrel skulls she had wrapped in a tissue. They were a present from her grandfather. For as long as Clair could remember they had sat on the shelf above her dresser. Her grandfather had been on the road a lot. He picked up everything, and eventually found a use for it. At first he returned home with broken chairs, empty crates, and old mattresses. Clair remembered her grandmother's voice being both excited and disgusted when he returned. It was a high, tense voice, and when she saw his face, it was like the wind took her voice away, her words trailed away into nothing. "Oh, Gene, I thought..." But as soon as she saw the junk piled in the back of the pick-up, her voice returned, full of venom. "What the hell do you plan on doing with all that trash? Good thing you brought your own mattress, cuz I don't sleep with no garbage man. I ain't that desperate."

"He didn't start bringing home the road kill until a while after Grandma got used to the junk. Grandpa believed that everything had another use, deserved another chance. Clair rubbed the skull with her thumb as she held it in the palm of her hand. He had dried the skulls, and with oil paints gave the skull a shiny, iridescent finish. A little morbid, but beautiful.

It was Clair's turn to use the phone. Dialing the number carefully, Clair's stomach felt like it did on the roller coaster.
Rinnng...Rinnng...Rinnng..."Hi. You've reached..."

Clair hung up. She wasn't going to leave *two* messages. As Clair left the station, she was careful to put her wallet and the two skulls away. Across the street from the station was a little street fair. Clair walked across the intersection to see if the vendors were selling fried cheese curds or corn dogs. Amanda was standing in front of the first cart, nibbling on a corn dog, a second one coated in mustard propped on the top of a coke.

"You read my mind!" Amanda handed the corn dog and coke to Clair. "I was just hoping you would come this way. I bit off more than I could chew, literally speaking. Could you carry my purse, dear? I've never been very good at eating things off a stick." Amanda lead the way deeper into the fair.

"Hey, Amanda, I think the bus is back this way." Clair was careful not to get mustard on her shirt as she weaved her way through the crowd.

"I know that, dear. The bus doesn't leave for another thirty minutes, so I thought we could stretch our legs a bit." Amanda continued cutting through the crowd at a pace Clair could barely keep up with. She just watched for the silver head bobbing in and out of the crowd of young kids.

As they reached the center of the fair, Amanda slowed down and looked up at the sky. Clair glanced up to see what she was looking at. It was a ride. It had swings on long chains, so that when you got going, they swung out, nearly horizontal to the land. Without giving it a second thought, Clair walked to the counter and bought tickets for the ride.

"Here Amanda, let's go."

"What is this for? Clair, this isn't for a ride, is it? I don't like rides."

"Aw, come on. I saw you staring at it. I know you want to go, so come on."

"But dear..." Amanda couldn't tell her that she was looking for the north star. The night was clear and somehow, even with the lights of the fair, the stars were shining brightly. Harold had called himself her "north star" when they were courting. She hadn't even seen the ride, until now.

They got in line, and within a few minutes were strapped into their swings, side by side. The ride started up slowly, smoothly swinging them in the night air. The breeze felt good on Clair's face. She looked over at Amanda, and noticed that her eyes were closed, and Clair could picture what Amanda had looked like as a child. The swings went faster, higher until Clair got that feeling in her stomach like its flying higher than the rest of your body. Clair and Amanda exchanged glances, and without even thinking, reached out and held hands. Clair closed her eyes. All she could feel was Amanda's warm hand, the cool breeze blowing her ponytail straight back, and the pumping of her stomach. When she opened her eyes, Columbus passed below them in all different directions.

As the ride slowed, they let go of hands, but Clair could still feel the warmth of Amanda's skin in her palm.

"I shouldn't have eaten that corn dog." Clair rubbed her stomach as she climbed off the ride.

"That was terrific, Clair. I had almost forgotten how good it felt to be a child. I feel as if I have truly begun my trip back home. Thank you." As they walked back to the bus, Amanda bought salt water taffy and mini donuts for the ride.

Boarding the bus, Clair and Amanda switched seats, so that Amanda could look out the window for a while. Before settling in, Amanda used the lavatory.

It was then that he got on. He was the type of guy that usually sat in the back of the bus, but for some reason he sat down across from Clair. Both seats were open, but he decided to sit in the aisle seat, placing his green duffel bag by the window. He sat down and stretched out his long, thin legs. He was wearing mirrored glasses.

Silly, thought Clair, to wear glasses on the bus at night. It made her nervous though, not to be sure where his eyes were looking. If eyes are mirrors to the soul, then mirrored glasses made one soulless. Adjusting her bra strap, Clair felt his eyes piercing through her clothes, searching out what was underneath.

"What are you looking at? Haven't you ever seen a girl adjust her bra before?" Clair stared directly at the glasses and then glanced away when she saw her own reflection.

"Its what's inside that's caught my eye. Just hoping you had a little extra to share. You know, giving to the needy."

"Needy? What exactly is that you'd be lacking?" Clair stared at his crotch until he pulled in his legs, turning his body toward the seat in front of him. Amanda approached the seats.

"Why thank you. I love a gentleman, don't you Clair?" Amanda paused a moment as she waited for Clair to get up, and thought, mirrored glasses, how vain.

Settling in, Amanda offered Clair a donut.

"Amanda, when was the first time you left home? I mean, really left?"

"I don't know if I ever did leave home, really. I guess I must have, if I am now returning. You see, my father died of pneumonia when I was twelve. I was the oldest of five siblings and felt that it was my duty to help my mother raise them. She was so fragile after my father's death. She still looked composed on the outside, never shed a tear in front of any of us children, but there was something missing in her voice. She sounded hollow."

The bus pulled away from the station. The fair passed by the windows as blurs of neon lights.

"Ted left in 1938 to follow his pregnant fourteen year old girlfriend, Charlene, to Wyoming. That left another hole in our family, so I felt I couldn't walk away from Maria, Eliza and Nick. Eliza was still young, eight or nine. Nicolas was eleven and Maria was fourteen. The same age as Charlene. Mother watched Maria with an accusing eye, certain she would end up like Charlene. She didn't. She joined a convent right after high school. I was thirty before I even thought of moving away. I had been working as a secretary in an office at the time, using most of my money to pay the bills at home. But then Mother's health took a turn for the worse, so I ended up living at home until her death. I guess I was thirty-eight when I really left home. Shortly after the funeral I decided to visit Eliza and her family in Duluth. That's when I met Harold."

"So you were old when you got married?" Clair reached for another donut.

"Thirty-nine, actually, if that's what you mean by old."

"Sorry. I didn't mean..."

"It's alright, Clair, I never expected to get married--not once I turned thirty. I believe it's Oscar Wilde who had convinced me how useless a woman over thirty is. It was years later that I found out he was gay. What use would women be to him?"

Clair didn't know who Amanda was talking about. "Was he a friend of yours?"

"No darling. I'm not that old."

"So you had your children when you were in your forties?"

"I never had any children."

"But you said you had grandchildren?"

"Harold had been married before he met me. He and his first wife had two children. His wife died in childbirth."

"How long were you married to Harold?"

"Forty-one years. Almost half my life."

"Jesus, that's a long time. When did Harold die?"

"Three months ago." Amanda looked out the window. The city of Columbus was now off in the distance. The city lights flickered like candles. Columbus was just far enough away for the bus window to frame it perfectly. Perhaps always looking out, or ahead could keep her from looking back, could keep the sadness at bay.

"I'm sorry. And I'm a little bit jealous." Clair glanced across the aisle and noticed that the guy sitting across from her was wearing a Walkman, but the tape wasn't moving. Eavesdropping. Figures.

"Jealous of an old woman?"

"I don't think I have a clue about love."

"Clair, you are young. Love matures as people do. You can't expect, or for that matter deal with, mature love when you are still a child. Don't rush things. Enjoy life, enjoy your youth and innocence while you still have it."

Clair thought about Amanda's words. As much as she knew they were true, they didn't feel like words she could use. She wasn't young or innocent. She was running away from her mother, hoping if she got far enough away, she would be free of her, and maybe free to become someone else, although Clair had no idea who she wanted to become --just knew she didn't want to turn out like her mother, going from man to man, never sure of what would make her happy.

"Where you headed?" He had taken his earphones off, but left them sitting around his neck.

"Portland. You?" Clair felt short of breath. He had handsome eyes, deep, perfect ovals, the color of a lake at dusk. He was probably nineteen or twenty, his body looked solid, filled in.

"Springfield. It's the first stop in the morning. I'm going to stay with my dad. He and Mom split up a few years ago. So I spend the school year with my Mom in Columbus, and go home for the summer to Springfield."

"My name's Clair. Sorry about the comment earlier."

"Hey, no problem. I deserved it. I would never have said anything to you if your grandma had been here. Sometimes I can be a jerk. I'm Jake."

"Want a donut?"

Amanda had fallen asleep. Clair carefully marked the page of her book and put it into Amanda's carry-on. She thought about talking to Jake again, but wasn't sure what she would say. As she glanced over at him, Amanda rested her head on Clair's shoulder. Jake smiled, and said, "I was just going to ask you if you wanted to sit over here, by me, but it looks like your grandma's gonna keep an eye on you-- awake or not."

Clair reached across the aisle, handed him a donut, and brushed her hand against his pinky. She felt an electric charge surge through her body. He popped the donut in his mouth, and then slid his hand into hers. His skin was smooth and dry. A few minutes later, she fell asleep, but not for long. Each time Jake's hand started to slip, she squeezed it harder, and smiled, hoping that no one could see them.

She dreamed about crossing the aisle, climbing on his lap, feeling his lips searching for her breast. She pictured them, arching and swaying as the bus flew down the jet black asphalt. She imagined the sweeping feeling, the rippling of her skin as the rest of the bus slumped snoring. His breath would be sweet, his skin as soft as a dog's ear. He was like an angel in the dream, allowing her to enter heaven.

His kiss startled her. It was firm and warm. She started to kiss back, but his lips were moving away. "Don't stop," she said, opening her eyes.

"Gotta go. Dad's waiting for me. Here. If you're ever in Springfield, look me up. I'd love to spend some time with you alone. Sorry. You seem nice--anybody our age who travels with their grandma has to be. You've got quite a grip. I don't know if my hand will ever be the same." He handed Clair a napkin with his name, address and phone number on it, grabbed his duffel bag and walked down the aisle. I could follow that ass anywhere, she thought.

"What the hell am I doing?" Clair felt her whole body tighten. I spend the night before my wedding holding hands with some college kid from Columbus. Walk down the aisle. That's what I'm going to do. Clair jumped up and rushed down the aisle, asking the bus driver how much time she had. Eight minutes.

Rushing through the station she looked for Jake. The station was crowded, full of men in business suits, and old ladies with their grandchildren. Unsure of what she would do if she did find him, Clair stood in the midst of all the movement talking to herself. "Got to make up your mind, Clair. What's it gonna be? After a long pause, she ran to the phone, and dropped in enough quarters to make her call. Once again she got Doug's answering machine.

"This is Clair. I'm in Springfield. I will be at the Portland bus station in three hours. See you there?"

Clair bought two jelly rolls and a cup of coffee for Amanda. They switched seats, so Clair could watch the scenery, green rolling hills dotted with trees, and glimpses of the ocean. Clair had never seen the ocean before. It was a giant grey blue haze in the distance, mingling with the sky. The roads twisted and turned, offering her dozens of vantages from which to see the sea.

As they pulled into Portland, Clair gazed out the window at all of the industrial buildings. It wasn't what she had expected. It looked a lot like Minneapolis and Columbus. She didn't feel excited or giddy, just tired.

"What are you thinking about, Clair?"

Clair could feel Amanda's eyes on her cheek. Still looking out the window, Clair said, "That as far away from home as I am, it's still here. It's still with me. I feel the same. Everything looks the same."

"Some things never leave us. Our pasts, like elbows, are always there whether we think about them or not. Sometimes it takes a good bump to remember that they are there. And believe me dear, amputation isn't the answer. But, I do believe upon closer inspection, you'll begin to see some differences in both the landscape and yourself. Give it time, Clair."

"Amanda, what is fate?"

"Fate dear? Fate is the explanation we humans give to the unexplainable. It's the belief that somebody or something is looking out for us. Why do you ask?"

"Because Doug my boyfriend, said our meeting was fate. I just wanted to be sure I knew what he was talking about."

"Will you marry after traveling all this way?"

"If he is at the station, I believe it's my fate to marry him."

"That's fair enough."

Clair looked at Amanda, trying to detect disappointment, concern, something from her face, for her voice revealed nothing. She saw the face of her grandmother in Amanda's. It looked worried in a confident sort of way. She thought about the eight hundred dollars and the gold ring her grandmother had left her. It was her grandmother who had looked out for her, made sure she had shoes that fit, a decent meal each day, gave her small presents that made her feel special. Her mother never noticed when Clair's clothes were too ragged to wear, never asked how school was, never said a word about Eddie.

Clair felt terrible, remembering the watch she had lost. She wished she could go back to that spot in the woods and search until she found it. She wished she had never met Eddie, had never learned about love. She didn't deserve her grandmother's kindness. If her grandmother was still alive, Clair thought she probably wouldn't be on the bus right now. Her grandmother would have noticed her leaving. She would have stopped her.

As the bus came to a stop, Amanda reached inside her hand-bag and offered Clair her books. Clair handed Amanda the harlequin romance since Amanda had never read one, and one of the squirrel skulls.

"My grandfather made this. It's kind of gross, but it's something I've had for a very long time. I want you to have it."

"It's exquisite."

"Granddad believed everything had at least one other use, another life. It was as if he was searching for something to turn himself into--but Grandma loved him just the same. Rambling, road kill and all. Although as hard as I've tried, I can't think of a use for a painted squirrel skull..."

"To remember you by." Amanda put her gifts carefully away.

"Do you know what your gentleman looks like?"

"I have this newspaper picture of him somewhere." Clair dug in her purse for the clipping.

"Do you want me to wait with you? Oh probably not... you don't need an old woman hanging around..."

Clair wanted to say yes, stay, but her lips wouldn't move.

Waiting for the seats to empty in front of them, they said nothing. Finally it was their turn. Amanda got up, and stepped back to let Clair go first. As they walked down the three steps and across the parking lot to the station Amanda breathed in the bus exhaust, and said to herself, "exhaustion" as Clair said, "At last, fresh air."

Once inside the station Amanda took Clair's hand and said something to her, but Clair didn't catch a word of it. She hugged Amanda and watched her walk away. Clair decided to stand by the arrivals sign. People swarmed by, bumped into her luggage, but no one stopped. As the crowd thinned a young man got up from his chair on the other side of the station and made his way towards her. Clair's underarms moistened. As the man got closer, Clair took a deep breath and practiced a "Hello Doug, hello Sweety," but the man walked right passed her, his arms outstretched to a young woman behind her.

Fifteen minutes passed. The station was emptying out. She picked up her suitcases and walked over towards the phone. Amanda stepped out of the first booth.

"Ah, dear, you're still here." She smiled at Clair. "My taxi didn't show. Besides, I had to see how your story ends. I couldn't leave so close to the conclusion."

"He didn't come."

"Why don't you try calling again..."

"I can't. He knew I was coming and I said if he was here I would marry him. He's not here, therefore..." Clair held the piece of paper in her hand that she had scribbled his number on at Sears.

"Clair, dear, may I see that?"

Handing the paper to Amanda, Clair took one last look around the station, not sure if she was happy not to be getting married, or angry because she had been stood up--big time. Fate either way though.

"Clair. There has been a horrible mistake. This isn't a Portland number, the area code is all wrong. Portland's area code is 207. My god, honey, this is a Portland, Oregon telephone number. I'm sure of it. You're in the wrong Portland."

"The wrong Portland? There is more than one Portland? Shit. You're telling me that Bea got me a ticket to the wrong Portland?"

"Yes, that's what I'm telling you. Maybe this isn't so...horrible. You may not have been jilted, and you've got your whole life in front of you now. This is a new start, a chance to figure out what you really want to do. I believe it's fate, dear, for I could use a traveling companion almost as much as you could use a lesson in geography. Grab those bags, will you? The taxi should be here any minute. Welcome to Maine, Clair."

Road

Diane Glancy

*The fire of God is fallen from heaven,
and hath burned up the sheep.*
       Job 1:16

*Behold now, I have two daughters which have
not known man; let me, I pray you, bring
them out unto you, and do ye to them as is
good in your eyes.*
       Genesis 19:8

She was on the road all the time. She couldn't stop traveling. She had to feel the land passing under her. She had a daughter with a sick child. She had an aging aunt. She had to keep moving between them. She could talk to her companion on the phone. How could they be close when she was always gone? He would ask. Well, she had to keep traveling and he couldn't always follow.

The road pulled against the hard things she had to pull against. The twenty-pound turkey her daughter had bought when there were just the four of them and one was the sick child. She'd thawed the frozen bird in the bathtub in cold water all night. Her daughter's sink in the kitchen was not deep enough to cover it. She remembered her daughter's frustration and impatience. Her temper at being constrained a small box of a life. She wanted to kick against the walls of the apartment. Knock it down. Start over.

She had felt a tearing in herself as she worked in the kitchen with her daughter. She was angry because she'd worked hard to sew her life together and her daughter's problems were pulling at the stitches.

When was she coming back? He asked on the phone.

She remembered she'd watched television as she talked to her companion. Switching back and forth between the channels. There'd been a drought in Australia. Another drought in Africa. She remembered the kangaroo running. There were brushfires in the Blue Mountains. Then she watched a baby elephant who couldn't stand.

I thought the lions were going to eat him, she said on the phone.

She remembered the mother tossing him with her foot to get him to stand. But the little elephant couldn't stand. He had tried pathetically to follow the herd, walking on the knees of his front legs. Not even able to reach his mother to nurse.

She loved calling him her boyfriend. They were both grandparents. Their lives were established, yet there was that longing for companionship, for otherness. But their lives were separate. She was always traveling. She even went to church while he was content to read the Sunday paper and say he'd like to go. Maybe someday he would go, but for now she went to church by herself.

There's been another calf born. Was it Australia? Africa? He was hardly breathing in the hot sun. She remembered the drought again when she talked to her boyfriend from the road. The mother had lifted him in the air in her trunk and carried him above her head to the shade of a scraggly bush.

There'd been another elephant in labor. Her thin tail high in the air as she stepped backwards. She wouldn't go near her baby when it was born and another elephant removed the sack and saw it was stillborn. Still another elephant touched the dead calf with her back feet in an elephant ceremony, kicking up the ground as if searching for roots in drought.

The little elephant who couldn't stand was bigger than any calf the commentator had seen. He'd been cramped in the womb with his legs under him. He couldn't straighten his front legs. He'd rub his knees raw trying to walk that way and they'd get infected. And the little elephant still couldn't stand. He'd still fall over when he'd try to reach his mother for milk.

But wildlife regulation and objectivism prevented the commentator or the park officials from doing anything.

She had looked away from the television. It reminded her of her daughter's child. The burning African fever she'd felt when she held her. Her daughter's father had come. Her former husband who'd left them stranded. She'd been in church when she heard a minister read about Lot who offered his daughters to the crowd instead of the men they wanted. But the men were really angels who only looked like men. They had come to tell Lot that Sodom would be destroyed. Lot gave them lodging in his house for the night and the Sodomites came asking for them. Lot had offered his daughters instead. How could he? The angels could take care of themselves. But the Bible was real life. She knew a man could give his family away.

Then there'd been a fire. She said to her boyfriend on

the phone when they talked again. Just like in Australia. The grasses crackled. Maybe the whole continent would burn. The animal herds stampeded. A lizard climbed a branch.

She wasn't one for observation. She would have gotten in there and kicked dust,

She passed a shed on its knees like the little elephant. The thickets of bright yellow leaves. A thin white dog walking beside the highway. The flock of geese. A splatter of birds.

Yes, on the road she was in the outback. She was in the jungle. She was on a safari of fast moving cars. Switching between her daughter and aunt as if they were television programs. She loved the migration over the road. It gave her a chance to think. To get perspective. To see where she was going. Cars were the parade of the highway.

She remembered the intelligent look in her daughter's eye, but she hadn't developed her intelligence. It was there. It was just something she wasn't using. For now she seemed dull. Maybe it was the dullness of her marriage and the no-way-out life she lived. The demands of the sick child. An uncaring husband and father.

Her own father had also traveled. How often had he been gone? How he had wanted to fly. Then she'd had a husband who was the same. Did everyone want to be away from her? She'd had a relationship since her divorce many years ago. She'd had several relationships. But she felt that final life with someone wouldn't happen. That final man would not come into her life.

The aging aunt had a husband, her uncle by marriage. They'd been together over fifty years. It was strange how some people came into the world in pairs. They only had to spend a few years of childhood on their own and then they were with their mate all their lives. They only had to meet one another. They were so much like one person you knew when one died the other wouldn't be far behind. Following into the beyond.

In her aunt and uncle's house there was order. The glasses for company had been unwrapped and boxed again with the cardboard sections. Everything was in its place.

They could wait all day to read their paper because they had such generous amounts of time. She had to grab what would be hers.

She felt their little vacuum she carried with her in the car.

The ticking clock in their house. The quietness. The turning of a page. Cathedral cookies and Divinity her aunt made, her cane hanging over the chair.

The morning sun was brilliant on the clouds. The geese and the sprinkle of birds in the clouded sky. The usual autumn when the cold mornings caused the sap to rise. Isn't that what made some leaves turn red and yellow, and others a shiny brown as if they were made of iron and rusted in the damp autumn mornings?

She heard a rock thrown up on the windshield. A truck passed on the interstate and she picked up speed to follow. A Batesville Casket Company truck with an evergreen on its side. She passed some farmhouses, a flash of cattle, the lovely air.

There was a band of sky through the clouds. Sometimes she'd be thinking and the time would travel. Other times it took forever. A mile was a long way. And she traveled hundreds. She put her blinker on and passed another car.

There was a harvester in a field with a long nose. She remembered the lizard crawling up a branch to get away from the fire. Her legs felt hot and she turned down the heat.

The spitting fire of the African grasses. She was that lizard clinging to a branch. She was the elephant on her knees. Isn't that what living did? With its tongue of fire. Its cramped situations. She had gotten singed. She had gotten burned. Her daughter was in line for the same.

Her former husband had come to her daughter's apartment looking like he'd been to the Australian outback. How much had his jacket cost. How much had he withheld from them? The lawyer she got once had cost her more than the court had awarded her. Then her daughter had turned eighteen and his meager payments were over.

He hardly looked at his sick grandchild. His daughter made him a turkey sandwich and he ate in the other room. Away from her, his former wife. Why had he even come? He only stirred up old ground. She could take him between her hands. Tell him she was more of a man. She could rip off his jacket and wear it herself. She could make him an ash with the heat of her words.

But it was in church she had dumped her anger. It was in prayer she had spoken her hostility. The unfairness of it all.

In their prayer meetings at church, there had been

other women who cried, still in love with their husbands. At least she was over that. Yes, she could crawl up his arm like a lizard. She could eat his eyes.

Faith was a companion more than her husband had been. Faith was more than her boyfriend. It was faith that held her like the sun coming up on another field. The cornstalks in the field with their arms lifted as if asking the sky to pick them up.

She heard the men in her church group talk about their anger also. Sometimes it worked both ways. They didn't always get off either.

They all had feet like the little elephant with his tendons not stretched, walking on their knees. But the elephant finally stood. He'd finally nudged his mother for milk. She had thought, watching television, he'd probably die from the lions. She felt every effort he made. Probably her son-in-law had noticed how intensely she watched the program. But she had struggled like the elephant. It was what she had found out. She would have to bow her knees before God to get anywhere. That's why she had knees so they'd bend. That's why she liked driving. It kept her knees bent. She was such a combination of hate and love. Weakness and strength. Triumph and failure.

She was full of bitter memories. Bright expectations. She'd had a husband who had let her down. A boyfriend who wasn't as adventurous as she was. A daughter who was locked in frustration. An aunt and uncle facing old age and death. A television which could jump all over the world. A minister who said God's love rested on them all. A God who understood their ambiguity and hurt. Their humanness.

She'd thought about her boyfriend that night she'd slept on her daughter's couch. After her son-in-law had gone to bed. Wakened at times by the child.

She felt brittle as leaves about to fall. Maybe she'd walk only a short time in the history of the upright, then return to her bed like an old aunt or a sick child. And her spirit would separate to her maker like the interchanges on the highway. The forks in the road. The bypasses.

She drove on the highway and saw the cattails along the ditches. The thickets along the fences. The farmhouses. The crowd of cows in the harvested cornrows. Fields. Pastures. The flock of birds. The spattering of geese. The sky.

It wasn't that her boyfriend didn't want to go with her, but there was something missing in their relationship that she thought about and he didn't when their brittle bones embraced.

She wondered what she'd do with her aging aunt. They had no children. After her parents' death, they thought she was their child. She was glad the road was between them. She felt choppy as the silvery surface of a cold lake she passed.

Was she becoming a man as she aged? She could keep up with them on the highway. She could drive with them after dark and keep going, rise early, move on. She could be part of the momentum of migration over the land. Not some wiggler over the road.

She had learned to change her oil. She knew where the crankshaft was.

But why did she define that independent part of herself as a man? Her ability to drive. Her willfulness. Her self-centeredness. It was what she'd seen in men. She wasn't going to move over and make room for someone. She didn't have the patience to start over. To do all that again. Maybe she was becoming like the former husband she didn't like.

Maybe she could see her anger and strength as part of her womanliness. She had not discarded her caring for others. She felt her gentleness. Religion.

Where the divided highway was separated by some distance, the oncoming traffic move like farmhouses along the road.

But it was a man whose voice emerged from her now as she traveled. She was her own friend. Women were women for a while, then the man in them took the wheel.

Soon she'd stop for gas and call her boyfriend again from the road and they'd talk and there'd be that closeness she longed for. But when it came down to it, he would stay in his house and she would stay in hers. She'd still be on the road alone. The oneness of her aunt and uncle would not be hers. When she put her hand in her glove on a cold morning, it was her own glove she put her hand into. It was herself she fit into.

She would have to be satisfied. Otherwise, if she asked for a chair, she'd be asking for a table.

A room.
A house.
A country.
A name.
A story with meaning.

An afterlife.

She'd be asking for a God who heard and answered. Who wouldn't rage fire across the African and Australian plain. Who would convince the world more clearly he was there.

Yes. Now the trucks were teepees moving on the hill. She could identify with Burlington and other names of migration. Tarps flopping like the loppy run of a young elephant. His penis nearly reaching the ground. Ribbons of clouds over the fields. The little white pebbles of the cows. It was like switching television channels.

What would Africa be like in frost, muted more than it was by drought? The lizard shivering under his thick plates of skin. How could the continent prepare for snow?

Every time the man ahead of her got on his car phone he slowed down. Why couldn't he talk and drive at the same speed? She took the mantle of her father and uncle who had been drivers an put it on her shoulders. Now she imagined her father as a pilot over the humps of air. Those mounds in space the mound builders left when they traveled to the beyond. Those humps in the air a plane bumped over.

For a while she followed a man in a pickup with a sense of order. She felt the leaves. The shiny road. The precision of his driving.

While God was in his aloneness above the clouds, hoarding unanswered prayers on his lap, his wholeness sat on the road. The farmpond and fields. God of Lot who offered his daughters to the mob. Who made people full of flaws. Or let them get that way on their own. Who filled the earth with the autumn trees soaking in the light

Sometimes a little elephant pulled through. She remembered his first wobbly reach to drink from his mother. The tears in her eyes. Her thought that her daughter and granddaughter and aunt would pull through. She would also.

Because somewhere over the fields she traveled, the minister said there was a God of the highway.

A God of the road.

She felt as if she'd turned into the universe crisscrossing the stars. Yes, if there was one road left, she'd take it herself.

Bitter Wine

Carol Mohrbacher

Retsina is a wine native to the island of Hydra, which is about one hour south of Athens by hydrofoil. The wine is as harsh as the rocky island itself. Just as no sweetness relieves the bitter taste of the tanin in the wine, no gentle field or green forest interrupts the island's angular grayness. In Tassos' Restaurant, the retsina is plentiful this wet and windy December 26th. Each table is marked by a rust red pitcher of the pink wine and a checkered table cloth. Bouzouki music bounces off the white stone walls and sound of conversation and laughter fill the large room. Tassos, the proprietor, visits each table, cigarette growing from the corner of his mouth.

"*Kahleespehrah*, Vlasi. So these are your young American friends and this must be sweet Gena," Tassos' eyes roam over Gena's tall, athletic body. They stop at the bottom of her low cut blouse.

"Don't get any ideas, Tassos," Vlasi warns. "You have a wife, who is watching you as you speak. Besides, Gena and David will soon be married and Gena is a good girl. Right David?"

"That's what *she* says," David mumbles and sullenly continues to write on the back of a picture postcard. No one listens to him. No one ever listens to him when he's with Gena. Gena is a large-boned, vivacious 22 year-old and, in comparison, David appears nervous, spare and almost colorless.

Linda, Vlasi's American wife of seventeen years looks on soberly. She won't drink alcohol on the island, only in their apartment on the mainland. She'd made this decision after having had a drunken one-night affair with Dimitri, a donkey driver. The next day Dimitri triumphantly revealed the affair to all who would listen in the men's bar in town. This was two years ago and a bitterness changed the marriage and made Linda an outcast among Vlasi's extended family. Vlasi used the incident to hurt Linda and garner sympathy for himself when he was drunk or angry.

"Gena, this is Tassos, owner of this high-class establishment, Hydra's perennial host and also its biggest letch," Linda says, winking at Gena, as she reaches for her Bic to light a Marlboro.

Even though American cigarettes are almost three times the price of Greek cigarettes, she still buys them. She clings stubbornly to small pieces of her former life. Vlasi and Linda moved to the island, Vlasi's birthplace, five years ago, after he'd retired and sold his business in New York City. She did not want to move but she and Vlasi had decided before they were married that when they had enough money to retire, they would return to care for his mother. Linda is desperately lonely for the U.S., so when she met the backpacking young couple on the mainland, she enthusiastically suggested that they come to the island and spend Christmas day with her and Vlasi. Linda had gotten them a discounted rate at the hotel where she works. David said that the hot shower and comfortable bed were exactly what he wanted for Christmas and showed his thanks by giving Linda a lighter with a picture of the Eiffel Tower on it. Gena and David were to leave tomorrow to continue their travels and this night was sort of farewell.

Although Linda liked them both, Gena was beginning to get on her nerves. Linda had watched as Gena's relationship with Vlasi changed from a filial one to one of flirtation. Gena insisted on calling Linda and Vlasi mama and papa. While at first this was charming, now it irritated Linda.

"Papa, papa, how do you say please in Greek?" Gena asks.

"*Pahrahkahlo*, Gena. And just why do you want to say that?"

"I want to ask Tassos for more retsina."

"Tassos, more retsina for Gena." Vlasi's booming voice can be heard through the restaurant.

Gena is beginning to get drunk. Her eyes are glassy, two pink spots color her cheeks and her words trip over one another.

"Gena, you need to slow down," David says, knowing it is useless to say anything. She thinks that he is far too conservative.

"Oh, David, relax, have some fun, do something. Sometimes I think you were born old!"

Tassos' wife, Vasiliki, goes from table to table searching for recruits for a women's handkerchief dance.

"Gena, will you come dance with us?"

"Oh yes, I'd love to. Mama, will you dance with us?"

Linda winces at the word, "mama." No dear, go ahead. I'll just watch you dance and keep David company."

"David doesn't want any company. He doesn't want to enjoy himself. Come dance with us. Pleeease!!" Her whining voice is like a fingernail on a blackboard to Linda.

"No, thank you, dear. I really don't feel like dancing right now. Maybe later."

The Greek dance is subtle, the arms raised, feet moving slowly and deliberately. The women dance in a circle, lightly holding each other's hands in the air. Vasiliki is the leader. She and the woman on her left hold a white handkerchief in the air between them. They begin slowly, and gradually pick up speed. This is the same dance that their ancestors danced a thousand years ago. Gena dances in a grand, noisy, American fashion, all arms and legs, looking like she'd be more at home with rock and roll. The women try to teach her, to subdue her. This does not good. Toward the end of the dance she is dancing, or rather, flailing in the middle of the circle, convinced that she is turning in her most superb performance.

"Oooo! This is painful to watch," David moans as he covers his eyes.

Vlasi scowls at David. "She's just having a good time, David. Leave her alone. Let her have her night." He is watching Gena with glee and clapping his hands in time to the music.

"I'm sorry, Linda," David apologizes, "Gena's not a very good drunk."

"Don't worry about it. Are you O.K.? You're very quiet tonight."

"Yeah, well sort of. I've just been thinking about Gena and I. *She* decided we were going to get married and *she* decided to buy a ring. She decides everything. I'm confused. I know this sounds crazy but I'm not even sure that I want to marry her. I love her but sometimes I don't really like her."

"No, it doesn't sound crazy. I know exactly what you mean. So what are you going to do about it?"

He shrugs his shoulders and sighs. "Punt," he says softly.

Gena finishes her performance and heads back to the table, more flushed than when she left. She is waving her hand to cool her face.

"Vlasi, papa, come dance with me."

"No, Gena, I'm sorry but I can't. Your papa has a bad leg. I haven't danced in many years."

"Come, Gena, I'll dance with you." Tassos has

appeared from nowhere, seizing the opportunity to dance with the voluptuous and very drunk girl. He pulls her to the dance floor and locking hips, they begin to dance seductively.

"He will take advantage of her. I just know it," says Vlasi, tensely, with a jealous edge to his voice. He watches their every move. They are dancing much too closely, American style and Tassos' wife sits on the edge of her chair watching, wearing a straight line smile, while her women friends whisper in her ears. The dance finally ends and Gena returns again to the table, sits heavily in Vlasi's lap and downs another glass of retsina. Drops of the wine roll down the corners of her mouth and onto her white blouse.

"More retsina, Tassos. Papa dance with me, please," she whines.

Vlasi no longer feels the constant pain in his leg. While Gena danced with Tassos, he had finished a pitcher of wine. He has lost his clearheadedness and gained a youthful bravado.

"O.K., just for you, dear Gena, your papa will dance." With that, they both stagger to the dance floor. They dance, leaning heavily against each other, occasionally stumbling.

"Oh brother, this is embarrassing, Linda."

"David, you don't have to feel guilty about this. It's not your fault. She's drunk. Tassos is drunk. I think maybe you had better take her back to the hotel, though, before she makes every woman in here jealous enough to kill her."

"I don't think she'll come."

"Well, we'll just have to convince her."

The music ends and Vlasi and Gena move toward the table, laughing, oblivious to the eyes that follow them.

"Thank you, papa. This is the best night of my life." says Gena thickly as she and Vlasi try to untangle their chairs and coats and sit down.

"Papa, do you love me? Do you love your Gena?"

"Yes, Gena, I love you."

"Then kiss me, papa."

Vlasi looks into Gena's deep eyes for a moment. Then they kiss, not a father/daughter kiss but lover's kiss, a lingering, deep lover's kiss. Vlasi and Gena ignore everyone and everything but each other. Their drunkenness has made them forget where they are.

"ENOUGH!" David shouts. "Get your coat on. We are going back to the hotel." For one frozen moment, all conversation ceases. Everyone watches David.

"NOW!"

"David, we're just having fun. Just because you..."

"NOW!"

"David, don't be so hard on Gena. She's young. She brings life to this place," Vlasi says meekly. He is clearly surprised at David's outburst.

"Vlasi, SHUT UP!" Linda says in icy measured tones. "It's between them. It's none of your business." Vlasi starts to protest, but catches his wife's malevolent glare and backs down.

David helps Gena with her coat as he mumbles an apology to Linda. He promises to write and also to send he some Lipton's Onion Soup when he returns to the states. She can't find the soup in Greece and she needs it to make the gravy for her American pot roast. David supports his wobbling fiancee as they walk towards the door.

"Bye everyone, good-bye Hydra. I love you all," Gena gushes as David herds her toward the door. She is still bidding her farewells as the door closes behind them. The life drains from the restaurant at their departure. Tassos has turned of the music. People begin to leave.

"Tassos, more retsina!" Vlasi booms, pounding his fist on the table. He doesn't want the party to end.

"No, Vlasi, you're drunk. I don't want to carry you up the hill," Linda says with a parental sternness as she dismisses Tassos with a wave of her hand.

Vlasi is complacent as Linda zips up his jacket, arranges his hat on his head and guides him to the door. They leave the restaurant without speaking and begin their long ascent through the ancient, narrow, cobblestoned streets.

After walking for a few minutes, Vlasi ducks behind a low stone wall to relieve himself. He is angrily mumbling to himself. Linda watches and smokes. Suddenly he drops from sight.

"Linda, help me! I fell. I smashed my face."

She rushes behind the wall to find a very disconcerted Vlasi sitting on the ground, holding his nose. There is a gash across the bridge and a lot of blood. There is little doubt that he will have two black eyes in the morning. Linda sits on the ground next to Vlasi, retrieves a dirty kleenex from her purse, and shoves it at him.

"Here, hold this on the cut till it stops bleeding. Now come on, get up. Let's get home so I can see your face in the light."

Vlasi won't budge. "Linda, you shamed me in front of my friends when you shouted at me in the restaurant. This is Greece, not America. Women don't do that here."

Linda rolls her eyes. She's heard this line before. He wasn't the same Vlasi that she had married, the Vlasi who encouraged and loved her independence, the Vlasi who affectionately called her his "sassy American wife." The island had changed them both. She had become sullen and subdued and Vlasi had begun to brood and swagger as though some ancient Greek sailor possessed him.

Vlasi reaches into his pocket to see if his wallet is still there after the fall. He looks inside.

"Linda, where's my money? Who took my money? That Tassos is a thief. He took all my money."

"You spent your money trying to show off, buying drinks and food for everyone, trying to be a big man. Tomorrow, you will be a small man with a smashed face."

"Linda," Vlasi says softly, "did you love that son-of-a-bitch donkey driver?" Even though he has known Dimitri since childhood, he refused to speak his name since he found out about the affair.

"No, Vlasi. I was drunk like you are now. I made a mistake."

She brushes some dirt from his shoulder and kisses him lightly on the cheek. He puts his arm around her. A calmness settles on both of them as they listen to the night and to each other's breathing.

"Let's go, darlin'," Linda whispers as she helps her husband to his feet.

It has stopped raining. The half moon reflects off the stone street. In silhouette, the pair appear as one, as they make their way up the hill.

Eventual Revenge

Peter Gilbertson

I know what you're thinking. But you've got it all wrong. People keep wanting me to say it, that I'm crazy, but I won't. That would be the quick way out and everything would be neat and tidy. But that would also be a lie. Sometimes I can hardly believe it happened myself. Yet it did. It was real. And not in some far away fantasy land, either. No way, it was right before my eyes, in a place I practically call home.

Okay, wait, I'll admit I pulled the trigger. I didn't mean to, but I was scared. Hector was a good friend of mine. He and Clutch were the only two friends I had. Hector and I really got along. He was usually the loud, smiling guy who knew everyone when we walked into a pool hall, or at least everyone knew him. When the three of us would go out, Hector would chum with everyone, and introduce me to people as his friend. But sometimes he had a real temper. We'd get into bar fights all the time just because Hector was upset with how some "cock" looked at him.

While Hector was a pendulum of emotion, Clutch was pure stone. We called Johnny Ray "Clutch" because he was always so cool under pressure. What made Clutch cool wasn't his look or attitude, but what they complimented--his eyes. They were deep, man. He never flinched. You'd look at the shape of sapphire, like thin ice, right at the edge of his eyes. Then, Bam!, all of a sudden you'd break the surface and plunge into that numbing, midnight pit of the unfeeling centers. He'd stare, his eyes would penetrate, you'd cringe, and he wouldn't even blink. Johnny Ray was always in control. Nothing fazed him. We always said, "Johnny comes through in the clutch."

"Count it."
"What?" I mumbled. My head was throbbing. My whole everything was shrouded in a dull ache. It was as if a thick, fat, gelatin, glob of solid confusion was draped and clinging to my head and hanging down my body, forcing me to slouch. The glob of confusion absorbed half of everything I thought, and half of everything I heard. So even though my mind was racing, I was only hearing and speaking half coherent thoughts. I was barely aware Johnny

spoke.

"You deaf? I said count it." Clutch finished his sentence by taking a swig out of his bottle of cheap malt liquor. He kept one hand on the wheel, the other hand firm around his bottle, and both eyes on the road. They never moved. Sometimes I got the shakes just watching or listening to him. I've heard that the eyes are the windows to a person's soul. You could see how a person's essence by looking through their soul windows. But all I ever saw in John's eyes was unfeeling blackness. It was an empty void. Anything in there was buried deep.

His voice had the same effect. No emotion. No inflection. Only a dead bass. It allowed him to speak in hypnotizing sermons.

I glanced over again and watched him drive. I couldn't believe it. He was still the same. After what we did he was still in control, acting like nothing happened. I could see it in the way he drove. His eyes and tendons were one, operating like a machine. His arms and legs reacted to what his eyes told him.

We were doing 80 down some dusty Arizona highway after midnight with the high beams on and not another car in sight. Man, I was sick. Those half-thoughts kept whizzing through my head as fast as the dotted lines sped under our car. Maybe it was only a bad mix of all the booze and pot, but I was beyond gone. This wasn't an ordinary high. I wasn't even close to being in touch. All I could do was blink.

"You gonna count it?" John asked in the same cool even tone. This wasn't the first robbery we pulled. Not that we were big time thieves or anything. Usually we'd just take small convenience stores near the highways or hit a restaurant for some pocket money and jewelry. The irony is that the only gold we got was mostly those free junk necklaces you get for signing up for credit cards.

"Danny, roll down you window," Clutch said.

"What?" I breathed. My eyes were barely open.

"I'm hot. Roll down your window a crack."

"Sure," I said. My hands fumbled for the handle. I couldn't roll it down. It wouldn't budge. The motion was too awkward.

John leaned forward and popped in a cassette tape. It wasn't to his liking. "This tape sucks. Where's that Serpent Doom tape of mine?"

I almost passed out instantly. I knew where it was. "Ah, I think Hec's got it."

Clutch didn't even flinch. "Hec's dead, Danny.
"Screw it. Let's listen to the radio."

Some punk DJ call in show was on. You know, the kind where they take requests live and talk real primitive on the radio.
"Hey, this is KBUZ 660. You're on the air."
"Hello?" said the caller. It was a male voice
"Yeah, what's your beef?"
"I'd just like to say to my buddy, Little Junior, 'I've got your tape and I'll get it back to you tonight.' Meantime, please play 'Next Time' by Serpent Doom for him. Thanks."
I shit my pants. I literally almost shit my pants. Hector used to call Johnny Ray, 'J.R.' or 'Little Junior' when they'd get into fights. But nobody else dared to sat that to Clutch! He pulled a knife on one guy for saying it. It had to be Hector.
Clutch didn't bat an eye. He just switched off the radio and pressed the cigarette lighter and waited. The whole time I just sat there gaping at him. Seconds passed, and then John calmly lit his smoke, took one drag and said, "You can relax now, Dan. You didn't kill Hector."
This time I didn't have any trouble with the window handle. I launched my head out the window, and I puked real hard. When I stopped dry heaving, I was bent over outside the door groaning, with my hands braced, but buckling, against the outside of the car door. My stomach was knotted so tight I couldn't pull my self in. I was stuck, upside down and helpless, leaning outside the window. I could feel the oncoming of a severe blood rush in my head. At the same time I felt all of the fluid in my nose and mouth was draining out of my skull. My head swelled until it felt like my heart was pounding in my head; I got woozy and my hands slipped off the door and my chest slammed back to where my hands had been supporting me. Pain shot up my arms as I watched my knuckles dance and leave behind pieces of flesh upon the road as they grazed. The oncoming blur of gravel below was getting closer. I felt myself helplessly slipping out of the car head first, at a slow, stupid rate. I remember thinking, "Here it comes." Before I was about to hit, Clutch leaned over and pulled me in by one of the ass loops on my jeans. I was a mess. I was so bad I couldn't even wipe the snot and puke drool off my face, let alone say, "thank you." I just sat there dumb.
We kept driving and my half-thoughts continued. I

kept seeing the blood. All that blood. Why'd Clutch make me do it? It made sense when he explained it before, but not after I did it when we were riding in the car; mostly because I couldn't remember how Clutch had explained it. See, Clutch had caught Hector skimming money on the last job. It was like ten bucks or something. Anyway, a few days before we were going to pull the last job, I was with Clutch in his apartment. It always smelled like a combination of soiled laundry from the garage John worked at and incense. We were smoking up and drinking some Venom Bite tequila. John's apartment was pretty dark in the first place, and all the smoke we were creating didn't help. The only light he had on was his blue lava lamp. It cast an eerie glow on everything, including John's face which I could barely see through the thick smoke and incense. The place reminded me of some spooky oracle from the movies. But I didn't need to see him. I just liked listening to him. He used to tell me things about life, like a sage would. I was just out of high school, living with my folks. I thought he was everything I wanted to be.

When I had talked to him on the phone he told me to come on over for some smoke and Bite, and to bring "our" gun, and later on we'd meet Hector at the pool hall. When I got over there, Clutch had already started smoking and drinking. We always did this. It was like some kind of event or ritual. I grabbed a glass and we started talking. That's when Clutch told me about the missing money and said Hector would probably steal all the money next time.

"You think so?" I asked.

"Shit, yeah. What's to stop him?" Then he explained other things about Hector, and reasons to kill him, while he got me good and stoned. I looked at the gun in my hands and started thinking. I was sure Clutch was right. He was always right. I looked up and saw him just sitting there staring at me through the smoky haze. I'd swear he had a grin.

"You think you're pretty invincible, don't you?" I asked.

"Yeah, pretty invincible," he replied and took a swig out of his bottle.

At the time I was drunk, stoned and pissed off. The way Clutch told it to me, man I wanted to kill Hector on the spot. But Clutch told me to be cool, and wait. I wanted to be just like Clutch. Who didn't? Everyone did, except Hector and Hector's sister Cassandra. They were the only ones I knew who didn't idolize the guy. So I waited. Man,

I was cool. You should've seen me. I was just fucking beautiful.

This is how it works when we do a job. Hec grows out his beard before the job, then shaves it off after. So first, he goes in there disguised and bullshits with the cashier, while Clutch and I pull up to the pumps. As soon as Hector's got the cashier's attention we head in and leave the car running. We both had to go in because Hector didn't trust leaving anyone in the car during a crime, especially when the car was supposed to be running. Just before we get in the store, John and I pull up our handkerchiefs from our necks and put on sunglasses. That's when I pull the gun and cover the cashier. Hector then ties him up with duct tape and grabs the cash while Clutch checks the place for any other attendants. Hec usually grabs a couple of cartons of smokes and a porno magazine on his way out. Meanwhile, I just stare the guy down, keep him covered, and act mean. Hector told me to do the mean part.

I was the only one allowed to touch the gun. Neither Hector nor Clutch trusted each other with the gun. Somehow I was oblivious to this fact. I rationalized they trusted me and it was an act of friendship, or something like that.

Once Hec has the money, Clutch walks back to the car and makes sure no one else is out there. Hector finishes grabbing the other stuff, does his "business," and says he'll follow me out in a second. Hec liked roughing up people he duct taped. He would start molesting them and stuff. I'm glad Clutch always made us hurry up. I didn't like some of the things Hector did to those people.

"Here, drink this. Rinse your mouth out." Clutch twisted the top off and handed me the 20 ouncer of some yellow soda he swiped from the store. I tried wiping my face before I drank, but I couldn't get the crap off me. It just spread over my face and hands and jacket. I took a sip and almost gagged. I had a headache spasm and saw head lights in the mirror.

"Clutch, why'd that kid pull a gun?"

"You scared him, Danny. What would you do if someone pulled a gun on you and you had a gun?" he asked.

I changed the subject. "Is Hec still alive?" I asked.

"What do you think? He finished with another swig on his malt liquor; his eyes were forward the whole time."

All that blood in one night. I was going nuts. That kid didn't need to die. Why didn't he cooperate like everyone else? Hector, man, he yelled at the kid for getting shot and then kicked him. All I could do was stare at the pool of blood spreading over the floor behind the counter. Hector yelled, "Nice shot Danny!" and smiled. It was point blank, anyone could have done it. Still, I wouldn't have shot the kid if he hadn't reached for his gun under the counter after Hec hit him. I hunted snakes and birds with my brother before, but killing a person? That was something I never experienced before.

"No way," I whispered. "No way. I shot him in the heart. Hector has got to be dead. I mean, all that blood."

"Then he's dead," said the cool even tone.

"But that voice! On the radio!" I pleaded. "What about that?" Clutch too a long sip, eyes forward. This time, though, his hand was trembling. I could see the liquor in the bottle making minor ripples back and forth. I knew what he was thinking. "Clutch, I know that was Hec."

"Cripes, Dan, we don't even listen to that show. I think Hec, if he was still alive, would have better things to do now than call a radio station from the damn hospital to threaten us. So just cool down!" Clutch took a quick swig, his hand was really shaking now. "See, you know we can't stick around. Robbery is one thing, but you committed a double murder, Dan. That brings the roof right down on top of us."

"But you told me to!" I screamed. I sat up. My head got dizzy.

"That's you defense?" said the Voice. "Dan there isn't a court in the world today that wouldn't convict you with a plea like that." We were both quiet for a long, silent second. "I guess we'll be leaving the state for a couple days. Go to Utah or something."

My half-thought repeated. "That voice on the radio," I whimpered in fear, "You know Hec was into that exorcism shit."

Clutch blinked and checked the rearview mirror. "Man, this guy is on my ass. Where'd he come from? I'm doing 90. Look, we'd be okay, but cops know we're Hec's friends. They'll come looking for us asking questions. My cousin lives on the border. We'll shack up there and that'll be our alibi, going to the bar with my cousin. I'll make a few phone calls and find out what people are saying. Cassandra will go crazy, but we'll deal with that later..."

I started thinking about Hector's death over a lousy ten dollars. What did I care about ten dollars? Maybe Hector needed it. What if his sister needed glasses or something?

"I'm sorry Hector's dead," I interrupted.

Clutch looked through me, "Yeah, it's a crying shame."

He continued rambling on about what we had to do. I couldn't stop half-thinking about the heist. It was just a nod. That was out signal. I almost forgot about the agreement Clutch and I had made.

"Let's go," said Clutch.

"Would you wait!" yelled Hector. "I haven't got all the money yet. There's blood everywhere, man." The blood was dripping off the counter, splashing on Hector's boots. Hector was squatting behind the counter filling a paper bag with the money from the cash register drawer that Hec had set on the kid's chest.

"Get the money and let's go. Don't waste any time. Drop that gun Hector! You know our agreement!" I didn't know it at the time, but I found out from some "friends" that Clutch and Hector agreed to let me have the only gun on the jobsand if either one found any gun, no matter how expensive, they'd leave it. Clutch had caught Hector holding the cashier's gun.

Hector recovered quickly. "Danny's supposed to count it!" he shouted as he wiped the piece off with his shirt and threw it in the garbage can next to the cashier's head.

"Give it to him in the car like you always do.. We've got to go now." Clutch sprinted out the door. I was still panicked from the shooting. I glanced at Hector and then followed Clutch. When I got outside, Clutch was already standing on the driver's side with the car door open and one foot inside. I was sprinting toward the car and Hector was a little behind me. He had the bag of money in one hand, his standard carton of cigarettes and handful of porno mags in the other, and a big, old smile on his face. The kid's blood was over Hector.

Clutch just smiled at me as I approached the car and gave me a simultaneous wink and nod. It was body language loud and clear. I smiled back, and remembered out agreement. Suddenly I wasn't scared anymore. I was angry all over again. Angry about the money, angry about the kid, about the blood, the betrayals everything. I spun around and fired without hesitation. Hec was grinning at me when I squeezed the trigger. His whole body exploded. It was on me now too. More blood, flying everywhere. Hec was dead before he hit the ground.

I was stunned. I killed one of my best friends.

Clutch told me to get in the car. I stumbled toward it as Clutch quickly slid across the hood and grabbed the paper bag. Hector's blood was smeared on the ground, his clothes, and money bag. Clutch even got some on his hands going for the paper bag. "An eye for an eye," Clutch mumbled as he took Hector's money.

"Are these kids out for a joy ride? I'm doing 120!" Clutch leaned on the horn and snapped me out of my daze. "Fuck this! Danny grab the wheel. Keep it straight." Clutch smoothly placed my hands on the steering wheel and removed the gun from my inside pocket. I couldn't believe it! Clutch gave me control of his car. The car behind us was clicking its high beams and revving up its engine. Clutch rolled down his window, leaned out and squeezed off two rounds. One hit the windshield and the other hit the hood.

Clutch was climbing back in when the car rammed into our bumper. "Son of a bitch!" he swore. "You hold it steady Dan. Keep it under control." John went back out the window. I was leaned over sideways, barely stable, with my hands on the wheel, and my eyes barely over the dash board. Suddenly the radio clicked on by itself. Static was blaring out of the speakers with high pitched squeals of feedback. In the background the damn D.J. was laughing at something. I flipped the knob, but he kept laughing. The radio wouldn't turn off. Then the sound of the voice slowly changed. It became Hector's voice laughing. I stopped breathing.

The car rammed us again. "Bastards!" yelled Clutch. "Let's make it three or four dead tonight, huh?" Clutch finished off the rest of the clip, but the car never stopped coming.

I didn't have time. Clutch was standing on the gas. We were going full bore. I was fighting with the radio. Clutch's legs were in the way. I couldn't reach the brakes. I could barely see the road. The car rammed us again. I started to dry heave, again. My half-thoughts, visions of blood. The noise. The gunshots. The drugs, the booze! Everything, my mind, my body, froze up. Overload.

I missed the curve and we went flying off the road.

I woke up and we were lying in a shallow ditch. I was some ways off from the car. I had gone right through the windshield and I landed upside down on top of some shrubs on the other bank of the ditch. My eyes were facing the car. I don't know how I was conscious. Clutch was still looking back at the other car when we went flying. He smashed his back against the door rail, and snapped his spine in two. The impact threw him sideways a bit, and he barrel rolled across the ditch. I could barely see him. He called out for me. I heard him screaming, but I couldn't speak or move. My body was getting frigid from the loss of blood and the bite of the night air. A cool, narrow trickle ran along my upside down scalp. I would feel each drop, like a pulse, flowing, and then hear it drop into the growing pool beneath me. An occasional cool breeze would rustle through my hair, up my shirt, and change the direction of the mist of breath passing from my motionless lips. For a half hour the two of us lay there, dying.

From my upside down position, I had a crystal clear view of the road, and soon I saw a shadow coming up on the horizon. A black outline of a figure against the night sky. I think Clutch saw him too. Either that or he just knew. It was impossible for me to move, I couldn't look away. The shadow just kept coming with a slow, steady, even stride. I tried to convince myself I wasn't seeing him. This wasn't happening. The terror overwhelmed my pain. My mind became frantic, yet my body was still paralyzed. And he just kept on coming at his steady, ominous pace. I never thought I'd literally see death coming to get me. Especially not with the face of Hector.

He made it, eventually. Hector's skin seemed lighter, dusty. His eyes, though. Man, the skin made his solid black eyes shine. They were two empty pits of complete blackness. He stood right over Johnny Ray and grinned. "Hey Little Junior. Here's your tape back." Hector crammed the cassette into Johnny Ray's mouth. I heard his teeth break. "Come on junior, let's go. Oh, yeah, I've got something else for you to see. Here, take a look." Hector lifted Johnny Ray's head off the ground by the hair. Hector smiled, and spit on Johnny's forehead. Then Hector raised his right hand and drove his fingers into Johnny's eyes. I could hear Johnny screaming--even with the tape in his mouth. Hector laughed and started dragging Johnny away by the head. It was almost like he was holding a bowling ball.

Then Hector looked at me. My eyes zoomed in directly on his face. Hector smirked at me, flipped the hair off his brow with his bloody fingers, and then started dragging the person I called Clutch toward me. Hector started giggling. The pace was the same. I couldn't blink,

I couldn't breathe. I wanted to look away, but I couldn't. He kept approaching, smiling. I watched the whole way until Hector was standing above me.

"I'm not going to hurt you Dan." My hand suddenly reached up and touched his stubbled chin. "I believe you were innocent. Mostly." His brow wrinkled and his eyes drew close. My heart stopped beating as he lowered my hand and then stroked my chin with his own hand. He giggled as he slid his hands slowly over my eyes, hesitated, and then gripped my forehead with his free hand. It was like a vice. Hector squeezed until I heard bone crushing and saw galaxies. I passed out for a couple of seconds and woke up to Hector dragging Johnny over the curve and into the sand. John's boot heels left a trail, but his head was so high that his knuckles didn't even touch the ground.

The cops found me the next day and rushed me to the hospital. They told me I was under arrest for armed robbery. They didn't try for murder though, I was surprised. I heard that they followed the trail of Clutch's boot heels until the trail just ended. There was no body. I got a shiver when they didn't mention his knuckles dragging in the sand. Right where the trail ended, the police found the gun I had used the night before, except it only had Clutch's finger prints on it. I guess the security camera didn't catch me shooting the cashier. I found that kind of ironic, because the cameras nailed me on the other 14 counts of armed robbery. When I came to trial, the judge didn't have one look of sympathy in his eyes. He gave some public sermon about scum like me, but before he could finish I started giggling. Right in front of God, my public defender, and everyone in court, I started laughing. That look the judge gave me, I'd seen it before. I suddenly knew a lot more about him than he knew about himself. A couple people in the audience had a similar look that made me smile. Remember what I said about windows and peoples' souls. I see that much better now. Something Hector gave me. If you ever see some dark eyed, black haired kid, in some coffee shop or gas station along a highway, staring at your face, and for no apparent reason laughing directly at you, look out. He might know or see something you don't. I know to some of you this story sounds far out, like it was in a distant land; well let me tell you, honestly, it's all Arizona to me.

Party of One

Jess Lang

Lloyd Burton awoke still hearing the voices.

He fought his way out of the recliner, struggling against his own bulk, paddling his feet toward the floor. At first, he thought the chant came from the ice-covered porch of his house. At first, the chant seemed real.

"Burt-o! Burt-o! Come out and skate. Burt-o! Burt-o!"

My skates, he thought, his mind sixty years away. *Where are my skates? Maybe Mother knows, or Aunt Ellie.* He blundered out of his chair toward the kitchen (*the guys will leave without me if I don't hurry, I'll have to catch up and I'll be IT!*), where the coldness of the tiles under his feet pulled him out of the fog, back into the real world, where his friends were long dead and he was too fat to go ice skating.

Lloyd rubbed his chins with the back of his hand and peered at the yellow dial of the clock on the stove. Three-thirty. He had fallen asleep in front of the television again. *Night Owl Theater* was long over, and the unsteady light from the snow on the screen guided him back to his chair and helped him find the remote control. He tilted it toward the light to find the right button, and silenced the crackle of dead air.

On his way to bed, he paused on the tenth stairstep. *Burto, they used to call me Burto, all the boys, what were their names? No one knows I was once Burto, I could run, girls smiled at me. I hardly know it myself.* He listened for the voices, unexpectant but hopeful. Hearing nothing, he continued up the stairs.

Before Lloyd awoke in the morning, his feet were already touching the chenille mat beside his bed. In his mind--as clear as a Polaroid snapshot--he saw a pair of steel ice skates with screw clips and leather ankle straps. *They're somewhere in the house, I've just got to find them, maybe in the garden shed? I can get to the yard and catch up with the guys...*

He rushed toward the door, but ran into a dresser, catching his knee on a drawer-pull. The pain dissolved the mist and made him wonder where he was going. Rubbing his leg, he frowned and made himself think of breakfast.

While in the kitchen, pouring beaten eggs into a pan, another wave of fancy swept over him, closing dark and soft over his bald head. He stood by the stove, slack-shouldered. This time, he saw not only his skates, but where he had left them. *The root cellar, where they would be out of the way in the summer. In a sand crate, to keep the blades sharp. When the apples were harvested, after the late frosts, that's when the skates came out.*

He hurried down to the basement, where the packed earth under his slippers felt harder than the tiles in the kitchen. He groped past the electric furnace to the root cellar and opened the door. It pulled open with difficulty, but no sound.

A beam of sunlight slanted into the room from a window streaked with grime, high up on the opposite wall. Puffs of dust sifted down from the doorframe, and for a second or two he imagined he caught a fruity scent in the air. *It's the apples, I can still smell the apples, Winesaps and Jonathans, wrapped in brown paper.*

The table in front of him was loaded with sand-filled crates. Digging his hands deep into one of the crates, he probed the sand with his fingers. It felt warm--like the top of a television set--oddly warm in the cool air. *I know they're here, my beautiful skates with red leather straps. Aunt Ellie bought them for me in LaCrosse, my thirteenth birthday. Mother said they probably cost too much, at least five dollars. "Eleanor, you've no more sense than a child, but look at his eyes, how they shine," she said.*

His fingers closed on a tangle of metal plates, buckles, and strips of leather. They were men's skates, dull silver, with cranberry-colored straps. He clutched them against his body hard enough to feel the press of metal into his chest. *I haven't seen my skates since I went away to school. I was fifteen.* He left the cellar whistling, the notes fading as he walked up the stairs, one step at a time.

An hour later he sat on a stool in the mudroom, pushing his feet into a pair of thick-soled boots. The voices had returned; they were much louder than before, and he could hear them everywhere, in his kitchen, in the bath. High voices, young voices, all chanting the same few words.

"Burt-o! Burt-o! Come out and skate!"

He had stopped questioning whether the voices were real.

"Please! Wait for me, I'm coming right over," he assured the coat rack, and pulled on a green knitted cap.

His fingers remembered the stylish way to fold the brim, and his thumbs ran across his bare forehead as if tucking away strayed hairs. *They'll start without me if I don't hurry, they'll pick teams, everyone is at the school already, everybody but me!*

He rose from the bench too quickly, and had to sit down again, gasping. He wound his fingers into the skate straps and squeezed. *The ice is ready, Clovis and Gus have been hosing down the yard for weeks, the ice is thick and smooth, there's no school today and the sun is shining.* Standing up--slower than before--he passed out the door and headed down the sidewalk toward Bombay Junior High.

Geography was about to begin in the classroom facing the schoolyard. Students circled the desks, repelled from their seats, negative poles. It was still early, and the teacher had not arrived. A few boys congregated at the window, fencing with Bic pens.

"Hey, check out the fat dude," said the tallest, Jeremy Cross, nudging the others toward the glass.

Stacy Harris and Chip LaPointe turned to look.

"Over by the ice." Jeremy folded his arms and leaned toward the window. "Y'know, I think he's going to skate."

Chip frowned. "No way! Me and Stace just ran the hoses last night, must've been for two hours."

"Yeah," said Stacy. "My dad's got the shed keys. We ran a new cover last night and that fat dork better not wreck it."

"You and Chip? All alone in the moonlight? How roe-mantic."

"Shut up, Cross, you hermaphrodite. That ice is *perfect*. We looked at it this morning, there isn't a mark on it." He poked a finger at Jeremy's chest. "And you can't use my stick tonight. Remember your own, dammit, you moocher."

Jeremy watched the man strap runners to his boots. "He's about a hundred years old, and he's talking to himself."

There was no answer. Stacy and Chip had resumed the ballpoint war. Jeremy drummed his thumbs on the window-sill and smiled. "Don't crack the ice, big dude," he said, and went away from the window.

Lloyd sat in the center of the bench, squinting at the forsythia bushes at the edge of the rink. He wanted to stand, but his legs wouldn't move. He felt cold and tired. *Where did they go, am I too late? I was too slow, they've gone away, and--*

"You're it, Burto!"

A hand slapped his shoulder, hard, and he rocketed from the bench after the boy who had tagged him. His flesh felt firm and good as he raced through throngs of skaters, teetering beginners, groups of boys playing tag, and a string of little girls pulling each other along by a blue scarf. Myriad sounds echoed and spun in his ears: shouting, laughter, the rhythmic hiss of skateblades on ice. In the clear air he saw the retreating jacket of his best friend, who lived over the drugstore. *Ivo Detterman! Ha! Sneaked right up on me, I'll fix him!*

Lloyd caught Ivo easily; he was short, and his legs couldn't carry him with the efficiency of Lloyd's. Lloyd bashed into Ivo and knocked him into a snowbank. They landed in a tangle, pummeling each other and whooping.

"Thought you'd never get here!" Ivo rose first, and yanked Lloyd to his feet. The boys slapped snow from their clothes. "What's the matter, Burto, you got lead shoes?"

"Sure, lead shoes," Lloyd said. "Good enough to catch you."

"Geez, it's about time," said Hal Jefson, who kept lunch in his pockets and smelled of herrings wrapped in paper. He smacked Lloyd with his cap. Gus Cloutier and Clovis Westphail started a chain, and when the whip extended into the middle of the ice, girls and younger boys migrated to the north edge for safety; the afternoon had begun.

They played Maddog. Hal was the dog first, snarling and lunging, and everyone he caught and "bit" turned mad also. Next was Runaway Train. Since Lloyd was the largest, he stood at the head of the wall of bodies, boys with arms linked, tensed to withstand the assault of the train--a trio of skaters smashing through to the other side. When everyone was bruised, they played Crack-the-Whip.

Late in the day, Lloyd saw a girl in a green wool coat sitting on a log. She looked smooth and round, like a pigeon, her hair swinging in a braid while she tightened her skates. She stood up, shaking flecks of bark from her skirt. *Alice Weems. Her father let her come skating today.* Lloyd pulled his collar straight and headed toward her. *I could ask her to skate with me, she's smiling at me!* He stopped in front of her, but couldn't think of anything to say. He seized her hands, soft in mittens, and they circled the yard in a leisurely arc.

Lloyd ignored the whistles and calls from Hal and Gus, but when Ivo stuck his thumbs alongside his head and wagged mule ears the insult was too great. He broke away from Alice and picked up a handful of snow to hurl at Ivo. He missed, and when he looked back Alice had skated away to the other side of the yard.

Lights came on in the houses nearby as the sky darkened. The crowd thinned fast as more kids left for home, waving at those who remained behind to brave the worsening chill. Snow fell, sharp and crystalline, spiraling across the ice.

Lloyd and Ivo watched the party disintegrate. Ivo's face was serene, smiling, but Lloyd felt distressed. *They're leaving, I wish they would stay, I don't want to go, I want to keep on skating, never stop, never again.*

Ivo turned to Lloyd and frowned. "Say, what's the matter? You look like you've got a toothache."

Lloyd tried to clear the hum starting in his brain. It was getting louder, and starting to hurt. "I don't want to leave," he said. "It's too far."

"Far? I can see your house from here, dumbhead."

"You don't understand," cried Lloyd He gripped Ivo by the shoulder and shook him. "I don't know if I'll ever come back!"

Ivo gazed at him. "You're the one who doesn't understand. Listen to me. It's better this way, you'll see. You live closer to this place than anyone else"--his voice fell away, as though it were coming through a wall--"and you have your skates. Don't lose them again, Burto."

Lloyd looked down at his feet. The flakes were falling faster and faster, so he could hardly see. He closed his eyes to protect them from the driving snow. A chill gripped his ankles like fists and traveled up his legs.

When he opened his eyes, the air was clear. Streams of students trickled from the doors across the yard, their jackets glowing in the late-afternoon sun. The bright colors, purples, blues, and yellows, made him remember, and he looked down.

The straps are faded again. Or maybe they weren't ever red, maybe I was mistaken. The numbness of his fingers made undoing the skates difficult, but he pried the buckles apart. *I should get home, I probably left the door wide open. What was I thinking?* "Memory isn't simple," he said.

Lloyd hoisted himself from the bench, slinging the skates over his shoulder. He grunted as pain rippled through his stiff arms. Another image was imprinting itself on his brain, a picture of a white china pot with a high neck and purple flowers. He could almost feel his mother's hand patting his head as he sat next to the stove, while his aunt made buttered toast. *Say, I wonder what happened to Mother's hot chocolate set? I think it might be in the hall cupboard, behind a box of odd spoons.* His teeth felt cold, and he realized he was smiling.

Jeremy Cross and Chip LaPointe stood by the edge of the rink, shaking their heads.

"I thought you said he just sat here all day, Cross."

"He did! I looked out here a lot. He never even moved, I kind of thought he was dead."

"Yeah, right. So who did all this? Looks like an army's been romping around on here."

"Maybe some other people came. I couldn't watch every single minute."

Every inch of the ice was scored with skate tracks, swirls and curlicues which glistened in the light. The boys turned and watched the old man pick his way across the street. He was whistling. The wind carried a few notes back across the yard, and his skates rolled against his back like a caress.

Skeeto Bites

Jim Palmer

Most of the kids are swimming at the lake, playing tetherball, or taking a nap. Not us. Me, Boots, and Chumley are busy breaking "Camp Law"--leaving the boundaries without a counselor. Yesterday our counselor Larry took us back in the woods on a nature hike. That's how we knew this river was here. Actually it's more like a creek, not like the Mississippi or anything.

Me and Chumley each have a tube sock wrapped around our heads like Rambo. Boots is wearing a large gauzy bandage on his forehead. He got cut this morning canoeing. A kid was swinging his paddle around on the shore and Boots got smacked and was knocked to the ground. The kid started to hyperventilate when he saw Boots was bleeding. Boots is still wearing his "Styx" T-shirt, even though the front is spotted with blood drips.

Me and Boots are bunk mates. I'm on the top bunk. I just found out his first name today. His mom sent him a letter in the mail and it said "Ronald Boots" on it. He don't look like a Ronald though. His face looks like Chachi's from "Happy Days," and his hair is curly and long in the back. He wants people to think of him as a tough guy, and most people do. I'm the only one who knows about the teddy bear he keeps stuffed in the bottom of his sleeping bag.

"Chumley, what time is it?" I say. "Free time is over at four."

"About 2:30," Chumley says looking at his watch. He's got one of those calculator watches. He brought it so we'd get back to our cabin in time. I've seen them watches in magazines before, but never knew anybody that owned one. During campfire last night he showed me how to spell words on it by typing certain numbers and turning the watch upside down. He wrote LOOSE, SLOb, hELL, and bOObS on it. I'm gonna get a watch like that and show my friends when I go back home.

Boots is wearing his blue jeans in the water. He didn't bring any shorts to camp. Me and Chumley are wearing swim suits and tank tops. We left our shoes on the shore downstream when we jumped in. The water is just over knee deep--I can tell by looking at Boots's jeans. Chumley is wearing an unbuttoned Hawaiian shirt over his tank top. I think he has wore that shirt every day so far. He told me his mom got it at Woolworths for nine bucks.

"Boots," I say, "don't move. Chumley, check this out." A huge caterpillar is crawling on the back of Boots's shirt.

"It musta fell off a tree and landed on your back," I say.

"Smash it," Boots says.

"No, don't. Leave it," Chumley says. "Save it, you saved its life, so some day it might save yours."

"What?" I ask.

"Reincarnation," he says,

"Oh," I say, but thinking, what the hell is reincarnation?

Chumley brushes the caterpillar into his hand and sets it in the grass on the shore. Boots takes the lead as we trudge ahead.

The river is starting to get deeper, and cold too. Seems like all the water is cold here. I went swimming the second day and it was freezing. It took me twenty minutes just to get my trunks wet. Then as I finally got enough courage to put my head under, one of the lifeguards yelled, "Buddy check, find your buddy!" This camp has the "buddy system" where you're assigned a partner and every so often the lifeguard yells and you have to find your partner and raise their hand high in the air. Usually they match up boys with boys and girls with girls, but I was assigned Carol. I guess we were the leftovers of the boys and girls so we had to be partners. When I lifted her hand up, everyone in the water started chanting that me and Carol were sitting in the tree k-i-s-s-i-n-g. Carol turned to me and smiled, making her nose plug go crooked and it nearly fell off. I haven't gone swimming since. Maybe I'll go tomorrow.

Behind Chumley's twisted teeth and untanned body is a darn smart boy. I look up to him for words of wisdom. As much wisdom as a ten year old has. He's bigger than most of the kids here and says his dad is a scientist. I'm not sure what his real name is, but the first day he told everyone to call him Chumley. He was at camp last year, so he knows the ropes. The other day I saw him shoot his bow and arrow that he brought from home. Larry brought us back to shoot at the targets that were tied to hay bales. Chumley's bow was twice as big as the ones we had to use. We had these red, flimsy, plastic bows while he stood there with a massive, sturdy, arrow-blasting machine. He was good with it, too. He hit the targets every time he shot and once even hit the bulls-eye. All the kids called him Robin Hood the rest of the day. I told him he should try out for the Olympics. He told me he might get a crossbow with his birthday money.

We planned this sneak away at breakfast. The last couple of days the free time period was getting boring, so we decided to liven it up a bit. Some kid at the table next to us found out there were ants in the syrup after half his pancakes were gone. Chumley told me his uncle once made chocolate covered ants for him. He said he ate them and they tasted like a Crunch bar.

"Hey Skeeto, come here," Chumley says. The first day of camp I wore my tie-dyed shirt that said "Minnesota State Bird" on the front and had a big black mosquito on the back. During roll call Larry called me "Skeeto" after I raised my hand. Everyone forgot my real name.

"Come here," Chumley says.

"What?" I say, coming closer.

"Chumley looks me straight in the eye, rolls his tongue, and without jerking his head, blows a phlegm chunk right at me. The chunk whizzes past my ear so close I can hear it. After a second of confusion, a smile rushes to my face. Boy, this kid is gifted.

"Holy shit, Chumley, how'd you do that?" Boots says.

"Yeah, how did you do that?" I say.

"It's easy," Chumley says, "you just go like this." He rolls his tongue and unleashes another chunk that just misses the other side of my head. "Hold still. I'll shoot one right over you."

Chumley reloads, and with a short tongue flick, fires again. I'm not sure if his aim is on or off, but he pegs me right on my cheek and it just sticks there. Boots laughs so hard his face turns red and he loses his breath. I think he's peeing in his pants but I can't tell for sure 'cause he's dipping his waist in the river. Chumley starts laughing after he sees I'm laughing and tears flush his eyes. The tears leave clean lines down his dirty face. He snorts a couple times, too, which makes me laugh harder.

As I wipe the spit from my cheek I can smell his breath on my hand. I rinse them in the river and dry them by running my fingers through my hair. Boots starts breathing again and Chumley smudges his tears across his face. We're ready to move on.

"Hey, guys, look at this," Boots says pointing toward shore at a turtle sitting on a log.

"Stay back, it might be a snapper," Chumley says. "Them are dangerous."

We slowly walk through the water past the turtle. Boots throws his gum at it after we pass it. It just sits there.

"Me and my brothers went tubing once," I say. "We were just floating and relaxing and all of a sudden my brother jumped off his tube. He said something bit him on the butt. We figured it was probably a turtle. He told me he had teeth marks on his butt for a week."

"Really?" Chumley asks. "How could he tell?"

"He checked every day with a hand mirror," I say.

We all look back at the turtle, but all we see is a log.

"Shit! Turtle on the loose!" Boots yells and takes off running, splashing water everywhere. He's not going that fast 'cause the water's about thigh high, but he tries bringing his knees up out of the water. He looks strange, but we follow him. It's sandy on the bottom, so it feels good on the feet to run.

After about ten steps Chumley stops and rests. We go back to our sluggish walk. Bits and pieces of light show through to the narrow river. Most of the river is in the shade from tree branches hanging overhead.

The other day it was hailing in the middle of the day with the sun shining. We've had hail twice in one week here. It's weird.

"Skeeto, come here," Chumley says.

"Why," I say, knowing what happened last time.

"I gotta show ya something," he says.

I move closer to him, aware that at any second I could be struck by flying mucous.

Chumley grabs my arm. "If your name is Skeeto, you gotta be able to give 'skeeto bites.'"

"Huh?" I say.

"Here, I'll show you." He sticks his thumb between his pointer and his middle finger, places it on my forearm and pushes his thumb down against his middle finger. I yank my arm away. It feels more like a bee sting than a mosquito bite. I try it on my own arm. I must be doing it right because it hurts like hell.

The water deepens and tiptoes keep us moving. We look like zombies with our hands on the surface of the water in front of us. The water is cold, but I'm used to it now.

"We better get back to the cabin," Chumley says. "It's almost four and I don't want to get my watch wet."

"Yeah, you're right," I say.

Boots jumps up, turns in mid-air and lands facing the other way. Me and Chumley do the same. Chumley nearly falls. We start our way back downstream to our shoes and the trail that leads us to camp. The small current pushes at our backs making us walk faster.

"What time is it now?" Boots asks.

Chumley looks at his watch. "Geez, it's already ten to."

"We better hurry," I say.

"Nah," Chumley says, "we'll just sneak in when we get to the cabins. Besides, Larry usually doesn't take counts 'til quarter after."

I think we should start running but Chumley knows the ropes, and what he can get by with. He also can't run very fast or far. He's got a strong kicking leg, though. We played kickball the other day and he kicked one way over everyone's head. The bases were loaded and they all scored on the play, except Chumley. He got thrown out half-way to second.

"I'm gonna start running," I say.

"Yeah, me too," Boots says.

As the river gets shallower, the faster we go. Me and Boots are jogging next to each other. Chumley is fading back quickly.

"Race ya," I say.

Boots slows down, and as I ease up, he sprints ahead. I start closing on him right away. His waterlogged jeans give me an advantage. I finally pass him after the third curve in the river. The second I pass him, he stops.

We hunch over, sucking for air. I turn back and look for Chumley. I can't see him.

"Chumley's way back there," I say on an exhale.

The square bandage on Boots's head is peeling at one of the corners. It looks soggy, too.

"I got an idea," Boots says.

"What?" I ask.

With a mischievous grin and raised eyebrows he points up. A branch hangs directly above us. It's about fifteen feet up.

"I'll get him back for you," he says.

Boots is the best tree climber I've ever seen. We played hide-and-seek the other day where the counselors had to try and find all the kids. Boots was the only kid not found. He climbed to almost the very top of the biggest evergreen tree in camp. After the time ran out, Boots climbed down. Larry told him it was very dangerous and he'd be peeling potatoes ain the cafeteria if he did it again. I gave him a high-five and we nearly stuck together from all the sap on his hands. He scrubbed with Lava soap to get it off.

"Keep walking, Skeeto," Boots says. He leaps on the shore and scales up the tree like Spiderman. I'm walking backwards, slowly. Boots is laying on the branch looking down at the water. I can see Chumley coming around the corner.

"Where's Boots?" he yells.

"He's up ahead somewhere," I say. Chumley is almost right under Boots. I'm still not sure what's going to happen.

Boots slowly leans his head over the side and drops a pool of spit from his mouth. It musta hit Chumley on the head 'cause I see him flinch and duck down. Boots's face flushes red and he giggles like a girl. Chumley lifts his chin up and sees Boots. I don't know where he stores them, but without reloading, Chumley sends a phlegm chunk up at Boots. It doesn't reach its target, about a foot short. Instead, the chunk drops right back down on Chumley and lands on his chin. He quickly wipes it off with the shoulder of his Hawaiian shirt sleeve, and then walks past me with no expression on his face. He rips the sock off his head and holds it as he walks. There is still a wet spot on the top of his head from where Boots's spit landed. Boots climbs down from the tree. He isn't laughing out loud anymore. We stand in the river and watch Chumley until he's out of sight.

Me and Boots sing "Puff the Magic Dragon" the rest of the way back. He knows all the words to it. Boy, this kid is gifted.

We Oughta Write a Book

Grace M. Sandness

Now this is more like it. You've finally got what you deserve, Luke Baxter. First Class at that. Luke looked down at himself admiringly and brushed a peck of lint from the leg of his black leather suit. *Five hundred big ones sure did the job. And these boots--class, man, class. There's no stopping us now.* He ran his hand through his tight, greased curls and pulled one down on his forehead, imagining the "right angle". His lanky, black-clad legs were stretched out as far as they would go, which was pretty far. Couldn't do that in Coach.

Beside him Keli had fallen asleep, her blonde hair with its new frizzy perm crushed against the window frame where she'd been staring out at the Dream Whip tops of clouds. That's what she called the--Dream Whip. Her leather suit matched his and her black high-heeled boots stretched her five foot two closer to his six four. *She looks like a little kid, sleeping there. A minor. Hah! Here I am, twenty-two years old and chasing around with a sixteen year old kid. What a joke. But if she was dumb enough to come with him--Green as they come. But sexy.* "Hey, Kid. Wake up."

"Huh? We're there? At L.A?" Keli stretched, looking delicious. He'd noticed that the excitement of their whole escapade had seemed to keep her on a perpetual high. She hadn't needed the speed to keep her floating.

"Just about. I saw the smog blanket ahead about five minutes ago. Say, did I tell you I called for reservations from Houston? The Hilton Seaside. A suite--Four hundred bucks a night. How's that for living, Kid?"

"Don't call me kid. Got enough trouble worrying about that part of it. We're in plenty of trouble already."

"Hey, will you cut that out. By the time anybody catches on we'll be gone! *Relax*, Kid. *Enjoy*."

"No serious, Luke. Think the old lady's missed her card yet?"

"Naw, she's probably still too drunk to notice. Anybody driving that drunk deserves to lose more than a credit card. Specially when she hadn't even signed it. She was just asking for somebody like us to come along."

"Well, she did give us a ride. It was hot on that

highway." Keli wrinkled her nose. "Kinda mean to do her so bad. Say, lemme out. Gotta go fix up if we're almost there." As she slid across Luke's knees he gave a sharp slap to the roundest part of her tight leather pants. Grinning, he watched her swing retreating down the aisle to the lavatory.

Yeah, getting away from Cleveland was one good idea. Specially with that cop business, nosing into where I was when that Jiffy Mart was hit. Now things are really moving. The pickup by that redneck trucker helped, he thought, even though he kept looking at them suspiciously and said something about Keli and Laws. That got them to St. Louis, anyway. And the other one to Texarkana. Then the walking did get a little hot. But taking the hitch from the old broad in the Continental--that sure changed things. *Leaving her purse open beside me. Fool. Making it so damn easy. When she dumped us in Houston she hadn't missed her precious card yet. Too hung-over. After that it's been First Class all the way.* "The way it oughta be," he said out loud and, being Luke, saw no reason to think differently. Almost purring, he pushed the call button and ordered a scotch. What a way to go.

When Keli returned she'd wiped away traces of the black mascara-smudge that sleep had left beneath her eyes, and applied another coat of eyeliner and more of that Hot Scarlet stuff she'd bought in Houston for her lips. (She'd been a mess, leaving Cleveland without anything. Just taking off with him that night they got high and decided to split). Her hair didn't look much better after that $80 perm, but she was still a doll. Even if she was a dumb blonde. What a blast she must have had that day in Houston, when he'd given her the card and told her to have fun. The clothes in that bag of hers must have cost nearly a thousand dollars.

Keli slid back into her seat by the window. "Boy, this is cool. If Ma could only see me now."

"Do you think she's gotten around to looking for you yet?"

"Prob'ly thought about it if she'd been sober long enough to--specially if she's figured out I'm with you. Black guys ain't her idea of okay."

"So, do we care?"

"Sure not me. She prob'ly ain't been off the bottle long enough to do nothing about us, anyway."

"Let's just forget about her, okay Kid? She's depressing."

"Sure," Keli took out her compact from her Gucci purse and checked her eyes. "Only thing is--if she does do anything she can git you for kidnapping a minor, statutory rape, and a few other things."

"Rape? Kidnapping? That's a joke, right? I told you, forget about all that stuff. We can prove you were willing. Anyway, the law can't touch me. It never can because I'm too smart for those bozos. You know that."

"Sure, Luke." *Sure, Luke. Sometimes I wonder--*

"You doubt me? You'll find out. Besides, you're having fun. Right?"

"Uhhuh."

"Then that's what counts. Luke Baxter shows *his* women a *good time*. Treats em *right*!"

After they'd collected their luggage, (matching burgundy leather) at LAX, Luke rented a Corvette convertible from Hertz. Red, with an eighty watt quad system. On the freeway to the hotel the hot wind of speed stung Luke's eyes and flattened Keli's perm into straightness. She held her head with both hands like it was ready to fly off. "Wow! Yuh sure know how ta handle this baby!"

"Of course. Luke Baxter understands *his* cars. You like speed, Kid?"

"Fast people fast cars--you're really flyin low!" Keli grinned, stretching into the California sun. "Lookit the smog, Luke. That's smog, huh? Plenty of palm trees, anyway. Gi*gan*tic. Hey, there's the ocean!"

"Sure is. We'll have to get you a suntan tomorrow on that sand. You can start catching up with me."

"Oh sure. You joker."

"Anyway, that new blue bikini's the most."

"Think I look like California?"

"Kid, you look just like a Valley Girl."

"Whut's that like?"

Luke shrugged. "Dammed if I know."

When they pulled around the curve under the white-and-gold portico of the Hilton Seaside, Luke released the keys of the Corvette to a gold-coated attendant. And tipped him ten dollars. Keli trailed behind him, staring around her at the palms and the rushing waterfall in the center of the lobby under the high glass ceiling. "Oo-oh, Lukie, lookit this place!"

"Cool it, Kid. Don't act like a greenhorn." He led her to the registration desk, hand reaching for his wallet, and pulled out the car--the card with the woman's name, Margaret Coleridge. Somehow they never remembered that name between charges. "Mr. and Mrs. Coleridge?" The clerk eyed the couple and glanced back at the car.

"Yes sir. Luke and Margaret Coleridge. We have reservations." Keli stood back a little by an elephant ear plant that was taller than she was. Looked apprehensive like she always did, as if she wanted to run. Luke's steel remained unbent.

"Suite 2008, Sir." The clerk tapped the bell; a gray-haired bellman in a gold uniform piled their luggage on a cart and walked toward the glass elevator. They followed him, Keli giggling softly. Sir, the guy'd said. Luke grinned. It was about time.

"Where'r we goin' next, Luke?" Keli had stretched herself on the king-size waterbed, wearing the black lace bra and bikini panties she'd been saving for California. Sexy kid. Luke pulled the drapes against the sun and flopped down beside her, his probing fingers dark through her black lace. "Stop it, Lukie! I asked you, where'r we going next?"

"Oh, we can swing around here awhile--like Rodeo Drive and Laguna Beach. A few night spots. Couple of days, anyway."

"An Hollywood?"

"Sure. And Hollywood."

"An Disneyland? We gotta see Disneyland, Lukie, puleeze?"

"Sure sure. But we can't stay too long, in case the old lady blows the whistle. But we can drive up Highway One to Frisco or something. Look around there."

"Okay," Keli arched toward him, waiting, her fingers twisting the curl on his forehead. "Then whut?"

"Who knows? Who cares--now. We got more important things to do. Much more important." Keli's arms slid around him. Clung to him as his lips forced down on hers. Clung to him. Tighter.

"Lukie--" She'd been watching him lying there staring at the ceiling. Long mute minutes when it seemed as though he'd forgotten her or the intensity of the way they'd made love. "What'cha thinking about?"

"I don't know. Just way back--"

"Like when you wuz a kid. You never talk about that. About your folks."

"Maybe because I never had any. How's that."

"Aw, sure you did. Who yuh kidding?"

"Never a father, anyway. You're looking at a real live honest-to-god bastard."

"Lukie, don't! Don't say that stuff. It's *awful*!" Keli stretched her arm across his chest, soothing the child in him.

"Well, I heard it enough, anyway. And worse. From Maw every time I screwed up. And the neighbors. Until I was five."

"Why five?"

"That's when Welfare wised up and noticed that the money my sainted mother was getting to feed me with was ending up in the pocket of some pusher. Maw was really heavy into the stuff. So they blew the whistle on her and I ended up in the System. Neglect. Boy was that neglect."

"You were a Foster Kid?"

"You're looking at one. Five so-called Homes in thirteen years. And when eighteen came they said 'you're a big boy now. You don't need us anymore.' And they were right. I don't need anybody." Luke rolled toward her and rumpled her hair. His voice had the hard brilliance of a diamond. "Remember when I said 'it's you and me, Kid'? Well, who else is there? Now I've got somebody."

The sable coat he bought her on Rodeo Drive was sensuous to his fingertips. Its touch made him feel what-- triumphant? Once back at the hotel she slid her fingers deliciously through its luxury and danced around him, teasing. "Oh, Lukie! I feel just like a model!" When he fastened the diamond watch like a circlet of sparks around her wrist she gloated, standing by the window and twisting her hand around to watch the diamonds catch the sun. When she modeled the new lingerie from Fredricks of Hollywood, swinging her hips and giggling, he chased her, teased her, and carried her squealing to the bed.

He'd known she was for him the first time he saw her walking along Jefferson with that sexy swing. And that blond hair shining like gold thread in the sun. His kind of woman. And, when he pulled up in Josh's red Camaro convertible and opened the door, he hadn't even had to coax her. Nothing hard to get about her. Showed right off she was dumb. But he looked good with her. And she's been lapping up the expensive stuff like a hungry puppy. Lapping up the Good Life. They had it coming, both of them, he thought. The world owed it to *him*, at least--young, good-looking, smart.

If he weren't smart they'd've been caught a long time ago. Even back in Texas when they'd hitch-hiked for hours on a road with no end and no traffic, where a patrolman could have come along any time asking what a black dude like him was doing out there with a blond-headed kid.

Keli had sure looked a mess then. Hair blown in knots and glued to her forehead by sweat. Face burned red by too much sun. She'd unbuttoned her blue shirt and tied the ends together in front. Everything the sun hit looked red. Those blond types never could take sun. She'd been dragging along silent and barefoot beside him down the highway. Then she stopped still, standing there with that helpless look, carrying her spike heels in her hand. And started hopping from one foot to the other, moaning about the blistering pavement. That Texas road stretched on and on like a white-hot cement ribbon. And all along the cement the cactus and thistles were growing rough in rocky gravel. She should have kept her shoes on. Dumb kid. "Lukie, I can't go no farther. I'm dying. I'm just dying'!"

"Didn't think I brought a squawking baby along. Cut it out, will you! I know this is no picnic."

"Well, I din't think I'd be stuck out here in the godawful place. Some bigshot you are. 'Travel in style. See the world.' Just a buncha crap!"

"Look, Kid, if you're too much a baby to put up with it then take off. Who cares. But something'll come our way. I got luck, Baby. Just stick with me. You'll see."

"Sure sure. You'll fix everything. Think yer God or sumthin'. That's the trouble with you. You think yer the greatest thing in the world!"

He'd thought a minute, then stopped right there on the highway and given her a big hot sticky hug. And put honey in his voice like only he knew how, "Keli Baby, hang in there. I said I'd take care of you and I meant it. I always take care of my good stuff. And you're the best." All that complaining could spoil things in a hurry.

She'd twisted away from him and stood there in the gravel with her face twisted in that little-girl pout. "Yeah, tell me about it."

All they could see were corn fields and flat, emptiness. He'd never seen so much nothing in his life. Helluva place to live. There wasn't a cloud in the sky. Sun had been searing their faces white lead and almost blinded him. He'd left his shades at that gas station where they'd stopped for a beer, and now that stupid red-necked pump jockey would be sporting forty-dollar shades. What a waste.

Then a white Lincoln pulled up and that drunken old cat leaned out the window. "You kiddos want a ride?" And Keli'd almost cried. She'd crawled into the back seat on the white real-leather cushions and stretched her legs out in the air conditioning. "Oh-h-h, my feet!"

"You been out here long, Baby?" The old lady had dyed red hair and the skin over her bones looked like crushed brown leather from too much sun. She'd looked him up and down and slid her purse over between the seats to make room for him. "You sure are tall. Han'sum guy, too. Y'all goin' far?"

"We're going to Houston, Ma'am. We're on our honeymoon, you see, Ma'am, but my wallet got stolen in Texarkana and we sort of got stranded." He heard Keli make a choking, sputtering sound. Like she was swallowing something. But the old gal didn't hear.

"Too bad. Nice young couple like y'all."

"We have reservations at the Sheraton Towers in Houston, Ma'am. The bridal suite. My wife here, she likes fancy places." He grinned back at Keli and winked. The old lady smiled that spaced out sort of smile and kept driving along.

Her and her wide open purse sitting right there between them. Wide open with her cigarettes hanging out and her wallet gaping and that card sticking right out there. She just kept talking and talking. "I got a cattle ranch. D'jou guess that? Almos' a thousan' acres. Sure. I'm a rancher but I can't stand the country. Too quiet. Y'all want a cigarette?"

"No thank you, Ma'am. We don't smoke." He winked back at Keli again. She shook her head, grinning.

"Yep, even after my husb'n left me for that painted-up kid in Fort Worth I kept ranchin'. Got me a hired hand, o'course. It's a good life. Money, too. Plenty of it." She talked on and on, sucking on that Budweiser can. Like she didn't really see him or care what was going on. Except that once in a while she looked him over like she was picking out a steak. Most of the time she just talked away like she was talking to herself and not even listening. Old Lady Coleridge, she was the dumb one. Dumb ones deserve to get taken. And they'd sure taken her. Her and her top-o-the-line credit. Three weeks of living high on *her* American Express, seeing the world, just because she was too soused to notice. Now here they were with a world of sun ahead. And nothing was impossible.

"Mm-m-m. I could lie here forever. Jus' you'n me, Lukie. It's like bein' on a desert island, isn't it, Lukie?" Keli'd been stretched out on a bright orange deck chair for nearly an hour. Five days of sun and Hawaiian Tropic Formula had turned her a honey brown. Made her newest white bikini glow. Luke loved buying her bikinis.

"What do *you* know about islands, Kid?" Luke was beaded with pool water that clung to him like crystal on brown satin. *Gee he looks good,* Keli thought. *Too bad he knows it.* "Cruise ships are more expensive than islands, anyway. You need to learn to keep your priorities straight if you're going to live big time. Like this." He rubbed the beach towel over the satin. "You need a drink, don't you. I know I need a couple of beers."

"Sure. Anything you say." She watched his stride toward the lounge, drops still clinging to his permed hair. *Always puttin me down. Keep my priorities straight? Huh. He's just plain arrogant. When he's around me it's like he's watchin other people watch him.* What she was learning, a little more every day, was making her more and more uneasy. *And every night the dancin'. Doesn't even ask me if I want to. Like maybe I wanta just sit out here in the dark and feel him hold me. Like he was a real lover, not just a phony. Now he's comin' with the beers. And glasses even. Who needs glasses anyway?* He was getting more and more that way, she though. *Like he owned her. Always shoving that white powder at her.* Always asking her, "Having fun, Kid?" Waiting for her to say, "Oh, Lukie, you're the greatest!" *And he always believes me, of course. Cuz that's what he thinks, anyway.*

That night they went to the Mexicali Lounge. Keli had begged, "Let's do sumthin diff'rent tonight, Lukie, please!" But they still wen to the Mexicali.

"Come on, Kid, let's grab that table in front by the dance floor. Gotta get a good look at that meat in the dance line." Luke had already drunk too much.

"That's gross, Luke. How about that table over there in the corner? It's more romantic."

"Romantic, hell. Gotta chance to see some good stuff up in front an' *you* wanta get romantic? I got *you* any time I wantcha!" *Why does he have to talk so loud?* The couple at the next table stared, started to whisper. About them, of course. About them. *He always gets so nasty when he's drunk. Nasty and ugly.* He'd been getting meaner and meaner every day, anyway. Oh, not always, she thought, but when he was high on coke and figured somebody didn't like him. Then he'd get that steel look in his eyes and the snarl.

"Hey Señor!" Luke waved his fist in the air and shouted across the room. "Gimmee a couple'a scotches!" The raucous insulting voice. "Bring on the skin! I'm waitin'." Keli wanted to be so small nobody could see her.

"Luke, please don't." She wanted to scream, "*Shut up!*" But she knew the steel.

"Hell, kid, wudya leeme alone! I wanna see a little action. Watch a littl' piece o' action! Whatsa mattah? Sacred ta ha'me lookit other wimen? 'Fraid they got sumthin *you* don got?"

"Sir--" A latino officer in the white uniform laid his hand on Luke's shoulder. "We must ask you to leave, Sir. You're disturbing the other guests."

"Disturbin *what*? Hey, I *paid* tuh be here. You can't--"

"I'm sorry, Sir, but you *are* creating a disturbance. Please come--" He put his hand firmly under Luke's arm.

"You sonofabitch. Take your hands offa me!" Snarling, Luke lashed out with his arm, smashing his chair backward. Its red-upholstered back thudded against the carpet. Shouting, he stumbled toward the door. Keli looked at the steward helplessly, then followed Luke with her eyes on the ends of her shoes.

Now the cabin was black except for a single shaft of the commanding Pacific moon stabbing the far wall. She could hear Luke's heave drug-weighted breathing in the bunk below her. No sign of restlessness. He was sleeping like a baby.

On the first night out she'd argued when he said, "You take the top bunk."

"Oh, Lukie, I'm scareda heights. You know that!"

"Sure. But what if I fall out trying to roll over? What would you do if *I* broke *my* leg, huh? Not too smart."

"Oh you poor baby. Luke, sometimes you're just plain mean." She'd given up then and crawled onto the narrow top bunk, turned her back on him and wouldn't talk. But soon he'd made her forget.

Now she lay staring toward the porthole, her mind on the scene in the lounge, trying to forget it and her smallness, to concentrate on the nearly imperceptible rolling of the ship. Like a lullaby without music. *Like when Ma used to rock me. Before he left. Before I woke up that morning when I was only eight and found her just standing there crying in front of his empty closet and there wasn't any note or phone call or anything. Before she started getting crazy and drinking herself unconscious and life started falling apart because she said she didn't know how to make it alone.* (When she let herself think about that--when she let herself wonder). *Maybe that's when I started to hate her--when I started figurin out that she really was too weak to make it without a man. Just helpless and a fool.*

Sleep wouldn't come but doubt did. *What'm I doin here, anyway?* She shifted on the narrow mattress, her elbow bumping the wall, the shadows in her head making thinking blurred and elusive. *Chasing around with this guy I hardly even know. Who acts like a total jerk. With no time even to make sense of things. Bet he tries to keep it that way, keep me so busy and foggy I can't think. Always off balance. Like I'm never sure of anything. Making me depend on him. And every time I ask, "Lukie, aren't you scared?" or "Shouldn't we go back, Lukie?" he changes the subject. Gives me something to "calm me down." Says he's not worried. Says the law can't touch him cuz he's too smart for em. But he's not. He's running!*

She turned onto her side and groped for her watch fastened to the rail of the bed. Three-thirty and still not sleeping. Listening for any change in Luke's breathing, she raised on one elbow. Her head nearly touched the low ceiling. She slipped her legs over the side of the bunk and lowered herself to the floor. *Big Mouth should've wised up and gotten a stateroom. With a real bed. Even I know about staterooms.* Groping for shorts and shirt, she slipped into the bathroom to dress.

The lounge was now subdued and candle-dim A couple sat off in a far corner, low-voiced and oblivious. Keli chose a table in the shadows, as far as possible from where she and Luke had sat, lit a cigarette and ordered coffee. She watched a single red tear edge down the candle in the round glass bowl in front of her. Picked at it with a discarded match. Watch it change direction and keep crying. The flame shed gold over the red cloth and caught and held the brightness of her hair. But the brightness inside her had died. When she buried her face in her arms it was shining with tears. *They're gonna get him, I know they will cuz he oughta get caught.* The thought had been throbbing through her for days, echoing and re-echoing like through a huge empty room. *They're gonna get us. I'm in this too. But at least I'm smart enough to be scared. He's such a fool. Doesn't have sense enough to be scared. There's something wrong in his head but I sure don't understand it. And he thinks I'm dumb. Sure. I know he does. Sometimes he talks to me like I'm some kind of stupid dumb doll. All he really wants is sex. And that we "look good together" like he keeps telling me. So he dresses me up and leads me around like a pet poodle. Thinks I don't know what he thinks he's doing.*

She wiped her eyes and picked up the coffee cup. It was cold. *Stupid, letting him pick me up like that. Like some kinda tramp. Stupid. I gotta get out of this. It's all wrong. I'm starting to depend on him like Ma did on that guy. Even if he does treat me like dirt. I can't do that. I'll never do that. Wish I could just go home. Home to Ma and her bottle. Maybe she'll change. Be like she useta be. When she loved me. Maybe we'll have fun together again. Go to movies. Maybe she's got a new guy and ain't scared no more. Or got in AA or something. But even now she's better than this. I should just take all this good stuff he's givin' me and go home. Just blow the whistle an call it quits!*

When the ship docked back in LA, they chose a different hotel, this time in San Diego. "We'd better keep moving." Luke had explained when she'd wanted to stay in LA, at the Seaside. "Don't need the long arm of the law reaching out for us--or your mother, either. If we're shrewd nobody will put it all together."

"Sure, Luke. But maybe--"

"Maybe what, Kid?"

"Maybe we should give it up. Turn ourselves over to the cops before they--"

"Are *you crazy*? Now listen, Dummy. Don't say that any more! Use your head. Pretend you're intelligent. If we stick together everything's going to be fine. Don't you turn chicken now and mess this up for us."

"Okay, but I'm beginning to think you're really nuts!"

There was in Luke's face, for the single flash of a thought, a look so perilously close to hate that Keli gasped and was silent.

The sun followed them along the highway to San

Diego, pausing when Keli squealed at Luke to stop at a T-shirt booth along the beach. "I really need another souvenir," she coaxed, "something to remember this by." Crazy kid, Luke thought, watching her and thinking of the sable and diamonds and the stuff she bought in Puerta Vallarta. There was something different about her, he thought. Cooler. She's pulling away from me, he thought. Stupid kid can't take the heat. And still never satisfied. He glanced down at his new $500 black boots with silver and honest-to-goodness rubies around the top, and patted the video camera case between the seats. At least *he* knew how to do it. Pretty hard to keep up with The Big Man. Old Lady Coleridge should love the bills.

In San Diego they checked into a resort hotel on the beach, a Hilton, of course, Luke's idea of luxury. And, naturally, a suite. Nothing but the best for Luke Baxter. The king-size bed had a brass headboard and a white satin spread. On the mahogany table two wine glasses stood by an ice bucket with a bottle of Chardonnais. You get what you pay for. Across the pale gold plush carpet the white-curtained doors open onto a broad tiled deck with a chaise lounge and umbrella'd table. The railing was edged with some kind of spiky plants. Keli ran to it and leaned over the edge, gazing down twenty-eight floors onto the tops of palms and the red-and-green carpet of bougainvillaea and ivy. Over the ocean there seemed no horizon, only the blue of infinity. "Lookit, Honey!" The voice was sounding fakey. "Ain't it bee-utiful?"

"Um-hum. Our kind of place. Right, Kid?" Luke had thrown his sport shirt on the bed and followed her to the deck. Looking down at the world made him feel like a king. He looked down at Keli's hair, inches below his shoulder. It was bleached white by the sun and hovered on the breeze. Like a halo. He pulled her back against his dark, bare chest, waiting to hear her sigh and feel her wilt against him as his hands slipped around her. Wondering why she didn't. Feeling her softness. Stroking the places that usually made her come alive. Dumb kid. Sixteen years old and still innocent as a baby. But he looked good with her.

"Hey, are you going to get yourself prepared for a glamorous evening?" He gave Keli a squeeze. She sure looked better than she did on that highway. Luxury agreed with her.

Keli pulled away, looking at him with a strange sort of

half-smile. Something was different. The difference he'd seen that last morning on the ship. "Ready for what?" Like she didn't know.

"Hey, I told you. Tonight we go to the Lanai Room. That's rich man's territory, Kid. I'm ready for some lobster. Or filet mignon. And some really good wine. Wear that red satin dress you bought in L.A. And those diamond earrings I bought you. We'll wow 'em Kid."

"Lukie, really, d'you think we ought to?"

"Why not, Kid. That's what we're here for, is it not-- to live it up?"

"Yes, but--"

"Yes, but nothing. Just go and get ready like I told you."

"Did you ever stop to think that maybe I don't want to? You never ask me. Always boss me around like you own me."

"Because I do. I own you now, Kid, and *don't you forget it*! Where would *you* be if *I* pulled out? Dumb kid can't even think for herself and *she's* telling *me* what to do!" His fist tightened on her arm. Keli looked at the fist that had almost struck--looked down at the purple imprints of his fingers. Then jerked the satin dress from the closet and slammed the bathroom door behind her. He stared after her. Puzzled. Angry.

At the linen-covered table, she in her tight red satin, Luke in his tux, Keli even giggled when the champagne bubbled against her nose. An obedient giggle. Luke thought the rebellion he had stifled back in the room had vanished. Treat 'em rough and they know who's boss. Yet there was a deliberateness to her laughter that confused him, and he didn't like being confused. She hadn't gotten high today, either. She was a blast when he got her high, but-- "C'n I git lobster, Lukie Baby? I want lobster, too."

"Sure, Kid. Anything for you." The sun was low over the water, streaking its far blue with the pink and orange promise of approaching night. Night came early there. City lights had begun to spark their own diamonds; Keli's sparkled under the stars of the chandelier overhead. Luke's hand covered hers on the white linen, squeezing it possessively. Tan and young and full of promise. His kind of girl.

Keli pulled her hand away. Abruptly. "Gotta find the lavatory. Be right back."

"Want the room key?"

"No, there's one down the hall there. By the phones." Again he watched her walk away. Not sassy swinging, but stiff. Like she was determined or mad or something. *Women.* He ordered another scotch.

When the Lanai Room closed, shutting off their dancing and the heightening passion Luke was feeling, he walked close to Keli, his arm across her satin-covered hips, leading her to the elevator. Three whole weeks, he chuckled to himself. Hilton, Sheraton, all the big ones. "Having fun, Kid?" He never tired of asking. Each time gloating with her affirmation. Obediently, Keli leaned her body against him, offering the kiss she knew he would demand. The elevator doors opened.

"Oh, Luke--sometimes I wish this could go on forever." There was that strangeness again, as if there were quarreling inside her. As if she were--"Just us, living and traveling and not fighting, just lovin--specially the lovin."

"Who knows? We got Now, Kid. That's all any of us can know about. The old lady's card has taken us a long way, hasn't it, Mrs. Coleridge? A long way."

When the doors opened they were still deeply together. The world had stopped for Luke in another of those never-ending minutes that had become for him a way of life. "You're my woman, Keli. Mine. As long as I want you. Don't you ever forget it." Still they stood, bodies together, when the waiting uniformed men separated them and read them their rights.

It's easier just to tell part of it, Keli told herself on the plane back to Cleveland beside the paunchy, bald police officer. She sat there in Coach in the seat by the window, staring out at Dream Whip clouds that were now dull and deflated. *There's Luke right across the aisle with that other cop. He keeps lookin at me. I feel it. He knows all about the phone call. I know he does. An they're puttin him in lock-up til his trial. He thinks it's all my fault. My fault? I don't want him to look at me. Wish we'd get there.* But as she huddled inside herself, silent and powerless, she knew Ma would be waiting, knew she would need explanations, answers, reasons. And for a dozen of those mixed-up reasons, the three-week-old balloon she'd been riding had collapsed in a pitiful tangle of reds and golds.

There in the waiting area Ma was walking almost straight. "So, you're back." Keli searched her perfunctory hug for some hint of her little kid days, but it felt empty. There was nothing to say. Lugging her burgundy leather suitcases, she followed Ma meekly from the terminal. Then through all that endless hour driving home came the lies. "It was great, Ma. Lukie was real good to me. Treated me like a lady! We had us the greatest time in the world!" Nothing about the doubt and the agony, the humiliation. Only the frosting of a bitter cake. "An that old Mrs. Coleridge. Bet she had a stroke when the bills started coming." When she heard herself she realized how much she sounded like Luke.

The diamonds and sable had been confiscated. But even Ma's eyes glistened when Keli showed her the new bikinis and sport clothes, the black leather suit and the red satin evening dress. Maybe because Ma wore the same size. And every time she told her story it became more preposterous. "Luke was a real gentleman. Treated me like some kinda queen. And he was hot, man. Was *he hot*! Y'know--we oughta write a book!"

She was soon seventeen. Luke had never contacted her. Not once since his arrest. Once in the deep-night misery of sleeplessness she started a letter. Wrote it with her neatest script in violet ink on her best orchid stationary. She even sprayed it with a hint of Intimate, the first thing he'd bought her, back in Houston. But she couldn't think of a thing to say that was real; the weeks they'd shared loomed too threatening--were still what they had always been. She felt demeaned. She read the letter again. And Again. And crumpled it into a tight orchid ball in her fist. The entire year Luke spent in prison she never went to see him.

Attention Writers

Stories for the 1997 Collection of Minnesota Writers Will be Accepted Until May 1, 1996

Write:

```
Crowbar Press
P.O. Box 8815
Madison, WI 53708
```

Please include self address stamped envelope.